I0673081

Blind Sight

PSI Sentinels: Book Two

Pamela Moran

PSI Sentinels: Guardians of the Psychic Realm
Extraordinary senses in a world full of danger.

Protectors and hunters, PSI agents lay their abilities,
sometimes their lives, on the line.
They defend and shield unwary victims against the
twisted underside of a psychic society bent on
exploiting an unsuspecting, mundane world.

Acknowledgements

M.A. Taylor, Janelle Denison and Stephanee Ryle

Ladies, you're the best!

HelenKay Dimon, for the Challenge.

Warren – as always, my heart.

Dedication

My sister, Karen – love you so much.

Chapter One

GABRIEL NICHOLETTI STRETCHED out on the bow of his sailboat. He crossed his bare ankles and linked his fingers behind his head. A shooting star arced across the black, pre-dawn, winter sky.

The gentle lapping of the warm, Caribbean water against the hull should have been enough to rock him to sleep.

Under normal circumstances.

That same water should've been enough of a barrier to stop the visions plaguing him, disturbing his sleep. Keeping him awake.

Again, under normal circumstances.

Those visions of the last three nights had been troubling. Water, a natural deflector and normally his salvation in such times, had failed him. Miserably.

Right. Who was he kidding? Dead bodies were always troubling. Always miserable. He'd seen his share. More than any sane man should see.

This one, though, for whatever damn reason, was different. This one called to him. Stronger than any in the past. The beautiful blonde stretched out at the edge of some forest floor, her lifeless green eyes staring at him. Through him.

Above, the ship's flag flapped in a sudden gust of balmy wind. Rain was coming, the hint a bare scent in the briny air. In a few hours though, by the time he made it back through customs, the hint would be a full blown, Caribbean winter squall.

He stared up at the American flag, lit by a small mast light. And sighed.

He was heading back to the States.

GABE ROCKED BACK in the chair, contemplated settling his feet on the polished mahogany desk in front of him. Reconsidered. Rogue agent or not, his feet propped on Boss-Man's desk *might* be going too far.

If the man didn't hurry and get his ass in here soon, though, he'd rethink that scenario. These chairs weren't built for comfort, especially not for someone as tall and wide as him.

Behind the desk, positioned on the credenza to stare back at him, sat a single, silver framed 8x10 group shot. A wedding. Everyone smiling at the camera.

Happy.

His hands clenched, he squeezed his eyes shut against the photo.

Out of here. God, he wanted to be gone in the worst way.

But dammit, that photo sealed his fate.

He needed to be *here*. For now. For answers.

Somehow Ben Garrett, his boss, agency head and one time mentor, tied Gabe to the woman he saw dead in his dreams.

There was always a link. A tie.

He didn't normally know the people in his visions, but there was always a connection, somehow, to someone Gabe knew. Always.

This time, Ben was the reason Gabe couldn't sleep more than a few hours at a stretch. The reason the woman's face haunted him. Her green eyes ….

Gabe shoved up from the chair. With his hands fisted in his front pants pockets, he paced to the far window. Floor to ceiling, plate glass lined the entire wall. A false barrier to the threatening elements. Heavy blue drapes, tied back, framed the bleak Minnesota-in-winter landscape.

God, what he'd give to still be on his boat.

He stood with his legs braced apart and twisted his head to the side. Damn kinks. They'd taken up permanent residence these last several days. Disgusted, he stared out the window.

Boss-Man's third story office overlooked a small lake. The flat landscape stretched from the shore and faded into the forest, although the edge of the institution's property went far beyond the trees that could be seen.

Snow covered everything. Even the frozen lake.

There hadn't been any snow in his dreams.

Winter, though. He'd seen tall, thin, leafless trees interspersed with a few pines. And the sky had been heavy with grey, angry clouds.

But no snow.

So, not here. The green-eyed woman wouldn't die here. Not on this property. Probably not in Minnesota.

A small thing to be thankful of, that the woman wasn't tied to this location.

From the time he'd turned six, Gabe had lived here. Abandoned by a mother who couldn't cope with such a *gifted* child.

The Institute for Psychic Studies, IPS.

They'd taken him in, trained him. Studied him. The freak among freaks. Hell, they'd even made sure he had a job with the Institute's secret side agency. He'd sworn that once he got away from this place he wouldn't come back.

How many times had he broken that vow?

His hands still in his pockets, he squared his shoulders and turned to face the desk but refused to look at the photo behind.

He stared, hard, at the closed office door. Had Ben's secretary even bothered to tell him he was in here, not so patiently waiting? Probably not. The woman hated Gabe.

Her son had been an addict, had run with the wrong people. Had ended up dead. But it was easier to blame the kid who'd *seen* the vision rather than deal with the truth.

Gabe's gift. His curse.

Yet here he was, back in Minnesota because of another damn vision.

He settled in the uncomfortable chair. With another dark glance at the door, he set his feet on the desk, crossed his legs at the ankles.

And made sure his heels didn't mar the desk's shiny surface before linking his fingers over his belly. He willed his shoulders to relax.

The damn photo beckoned.

Hell.

The bride, her dark eyes holding a hint of somberness in spite of her wide smile, next to her protective groom who held her close. There was a definite story there, but they weren't why he was here.

Boss-Man flanked the couple on one side and Gabe's mystery woman stood on the other.

Except for Ben, none of the people in the photo were agents. Gabe would have recognized them.

Therefore, Ben's relationship to the people had to be personal, especially if the grin on his face and the arm he had loped over the bride's shoulders were any indication. The bride sure as hell wasn't Ben's daughter. That was another person Gabe would recognize.

From intimate, personal experience.

The scar at the back of his neck twitched. Not much, not the throbbing pain it'd once been, but enough.

Talia Garrett wasn't a memory he intended to dwell on. Not today, not with her father somewhere on the other side of the office door. Not when he needed answers from Ben.

Answers and not arguments.

Rehashing the past wouldn't solve or change a damn thing.

Again, Gabe focused on the photo. His mystery woman resembled the groom, so probably related. The shot was narrowed in on the people, without many background details to give a clue to location.

Here in Minnesota? Somewhere else?

Did it matter?

If the woman in his vision wasn't already dead, she would be within a matter of weeks.

That's how this worked.

He saw them dead. With nothing he could do about their dying.

Sometimes he was able to find the killers, sometimes not. But he'd never been able to stop the death.

So why the hell did he keep trying?

He rubbed his hands over his face before again lacing his fingers over his stomach. Sick bastard, that's what he was.

Idealistic fool, believing this cursed gift might actually save someone. Somewhere. Sometime.

The soft swish of the office door opening across the plush carpet scraped across Gabe's skin. He settled back in his chair, feigning a comfort he wasn't close to feeling.

"Fax that off as soon as soon you can." Ben Garrett's deep voice echoed through the room. "What the hell?"

Gabe allowed a small quirk to lift the left corner of his mouth, disappointed but not surprised at the alarmed expression, quickly shuttered, crossing his boss' face.

Even Ben Garrett wasn't immune to that initial reaction to seeing Gabe Nicholetti, the *Harbinger of Death* as the other agents had tagged him, sitting and waiting.

Who was going to die?

That was always the first thought his presence triggered in the people he sort of worked with.

"I figured your Bear at the gate neglected to let you know I was here." Gabe rolled his shoulders, steepled his fingers. "She's never forgiven me. But what have you done, lately, that she's so willing to just let you walk in here? Without any warning?"

"None of your damn business." Ben, his craggy face now a complete closed mask, pulled the door closed behind him, eyed Gabe's feet on his desk and raised a grey brow.

Gabe let his smile widen and, taking his time, lowered his feet to the floor. He took a few extra moments to straighten the crease in his pressed jeans. "How are you doing, Ben?"

The muscle along Garrett's left jaw tightened. Pulsed.

Indulging in a power play with Ben was dangerous.

Gabe didn't bother to check himself this time.

Too much history, too much between them.

Ben settled his tall, broad shouldered frame behind his desk, leaned back and mirrored Gabe's relaxed stance and steepled fingers. His mouth moved into a semblance of a smile and Gabe caught the flash of Grey Wolf just beneath the surface, hiding in the depths of Ben's dark, blue eyes. Watching. Waiting.

Totem Animal.

Seeing into another, seeing their core, their essence was another of Gabe's gifts, one he actually embraced.

Lone Wolf, Ben was a man whose wife had torn his pack apart early in their marriage. She hadn't cared or even looked back.

Gabe squelched the urge to glance at the photo behind Ben's head. But he wondered if the man was finally building another, looser family circle. After all this time.

"Cut to the chase, Gabriel. Talia?"

"As far as I know, your bitch of a daughter is fine. I haven't seen her, in any manner, in many months."

Ben's shoulders drooped a slight amount. So he still cared about her. After everything she'd done. To him, to Gabe. The wedge she'd carved between the two men.

"Then what brings you here, Gabriel? It's not like you're one for social calls."

"True." Gabe kept his gaze level. "Who's in the wedding picture?"

Ben, his eyes darkening, stared at Gabe for a long moment. Then the man rubbed one hand down his face. For the first time Gabe could remember, Ben Garrett looked his age.

"Gabe. They were just married last month. After everything they've been through –"

"Not the bride. Or the groom." Crap. Gabe held himself still. He would *not* let guilt eat at him. What he *saw* was not his fault. Ben knew how this worked. Better than anyone, he knew. He'd been the one to hammer that lesson home. No guilt for what he *saw*. "The woman on the other side of the groom. His sister, I'm guessing. Who is she?"

Ben's face paled and emotion swirled in the dark depths of his blue eyes. "Rily Carrigan."

RILY NOSED HER truck into the parking area of the roadside rest stop on the fringe of her small Oregon town. The rain had stopped, but her headlights did little to penetrate the fog

7

laced night. Even the bright red paint job on her truck seemed dim and muted in the thick fog.

Past midnight on a cold, damp December night, she should be snug in her bed. Asleep. Like most sane people.

Although there were a few not-so-sane out and about, if the number of vehicles parked haphazardly along the edge of the rest area was any indication. Damn lookie-loos with police scanners.

She slipped the gear shifter into park, let the vehicle idle for a few moments then shut off her truck. The soft ping of the diesel engine settling punctuated the night.

Not her choice to be out here, but no seniority meant she got the call when Eagle Crest's only other detective, the one with seniority, wanted to stay in his own warm, toasty bed.

But she really didn't mind.

Truth was, there were times she missed graveyards. Back when she'd been in uniform that had been her favorite shift.

Now she needed to get to the matter at hand. Shoving her truck door open, she jumped down, rummaged behind her seat on the floorboard of the extended crew cab area and pulled out her police-issued flashlight along with one of two SLR digital cameras she kept in her truck.

Dead bodies didn't turn up all that often and while the woman that had been found wasn't going anywhere just yet, Rily was sure the man who had found her wanted to be anywhere else.

She slung the camera strap over her shoulder, flipped on her flashlight and pinpointed the direction of voices along with a soft, barely there circle of diffused light just off in the distance. She stepped forward in that direction.

"Detective Carrigan?" Another low level beam of light, most of its glare sucked up by the fog, bobbed towards her. "Let me guide you in."

She recognized the voice, one of the uniformed officers, and stopped to turn in his direction. With her own flashlight pointed at the ground, she hunched her shoulders in her fake-fur lined jacket, zipped it up to her neck and shoved her free hand into the pocket.

"Samuels." She nodded and moved towards him when he seemed to materialize from the thick, soupy air.

He nodded in return and fell into step beside her. Both of their flashlight beams barely cut through the fog, but they kept them trained on the ground for a small semblance of guidance. Small comfort, but at least the ground was relatively flat in this area.

"You were first at the scene?" Rily stepped over the curb and onto the wet grass.

"Yes."

"Fill me in."

"Guy passing through this area stopped to let his dog piss –, I mean pee." Samuels blew out a breath, the vapor lit by the glow of the flashlight and mixing with the fog.

Rily sucked in her bottom lip to keep her smart remarks to herself. Now wasn't the time.

"The dog had to go so he stopped here rather than along-side the road." Samuels cleared his throat.

"So our guy had his dog out of his car, letting it pee?"

"Yeah. And the dog got away from him, ran off. Our guy goes looking for the dog and finds the dead woman, at the back behind the dumpster, just inside the line of trees."

"Where is this guy now?"

"In his car. Just over there." Samuels aimed his flashlight to the right where a small, grey vehicle was barely visible in the beam. "With his dog. I have his keys, just in case. The guy's pretty shook up."

"I imagine he is."

Voices again penetrated the fog, closer and just to the left.

"The body?" Rily stopped and turned to Samuels. "Did this guy touch her? Contaminate the scene in any way?"

"We're pretty sure his dog did, but he swears he, himself, didn't."

"What about all these extra people I hear out here? The ones those vehicles belong to? That don't belong out here. Who's keeping them away from the scene?"

"The entire night shift showed up, Detective. We've got a good handle on that."

"Right." For all their sakes, she hoped the rest of the night stayed quiet, it'd be hell getting anywhere fast in this soupy fog. "And the victim?"

"White female. Maybe early thirties. Whoever killed her –"

"Killed? You believe she was murdered?"

"Yeah, Rily. I do." Samuels sucked in a deep breath and exhaled hard. The mist from his mouth swirled into the fog. He glanced to the left, in the direction of the voices. "Whoever did this left her there, partially covered with pine needles, like maybe they were trying to hide her. I don't think she did that herself."

"Nude? Clothed?"

"Clothed."

"Any idea who she is?"

"No. Not a local. No one any of us recognize." Samuels waved his light to the right, away from the low drone of voices. "She's a few feet over there. You'll want to watch for the moisture dripping from the overhead trees."

Great. If there was any evidence not contaminated by the dog or weather, she'd be surprised. "Okay. Grab the other camera from my truck, see if you can get some pictures of the lookie loos, the surrounding area. Hard in this mucky air, but see what you can do."

"No problem."

"Reiterate to the rest of Night Shift about keeping my perimeter secure. And let me know when the State M.E. arrives. She's in town, so I called and woke her up. With any luck, she should be here shortly."

"Will do."

Rily watched Samuels retreating back. The slight bob of his light beam disappeared within a few feet and darkness swallowed him.

Was the fog getting thicker?

Hell of a night to find a dead body.

With her shoulders back and squared, Rily aimed her own light in front of her. She might as well get this show on the road.

Assaulted by the underlying stench of wet garbage, she scrunched her nose.

Dank. Rotting.

Helluva night.

A few feet ahead, in the swing of her light beam, lay a lump of something underneath a sopping wet pile of pine needles. Their victim.

Rily moved closer and played her light over the small area. Samuels had been right. The pine needles on this side of the body had been disturbed. Possibly from the dog pawing at the pile of needles. Muted yellow that might be bright in actual daylight, peeked from where the needles had been moved. The victim's shirt? Maybe a jacket.

Those pine needles covered the woman like a blanket, tucked up to her chin. Moisture from the night air had soaked the blonde hair, leaving it dark and tangled around the woman's head.

Rily knelt and aimed her light at the face.

Her insides knotted as if a fist had slammed into her gut.

No. No. No.

Rily wiped a hand over her eyes, but the face stayed the same.

Shit.

Allison.

Allison Davis.

Samuels had only been partially right. No one else recognized her because Allison was no longer a local. But she had been once. A long time ago.

She'd come back. To see Rily.

Chapter Two

RILY, WITH BOTH HANDS shoved deep in her jacket pockets and her shoulders hunched forward against the chill of the wee morning hour, kept her gaze on the Medical Examiner as the woman worked on the body that still lay on the ground.

Temporary overhead lights the officers had set up barely cut through the murkiness of the heavy fog. Fog that condensed and dripped from the trees, that gave everything an otherworldly feel.

And Rily still reeled from the realization the body was Allison Davis. Her best friend in high school.

The one person from her past she'd never wanted to see again.

Allison had called last week, left a voice mail saying she planned to be in town towards the end of the month, before New Year's. Two weeks from now. What she'd wanted, Rily hadn't been sure. The cryptic message could have meant anything.

Rily hadn't called her back. Had no desire to rekindle that friendship, open those old wounds.

Allison no longer had family left in the area, no one left to visit. So what was she doing here, this many days before her supposed trip to Eagle Crest?

What was she doing dead?

Shivers raced over Rily's skin, shivers having more to do with their shared past than the bone-aching cold of the pre-dawn air. She let her fixed stare drop to the body on the ground.

Allison had hung around some shady, weird people in the past. Had one of them gone over the edge? Rily didn't know who the woman associated with now, but she'd have to find out what her one time friend had gotten herself into.

And why she'd brought it back here, to Rily's turf.

"Hey?" Malory Quinn's husky voice pulled her from her circular thoughts.

Grateful, Rily pulled her hands from her pockets to run her fingers through her shoulder-length hair then rubbed her fingers over her eyes and shook her head once. Lack of sleep was catching up with her. Fast. She turned to the Medical Examiner. "Yeah, Mal?"

Malory stood, her hands at the small of her back, and stretched. Several of the uniformed officers still milling around stopped and openly watched.

Men.

Stepping around a couple of them, Rily shook her head again, this time in slight bemusement. Long, red curls, porcelain skin, big brown eyes and a compact, curvy body and males went stupid. Samuels was the worse. Smitten didn't even begin to describe the look on his face.

And Malory was oblivious.

Rily let a half smirk curl her lips.

Heaven help those men if Mal ever decided to pay attention.

"What do you have?" Rily stopped next to her.

Malory held up a key between her gloved fingers. In spite of the fog, the overhead lights managed to glint off the tarnished, brass colored metal. Rily slipped on her own pair of thin evidence gloves, took the key and turned it over in her hand then ran her fingers over the mostly smooth surface. Longer and narrower than a regular key, RSM was etched into the top of one side, 227 on the other.

"River Shores Motel, at the eastern edge of town." Malory shrugged. "I stayed there for almost a week the first time I came to town. Not a dump, not a palace either."

"And you found this on her?"

Malory nodded, her gaze skimming the body on the ground. "Nothing to confirm your ID, nothing except that key in one of those hide-away pockets inside her jacket. You almost had to be looking for it to find it."

Rily turned it over in her hand again. "Samuels?"

The man was next to her in mere seconds. Rily bit the inside of her cheek to keep her smart-ass remark to herself. Malory gave the man an absentminded smile before frowning and crouching down again next to the body.

"Head over to River Shores." Rily snapped her fingers in front of Samuels' face. "Secure this room, number 227, while I work on obtaining a search warrant."

She had to do this right. Completely by the book. For Allison. To avoid any questions of impropriety in her knowing the victim. To keep from having this case yanked away from her.

She hadn't wanted to see Allison, but she hadn't wanted to see her dead, either. She had to see this through, find out what had happened to her one time friend. Find whoever had dumped her like so much garbage at a roadside rest stop.

And why.

WITH ONE HAND loose over her truck's steering wheel, Rily settled back against the driver's door and sipped the steaming coffee Samuels had brought her from the café attached to the River Shores Motel.

Dawn was breaking over the tree line to the east, the colors a soft pastel and barely visible through the swirling ground fog. Although normally a peaceful time of day, dawn was even colder than the night had been.

The warrant had yet to arrive.

She sat in her truck in front of Room 227 and its Do-Not-Disturb sign hanging from the doorknob. With her covering the only way in or out, Samuels had opted to sit in the café, at a booth with a perfect view of Rily and the room. Warmer yes, but she had her heater running and alone time to think, to jot down notes. This was more conducive to her state of mind than breakfast and chatty waitresses.

Process time. Not that she'd come up with anything new, but her notes were complete, even if her thoughts were chaotic.

A large, dark blue sedan swung into the parking lot and pulled to a stop on the right side of her truck. Rily sat straight.

Why was Chief Hendricks here?

She had called him to fill him in, to request the warrant and to let him know she had been the one to ID the victim. But she hadn't expected him to show up, not here.

Her fingers fumbling a slight bit, she pushed her truck door open and climbed down, still gripping her to-go coffee cup. She slammed her truck door, the sound loud in the quietness of the morning.

Great. She needed to reign in her nerves. Fast.

"Chief." She rounded the hood of her truck and nodded at the large man now standing between the two vehicles.

She'd known the Chief since she was in diapers. He'd watched her grow up, had served as Assistant Chief under her own father when he'd been Chief. To say Hendricks knew her was an understatement. But she knew him almost as well. And the look in his eyes hit her low in the stomach.

"Rily."

The door to the café opened and Samuels hunched his shoulders before heading toward them at a brisk pace.

The Chief nodded at the uniformed man, tilted his chin towards the door of Room 227. "Officer, stay here while Detective Carrigan and I take a short walk."

"Yes sir." Samuels gave Rily a quick look of sympathy.

"Detective." With his palm open, the Chief indicated they proceed along the sidewalk in front of the motel rooms.

Her stomach a mass of unruly moths, Rily moved into step with Hendricks. "Is there an issue with the warrant, sir?"

"No." He patted his jacket pocket. "I have your warrant. But that can wait a few moments."

They took several more steps, reached the end of the sidewalk before the Chief stopped and faced her, his light blue eyes troubled.

"Ben Garrett called me late yesterday evening."

The moths in Rily's stomach died a sudden death, leaving the taste of decayed wings strong in her mouth.

She didn't hate Ben, most days she actually liked him. But anything he was involved in also involved that woo-woo shit. Stuff she wanted no part of, in any way or form.

Yet wasn't that exactly what she was afraid Allison had been involved in, with the shady friends she used to hang with?

Shit. She shoved those thoughts to the back of her mind. "What did Ben want this time?"

"He has an agent he wants to send out."

"No."

"Rily –"

"No."

"Detective."

Rily puffed out her cheeks then let her breath mingle with the fog. Dammit. Hendricks was the Chief, and although she wanted his job one day, that day hadn't arrived yet. "Sir."

"Yesterday Garrett wanted this agent of his to work with you on the cold case John Does." Hendricks nailed her with a stern look. "After your identification of Allison Davis this morning, *I* want the man to work with you on this case."

"Sir." Rily fought to keep her feelings from crossing her face. "Although I knew the victim, it was a long time ago. I do believe I can conduct an unbiased investigation."

"I'm sure you can, Detective. However, we can't be sure this case isn't related to the two John Does. Garrett has a vested interest in those cases."

"We don't know that there *is* any connection to those cases, either, Sir."

Hendricks turned to face the row of rooms and gave her a sideways look. "Rily, why turn away an offer of help?"

She could think of all kinds of reasons. But the look the Chief threw her killed the tirade of words springing full born from her mouth.

Dammit and double dammit. She didn't need an *agent*, one without any type of credible law enforcement credentials, getting in her way. And that's all he would do, get in her way.

"According to Garrett, his man should be here sometime this evening." The Chief began moving again, back towards Samuels and Room 227. He pulled an envelope from his pocket. "Here's your warrant. And Rily?"

"Sir?" She took the envelope, struggled to keep her face impassive, and stopped in front of her truck to look up at him.

"Play nice." He smiled, but it didn't reach his eyes. With a nod to Samuels, the Chief climbed into his car.

Dammit, when didn't she *play nice*?

"RILY?" Samuels' voice edged toward a low level of excitement. "There's a laptop under the mattress here."

She turned from the mostly empty closet to face the officer. "Paranoia because of thieves or hiding something she didn't want anyone to see?"

"Your guess is as good as mine." Samuels pulled the black laptop from between the mattress and box springs and tagged the computer. "Do you want me to fire it up here, or at the station?"

"At the station." Rily rotated her shoulders, turned her head side to side. "I think we're done here."

Except for a few sweatshirts and two pair of jeans, some underclothes in one of the drawers, nothing personal had come of this search warrant. No purse, no car keys, no ID. Nothing to say this room was inhabited by Allison Davis. Or anyone else for that matter.

Until the computer. If it was even Allison's laptop.

Although a uniformed officer, Samuels doubled as their department's Crime Scene Investigation tech. *Teach him to take a few classes in Portland and then brag about the fact.* He was good though, and Rily appreciated the fact he'd been the responding officer when the call had come in to the station.

"You've been up all night." So had she, and the lack of sleep was beginning to cloud her thoughts. "Your shift officially ended hours ago. Why don't we log all of this into evidence, catch some sleep then meet back at the station in a few hours?"

And maybe, after some sleep and then time on the internet looking into her old friend's past, she might have some kind of clue where to go from here.

GABE SHIFTED IN the flimsy metal chair, crossed his right ankle on his left knee. He wasn't going to complain about Ben's chairs ever again, not after the last hour sitting here at the Eagle Crest Police Department.

The Chief was a nice enough guy, easy to read. Much easier than he believed himself to be. A Bear of a guy, easy-going enough, with a steel core. But the Chief wasn't who Gabe wanted a read on, and the woman of the hour was nowhere around.

Conspicuously absent at the moment.

Rily Carrigan.

Her name had played in his head all the way out here. From the airport in Minnesota to the one in Portland, and the drive out from there along the Columbia River practically to the Pacific Coast, she stayed at the front of his mind.

Water was everywhere in this corner of the States.

Somehow he didn't think that would help keep the visions away here anymore than it had on his boat in the Caribbean. Not with this Carrigan woman out there, somewhere in the vicinity.

But then, maybe, once he met her, identified the direction of the threat that would take her life, the vision would back off.

He could hope.

His ankle still crossed, Gabe slouched in his seat, linked his fingers over his stomach. Stale, burnt coffee seemed to be the aroma of the early evening hour. Outside the front doors an early dusk had already fallen.

Those same front doors swished open and the room sparked with a sudden high energy level scattering to reach all corners of the room before being pulled back as suddenly as it had appeared.

Gabe lifted his head, eyed the tall, lithe woman striding into the building and containing all that energy inside her tight, well-toned body. Somehow, neither the visions nor Ben's photo had prepared him for the angry gold sparking out of those pissed-off green eyes.

Or the way his solar plexus tightened in response to the mere sight of her. Crap. Not good. In any way.

Rily Carrigan, very much alive at the moment, stopped directly in front of him. Her eyes widened, just for a moment. Gabe remained seated, his fingers still loosely twined over his stomach.

"Benjamin Garrett sent you?"

"Technically, no."

She narrowed those gorgeous gold flecked eyes of hers, obviously not caring who saw this little tête-á-tête of theirs. "But he's behind you being here."

"What do you have against Ben?"

Her brows lowered and her Totem Tiger glared out at him.

A Bengal. No wonder restlessness rolled off her in waves. And the green eyes that flared with gold heat. A true Tiger.

"I thought you were all one big, happy family." He knew better than to taunt a Tiger, had tangled with one and had the scars to prove that fact.

"Is that what he told you?"

"No. Actually, it's not." Gabe tilted his head to one side, looked up at the woman who even now made his insides clench. "He told me you were a piece of work with a chip on her shoulder. One with no time for anything remotely dealing with what couldn't be seen or touched. But once I got past that, we probably still wouldn't be able to stand each other."

She stared at Gabe for a long moment. Then a sharp laugh exploded from her. "Well. At least Ben understands me."

Gabe cocked an eyebrow. The assessing look she gave him ran over his entire body. Tingles followed her gaze, speared across his skin.

What the hell was that about? Whatever it was, he needed to apply the brakes. Take control. Do something.

He stood, offered his hand. "Gabe Nicholetti."

"Rily Carrigan." She eyed his outstretched hand before grasping it with her own. "But you already knew that."

"Yes, I did."

The firmness of her grip, the warm softness of her hand in his, seeped through his skin in those few seconds. Then she pulled away, her fingers curled and a frown marred her forehead.

He missed the contact. That fast, he missed her touch.

Trouble didn't even begin to describe this cluster.

"Well." Rily met his gaze, her own troubled. She cleared her throat, glanced around the quiet room.

Oh yeah. They weren't the only two people in the room. He followed her lead, met and held the gaze of two male uniformed officers. One looked away immediately but the other held firm. Gabe gave him a slight nod. He'd have to find out who those two men were, what they meant to Rily. Why the one had his hackles up and male instincts flaring.

And if either one would have any reason to want her dead.

"Why don't we continue this in my office?" Rily nodded to the stiff and alert officer herself, before turning to Gabe. "I'd like to know what Ben hopes to accomplish, sending you out here like this."

Save your life, stop my vision from becoming true, from happening. Something that had never before been accomplished. With his neck and shoulders in bunched, tight knots, Gabe followed Rily across the station to a small den of an office. She waved him inside.

He moved past, but the scent of her filled him, lingered in the air. Musky sandalwood, rich amber undertones. The kind of subtle fragrance that haunted a man, made him think of things he was better off not thinking about.

Not with this woman. Definitely not at this time.

Gabe set his shoulders, ignored the tingle in the hand she'd shaken and shoved both his hands into his pockets. He spared a quick glance around the cramped room.

One small window. That would drive him crazy fast. The office barely had enough room to turn around. The desk, stuffed in the back corner, faced the door with two of those uncomfortable metal chairs at attention in front. A definite den, all of it Rily's space.

One wall was covered with accommodations, the other with differing sizes of black-stained wood framed photos. Most were black and whites, for the most part capturing the same small group of people in movement, in joy of life, in grief. Gabe blinked and moved in closer to study the photos.

Ben stared out of one, a close up, with a huge grin on his face. Gabe, with his hands still in his pockets, rocked back on his heels. Except for the wedding photo, how long since he'd seen that look on Ben's face? Too many years.

A throat cleared behind him and Gabe angled his head to meet Rily's gaze. She stood just inside her door, arms crossed over her middle, a frown drawing her brows down.

"Nice pictures." He kept his tone neutral and his expression bland.

Her eyes narrowed. "Thanks."

He raised an eyebrow at that. "You took these?"

"Yeah. So?"

"You and Ben are frauds. Both of you."

"Excuse me?"

"The way you two take swipes at each other, you'd think you hated his guts."

"What makes you think I don't?"

"Ben wouldn't let his guard this far down unless there was a wealth of respect and even liking between you."

Her expression shielded, Rily eyed him then shrugged. "So."

His gaze locked on hers, Gabe let his mouth move into the semblance of a grin. "So maybe you'll learn to like me, too."

Her eyes widened, her lips parted then clamped close. She pushed past him to stand behind her desk. "Nicholetti, I wouldn't like you if you were the last man on earth."

Chapter Three

RILY RESISTED COVERING HER FACE with her hands. Last man on earth? How juvenile could she sink? If the challenge in Gabe Nicholetti's dark brown eyes was anything to go by, she'd just set herself up, but royal.

Dammit, why didn't she stop and think before she shoved her foot in her mouth? Still, those gorgeous, soulful eyes of his did have long sinful lashes. And those same eyes saw much more than he let on. She needed to remember that. Hunk or not.

"Have a seat." She waved to one of the chairs sitting in front of her desk, almost laughing at the distaste marking his face when he glared at the chair.

The edge of his lip quirked upwards in response before he pulled the chair back and settled his large frame in the now dwarfed chair.

He was tall. And broad. And rugged.

And she needed to stop. Get her raging hormones under control. How long had it been since she'd reacted this quick, this keenly, to any man?

Not wanting to go there, afraid Mr. Sharp Eyes would know *exactly* where her thoughts had wandered, she settled into her own, much more comfortable seat and pasted a fake smile on her mouth. "Back to Ben."

"Didn't realize we'd left him."

Bullshit. But she wasn't taking the bait. Not this time.

"Why does Ben want you assigned to me?" Rily picked up her pen, tapped it on her open notebook, more for something to occupy her fingers than to take any notes.

"Unexplained dead bodies." His dark gaze hooded, Gabe slouched in his chair, something she hadn't thought the chair would have been able to withstand, and laced his fingers over his stomach.

"As of this morning, with the newest dead body, cold cases aren't my priority. Not at this time."

"Again, unexplained dead bodies."

"That have nothing to do with you or Ben."

"True, in the strictest sense." Gabe crossed his right ankle on top of his left knee, lifted his linked fingers above his chest and ran his thumbs along his jaw. "However, your latest Jane Doe may be related to the John Does. Both Hendricks and Garrett want answers. I imagine you do, too. I'm here to help."

Her eyes narrowed, Rily leaned forward. "This is my case, Nicholetti. Understand the first time you get in my way, you're gone."

His gaze still unreadable, he held hers for a long, drawn out moment and then nodded. "Not a problem, Detective."

That was too easy. Rily leaned back in her chair, still holding her pen. The left edge of his mouth tipped up, but the rest of his face remained impassive. No expression. Even his eyes stayed neutral.

The man was too good at not being read.

And she was spending too much time sparring with him while a killer ran loose. She sat straight and pulled her notebook to her, ignoring the way Nicholetti's eyebrow lifted.

Screw him and Ben both.

"Since I seem to be stuck with you for the time being, let's get you up to speed on what we know about Allison Davis."

"You ID'd her."

"Yes. Knew her in high school, haven't seen her in close to fourteen years." Rily glanced down at her notebook, away from his probing gaze. She quickly filled him in on the key and their slim findings at the motel.

"So beyond a few changes of clothes and the laptop, she left nothing of personal consequence here in Eagle Crest?"

"Nothing." With a glance at the closed door behind Gabe, Rily ran her fingers through her hair, resisting the urge to fist her hands in the fine strands. "Samuels is working on the laptop. She had it pass coded, but he's already gotten past that."

Gabe's fingers still interlaced, he tapped the pads of his thumbs together and kept his unreadable gaze locked on her. "So Davis isn't from here, not any longer. You've found her current place of residence? Family?"

"Yes on the residence." Dammit. When the Chief had called to tell her Nicholetti was waiting at the station he'd reiterated the play nice comment, adding another about considering the man her partner.

A partner was the last thing she needed.

Rily picked up her pen and leaned back in her seat. "House in a small suburb on the southwest side of Portland. A rental. There doesn't seem to be an actual house phone, the only number we can find listed is for a cell phone. Which hasn't turned up and although it does ring, no one answers when we call it. No next of kin. Her parents are long gone. No siblings. It appears there's no one left to contact about her death."

"When are we heading to Portland?"

"Direct, aren't you?"

"When it pays to be."

"Tomorrow morning, bright and early. The warrant should be taken care of by then."

"We need a warrant?"

"Just in case. Allison may have had a roommate, a live in, someone we don't know about. Someone who could argue later about expectation of privacy. This way we're covered."

Gabe nodded.

"By then Samuels should also have whatever there is to find on the laptop."

"Samuels being your C.S.I.?"

Rily laughed, the sound dry in the small confines of her office. "Small town. Officially the only crime scene investigating is by me or the other detective and whatever M.E. we can convince to head over from Portland. Unofficially, we have an officer who has put himself through school and who, once he graduates, we're going to lose to some big city department."

"He would be one of the officers out front?"

"Yeah. Kyle Samuels. And this time I lucked out on the M.E. Malory Quinn is in town on other matters so I called her. We should have her report by morning, also."

"Is she here looking into the John Does from last year?"

"Partly. She's also trying to line up a County Coroner." She aimed a dark look Gabe's way. "We lost ours after Ben was in town last April and no one has stepped up to take the job."

"I heard something about all of that." He sort of smiled, but the expression didn't make it past the slight lift of his lips.

Full, firm lips. Lips that seemed to be immensely kissable.

Damn, she needed to reign in her thoughts.

Especially with the man's dark eyes remaining so expressionless. Rily kept her gaze locked on his eyes. No, his eyes weren't blank. There were depths swirling in that darkness. Deeper than she wanted to delve.

Depths he kept banked and guarded.

She really needed to get a handle on her wayward thoughts, especially the fanciful direction those thoughts wandered in with this guy. "Preliminary shows the body had only been there a short time. Essentially dumped. No one heard anything, no one saw anything until the guy with the dog found her."

Gabe nodded then covered a yawn with his hand. "Sorry. Long day."

"Yeah, changing time zones will do that to you."

"Try changing more than a few."

Rily raised an eyebrow. "You came in from Minnesota, right?"

"This leg." Gabe leaned his head back, his eyes half closed. "Started out early yesterday morning in the British Virgin Isles."

Rily blinked. She knew Ben wanted the cold cases solved, believed they had something to do with the case from last spring, although they hadn't yet been able to make a connection. But to bring someone in from so far away? "You're that good?"

A slow, lazy smile etched itself across Gabe's mouth. "Depends on what we're talking about, Carrigan."

"Solving crimes. Cold cases." She held his gaze, ordered her insides to quit the slow burn that settled low in her belly with all that maleness aimed in her direction. Crap and double crap. For good measure she narrowed her eyes and lifted her chin a slight fraction. There wasn't much she could do about the heat on her cheeks.

His smile widened. "Right."

"Where are you staying?"

His left eyebrow shot up.

"So I can pick you up for our trip to Portland in the morning." Dammit, she hated having to explain herself, hated the double entendre she wasn't sure she hadn't meant.

"Right." He stifled another yawn. "I have a room at the Pier Hotel."

"Nice place. I'll be there at 0700 hours. Be ready, Nicholetti. Meet me outside."

"Not a problem, Detective." He pushed himself out of the chair and stood, rotating his shoulders. "I need to grab something to eat. I don't suppose you'd be interested in joining me?"

"You suppose right." She tapped her pen against her notebook. "I was just finishing dinner when the Chief let me know you were here."

"Some other time then." He smiled, and damned if it didn't seem to actually reach his eyes. The man was lethal.

With her treacherous heart thumping in her chest, she gave him a tight smile of her own. "Maybe."

He held her gaze a moment longer than necessary before giving her a small mock salute and turned to leave. With a soft click, he pulled the door shut behind him.

Rily stared at her closed office door for a brief second before bracing her elbows on her desk and cradling her head in her hands. Forget the double crap, this just went off the crap-meter.

If she wasn't careful that man would have her wrapped around his little finger and every other part of his anatomy.

And what a fine anatomy it was … *stop*. This wasn't like her, not in the slightest bit.

Talk about skewed priorities.

Her old high school friend lay dead on a slab in the hospital basement and she sat here drooling over a man she just met.

Could life get any weirder?

GABE STOOD OUTSIDE the Eagle Crest Police Station and shoved his fingers through his hair. His palm still tingled. From touching her hand?

What was he thinking? Flirting with Rily Carrigan?

Wanting Rily Carrigan. In his bed, underneath him, on top of him. Any way he could get inside her. His erection pressed tight against his jeans and he shifted his stance, unable to get comfortable. He stared down the dark street, towards his hotel and the river.

There was no way this desire for Rily Carrigan could be anything other than trouble.

Another freaking Tiger.

Hadn't he learned his lesson the last time he'd tangled with a Tiger? He ran his hand over the back of his neck, over the long thin ridge of scar tissue that still ached with a sharp intensity, even after all these months.

Almost a full year.

Hadn't Talia Garrett taught him anything? She'd tried to kill him, left him scarred, his relationship with Ben damaged. In a real sense she'd broken both their hearts, his and her father's.

And now this Tiger, Rily Carrigan, played on all of his senses, called to him in a way he hadn't thought possible. Not for a freak like himself. But she wouldn't live to see the end of next month, maybe not even the start of the New Year.

No matter what Ben thought was possible, Gabe should leave. He couldn't save Carrigan, not from herself, nor from whatever was out there, wanting her dead.

Why was he bothering to try? Why go through the anguish of one more failure?

He was an Orca, his totem a sea mammal. He lived for the water, to be surrounded by the sheer liquid beauty. This Tiger, this cat, was a land animal. She was trouble and he wouldn't survive a skirmish with her, not intact.

He turned to study the building behind him.

What the hell was he doing here?

RILY PUSHED OPEN the side door and exited the station. Tonight the fog was lighter than it had been the night before, not as thick, although the air was colder. She flipped up the collar of her jacket, tossed her hair out of the way to let the soft, fake fur warm her neck.

Grateful her truck wasn't too far away, even though she'd be home before the heater managed to do more than blow a little hot air around the interior, she hunched her shoulders against the chill as she made her way across the small, asphalt lot backed up against the hillside.

They were too small a department for any kind of parking structure. Here, the vehicles were protected a little from the winds, but not the rain.

Next to her truck she tapped the remote and opened the driver door at the responding beep. Then stopped.

Prickles tingled along the base of her skull.

Something wasn't right.

A sense, heavier than the surrounding fog, hung in the air. Rily shoved her purse onto the seat, pulled her gun from its holster under her jacket and turned in a slow circle, her open truck door behind her. With her night vision almost nonexistent after being inside the well-lit building, she narrowed her gaze and scanned the surrounding area as best as she could.

What a time to *not* have her flashlight.

Nothing seemed out of place.

Still, she kept her weapon out and hopped into her truck, butt first. She swung her legs around, slammed the door shut, hit the lock button.

She had nothing to go by, nothing beyond a gut feeling. Something was out there, watching her.

Someone.

Something was just a fanciful term, brought out by her overwrought imagination. Along with Allison's aborted return to her life. *Something* was a place she wasn't going.

There weren't many places to hide in the parking lot. Not many vehicles left this time of evening. Maybe a cat, one of the big ones, up on the ridge above the station, but she doubted that.

This felt … intelligent.

And patient. Waiting.

Geez. Give her a little time and she'd be sounding like Ben Garrett. She scanned the area outside her windshield one more time.

Nothing.

With her gun on the seat, tucked just under her thigh but accessible, she shoved the key in the ignition, twisted it. Once she had the truck started, she revved the engine. With her headlights on high beam, she shifted into reverse and eased her truck from the parking space.

Shadows pushed back in the wide swath of her headlights, and still nothing appeared out of place. Rily shifted into drive, deciding to take the long route home. Just in case.

A HALF BLOCK from Rily Carrigan's two-story, Craftsman style home, Gabe stood in the shadows, a foot outside the circle of light cast by the old fashioned wrought-iron streetlight. Fog lent an eerie glow to the light and dampened everything.

His shoulders stooped against the night's chill, he debated between cursing Rily and her paranoia and applauding her instincts.

If she hadn't been so alert, he'd now be tucked inside his rental car with the heater on, warm and toasty on this hellishly cold night. But with her on high alert, the sight of a non-familiar sedan parked on her street was bound to arouse her suspicions.

And something had waited outside the station. Something or someone besides him. He'd felt the presence, weighing down the air. More than mere bone-chilling humidity.

The way Rily had come to attention when she reached her truck had impressed him, made him wonder briefly how anything would get past that attentiveness. But his visions never lied. Someone wanted her dead and that someone would succeed.

Gabe hadn't followed Rily himself. He already knew where she lived, already knew she was taking what she considered to be the long way home.

In her place, he would have done the same.

Whatever waited hadn't followed her either, hadn't done anything except fade away to nothing. Which didn't bode well at all, not to his way of thinking. Especially after being so intently focused on Rily. The question was *who or what* that something was, and Gabe didn't have an answer. Yet.

So he'd made his way to Rily's place, had waited for her to get home. Waited to see if the presence showed up as well.

That had been hours ago.

Now, with her big, red truck sitting square in her drive, Rily and her large dog were secure inside her home. The lights to what must be her bedroom had finally gone off and nothing stirred. Natural or preternatural.

She was in bed, alone. A fact over which he had no reason to rejoice. In fact, he should be wishing she had someone. Anyone. If she did, he'd find it easier to tamp down this overwhelming desire, this *need*, to join her there in her bed. He'd find it so much easier to ignore the *want* eating away at him.

Because he wouldn't poach. Not if she had someone.

Instead, his soul reveled in the knowledge she was alone and as aware of him as he was of her. Even while his brain screamed what a bad idea that awareness was, that nothing good could come of any of this.

He shoved the mental and emotional tug of war to the back of his mind. What kind of answer could he possibly find on this cold night?

With a wide yawn, he rotated his shoulders and stretched his senses throughout the neighborhood, specifically around Rily's house, one more time.

Nothing.

Time to round up his car, park it just down the street and see if he could actually get some semblance of sleep before he had to beat Rily to his hotel in less than five hours. And still be presentable. Or at least showered and shaved.

He set a mental sphere of protection around her home. Shields and wards weren't his forte, he wasn't *gifted* in that area, not like some of the other agents. His sphere wouldn't stop anything that seriously wanted in, but at least an internal alarm would sound inside him, alerting him to the trouble.

Trouble. That had to be the woman's middle name. With a capital T. A Tigress named Rily Trouble Carrigan.

A woman he wanted with an intensity that scared him.

A woman whose life he couldn't save.

Chapter Four

RILY, SURE SHE WAS going to have to go inside the hotel and hunt Gabe down, swung her truck underneath the Pier Hotel's portico. She shoved the gear shifter into park and adjusted her sunglasses against the bright December sun.

Beautiful day for a drive into Portland. Chilly, but without clouds or fog, a day meant for a drive. Too bad the circumstances weren't better. And too bad the company in question had her uneasy in ways and places she resented this beautiful morning.

The man in question leaned against one of the hotel's front pillars, his left foot braced behind him on the column. He sipped from one of the two to-go cups he held.

Worn blue jeans hugged his muscular legs, matching the worn work boots on his feet. The sweatshirt he wore looked suspiciously new. A light morning breeze ruffled his shaggy brown hair and black sunglasses covered those sexy, dark eyes.

Nothing hid the wicked grin he aimed her way, though, or stopped the fire from reigniting way down inside her belly. A fire she'd thought she'd banked last night.

After she'd gotten over being spooked by the thought of someone watching her, she'd dwelled on Gabe Nicholetti for a while, dismissed him as her mysterious watcher and had hoped, against odds, she'd managed to tie him up and shove him in the corner of her mind marked stupid.

Stupid was right, if just that lethal grin had her insides getting all hot and mushy. Stupid, stupid, stupid.

Gabe pushed away from the column and through the open driver's window he handed over one of the to-go cups. He rounded the hood of the truck, pulled open his door and climbed inside.

"Coffee?" Rily pulled the lid off and the steaming aroma filled the truck cab. She closed her eyes for a brief second then took a cautious sip of the creamy, sweet liquid. "Perfect."

Gabe gave her that wicked grin. Again.

"How did you know?" Rily squinted, more to stop her internal reaction than in irritation. Then she thought about what she'd asked and annoyance flared inside. "Ben told you how I like my first cup of the morning, didn't he? How did you know it was my first cup?"

"So many questions. Wait. How the hell does Ben know how you like your *first* cup of the day? Never mind." Gabe held up a hand and set his own cup in the front cup holder. He clipped his seatbelt, slouched in his seat and adjusted his sunglasses before he crossed his arms over his chest. "Wake me when we get to Portland."

Rily turned in her seat. "Excuse me?"

"With the questions again." He covered his mouth and the yawn. "Didn't sleep well last night. I figured I'd catch up on the drive over. If you don't mind?"

Well. She'd worried about carrying on any kind of conversation with him, without making a sex-starved fool of herself, and he wanted to sleep all the way to Portland. "Fine. Whatever. Sweet dreams."

The quirk of his lips when he settled further into the seat had her jerking the truck out of the Pier's parking lot a bit rougher than she'd intended.

The fact he never said anything, just let his chin drop to his chest had her fuming for half the drive to Portland.

Damn man.

THE SLOWING OF the truck as Rily pulled off the freeway pulled Gabe back to consciousness, although he remained still, his breathing even. Staying outside her place until dawn broke this morning hadn't done much for his sleep ratio, although he had actually managed an hour or so in his car.

Too many thoughts had kept him awake. Plus the fact the cramped front seat of his rental wasn't conducive to sleep. Nor was the worry about whatever had been lurking near the parking lot, watching Rily.

The sleep of the last two hours had been his most restive in days. Maybe due to the fact she sat right next to him, maybe it was the way her earthy scent filled him, had surrounded him while he slept. And maybe he was an idiot when it came to Tigers.

On a deep intake of breath he rotated his shoulders and straightened in his seat. With this kind of restorative rest, he should just sleep at Rily's place. Indoors. He could always take the couch.

Under cover of his dark sunglasses, he slanted a glance at her stiff profile. Or maybe not. For his sanity's sake, he'd be safer outside. In the cold.

"We have to meet Sergeant Ortega to pick up the warrant." Her tones cool and clipped, Rily swung the truck into the half empty parking lot of a coffee shop that looked as if it had been there since the fifties.

"Ortega?"

"My brother's old partner."

"Right. Craig, the brother you lost early last year."

Rily threw him a startled look.

"Ben told me."

"Ben has a big mouth."

If only she knew. "So you're still in touch with Ortega?"

A purely feline smile crossed her face.

He took that as a yes. And already didn't like the guy.

With the truck switched off and her door open, Rily jumped down and turned to look at him across the seat. "Come on. You can buy me breakfast."

Buy her breakfast. Here at this dump. What he wanted was to buy her dinner, then make her breakfast and serve it to her. In bed.

She shut her door and with a slight, almost imperceptible lift to her step, she strode to the front entrance. She must be impatient to see this Ortega guy.

Somehow he didn't think it was for the warrant.

Breakfast. With Rily and another man. Wonderful.

Gabe eyed the run down exterior, the faded and chipped paint that might have once been yellow. Maybe. Even the bright morning sunshine didn't help the color. Weeds and thick grass grew up along the far side of the parking lot, coming close to topping the two foot wall running along the perimeter.

With this kind of ambiance he didn't want to hazard a guess at what was on the menu. Was he ever going to get a decent meal in this forsaken state?

He slid out and closed his own door. The door locks beeped before he was two feet away from the truck. He, for one, wasn't in that much of a hurry to see this guy.

Not at all.

Gabe managed to grab the front door before it swung closed in his face then followed Rily inside. Fifties retro wasn't quite the word. Neither was dinghy.

His stomach twitched in protest.

"There he is." Rily gave Gabe's arm a slight punch and side stepped a family trying to fit six into a booth made for four. She took off down a side aisle to the back of the restaurant.

"Wonderful." Gabe followed her, leaving his sunglasses in place, figuring he'd take them off *after* he assessed Sgt. Ortega.

He almost got lost in the sway of Rily's jean-clad hips, but her eagerness to reach this guy kept Gabe scanning the back of the restaurant.

At the far rear, with his back to the wall, a black-haired man slid out of the once red leather booth. Sgt. Ortega. Craig Carrigan's old partner.

Wearing black jeans and a button down black shirt, the man was on the slim side, with more of a swimmer's physique than a football player's. Ortega stepped forward and wrapped Rily in a full body hug, with his cheek pressed tight against her temple.

The man's darker skin tone, much closer to Gabe's Italian/Indian heritage than Rily's English complexion, practically glowed a burnished gold in the light filtering in from the twisted blinds to the side of the booth.

With his eyes closed, Ortega seemed to inhale the very air around her. So, *not* just a professional relationship between these two.

Pissed to realize he'd wanted it to be all business, in spite of Rily's obvious desire to see the man, Gabe's insides tangled into a nautical knot that might never come undone. He *really* didn't like this guy.

From his vantage point behind her, Gabe watched Rily press her forehead against Ortega's and the man rub his long fingers over her shoulders, down her back. The tension in her body eased, almost as if Ortega had wiped it away.

Gabe took another look at Ortega.

Was Ben right in his assessment? That Ortega was a natural healer? One who, if Gabe remembered the facts Ben had rattled off, refused to use his gifts or even acknowledge their existence?

Interesting.

With a soft word to Rily, Ortega turned and tucked her against his side. He stared at Gabe with dark, almost black, expressionless eyes. "Who is this, *Mi Corazon*?"

My Heart? Behind his sunglasses Gabe narrowed his own eyes. Healer or not, he still didn't like him. Couldn't get a handle on his totem, either. Almost as if he was being willfully blocked. Predator, though. This man was no one's prey.

"Gabriel Nicholetti." Rily glanced at Gabe, held his gaze for a short moment. "You could call him my current partner."

"Really?" Ortega cocked his head to the side. "Such enthusiasm. Does Jake know?"

Gabe recognized that name. Her other brother. The one in the wedding photo.

"What's to know? Ben Garrett, Jake's new boss, sent him out here to annoy me." Rily aimed an insincere smile at Gabe, the dark green of her eyes flat. "This is Sergeant Ramon Ortega."

"Ahh." Ortega smiled, the look predatory, not at all civil. "A work partner. Not personal, then?"

Gabe pulled off his sunglasses, let his own smile widen, knowing the look in his eyes matched Ortega's. The man grinned and humor lit his eyes for a brief second.

Rily, frowning, looked between them. She eased away from Ortega and slid into the booth on his side. "Let's eat and get this show on the road."

Ortega, his now shuttered gaze never leaving Gabe's, nodded. "Whatever you want, *Mi Corazon.*"

Gabe sat at the same time as Ortega, and leaned into the corner so his back wasn't completely to the room. He didn't care for Rily sitting next to the man, but at least from here he could watch them both. Gauge their interaction.

Decide if he needed to strangle Ortega with his bare hands. Or just beat him to a pulp with his fists.

If this was the guy who would ultimately be responsible for Rily's death, then he would do both. Beat him first then strangle him. With more than pleasure.

Although he'd only met her last night, he'd lived with visions of her for days longer than that. Visions of her staring at him with green, lifeless eyes. The gold completely leached away.

And after seeing that flash of gold, the anger and passion it brought with it, the thought of it gone squeezed at something deep inside his chest.

He forced the image away, focused on the very much alive Rily sitting across from him and his memory of the way her green-gold eyes sparked with frustration. With temper. With life.

The waitress, an older woman with greying blonde hair and a smile as bright as her light, blue eyes sat two empty mugs on the table along with two menus. She filled Ortega's cup from the coffee carafe she carried and then the two empty ones.

"I know what Ramon here is having." The waitress smiled. "But I can come back in a few, if you need time."

"I'll have the same." Rily handed her menu to the waitress and three sets of eyes stared at Gabe.

He glanced down at his unopened menu. "And just what is *Ramon* having?"

"Huevos Rancheros." The waitress beamed. "Best in the state."

Gabe took another glance around. Who knew the place served Mexican food? As far as he could tell, the establishment didn't even have a name. He handed the waitress his menu. "Then make it unanimous."

"Three orders it is. Coming right up." Her smile still spread wide across her face, the woman patted Ortega's hand before she moved away.

"You have the warrant?" Rily leaned back in her own corner, her coffee mug lifted to her mouth.

Gabe's gaze caught on her face as she blew steam across the surface. He yanked his gaze back to the table. Shit, he had to get a handle on this, whatever *this* was.

Ortega's mouth twisted slightly and one eyebrow lifted, but he touched his shirt pocket, checked his watch. "My team will meet us there in one hour. The place is maybe five minutes away."

Rily tapped the fingers of her left hand on her mug. What could only be anxiety clouded the gold flecks in her eyes. "You're going with us?"

"Wouldn't miss it." The line of his jaw tightened a fraction then relaxed. Gabe would have missed it if he hadn't been intent on watching their reactions to each other. "No worries, *Mi Corazon*. I've been cleared for active duty for several months now. I'm fine."

Gabe, his eyes narrowed, glanced between the two of them. This was something he would have to get to the bottom of, Rily's worry about this man and his health.

Rily held Ortega's gaze a moment longer then nodded. "You've been by this house? Any idea what we'll find?"

"Did a covert run last night. The whole neighborhood is quiet. Didn't seem to be anyone at your victim's residence. No lights, no activity."

"Maybe she lived alone, then. No roommates."

"Or they're out of town." Gabe shrugged. "Running maybe."

"Possibly. No next of kin, no one listed on the utilities except her." Ortega nodded and leaned back to let the waitress slip Rily's plate past him before she set his in front of him. He touched the woman on her arm. "Thank you."

The man was a touchy-feely sort. Because he was a healer, or was there another, uglier reason? Gabe nodded his own thanks to the waitress when she sat his plate down. She beamed at them all then rushed off to bring the carafe of coffee back for refills.

The scent of spicy green chilies mixed with the coffee's warm aroma and Gabe's stomach growled.

Ortega laughed. "You won't find better unless you head a lot farther south than here."

Gabe sent him a suspicious look, but the appetizing smell enticed him and he dug into his plate of food. Paradise on a plate. Silence reigned at their table while the other two did the same.

Gabe took back every dark thought he'd had about this place.

Rily, her food devoured, pushed her plate forward and checked her watch. "Come on guys. Time to roll."

"Man, woman. Give a guy a chance to enjoy his coffee." Ortega took a long swig from his cup.

"Time enough." Rily pushed on his shoulder. "Nicholetti's getting the tab."

Right. He was buying her breakfast.

With Ortega out of her way, Rily stood, her gaze on Gabe. Although the curve of her lips was harmless enough, the look in her eyes was anything except benign.

"Anytime, Sunshine."

She blinked once, opened her mouth then shut it before she gave a sharp nod and moved past him. He pulled a few bills from his wallet, making sure there was a good tip for the waitress and handed it to the woman. Then he followed the other two out of the restaurant.

A few feet outside the door, Ortega turned. "Thank you for breakfast."

Gabe glanced at the hand the man held out, then back up at his face. The eyes of a Jaguar shone in the depths of Ortega's eyes. Dark, cunning and aware.

Just how aware was the question.

Gabe inclined his head once before grasping Ortega's hand. Electricity sparked at the skin to skin contact. Ortega's eyebrows went up, along with the edges of his mouth.

"Interesting." With a slight grimace and one eyebrow still arched, the man pulled away.

"Very." Gabe curled his fingers into his palm. What the hell just happened?

"I walked here, so I'm hitching a ride with you and Rily to the Davis' residence. We can talk there, if you'd like."

Gabe held Ortega's gaze. "Count on it."

RILY GAVE A curt nod to the two men standing next to her and then to the uniformed officers behind them before she pulled her weapon and eyed the door of the small, tidy little house.

Ortega had been right, the place *felt* empty. Lifeless.

She made eye contact with Ortega and then Nicholetti before she spotted Gabe's gun. *Son of a bitch.* Where the hell had Nicholetti gotten that weapon? She hadn't noticed him carrying. And that wasn't the sort of thing she'd normally miss. She raised a brow. If things went bad, she didn't need him screwing it up worse.

"I'm legal to carry." His dark eyes direct, he held her gaze.

"We're going to have to talk about that." She slid a glance to Ramon, who had his own brows drawn down and then she glanced between the two of them. "Later."

Gabe smiled, the look lethal, and nodded at the open door. "Ladies first or shall I?"

"As if." She knocked on the door. "Police. Search warrant."

No response from inside. Rily reached down, twisted the knob and the door eased open.

Unlocked.

Okay then. That was a little too easy.

She nudged the door wider. The place was dark, heavy curtains pulled over the large living room windows they'd seen from the street.

And quiet.

"I'll take left." She stepped over the threshold, a faint hint of incense heavy in the air, along with cinnamon and cloves.

"Got the right." Ramon veered off to the side.

"I'll cover Rily's back. The uniform is yours."

How the hell did Gabe know entry-protocol?

She so wanted to spare that one glance over her shoulder but didn't dare. Not without knowing what waited ahead of her.

Nicholetti was full of surprises, in this instance a good surprise. Between this and his cop eyes, eyes that catalogued everything and everyone, maybe she wouldn't have to babysit his ass as much as she'd expected.

Their side of Allison's home included a small kitchen and an enclosed patio area, just as empty of life as the front part of the house. Awareness of Gabe, just behind her, pulsed underneath Rily's skin. She barely resisted rubbing her left arm.

That wasn't normal, not right, to be so aware of someone she could *feel* his movements. She didn't want that. Not with any man, and most definitely not with one of Ben's woo-woo agents.

And not on the job.

With the two rooms clear, and empty, she turned back and made quick eye contact with Gabe, contact that left her knees wobbly, damn him. She jerked her head to the side, more forcibly than she intended, indicating they head back to the living room.

Gabe, his dark eyes shuttered and completely unreadable, nodded once. With his free hand he rubbed the back of his neck and then motioned for her to go ahead. He fell in behind.

"Clear." Ramon entered the living room at the same time. He gave the room a quick scan, then turned to his men, the one who had followed him and the ones who had come in behind. He took a clipboard from one of the officers. "The house is secure. Figure out who to cover the perimeter. The rest of you can leave."

"Next round of drinks are on Sgt. Ortega, guys. Thanks for the help." Rily slipped her gun into its holster and walked with the men to the door. She hid a smile at the calls of where those drinks would be bought and paid for and ignored Ramon's good natured growl to get back to work.

She shut the door behind the uniformed men and turned to Ramon who stood in the center of the living room. "What did you find?"

"Two bedrooms." Ramon, his legs braced apart, glanced down at the clipboard. "Just as the floor plans indicate. A master and what looks like an artist studio with a twin bed in the corner. One bathroom."

"Allison was always artistic, so I'm not surprised she kept that going." Rily turned in a small, tight circle and focused on the roll-top desk tucked in the corner. And the little fake tree on top with several packages under its decorated limbs.

For a Christmas Allison would never see.

Rily turned away to address the two men still with her. "Ramon, can you do up our own rendering of the floor plans and Gabe, start in the master bedroom?"

"Already on it." Ramon held up the clipboard and a pencil.

"No problem, Detective." Gabe, his weapon tucked away at the small of his back and under his sweatshirt, gave Ramon an unreadable glance before heading out of the room.

Rily watched his retreating back for a moment and let her gaze linger on the curve of his butt and the way his worn jeans hugged his muscular thighs. She barely resisted the urge to sigh.

At the loud sound of a throat being cleared she swung her head sharp to glare at Ortega. "What?"

"Nothing, *Mi Corazon*." Ramon's dark eyes sparkled.

She may have resisted the sigh, but this was worse. Caught all but drooling. Damn them both. "Little heavy with the Corazon stuff, don't you think?"

Ramon smiled, the dimple in his right cheek deepened. "Never. We both know if not for your brother, you and I would have danced."

Her eyebrows drawn down, Rily tilted her head to the side. She was not going to admit the juvenile crush she'd had on this man from almost the moment they'd met. Not when he'd turned into a good and caring friend instead. Where he was going with this, she wasn't sure she wanted to know, not with her lusting after the big guy in the other room. Still, curiosity and all that. "Really?"

Ramon sighed, the sound rich in his chest. "It wouldn't have lasted, but we would certainly have lit up each other's world."

"Major problem with that." To avoid the over-the-top amorous look he sent her way, Rily moved to Allison's roll top desk.

She pulled white evidence gloves from the pocket of her jeans and slipped them on her hands before yanking back the curtains hanging behind the desk. Weak sunlight spilt into the room, glistening off the tinsel draped across the little tree.

With a stealthy sideways glance, she looked back. "Craig's been gone almost two years now. He's no longer between us."

"Ah, but he is." Ramon shifted the clipboard in his hand, the smile on his face almost sad. "In spirit if not in body."

"Ramon —"

"And since he's not here, and Jake is —" He frowned and drummed his fingers on the board. "Where is Jake?"

"Minnesota."

"With this Ben character?"

"Character is right."

The edge of Ramon's lips lifted. "So as your surrogate brother —"

Rily choked on the laugh suddenly bubbling in her throat. She didn't know of a single woman who would possibly think of Ramon Ortega as a *brother*.

He grinned, the look dangerous. "As your surrogate brother, let me say that if this Gabriel Nicholetti allows anything to happen to you, I will kill him."

Chapter Five

"KILL HIM?" Rily faced Ramon, her search through her one time friend's roll top desk momentarily forgotten, she fisted her gloved hands on her hips. "That's a little drastic. And what do you mean by *allow*?"

"Word choice only." Ramon's expression serious, he glanced towards the hallway. "If something happened to you I know Craig would want me to take care of the man responsible."

"Happen to me?" Rily screwed her eyes closed for a brief moment. "Why are you talking like this?"

"Because you are my responsibility now that Craig is no longer here and Jake is in Minnesota. No arguments. That is just the way it is." He shrugged his left shoulder. "Craig would want you safe. Wrapped in cotton. However, I don't believe that is possible."

She frowned. How had they gotten on this subject? More important, how did they get off it?

"The man down the hall, this Nicholetti, he wants you." Ramon cocked his head to the side and tapped his board again. "You get under his skin and he doesn't like it."

"Too bad."

A deep, pure masculine laugh erupted from Ramon, but the glint in his eyes stayed serious. Dark. "Be careful, Rily.

Death is Gabriel Nicholetti's companion. It stalks those close to him."

Shivers, too large to deny, ran several races up Rily's arms, down her spine. "I'm not going to let him hurt me. My heart is intact and I plan to keep it that way."

"And if something worse than a broken heart is involved?"

"Ramon. You sound as if you think I'm going to die."

"And if you do? You wouldn't want me to avenge you?"

"I'm alive and I plan to stay that way." She frowned, blinked once and wrapped her arms around her middle. As if that would keep the tangle of knots from coiling tight in her stomach, like a fist intent on doubling her over. She wasn't going to die. Not any time soon. "Vengeance is what got Craig killed."

Quiet for a long stretch, Ramon kept his gaze locked on hers. "My great regret is that he went after those bastards without me."

"You were in the hospital. No one thought you would make it, much less walk out on your own." The intense pain in his eyes struck that knotted cord in her gut. Tension reverberated through her entire body. "Craig shouldn't have done that. He should have –"

"I still owe the ones in charge of that scum. For my partner."

"Don't you dare go there. The two that killed my brother are also dead. What good is a vendetta now?"

"There are things you don't understand."

"Ramon."

"There are times even I don't understand." He shrugged both shoulders this time, a faint smile on his face. "Nicholetti, he is different. Death –"

"You're freaking me out here." She poked a finger against his chest, quick to blink back the tears wanting to well in her eyes. Stupid, girly emotions. Geez. "You're not pulling that psychic woo-woo shit on me, are you? Come on. You're my rock. Don't go all Ben Garrett on me."

Ramon covered her gloved hand with his and lifted her hand to his cheek, pressing her palm against his skin. A flash of something dark, something that might simply have been a trick of bad lighting, glinted in his eyes for a brief second.

"Ramon?"

"Watch yourself with Nicholetti, *Mi Corazon*."

"You don't like him?"

"Actually I do." His grip light, he squeezed her fingers and let both their hands drop. "But that won't stop me from killing him if anything happens to you."

IN THE MIDDLE of Allison Davis' frilly bedroom, Gabe wiped his hand over his mouth then rubbed the scar on the back of his neck.

This wasn't good. At all.

He scanned the room, visually and psychically, but he wasn't mistaken. Talia Garrett's signature, one he would recognize *anywhere, anytime*, was as strong as if she'd just walked out of the room.

Shit.

He had thought he'd picked something up the moment they'd entered the house. And once again in the kitchen. But until the very *feel* of her hit him, here in this room full of lace, sunshine and silk flowers, he hadn't been convinced Talia had really been here.

What he'd felt in the other parts of the home, he hadn't been sure. Until now. Talia had spent a considerable amount of time here, in this room. As recently as a few hours ago.

She may even have been the one to leave the front door unlocked. If so, why had she done that, and why had she been here, in the home of a dead woman?

He'd question how the sentry Ortega had on surveillance this morning had missed her, but breaking and entering with no one the wiser had always been nothing more than a game to Talia. One she always won.

From his back pocket, Gabe fished the evidence gloves Ortega had given him and snapped them over his hands. What had Talia been searching for, here in this room?

There was something, that woman never did anything without a reason. Including screw him, in multiple ways, the last time not at all pleasant.

He stood in the center of Allison Davis' room, letting the winter sun filtering through the filmy curtains warm him. With his senses stretched outward, he slowly reeled them back.

Echoes of protection surrounded the house, levels of warding that should be stronger than they were, even with the owner dead.

Had Talia stripped the wards? Made them nothing more than mere shells of their intended purpose. She had that ability, but again, the question was why?

Another quick visual scan of the room showed nothing remotely out of place. Allison Davis had been neat, the dust no more than a few days' worth. Yellow and pink roses splashed across the ivory material of the bedspread, the curtains. The lamp shade. The room even held a light scent of rose.

Here, in her own sanctuary, Allison had loved the feminine.

And Rily? What did her bedroom look like?

His gut clenched on that thought. No. He swiped his hand over his face again. What he needed was to stay focused on now. On here.

On what the hell his ex-lover had been doing in this home, in this room. A pretty room belonging to a dead woman.

He twisted his neck, rotating his head to each side. The scar on the back of his neck throbbed.

Talia.

Things kept circling back to her. And not in any kind of a good way. What the hell did she have to do with Allison Davis' death?

Murmurs from the other room, Rily and Ortega talking, drifted down the hallway. He had maybe a few minutes before one of them joined him.

Probably Ortega. Rily didn't trust Gabe knew what he was doing. He could understand that, but he didn't need the guard dog, or rather guard Jaguar, getting in his way. Especially one that had the psychic nuances Ramon Ortega did.

If he wanted his own kind of answers, Gabe needed to get a move on. Now.

In the center of the room he stood, a sphere of protection surrounding him, and again he stretched his senses outward. This time, though, he focused on the *why* of what Talia had been doing.

Through a deliberate, complex, mental weave of misdirection, he found their connection, the forged bond linking them, and in his mind he strummed his fingers along a short length.

Nothing.

His chin dropped to his chest and he rotated his shoulders. She'd blocked him. Because she knew he was in the area or just standard operating procedure for her now that they were no longer a couple?

He had no idea, it had been months since he'd touched the thread connecting him to the bitch. There had even been a time when, if he could have, he would have destroyed the link between them.

And that time hadn't been all that long ago.

Short of one of them dying, he now understood the connection could never be severed. Dampened, but not destroyed. The question of the moment, though, was how could he get through her block without her knowing he had?

How did he keep her from realizing he, himself, was in the area? If she didn't already know. Talia had always been better at shielding, hell most of the other agents were better at that than he had ever been. Not his *gift*.

What he needed was to find Talia first, keep the element of surprise on his side. Find out what she was doing and stop her.

If he could.

God, he hoped whatever she was up to had nothing to do with Rily and these damn visions. His stomach clenched tighter than if someone had slammed a hard fist into his gut.

No. He wasn't going to examine that. Not yet.

His legs spread wide, Gabe closed his eyes and leaned his head back. The mumble of voices from the other room faded to simple background noise.

Light, with barely a touch, he mentally stroked the link. *Where was she?*

"Funny way to search a room." Ramon's deep voice cut across Gabe's skin, abrading every nerve ending.

Shit. He pulled back from the connection to Talia, severed his intentional strumming of the link. With his movements slight and unobtrusive, Gabe shook out his hands, letting the energy centered at the tips of his fingers dissipate.

"Didn't your mother ever teach you *not* to interrupt someone when they're meditating?" Gabe half turned and set his hands on his hips.

Ortega stood at the door, his right shoulder braced against the door frame, ankles crossed and arms loose with his thumbs hooked in his jean pockets. The piercing, dark and watchful eyes of a cat waiting for his prey to move stared at him. "Meditating?"

"What do you want, Ortega?"

Although he didn't smile, humor lit the man's eyes. "I can see that Rily has her work cut out for her."

"What does that have to do with what you're standing here wanting?"

"I sense a problem lurking on the fringes." Ortega shrugged his left shoulder. All traces of humor gone from his face, his lips moved in a faint parody of a smile. "Something more than just this case. Rily gets hurt, I'm coming after you."

Hurt? Gabe cocked his head to the side and studied Ortega from the corner of his eye. *How about dead?* "Direct. To the point. I get that."

There wasn't a way to save Rily, from herself or whatever was after her. He would have to watch his back when it came to Ortega. But a pact, along with the loyalty he saw shining deep in Ortega's black eyes, that was something linking the two men together. Gabe kept his promises, too.

Even when he didn't want to.

He ran his hand over his face, shoved his fingers through his hair. Ortega still watched him, his gaze not wavering.

"I am glad we understand each other." Narrowed, the gold outer rim of the Jaguar's eyes momentarily blazed from Ortega's black gaze. "The weight pressing on you is great."

Fan-freaking-tastic. Not only a Jaguar healer, but one who *saw* things others didn't want seen. He didn't have time for this. Not today. Never, if he had any choice in the matter.

With his head back and his hands on his hips, arms at an angle, Gabe closed his eyes for a brief moment. His chuckle was dry and bitter. "You always go around spouting doom and gloom?"

Ortega's laugh, quick and razor-sharp, cut through the room. "Always. Makes me quite popular around the precinct."

"I bet." Gabe rolled his shoulders. "You going to help me search this room? Or stand there all day?"

"I'd prefer an answer to what you were doing when I came in." Ortega pushed away from the door, his movements as fluid and lethal as the animal residing deep in his soul. "But you can enlighten me while we hunt."

"Meditating, Ortega. Meditating." Gabe pulled his thoughts tight, shoved the images of Talia and Rily to the part of his mind operating on automatic pilot and moved closer to the small amount of warmth radiating through the window. "I'll take this half of the room."

To Rily ... there when it started, and now when it ends.
Love, Allison.

Rily's stomach twisted in on itself. She stared at the carefully crafted script stretched across the little tag attached to the small, festively wrapped gift she held in her left hand. No more than six inches square, the box had no real weight to it and Rily had no idea what it could possibly contain.

Why the hell had Allison left her anything at all?

Rily ran the fingers of her right hand over the edges, across the shiny, smooth surface of the blue and silver wrapping paper, then along the thin, multi-strand, silver-hued ribbon tied around the box.

There when it started....

Rily didn't want to know what that meant. The past was buried, had been for a long time. She had no desire to revisit anything she'd shared with Allison.

Certainly nothing that had happened all those years ago.

As for ending it, what was over was already over. She wouldn't go back, even if she could.

Rily glanced around the confined, little living-room, at the simply framed original artwork lining the walls above the lawyer book cases jammed full of books. The art, pen and ink over watercolor washes, was delicate, the floral renderings almost lifelike.

All done by Allison. Rily had noted the style, checked the signatures. Hadn't been surprised. Although in high school, Allison's style had been a rougher version of these renditions, the talent had shown through, even then.

With the heavy drapes open and the soft, cool breeze blowing in through the window Rily had opened, the living-room shouldn't have felt as oppressive as it did. She turned the box over, switching it to her right hand.

As much as she didn't want to open the package, she needed to do just that. For the investigation and for herself. But not alone. The case was too sensitive and her role too pivotal to tuck this away and pretend it didn't exist. Or to open it alone and have the contents bite her in the ass later.

The guys had moved from the master bedroom to the room Allison had set up as an art studio. Rily needed witnesses present. Those two were probably the best she'd find. Not quite impartial, but vested in solving this case.

Her left hand shoved through her hair and resting at the back of her neck, she sucked in a deep breath and set the box back under the tree where it had originally sat.

May as well get this over with.

"Gabe? Ramon?" Rily strode down the hall and into the room, her fingers still threaded through her hair at her nape.

Both men turned from where they stood, side by side, in the center of the room in front of an easel. The protective fabric covering the artwork perched there had been lifted and draped over the back of the stand. Rily couldn't see the art itself, but the careful neutrality marking both men's expressions stopped her just inside the door.

The way they both masked their thoughts, their gazes shuttered, couldn't be good. At all.

She let go of her hair, braced her legs apart and set both fists on her hips. "What?"

A slight quirk lifted the left side of Gabe's mouth but tension radiated from his still body. She couldn't read the levels of meaning in those dark brown eyes but at least they were no longer neutral. Pissed, maybe. Cautionary, definitely.

She took a step forward. Gabe held up a hand and then rubbed it across his mouth, along his jaw, stopping to tap two fingers against his lips. "When was the last time you saw Allison?"

That stopped her forward motion. She swung her gaze between Ramon and Gabe. "Before yesterday morning? High school graduation. What are you two looking at? Something Allison painted?"

"Yes. Except for that voice-mail on your cell, she hasn't been back in touch with you?" Gabe dropped his hand from his mouth, his eyes sharp in the hazy sunlight filtering into the room. "She didn't make any quick visits to town? There were no invitations to join her here?"

"No." She rolled her shoulders but the tautness in her muscles refused to budge. "What are you getting at? What's on the easel?"

With a jerk of his head, Ramon curled two fingers, motioning her over. "The current likeness is remarkable."

Her stomach heavy and tight, lined with the same lead encasing her feet, Rily forced herself to join the two men. Without meeting either of their gazes, she looked at what sat on the easel.

Watercolor. Pen and ink. Three figures, the very edges of each image skillfully integrated, one into the other. And all three of the faces staring out from the art board could have been Rily at varying times in her life.

All three *were* Rily. Her own eyes stared back at her, three fold, from the painting.

Dizzying light swirled for a moment, leaving her unbalanced. Her hands balling into fists, she eased backwards. Away from the painting her gaze locked on.

She quit moving backwards when she bumped into something. Muscular male arms, clad in a sweatshirt, slid around her, holding her back firm against a broad male chest.

Sparks arched between their bodies, she swore they did. But she wasn't going to look. Nicholetti. The full, masculine spice of him surrounded her and she let herself stay where she was, her hands gripping the soft, thick material of his sleeves.

"Rily?" Gabe's breath, warm across her cheek, tangled in her hair and she let herself close her eyes, just for a brief second, blocking out the painting.

"Okay." Time for weakness over, she forcibly pulled herself together, pushed at his arms until they dropped. She stepped forward, away from the warmth of his embrace. Away from the electrical current connecting them. She wrapped her own arms tight around her middle. "I'm okay. How did Allison do this? This likeness? The first one I understand. Sort of. That's how I looked in high school."

And the yellow and black checkered scarf painted loose around her neck, a scarf her old boyfriend had given her, a scarf Allison couldn't have innocently painted.

One arm at her waist, Rily pressed a hand to the base of her throat, slipped two fingers under the neckline and pulled her collar away from her skin.

"The Tarot's Fool." Ramon, a bare hint of relief evident in this voice, turned from his impromptu search of the papers and photos stacked neatly on a makeshift bench tucked under the windowsill.

"Excuse me?" Rily's nerves raw, she sent him a quick, narrowed look.

The light breeze billowed the lacy curtains behind him and ruffled his black hair. He exchanged a barely masked, uneasy glance with Gabe, who had shifted his stance and now stood to the right of Rily. Their exchange of looks was too reminiscent of her older brothers for her to miss what had just passed between the two men.

She was fine, dammit. They weren't her brothers. She wasn't fragile. She was a cop. She didn't need to be coddled, smothered like some wimpy, female unable to handle the things thrown at her. She was no longer that teenager who had just had everything she considered normal and safe ripped out from under her.

Normal. She barely stopped herself from biting her bottom lip. Allison's voice mail had torn that illusion to shreds, Rily just hadn't realized it at the time.

She did now. With one quick swallow, she turned back to the painting, her gaze zeroing in on that scarf. Dammit. Maybe it was long shot but she was going to have to pull the old case file. The one from her senior year.

Justin Doherty's death.

Her high school boyfriend.

Chapter Six

"THE FOOL?" *Back to business.* Rily, aware of Gabe and Ramon and where they stood in Allison's art studio, kept her fingers tucked into her neckline, kept her eyes on the painting. "What do you mean by that, exactly?"

"The image with the scarf. Card number zero in the Tarot." Ramon shuffled a few more papers aside on the desk underneath the window.

Of course. She stopped herself from rolling her eyes. Allison had become fascinated with everything esoteric after Justin had died. Then there were the boxed decks of Tarot cards Rily had found stacked on one of the bookshelves in the living-room. The ones with Allison's name on the fronts. As artist. "And the other two images?"

"The High Priestess and Justice." Gabe watched her. She could *feel* the weight of his gaze.

"Justice." The third figure in the painting, wearing a cop's uniform, stood holding a scale in one hand and a white scarf draped over the open palm of the other. Her green eyes stared, hard – without quarter – out of the painting.

Rily's days as a uniformed officer. Not all that long ago. The likeness striking.

When had Allison seen her in uniform?

Rily forced her focus to the center figure. Chills scurried over themselves, up and down her arms, her spine.

The High Priestess.

Her, but so much more.

The open gaze in the Fool's eyes was innocent, trusting even, in contrast to the cold, judgmental stare of Justice. But the High Priestess' eyes radiated wisdom, secret knowledge. Depths Rily wanted nothing to do with.

Shivers chased the earlier chills right to the core of Rily's stomach. Sourness threatened to close her throat. She pulled on her neckline again.

"She was good." Ramon shuffled a few more papers, held up a file folder. "Good enough to have several contracts to produce images for this company's different Tarot decks."

Gabe whistled, the sound low and soft in the room.

"There are several boxes of those cards in the other room." *May as well get this over with.* She spared another glance at the painting, hoping the small box under the tree didn't hold another bombshell. "There's also a package under the small tree. A gift with my name on it."

"A Christmas present?" Gabe pulled the protective cover over the artwork. "You going to open it?"

Her chin almost to her chest, she swung her narrowed gaze between theirs. "That's why I came to get you two."

"Witnesses?" Gabe held her gaze, his own unreadable.

"Always a good idea." Ramon waved his hand. "After you two."

Once in the cramped living-room, she pulled the small package from under the little tree and turned to face the men. "Any guesses to what's in here?"

Not that she had any ideas or even really wanted to know.

Light from the open window glinted off the silver sheen of the package. Gabe held out his gloved hand and she stared at his fingers, just for a moment. She sighed, nodded then set the box in his open palm.

His eyes widened a fraction then his lips compressed. A heavy frown pulled down his brows.

"What is it?" Ramon's footfalls almost silent, he moved to stand next to Rily. "What are you getting off that?"

"Getting off it?" Rily shot a quick scowl towards her friend.

"Geez."

"Not really sure." Gabe turned the box over, ran a thumb across the edges.

Rily's gut tightened. She'd done the same thing earlier, when she'd found the box and realized it was addressed to her.

Gabe read the enigmatic tag out loud then exchanged an unreadable glance with Ramon. Rily barely resisted the urge to roll her eyes.

Yes, it was cryptic. Yes, it was weird. Especially after the painting in the other room. The painting she wasn't going to think about right now. So no, she wasn't in the mood to explain something she wasn't sure about in the first place.

His chin down and his frown still in place, Gabe held out the box and nailed her with a direct look. "Since it's addressed to you, you open it."

Rily swallowed. She wasn't afraid of what was in the box. Not exactly, anyway. But whatever was in there was going to change things.

She could feel it.

Crap. Now *she* sounded like Ben Garrett.

She swiped the box from Gabe before she had time to check the impulse. Irritated, she ignored his lifted brow and the way his lip quirked in the corner. Ignored Ramon, too, and the look he exchanged with Gabe. Damn protective, smirking macho males.

Might as well get this over with. Pushing the ribbon to one side, she slipped it off the package and handed the dangling strands to Gabe. Then she slowly undid the wrapping paper.

Ramon groaned behind her. "My grandmother unwraps gifts the same way."

Gabe flicked a glance at him. Nodded. Rily continued to ignore them and pulled a white gift box from the paper.

Inside, nestled in sparkly silver and blue tissue paper sat another piece of art, this one less than four inches high and two inches across. Rily's stomach muscles contracted and her fingers tightened on the white box cover. She couldn't pull her gaze from the drawing.

Two naked figures, legs and arms entwined around each other, stared into each other's eyes, oblivious to the world around them. Pen and ink, soft watercolor washes. And a marked resemblance to Gabe and Rily.

She raised her eyes, met Gabe's and the dark, raw desire swirling there matched what Allison had painted. An answering pull, centered low in her belly, flared hot.

Need, the pain of it so intense it scorched her nerve-endings, consumed her. For just an instant, with her gaze locked on Gabe's, her free hand lifted to touch his face, to trace his lips. To pull his mouth down on hers.

"So." Ramon cleared his throat. "How the hell did our little artist capture *that?*" Stunned laughter coated Ramon's voice.

Rily tore her gaze away from Gabe's and wildly looked anywhere except at him, the box in her hand or Ramon. Where the hell had all that come from? All that need welling up inside? As if a spark had ignited spilt lighter fluid.

"No clue." Her voice, raw as if she hadn't used it days, sounded husky even to her own ears. Rily lowered the box and chanced a look at Gabe from under her lashes. He hadn't said a word. But heat, matching the fire inside her, radiated from him. Along with shock.

"You'd never met her, had you?" Ramon glanced at Gabe before he took the box from Rily's lax fingers, closed the lid and slipped the white box into a clear evidence bag.

"Never." Gabe shook his head then shrugged both shoulders. He twisted his head to each side. Heat simmered deep in his dark eyes. "Allison Davis might have had more than just artistic talent."

Rily closed her eyes, but the image of Gabe's naked body twined around her own singed her closed eyelids. Her eyes snapped open and she stared at the ceiling. Warmth tinged her cheeks. "So she picked this up from out there somewhere? In the ether? Is that what you're saying?"

"In a manner of speaking. The question, really –" Ramon cleared his throat again before he tapped the box through the evidence bag. "Is whether this is a prediction of the future or simply a possibility Allison picked up on."

Rily swallowed twice, sure she didn't want that answer. She swung to face Ramon anyway. "And? What do you think it is?"

The corner of his mouth lifted. "Judging by the two of you, what I was just witness to? I'd almost say it's a forgone conclusion."

CRAP.

Gabe stood just outside the precinct doors and watched some kind of bird of prey float along the currents of the light afternoon winds. He didn't know what type of bird, didn't plan on being in this part of the world long enough to care.

Dammit all to hell.

He'd used the pretense of making a few phone calls to escape the confines of Ortega's small office and the evidence booking area. Hell, the entire building had been closing in on him.

Allison Davis.

The Tarot.

The Lovers.

Rily Carrigan.

All of it played through his head, but the image of two people wrapped up in each other that the woman, the artist, had captured haunted him, wouldn't leave his mind. Nor would the way Rily had looked at him over the card rendering she'd held in her hand.

The Lovers.

Everything circled back to that.

He understood, intellectually, the cards themselves didn't always mean specifically what was depicted. Not literally. The Lovers was the sixth card of the Tarot's Major Arcana.

Choices.

But inside him, inside his gut, that argument wasn't holding water. Not on this matter. Not on Rily.

The Lovers.

What kind of choice was that?

God, he wanted her. So badly he hurt.

He wanted her to live.

Those were his choices. Rily to stay alive and be his lover.

Like he had a say in any part of her destiny.

Overhead, the bird of prey let out a loud shriek and dived towards the open fields on the other side of the building. The doors behind him opened and Gabe turned away from the bird.

"Found a note at the bottom of the gift box, underneath the tissue paper." Striding towards him, Rily snapped her cell phone closed and slipped it into the small holder at her waist.

"Basically it said I should see an Irene Trent about the rest of the deck."

"There are more cards?" Gabe glanced at Ortega who had followed Rily from inside.

"And I got a call from Samuels, on the laptop." She stopped in front of Gabe, hands on her hips and her eyes more green than gold in the chilled afternoon sunlight. "Turns out it isn't Allison's after all. The internal registry is to one Irene Trent."

"I take it Irene is local and we're on our way to see her?"

"You take it right, cowboy."

"Always preferred sailboats to horses."

The corner of Rily's mouth lifted. "Well then, sailor-boy, I hope you're done with your phone calls. We're headed downtown."

He'd had to leave a message for Garrett, but she didn't need to know that. He jerked his chin towards Ortega. "All three of us?"

"Si, amigo." The other man shrugged. "After that card Allison painted, I'm not sure I should leave the two of you alone. At least not on my watch."

"Geez." Rily, her hands raised and fingers splayed, shook her head, turned away from the two of them and headed toward her truck.

"And after we leave you here?" Gabe fell in with Ortega behind Rily. He watched the sway of her rear end.

"What I said to you earlier still stands."

Right. He was a dead man.

AT THE TRIM, little cottage tucked away from the busy main intersection, Gabe hung back. From where the three of them stood on the front walkway, the sounds from the street could barely be heard.

He planned to be just as unobtrusive. To observe only, keep his senses open.

For a brief instance, he closed his eyes and rolled his shoulders, breathing in the calmness the place exuded. Not that it helped the tightness twisting his gut. A tightness that had been there since he'd crossed Allison Davis' threshold.

Talia. If she was truly around, he was screwed. He touched the cell phone tucked in its holster at his belt, hoping Ben Garrett would choose an appropriate moment to call back.

Now wasn't that moment.

Behind Rily and Ortega, he eased in another calming breath.

In spring the small yard would be full of color in that green-thumb kind of way. Now, the hanging baskets were empty, the yard tilled and waiting. Tree limbs bare.

The entire place, building and yard, looked as if it could have been transplanted from England. At least there was no hint of Talia Garrett here. Not yet anyway.

Rily knocked on the heavy wood front door. They waited less than a minute before the door swung silently open. The woman standing there, her hands clasped at her waist over an off white apron, gave them all a cursory glance before settling her slightly cross-eyed, bright blue gaze on Rily.

"Irene Trent?" Rily had her badge out for the woman to see, but the woman didn't even glance at it.

"You're Allison's friend." Her voice, soft and almost melodic, practically purred.

Gabe blinked. A Siamese mix of some sort. Himalayan? The woman's body was soft and round, pug nosed almost smushed against her face, her cheek bones wide and her chin a small, stubborn jut. Narrowing his eyes, he caught the swish of her fluffed, dark tipped tail behind her.

"Detective Rily Carrigan. Sergeant Ramon Ortega and Gabe Nicholetti." Doubt lined Rily's voice, he could hear it from where he stood behind her. "How did you know who I was? The painting?"

"Well, yes. That and the cards." Irene peered behind Rily. "And these two are with you? Oh my. She really did capture their essences, didn't she?"

Rily twisted slightly to the side and sent the men a dubious glance. Gabe cocked one eyebrow. Essences? That didn't sound good.

A slight probing, nothing intrusive, more a gentle question than anything else, pushed at the outer edges of his personal shield. Those edges hardened in response.

Behind his senses, he noted the sudden tenseness of Rily's posture. Ortega widened his stance a fraction and settled his shoulders.

Okay then. This woman they'd come to see was interesting, he had to give her that. Definitely psychic. Definitely checking them out in more ways than visual.

Although assessing someone's energy was another area that wasn't his forte, he could feel the hum of her power from where he stood. And she knew it, didn't even try to mask her abilities. Curious.

"Mrs. Trent —" Rily's voice firmed.

"Irene, please. Come in, come in." She opened the door wide and stepped back, waving the three of them inside and then shut the door behind Gabe. "Let's settle in my kitchen, it's much cozier there. I have coffee made. Some cookies. And then you can tell me why Allison sent you here."

Behind her, the three of them exchanged perplexed looks. Ortega shrugged his left shoulder. Gabe motioned for them to go ahead. Once in the kitchen, Irene shooed them all into wicker backed bar stools she had tucked underneath a counter made with a wide expanse of earth toned granite.

Settling on the far side of the counter, Gabe let Ortega have the stool between him and Rily. Gabe ran his fingers over the stone and its energy practically buzzed along his fingertips. He glanced up and Irene caught his gaze, her own undecipherable. But the small play of a smile along her lips while she glanced at each one of them made her look as satisfied as if she'd just finished a bowl of cream.

Himalayan, indeed. Domestic kitty cats were such interesting people.

His own mouth quirked in a small response and her eyes practically twinkled before she sat three extra mugs on the counter next to her own. She poured piping hot coffee into all four cups and pushed one in front of each of them.

Gabe lifted his, let the steam waft over his face, the smooth aroma of fresh ground coffee fill his nose. Sunlight soaked into the room from three large plated glass windows lining the wall behind him. He was finally warm. At least for a while.

He took a quick glance around the room. A desktop computer sat tucked away in an alcove to the right. To the left was a wall with dual ovens and a large stainless double door refrigerator.

Domestic indeed.

"Allison." Irene pushed a plate of sugar cookies in front of them, along with napkins, and focused that sharp gaze on Rily. "Did she find what she was looking for in Eagle Crest?"

"That's why we're here, Irene." Her expression guarded, Rily leaned forward, her elbows on the counter, hands cupping her mug. "Allison –"

Irene's face paled, the bright blueness of her eyes faded to a dull denim. Gabe sat straighter. Ortega, between him and Rily, did the same.

"Oh, dear." Her gaze unfocused, Irene gripped the edge of the counter. "She's not … oh, dear."

Rily stood, but Irene gave a short shake of her head. Tears welled in the woman's eyes and she blinked them back, although a few escaped down her round cheeks. She let go of the counter and wiped her hands down the front of her apron.

"I didn't realize –" Irene stared out one of the sun drenched windows. "I probably should have, but I don't think I wanted to know."

Rily sent Gabe and Ortega each a short look before moving around the counter. She laid her hand on Irene's shoulder. The woman visibly shuddered, then covered Rily's with her own.

A frown drew Rily's brows down, just for an instant.

What had they felt, each from the other? Gabe sensed the look Ortega threw him, but kept his attention on the two women.

The three of them were here to discover what Irene Trent knew about Allison Davis' death, but he would bet his sailboat the woman had nothing to do with it. Knowledge, on the other hand, this woman overflowed to the brim with that.

About Allison and all sorts of other things.

With a final pat, Irene moved away from Rily and pulled up her own bar stool on the opposite side of the counter. She picked up a cookie, stared at it for a moment before she set it on a napkin and looked at Rily. "Tell me what happened, please."

Rily, still frowning, returned to her stool and again cupped her mug. "That's just it, Irene. We don't know for sure. We were hoping you could shed some light on what was going on in Allison's life and who could possibly want her dead."

"Oh dear." Irene, her eyes wide, swallowed once and gave them each a long look. "So the illness didn't take her?"

"Illness?" Gabe leaned forward.

"That's what she was in Eagle Crest for." Irene lifted her cookie, but didn't take a bite. "To see that doctor."

Her mouth tight and brows drawn down, Rily sat straighter. "I thought she was coming to see me."

Irene laid her uneaten cookie down and sent the three of them a scattered glance. "Well, yes, she was going to see you. But not until after Christmas. She had a second trip planned. Today, when you showed up, I thought she'd jumped the gun, so to speak. That girl doesn't know the meaning of patience. Unless she's engrossed in her artwork."

"What kind of illness, Irene?" A slight edge fringed Rily's voice. She gripped the counter, then let go and spread her fingers on the surface. "Which doctor was she going to see?"

"That one who works with gifted people." Irene met Rily's gaze. "People with special abilities."

"Allison had P.L.S.?" Ortega's voice, soft and low, cut across the room.

Irene broke her gaze-lock with Rily, blinked and nodded.

Psychic Leukemia Syndrome. P.L.S., slang for what seemed to be a genetic blood disease mimicking leukemia, but only affecting psychics.

From the file Gabe had read in Garrett's office, they'd come close to losing Rily's sister-in-law to that disease earlier in the year. Now, the sister-in-law's blood held no trace of the disorder.

Cured or in remission? Ben still had scientists and medical experts working on that question. If Rily's reactions were anything to go by, this doctor Irene mentioned had something to do with that case. At least from her point of view.

"From what I understand –" Rily sent an uncommitted look at Gabe. "That illness is hereditary. I don't remember either of her parents being … well, psychic."

"No, I don't think they manifested any kind of gift." Irene shrugged. "But her aunt, on her mother's side I believe, was a strong talent. And died of P.L.S. When Allison's artwork began demanding the use of her ability, her health started going downhill."

"Her ability?" Rily's fingers curled on the counter. Not quite fists, but no longer splayed. "How did she know about Dr. Sheldon?"

Gabe tamped down the desire to run his fingers along hers, to wrap his hand over hers. Unobtrusive, he needed to remember that goal.

"Oh yes. That is the man's name. Even the psychic community has its underworld, Rily." Irene pierced Ortega with her blue gaze. "Isn't that right, Sergeant?"

Ortega, his mouth a thin line, cocked his head to the side.

"I know your grandmama. Powerful lady."

The corner of Ortega's mouth lifted, although his eyes remained dark and flat. He inclined his head.

Interesting. Gabe leaned back, adding one more person to his list for Garrett to check. Ortega's grandmother.

"P.L.S. doesn't run through your family, though, does it?"

"No, ma'am, it doesn't." Ortega took a short drink of his coffee, his attention solely focused on Irene.

"Mine either. You and I are truly blessed. And you, young man?" Irene wiped her damp cheeks and her still mostly unfocused gaze settled on Gabe. He barely resisted the urge to squirm. "You don't know, do you, if it runs through your family?"

Chapter Seven

DAMMIT.

Gabe's neck and back muscles tensed. The scar throbbed, but he kept his hands loose around his mug. In Irene Trent's cozy and warm kitchen he lifted his left eyebrow, held the woman's slightly unfocused gaze.

You don't know, do you, if it runs through your family?

Innocent words. A wealth of meaning.

But his family, or rather lack of family, wasn't up for discussion.

Not here. Not now.

Not with Rily and Ortega sitting here, with Irene's warm sugar cookies and open hospitality.

Her eyes still out-of-focus, Irene blinked and nodded. "It's all right, Gabriel. The disease doesn't … it has left your family untouched."

A weight he hadn't realized he carried, lightened and he blinked. His muscles retained the tenseness, but without the edge that would send him out of his chair and into full fight mode.

"Unlike Allison." Irene picked up her cookie and, her eyes sharp once again, looked at Rily. "But you say the disease didn't kill her?"

"I haven't heard from the M.E. on cause of death, but it doesn't appear that way." Rily paused, but Gabe thought it was more to center herself than for any kind of effect. "She was left at a roadside stop just outside of Eagle Crest."

Her eyes wide, Irene gasped. "That just doesn't make sense."

The older woman frowned before pushing the plate closer to the others. She blinked several times, sniffled once before she took a tiny bite of her own cookie.

"Which is why we're investigating." Rily picked up one of the offered cookies, stared at it for a moment. She shifted her gaze to Irene. "Your laptop was found in Allison's motel room."

Gabe leaned back in his chair.

The other woman nodded. "Yes, well, I loaned it to her because her desktop computer was on the fritz. I'm in the middle of reinstalling everything for her and she couldn't be without a computer for any length of time. Neither one of us could be. May as well have tethers tying us to the darn things."

"You have her desktop?" Ortega sat his almost empty cup on the counter.

"Yes, well it's not fixed yet. But I guess that doesn't matter to her now, does it?"

"We'll need –" Rily leaned forward, the cookie still in her hand.

"Of course. But the hard drive is completely wiped clean. I had to reformat the darn thing. All of her files are backed up on my computer, though. I'd rather not be without mine, but I'd be happy to image it for you, if that will help."

"Yes. Thank you." Rily nodded. "That would help a great deal."

Irene nodded, sniffled once and looked at each of them in turn. "I know Allison is – was talented. But the resemblance truly is remarkable."

"Resemblance?" Gabe leaned forward. The artwork. She's said something along those lines when she'd first answered the door.

"Allison's Tarot deck, the one she started on her own."

"Without a contract?" Ortega raised an eyebrow.

"Yes. Have you seen the painting she did of Rily? As the three figures from the Tarot? From that painting the two of us brain-stormed the idea of her designing her own deck. Unfortunately, once she started, she began channeling something or another, something from her past I suspect, and the images she designed really are quite remarkable."

"Channeling something?" Rily's voice held a trace of hoarseness and she rubbed her thumb over the cookie in her hand. Sugar crystals dropped onto her napkin.

Something with close to the signature of what he felt last night, outside the police station? Gabe narrowed his gaze. The tail of the kitty that was Irene Trent switched back and forth, agitated.

"That's how it seemed to me."

"Allison left a note for me in a gift box –"

"She thought she was being so clever with that, giving you The Lovers card for Christmas." The corners of Irene's mouth lifted, the kitty and her cream look firmly back in place. "Now that I see you, Gabriel, I can see just how clever Allison truly was."

Dammit to hell.

Guilt twisted his insides.

He and Rily weren't lovers. He hadn't done a damn thing about their attraction.

Yet.

He risked a quick glance at Rily. The tight set of her mouth, the heightened color in her cheeks.

She felt the pull as strongly as he did.

He needed to get himself under control.

"Right. Well." Rily broke her cookie in half and broke one of those halves again. Sugar and cookie crumbs stuck to the pads of her fingertips.

The tip of his tongue touched his bottom lip before he could stop himself. His stomach tightened.

God, he wanted to lick those crumbs from each and every one of her fingers. Cookie crumbs, sugar crystals and Rily.

A woman he'd known less than twenty-four hours.

At least in the flesh. Dreams and visions were another matter entirely.

She glanced at him from under her lashes before she dusted off her fingers and turned her gaze to Irene. "The note Allison left me said I should see you about what I'm guessing is the rest of that deck."

"Oh, yes. I have all of her images in the backup I made of her hard drive." Irene glanced again at Ortega. "And I would love to know who some of the other people she painted are. You never met her, did you Sergeant?"

"No, I never had the pleasure."

"She never met your grandmama, either. As I said, the likenesses are remarkable. Let me show you." Irene eased down from her stool, gestured for them to follow and made her way to the alcove where her desktop computer sat.

Rily spared a glance for the two men. Both sets of eyes were shuttered and unreadable.

She pretty much shared whatever sentiment had their jaws so tight. There'd been enough surprises for one day.

She slipped off her stool. The two men followed. Irene settled into the leather, swivel chair and rolled her fingers over the track ball that stood in place of a mouse. Instantly the monitor powered on and a picture of Irene's yard in full bloom filled the space. She tapped a few keys and a page opened, one with icons that looked like small paintings.

After clicking the top one, the screen filled with a softly colored pen and ink drawing of a female figure dancing along a path, a small black and white dog barking up at her.

"Allison." Rily's insides twisted into abrasive knots. She swallowed once and gripped the top of the computer chair. "And Scrappy. The pup her dad brought home on her seventeenth birthday."

Irene looked up at her. "Yes. She painted herself as a teen representing The Fool. At first she didn't understand the urge, that internal push, to put herself in the deck, but later – after she finished the Major Arcana – she said it was because everything had started with her. Back then, in high school. That this journey wouldn't be in motion if she hadn't insisted."

"What did she insist on?" Standing next to Rily, Gabe's deep voice, quiet and firm at the same time, skittered along her nerve endings.

She so didn't want to go there, but didn't see a way around it. And she'd looked. Hard.

That long ago file would definitely have to be pulled when she got back to Eagle Crest. She'd have to ditch Nicholetti fist. There was no way she was going over that with him anywhere near.

Not only did she not want to share those details, hell – she didn't even want to think about those details or that time in her life – unless she was forced, but Gabe's very presence scrambled what brain cells she had left.

The Lovers. Geez.

That image was still stuck in her head.

"Allison wasn't ready to talk to me about it. The whole thing with the paintings –" In a quick, almost non-existent movement, Irene shrugged both shoulders and Rily yanked her thoughts back from the circle they'd been spiraling down. "Allison was bothered, to say the least. And I don't pry. I figured she'd talk about it when she was ready to."

Irene angled her head to meet Gabe's stare, pursed her lips and then sighed. The tremors echoed in Rily, all the way to her toes.

"Hindsight, I should have pushed." Irene reached up and laid her hand over Rily's. "But then, we all know about hindsight."

Irene squeezed her fingers. Warm and comforting, the contact seeped through Rily and she blinked back the moisture pricking her eyes. Okay … what did this woman *know*, what was she simply guessing at? Irene patted her hand and turned back to her computer.

"Let's keep going." Her voice all businesslike, Irene tapped a key and clicked a button on the track ball twice. Another image filled the monitor screen.

Ramon stared at them from the screen, his eyes dark and triumphant. Arms raised above his head, his hands open to the heavens. A figure eight glowed above him, illuminating the blackness of his hair.

Rily's eyes widened before she frowned. This was over the top of the weirdness scale. She glanced at Ramon, who stood on the other side of Gabe. Her friend's dark eyes were unreadable and intently focused on the picture in front of them. Gabe's were narrowed and just as focused.

"Remarkable, isn't it?" Pride laced the sadness in Irene's voice. "That she achieved this without ever meeting you, Sergeant."

"Eerie." Shivers ran down Rily's spine.

Ramon rotated his neck, set his shoulders. His gaze still locked on the screen, his mouth and jaw were tight. Rily could understand the perception of threat. She didn't know of another word to describe how she'd felt back at Allison's, staring at a painting of herself, done by a woman she hadn't seen in too many years for it to have that level of resemblance.

On the screen, power exuded from the figure that was Ramon Ortega, the lift of his chin, the angle of his face. The arched eyebrow dared the observer to challenge him.

"The Magician." Gabe shoved his hands in his pockets, hunched his shoulders forward. "When did she paint these?"

"Over the course of the last several years." Irene clicked the track ball again. "In between her other contracts, obligations."

The next picture morphed onto the computer screen. A dark haired woman, defiant in her beauty, sat – poised to stand – on a throne with two pillars stretching skyward on either side of her. A black crescent moon topped one pillar, a white moon on the other. A white dog and a black cat sat facing each other at her feet.

"The High Priestess. Your grandmama, Sergeant." Irene twisted in her seat to look up at Ramon. "If you look deep enough, past the fact she's your grandmother, you will see her for what she truly is. A woman of power who shares that power with you. Through the line of her blood."

"And if her gift is something I don't want?"

"There are many things in this life we have no control over, Ramon." Irene touched his arm. "You've learned this the hard way, I know. This is just another of those lessons."

The muscle along his jaw twitched.

Yeah, well, Rily didn't like this mumbo jumbo B.S. either. She glanced back at the computer. Ramon's grandmother? The resemblance was pronounced. She looked at Gabe from under her lashes. He stood between her and Ramon, but back a step, his hands shoved deep in his pockets and his face utterly devoid of any expression.

Irene clicked through two more images. Gabe stiffened.

He knew those two people, she was sure of that. How much weirder was this going to get?

The image on screen transitioned into a man in a similar position as Ramon's grandmother, although the colors were harsher, with orange and crème lining the robes he wore. One arm was held up, the palm forward. A shock of white hair covered his head and stark blue eyes stared out of the screen.

Garrett.

"Stop." Gabe rocked back on his heels and a frown marred his forehead.

"You know this man?" Irene braced her hands on one arm of her chair and twisted to look up at him. "The Hierophant."

"Ben Garrett. My boss."

Irene's eyes widened and she threw a quick glance at Ramon before once again settling her gaze on Gabe. "And the previous two people?"

"Agents I work with." His words tight and clipped, Gabe widened his stance. "Allison was quite talented. The resemblances are uncanny. This one of Garrett is spot on."

With a brow lifted, Irene switched her gaze to Rily.

"Oh yes." Rily scrubbed a hand over her face. "Spot on. I have no idea how the hell she did this, but that's definitely Benjamin Garrett."

And the man was going to get a call from her before this day was over.

GABE SLAMMED RILY'S rear truck door and winced at the echo across Irene Trent's small yard. *Control, Nicholetti, control.*

His was hard won this afternoon. Hard won and barely there.

He'd used the excuse of stowing Allison Davis' computer and Irene's imaged hard drive on the back seat of Rily's truck, but the honest fact was he had to get out of that house. Away from the images, away from Irene's speculating gaze.

Those images.

The Devil card. A naked, teenage Rily chained to a towering red beast. Flames spiraling upwards, licking her skin. And the naked boy/man chained next to her, who the hell was he?

There was a lot more to Allison and Rily's shared past than Rily was telling him. What did it have to do with Allison's death?

More importantly, from his point of view, what did their past have to do with Rily's future demise?

There was no question Allison had been a talented artist. Her work had captured the essences of people he knew with an honest accuracy that went beyond uncanny.

How had she managed that? Did she really not know *any* of them personally?

He'd literally grown up around psychics, hell he was considered one himself. But the one thing Ben had drummed into him from a young age was to question first. Don't assume paranormal until all other possibilities were ruled out.

There were a lot of charlatans out there. Although his senses told him Irene was the real deal, and he'd also been brought up to trust his senses, he was still going to get to the bottom of who and what she and Allison Davis were, apart and to each other. And what Allison's relationship was to Rily.

That was the kicker.

Gabe pressed his fingers against his eyes then shoved his hands through his hair. Everything in this case circled back to Rily.

At least for him.

Gabe rubbed the back of his neck, scrapped along the scar there, more out of habit than because he sensed Talia Garrett. He let go of the breath he'd held.

Talia. Her presence at Allison's home baffled him.

In her deck, the image Allison had painted of him as the driver of The Chariot, striving to control the two tigers lashed to the body of the rig – that left him the most uneasy.

More to do with the fact one animal had Rily's green-gold eyes and the other had fur as white as Talia's hair, with eyes the same intense Garrett blue.

Balance. That's what The Chariot usually represented, at least for him. How the hell was he going to manage that?

Now, though, he scanned Irene Trent's small yard and waited. He rested his forearms on the back of the truck, his hands hanging and his fingers interlinked. The other two finished with Irene, handed over their business cards and headed down the path towards him.

Rily's cell rang. She waved Ortega on and answered the call, pacing a short distance away along the small pathway.

Ortega made his way to the truck. Slipping his sunglasses on, he mirrored Gabe's posture, settling next to him near the rear of the truck. "Interesting afternoon."

Gabe let the sardonic smile creep across his face.

Ortega lowered his chin, but they both stayed facing forward. "You know most of those people this artist painted."

A statement, not a question.

"A number of them."

Ortega nodded once. "My grandmother. Myself. The woman is right. The resemblance is striking."

"And neither you nor your grandmother knew Davis?"

"I will be checking with *mi Abuelita*, but I don't think so." Ortega shrugged his left shoulder. "I, personally, have never met her. Although that doesn't mean she didn't know me or know of me. That cannot be ruled out."

Gabe slipped on his own sunglasses. He still didn't want to like this guy. But he did like the way the man thought.

"The World Card. You know this place Davis painted?"

Gabe sent Ortega a sideways look. "I.P.S. The Institute of Psychic Studies."

"Fancy name."

"There are a lot of hard working people there, trying to make sense of the paranormal, of the weird shit." This time Gabe shrugged. He personally didn't have a lot of fond memories of the place, even though, intellectually he understood the need. "You'd fit right into their criteria. They'd probably like to get their hands on you."

A purely predatory smile lifted the edge of Ortega's mouth.

"Or maybe not."

Ortega laughed, a quick bark of humor. "Ben Garrett runs this place."

"Yeah, he has since I was a kid." Gabe lifted his chin and watched Rily's progress back and forth along the small pathway. "But you knew that. How much does Garrett know about you and your *talents*?"

That predatory lift to his mouth belied the easiness of his shrug.

Gabe shot Ortega another sideways look.

Seeing Ben and Ortega together might be interesting to watch. From a distance. Jaguars didn't care for dogs. At all. Ben wouldn't appreciate his Wolf being called a dog, but he'd bet the Big Bad Kitty wouldn't differentiate between the two.

"Garrett is the reason you're out here." Again a statement. Not a question.

Gabe shrugged. In a circular way, Ben was the reason. But Gabe wasn't going to get into a discussion about his visions or Ben's link to Rily. Not with this man.

"Are you here to protect Rily? From whatever it is that hunts her?"

Actual questions? Gabe angled his head to get a better look at Ortega. The man's mouth and jaw were tight, the muscles in his arms bunched with tension. Hell, every line in his body screamed tension.

Ortega pulled off his sunglasses and stared at Gabe. His eyes, dark and demanding, swirled with something Gabe couldn't put a name to. Gabe pulled off his own glasses.

"I cannot protect her. I realize this." A muscle twitched in Ortega's cheek, but he held Gabe's gaze. "However, maybe you can."

Rily snapped her phone closed, pulling both men's attention her way. Gabe slipped his sunglasses back on. What the hell was he supposed to say to Ortega? To that statement?

He couldn't protect Rily any more than Ortega or Garrett could. Shit.

"Okay, boys." Rily strode in their direction, her face full of doubt as she glanced between them.

Ortega had slid his own glasses over his eyes and his face was now a smooth mask.

"That was the M.E." Rily stopped on the other side of the truck bed, her hands on her hips. "No cause of death. Allison was perfectly healthy. No sign of any illness, no physical defects. Healthy heart and vital organs. No wounds. Nothing in the preliminary tox screening. As far as the M.E. can tell, Allison Davis shouldn't be dead."

Chapter Eight

RILY SWUNG HER truck into the Eagle Crest Police Department parking lot. All she wanted was to lay her head against the steering wheel, close her eyes and pretend today had been nothing but a weird, bad dream.

She switched off the ignition and the headlights then sat for one long still moment. Darkness surrounded the truck, the few streetlights barely making a dent in the heavy fog.

December nights near the Oregon coast. Fog was almost a constant guarantee.

Gabe, sitting next to her, shifted in his seat. She wanted to forget he was there, too, but her awareness of his mere presence rattled her all the way to her core.

How could she be so frigging *aware* of one man?

"I'd appreciate your help hauling all this into evidence." Her voice was hoarse, even to herself, as if she hadn't used it in months. Instead of hours. Two hours. Neither of them had said much on the drive in from Portland.

"Sure."

Rily nodded. Not so hard. "Then you can go ahead back to your hotel. Logging this stuff will take me awhile, writing it all up will take even longer."

Gabe still sat there, not moving. "You need dinner. Why don't you log the evidence then join me."

"No —"

"You can spare an hour."

"I'd rather get this done." She didn't want dinner. She wasn't hungry for food. She wanted to jump him. Was desperate to jump him. And that scared her. "We can meet up in the morning."

Gabe sat for another long moment before he pushed open his truck door. She blinked at the sudden brightness of the overhead dome, how it set them apart in an isolated world, devoid of anything except the two of them. She caught the tightness of his face, the twitch in his jaw muscle.

Tough shit.

She pushed her own door open, hoped down and slammed it before yanking open the back door of her extended cab. Small flare of temper maybe, but the kinetic release of all that wound up energy *felt* good.

She didn't *want* to want Gabe Nicholetti. Not one damn bit.

And she sure as hell wasn't giving into that want, no matter what Allison had painted.

She snatched the nearest set of evidence boxes, leaving the desktop computer for Gabe to carry. "I have my keys, hit the lock button after you grab that."

She made half the distance across the lot before she stopped, a different kind of awareness prickling her skin.

The same *feeling* from the night before.

Something was out there, something heavier than the damp air, watching her, just beyond the hazy, mostly nonexistent, light cast by the street lamps.

What the hell?

She turned in a slow, tight circle, her gaze catching Gabe's. He had stopped three strides behind her and had also turned in a full circle. He raised an eyebrow, but she shook her head.

They had to get this evidence logged in, couldn't risk it being tampered with. Shit and double shit. Whatever was out there had to wait. For now.

She angled her head, indicating they should go on inside. He nodded and followed.

Once inside, the sensation dissipated. She rolled her shoulders and headed to the back of the station.

At the evidence locker she sat her boxes on the counter. Before punching the bell to call the receiving tech, she turned to Gabe, a question barely formed on her lips.

"You felt it too, then?" He beat her to the punch. "There's something out there. Something too interested in *you*."

"Me? How do we know it's not *you* it's interested in?" Geez, how juvenile could she get? "Whatever. After this gets logged in, I need to do a sweep of the area."

"We need to do a sweep."

She raised her own brow at him. "You're a civilian – Shit, I'm not arguing with you about this. That was probably nothing more than someone getting their jollies off spooking whoever they can."

"But you need to make sure. To sweep the area? Because you *felt* something?"

"You did too."

"Yeah, but I always feel things. Nature of the beast." The almost smile he aimed her way was full of sardonic humor. "You don't believe in things you can't touch. Or have you changed your mind?"

Ass. She bared her teeth at him in a fake semblance of a grin. "I believe in following my instincts, trusting them to keep me from getting killed."

A shadow crossed his face, there and then gone. "So I'll help you sweep and then you can join me for dinner."

"Not happening, Nicholetti. We can sweep and then I'll drop your ass at your hotel. Alone." She jabbed the button to call the evidence tech.

Gabe shrugged one shoulder and leaned against the door jamb, his eyes shuttered and expression unreadable.

Again, tough shit.

RILY LEANED BACK in her chair, stretched her arms over her head. She really should call it a night. Go home. Get some dinner, some sleep.

Utter blackness outside her tiny office window didn't give her a clue how long she'd been sitting there.

The file from her and Allison's last great escapade sat open on her desk. She shoved it across the surface, away from her.

Nothing in there. At all.

Either her father, as Chief of Police at the time, had white washed the case, or the men *investigating* had done that in deference to her father. In either scenario, the file yielded a big fat zero.

No truths to speak of, at all.

But then, her memories were sketchy at best. Shock, her father had said. Maybe someday the memories would come back, but even she could tell, then, he hoped she would never remember.

What he suspected wasn't in the file. Neither of them had ever sat around talking about it with each other. Her brothers had been off living their lives, one in Portland, one in the service. Mom had coddled her.

She sucked in a shaky draw of breath. Hindsight, not the best tactic, but they'd been trying to protect her. With her memories so fuzzy, they hadn't wanted to subject her to the horrors of whatever had happened.

According to the file, it was speculated the three teens, Allison, Rily and her boyfriend, Justin, were out at night when they shouldn't have been. That Justin had wanted more than Rily was willing to give and that in attacking Rily, her boyfriend had experienced some kind of rare seizure.

A seizure that had left Justin Doherty dead, Rily unconscious on the ground with her clothes shredded, a black and yellow scarf tight around her neck and multiple cuts and deep scratches over her arms and legs. None of which made any kind of sense. Then or now.

Allison had been incoherent and babbling. Later, she'd said Justin had attacked them both, going for Rily after he'd knocked Allison down.

The detectives hadn't included anything in the file about Allison's Talking Board, a homemade version of a Ouija Board. Rily knew the damn thing had been there. That memory was clear.

Nor did the file mention the fact the three teens routinely snuck out at night. Or that Justin hadn't had any kind of medical issues, nothing to account for the way he'd died.

He wouldn't have attacked Rily, she believed that in her heart. So who had ripped her clothes and left her unconscious on the ground?

Suddenly chilly, despite the steady flow of heat from the vent, she rubbed her arms.

Justin had bordered on delinquency, yes, and had attempted to lure her into his lifestyle. *The Chief of Police's daughter and the troubled kid.* Justin had gotten a kick out of that.

She still could pick a lock faster than anyone else she knew. But her youthful use of that particular skill-set had been only to break into her own home, to avoid her parents knowing she was out most of the night, most nights, with Allison and Justin.

The three of them.

Rily gripped the edge of her desk, willed her fingers to loosen and laid her palms flat on the surface.

At the time, the current M.E. had said seizure. The authorities, her father included, had run with that scenario. Justin had only a drunken father who'd always believed the worst of his son. The man had latched onto the medical reasons for his son's behavior. And then left town.

She vaguely remembered worry of a vagrant attacking the three of them, but according to the sketchy notes, that idea had been dismissed early in the investigation.

Vagrant.

Why hadn't they followed that one further? What would they have found if they hadn't been so quick to dismiss the notion?

Had someone attacked them? Left Justin dead.

What about that eerie presence outside tonight?

Could that be someone from their past, back for the same reasons Allison had reappeared? Had it – *he* – killed Allison?

Was whoever that had been after her now?

Why?

Geez, this wasn't getting her anywhere but paranoid. She rolled her shoulders, her neck, but the tension knotted there refused to budge. Dammit, she needed to remember what had happened that night.

But she sure as hell didn't want to face those memories.

Rily pushed against the desk and stood. She turned to the small window, stared out at the black night.

Seriously.

Did their past have anything to do with Allison's death?

She and Gabe had swept the parking lot area, but the *feeling* and awareness were gone by the time they'd gone back outside, and it hadn't returned. They'd come up with nothing.

A sharp knock rapped on the outside of her door. Her heart stuttered.

Shit.

Paranoia was definitely the flavor of the night.

She swung away from the window, scrubbed a hand over her face and glanced at her wrist watch. After midnight. With her elbow she touched the butt of the gun at her waist. Reassurance. Then she laid her palms on her desk, leaned forward. "Come in."

The door pushed open and Gabe moved into the room, pulling the door shut behind him. The aroma of freshly grilled hamburger filled her little office. She frowned, as much at him as at the white paper bag he held loose in his big hand.

"What the hell do you think you're doing back here?"

One corner of his mouth lifted in that sexy, almost smile, at once charismatic and lethal. Both at the same time. "Feeding you."

Instincts took over and she sniffed the air, the scent of beef even more enticing the closer he came. "How did you score burgers, here, in this town, at this time of night?"

"Buddies with the hotel chef. He hadn't gone home yet."

"You're a fast worker."

"You have no idea." He sat the food bag on her desk.

"And I don't want to know." She took in the faint dampness of his jacket, the way moisture in his hair sparkled in the room's light. Lord, she was a liar. She *did* want to know how fast he worked, and that *want* sat uneasy right in the pit of her stomach. "How did you get here? You walked?"

"It's not that far, Detective."

"If you think I'm playing taxi-cab, dropping you back at your hotel every time you get a wild hair to *walk* somewhere —"

"I'm not going back to the hotel tonight."

Rily stiffened. That uneasiness in her gut solidified, hardening to granite.

What the hell was he up to?

Her jaw tight to the point it ached, she straightened then crossed her arms over her chest.

"I'm staying the night on your couch."

"Like hell you are."

"There or in my car, parked across from your house." He settled his big frame in the poor chair in front of her desk, made a face and reached for the bag of food. "Your choice."

"Neither."

He looked at her from under his lashes, heat scalding her skin. "You're offering your bed?"

"Go to hell, Nicholetti."

"Been there." He pulled out a grease soaked bag of crisp fries and two burgers. "Cheese or no?"

She lifted her top lip in a snarl. "Cheese."

"Thank goodness." He grinned again. "They both have cheese."

Her stomach grumbled, and she snatched the burger he offered. She sat hard in her chair and bit into the food.

Ass. Even if he was buddies with the hotel chef.

GABE'S GAZE LOCKED on Rily's fingers as she licked a couple drops of wayward ketchup from the tips. He shifted in his seat, willed his libido to settle down.

Of course, that was like telling Fido not to fetch when his ball was thrown.

God, he wanted this woman. She could lick him –

Concentrate, Nicholetti. On anything except taking Rily to bed.

He tore his gaze from her fingertips and glanced out her small, office window. One in the morning and all was dark with the world.

As it should be. More or less.

"This file." He tapped the folder that sat on the corner of her desk. She'd flipped it closed and shoved it to the side earlier when he'd offered her the bag of fries. "Obviously a closed case. Whose?"

With her eyes narrowed, she wiped her fingers on a napkin.

No more licking.

Damn.

He could see the wheels turning though, her decision to come clean evident.

Scary how well he could read her, this fast. They'd only actually known each other a few hours over a full day.

"Justin Doherty."

Gabe raised an eyebrow. "And he is?"

"An old boyfriend. From high school."

He tapped the file folder again. "The Devil Card."

This time Rily raised her own brow. "You are quick."

One corner of his mouth raised and he shrugged his shoulders. "Want to give me the run down?"

"No." She slid the file towards him, shoved her hands through her hair and rested her palms, fingers interlinked, on top of her head. Eyes more green than gold, troubled, stared at him with barely repressed misery. "Read it. See if I'm missing something."

He nodded, opened the file. Justin Doherty stared back from a senior high school photo. Good looking kid with a tight smile. Hair not brown or blonde, with a tendency to curl. Dark hazel eyes.

No animal totem to speak of, but then Gabe's gift didn't translate to photographs. He had to see into a live person's eyes, see into their being.

And according to this file, this boy had died years ago. Yet Allison had painted him in The Devil Card, chained to that monster along with Rily. As teenagers.

Gabe read what there was in the few meager pages, closed the file and looked at Rily. "And?"

She stared back at him, unblinking. "What?"

"Obviously there's more than what is in here." With the folder on his lap, he crossed one leg over his other knee, gripped his ankle. "Enlighten me."

Her eyes closed, she leaned her head back and sighed. "Why not?"

He waited.

A visible sigh shuddered through her body, she lowered her head until her chin almost touched her chest. Her tongue darted out, wet her lips, then she looked directly at him.

His stomach muscles contracted in on themselves at the simple touch of her gaze.

Shit. He had it bad.

Concentrate, Nicholetti.

He listened to her words, pulled in what she said, watched her body language while he himself sat extremely still.

The three of them had been inseparable all through high school, right up until the night Justin had died. She didn't know who or what had killed the boy. Not that she said *what*, but the implication was there.

"That damn Talking Board." She'd stood and now paced the small, confined area behind her desk. She faced him, hands on her hips. "I keep coming back to that. Where did it go? And why do I feel it's so damn important?"

She had good instincts, even if she denied what and where they came from.

One corner of his mouth lifted. "You said it was Allison's board. That she'd modeled it after the Ouija Board, right? She didn't know where it ended up?"

"Allison and I—" Rily shrugged, blew out a breath. "We didn't hang any longer, not after Justin died. My parents —"

She shoved her hands through her hair again, leaving the ends standing out. He gripped his fingers together in his lap, otherwise he was going to smooth the strands for her. And *that* would probably get him shot.

Her gun, at her waist, was a little too close for comfort.

"I didn't protest about not being able to see Allison. Afterwards, I mean. She went weird, interested in all things hinky."

"Hinky?" He raised an eyebrow. "Her homemade Talking Board wasn't already weird?"

She shrugged. "Yeah. I guess so. But that was a board game. Or at least we thought of it as a game. Justin and I did, at any rate. Allison? Maybe not."

"And you never saw that board again?"

"No. Until now, realizing it wasn't mentioned in the report, I hadn't thought about it."

"This is the first time you've looked at this? The first time you pulled this report?"

In an instant her eyes shuttered, any trace of gold leached completely out. "Yes."

"You weren't curious? You've been with the department how long? And this is the *first* time you've pulled it?"

"Your point is what?"

"You've pulled this now because of Allison's death?" He shouldn't push her, shouldn't dig into what was obviously so painful. Except he had to push. What choice did he have?

Especially with how telling that this was the first time she'd actually looked at the old case. "Because she painted you and Justin chained to that monster in The Devil Card?"

And she'd pulled the report and looked at it all alone.

Ah, hell, Rily.

"Isn't that *Devil* card enough of a reason?" A flash of gold lit her eyes.

"So, now you've looked. There's nothing there. What kind of bearing do you feel this *old* case has on Allison's death?"

She held his gaze for a few moments, moments where her eyes practically scorched him. "I have no clue. None. She's dead. The M.E. says she shouldn't be. Not even a *probable* cause of death at this point. I'm grasping at straws and this is one of those straws. If you have any better avenues, I'm open to hearing them."

She didn't want his thoughts on that, especially when his thoughts were so far away from Allison's death. He rubbed his eyes with the thumb and forefinger of one hand. "This old case. You weren't –"

"No." Her jaw tight, she rolled her head. "I don't remember. But my father took us both, Allison and me, to the hospital. We were examined and no, both of us were fine that way. We weren't … violated."

An unspoken statement lingered in her eyes.

"What?"

She puffed out a breath, exasperation sparked along the lines of her mouth. "Justin wouldn't have hurt me."

"Lots of women, girls, think that. Just before and right up to the point they *are* hurt. Or killed."

"I know that, dammit." She spun around to look out the small window, into the blackness. Spun again to face him. "But he wouldn't have."

Gabe tapped the file on his lap. "Juvenile delinquent. Or, at the least, heading that way."

"I know that, too. I was there."

"But you don't remember. And Allison's later comments were damming to the boy." And if Justin hadn't attacked Rily, who had? *What had?*

She linked her hands behind her neck, her wrists covering her ears. Gabe settled back as far as the torture chamberish chair allowed.

He knew she didn't want to hear what he had to say. But the cop inside the woman, the one who had been that teenage girl, wouldn't let her deny the facts of either that old case or this fresh one. Such as they were.

The weird shit, she still wasn't ready for any of that. And that shit was only going to get weirder. Didn't it always? He smothered the sigh building in his chest.

"Tomorrow then –" He glanced at the wall clock. "Later today, we're going to see that doctor Irene Trent mentioned?"

"Yes."

"Will you show me where Allison's body was left?"

She nodded.

"And where you were attacked, where Justin died?"

Her throat muscles working, Rily sent him a sideways look. "What the hell do you want to go out there for? That happened a long time ago. There's nothing there."

He simply held her gaze. She wouldn't like his explanation. If anything, his reasons would send her running the other way.

Something *weird* had gone on out there.

With Allison now dead and Rily soon to be, he'd wager that long ago night hid more than just a damn game board.

Chapter Nine

THE SMALL CONFINES of Rily's office and the black night outside the tiny window closed in on her. Heading out to that damn field, the place Justin had died, was the last thing she wanted to do.

What the hell was Nicholetti thinking, asking her to take him out there?

Shit and double shit.

Hell, quadruple shit.

Gabe sat with his fingers laced loose together in his lap, that dark gaze with its unreadable depths locked on her. She wanted to squirm, wanted to scream. Instead, after a few long tense moments, she simply nodded.

Maybe going back out there would jog her memory.

Maybe she needed those memories. For Allison. For Justin.

And maybe having someone with her would be smart. Even if that someone was Nicholetti.

"Fine, we can add that to the Eagle Crest tour." Less than gracious, but then she wasn't up to minding her manners at the moment. Her mother would never know. She barely stopped her top lip from curling. "We'll need to start early, like in just a few hours. Come on. I'll drop you at your hotel."

"How quick you forget. I'm staying at your place tonight. On the couch."

Like hell. "No –"

"Yes. Whatever that was out there is malevolent. I can't let you just wander around out there alone."

"You can't let me? Like you have a choice."

He shrugged. "Your couch or the front seat of my car, right in front of your house. Those are my choices. And yours."

"Dammit, Gabe." She snagged her jacket and shoved her arms through the sleeves then settled the bottom of the jacket around her holster. "This is stupid."

"Maybe."

She yanked open her office door, stormed through the empty outer room and through the front sliding doors. The cold air hit her, dug its fingers through her jacket, and wrapped boney hands around her spine.

Underneath the chill lay a stickiness, a sliminess that trailed along her nerve endings, tapped at her skin. Under her skin.

She stopped, scanned the immediate area, and pulled her gun.

"That's not going to do any good." Gabe's voice low and his narrowed gaze scanning the area the same as hers, he stood close. Almost shoulder to shoulder.

"I'm not imagining that, am I?"

"No."

"Now what?"

"Get to the truck and get us out of here."

"It won't follow?" Not that it had last night. But tonight this seemed worse somehow. Stronger, more alert. Almost sentient.

What the hell was she thinking? It? Sentient? She'd spent too much time with the ghost of all things Allison today.

Gabe didn't answer, just motioned towards her vehicle.

Not willing to put her gun away, she nodded and the two of them sprinted to the truck. Her keys already out, she beeped the doors unlocked and they barreled in, slamming the locks behind them.

Once the diesel truck rumbled to life, Rily shoved the gear-shifter into reverse, not switching on the headlights until they were on the street. "Why don't you think it will follow?"

"Instincts."

She wasn't able to stop the short snort. "So you've dealt with this kind of *thing* before?"

"No. Not really."

"Well then. That makes me feel so much better. Makes me trust your sharp instincts." Her heart pounding in her chest, Rily eased to a stop at a red light. She glanced at Gabe, the glow from the traffic signal cast harsh shadows across the lines of his face.

His mouth tight, he scanned the area around them, returned his gaze to the external mirror on his side of the truck. She checked her rearview mirror for the tenth time and the external side mirror on the driver's side for what had to be the twentieth.

The heavy ickiness had disappeared.

Gone, as if it had never existed.

Still chilled to her core, she flipped the heat on full blast. Gabe held one hand at the vent in front of him, spread his fingers and closed his eyes for a quick second.

She swung her truck along a back road, taking the same path home as she had the night before. A longer way around, but she'd be able to tell if anyone followed her.

At least Gabe had felt that presence. She wasn't completely nuts. Her nerves had already been shot from the day they'd had. This just topped everything off in the weirdness department.

Joy of joys.

Gabe, rubbing his hands together in front of his vent and still watching the side view mirror, was silent. After a few miles of zigzagging through meandering back streets, Rily pulled into her driveway, stopped the truck in front of her garage door.

Behind the light drapes of her living room, lights blazed, the timer doing its job of switching lights on and off. Her home looked cozy. Inviting. Part of the reason she'd bought the house several years ago.

She wouldn't admit it to Nicholetti, but in the back recesses of her mind she was grateful for his presence tonight. The day had been too stressful, too taxing.

But she had no idea what to do with the man.

She knew what she *wanted* to do with him, but that was a path to nothing but trouble and heartache.

No matter how the deep timbre of his voice sent quivers along every nerve ending she had. No matter how that come-get-me look in those liquid dark eyes of his swamped her usually sane sense of self-preservation. No matter ... just no matter.

Jumping him wasn't something she was going to do.

Not tonight.

She slipped the gear shifter into park, letting the truck idle, and turned to Gabe. His eyes narrowed, his entire focus seemed to be on her home. After a moment, he blinked and gave a short shake of his head, as if he was coming out of a trance.

"What did you just do?"

One side of his mouth lifted and he cut his gaze to hers. "Checked the perimeter of your property."

Ah shit. So much for a calming presence. "Psychically?"

"Yes."

"And?" Was he going to make her drag every small, freaking detail out of his sorry ass? She might have to hurt him.

"Clear." He smiled. "Completely clean."

Rily pursed her lips. The impression he was beyond pleased settled uneasily over her. What was she missing? Besides the entire psychic parade?

She took a deep breath, wondering if the proverbial *they* were right, if confession was good for the soul. "I think whoever was out there at the station tonight was out there last night."

"So two nights in a row." One brow arched, his gaze swept over her. "Where, in relation to the police station, was Allison's body found?"

Rily blinked at the quick change of subject. She drummed her fingers on the steering wheel. "Across town. Closer to the far west edge of town, on the way out to the ocean's shore. Why?"

"What we both felt tonight seems to be emanating from that hill behind the station."

"Emanating." What was she, a parrot tonight?

"It's a big hill. Wide at its base."

"And?" What was he getting at with this? She ran two fingers along the top of the steering wheel, catching Gabe's attention. She folded her hands on her lap.

The look in his dark eyes echoed the tension throbbing all along her nerves. Having him stay *inside* her house truly was a stupid idea.

So why was she contemplating it?

Who was she kidding? They were parked in front of her house. He was coming in. The only question was where he would sleep.

She hadn't decided that one yet.

Gabe glanced out the side window, then back at her. "What's on the opposite side of that hill?"

Back to that.

Twisting her fingers together, she swallowed once. "Allison's old house."

Gabe nodded. Had he known the answer? Just suspected?

Rily stared out her windshield at her own home. The one she'd worked hard for, her one zone of solitude. Peace.

Shit.

She closed her eyes. "It's more rural on that side of the hill. Some farmland. From the top of the hill downwards, about three-quarters of the back side is covered in trees. Protected by the state. No logging. Allison's family worked a small farm at the base directly opposite the station."

Gabe was silent, his quietness almost a balm as he waited for her to continue. She could do this, even if her insides quivered at the mere thought of talking about that place.

How was she going to handle actually going out there?

Her breath shaky, she opened her eyes. The front steps of her home were still illuminated from the shine of light behind her curtains. She still sat here with Gabe.

Life still went on, she *could* handle this. "Although the farm is directly on the other side of the hill, by road it's a good fifteen miles around."

"That's a big hill."

"Like you said, wide at its base. Why the questions about the hill? About Allison's old place?"

"Did you go by the station this morning, before you picked me up at the hotel?"

"Yes."

"Anything then? Any weird vibes? Anything watching you?"

Rily blinked, pressed her lips tight together and thought back. She shook her head. "No. Nothing at all."

"And nothing anywhere else? Only there. Only at night."

"Right."

"How about earlier this evening, after you dropped me at the hotel and went back?"

"Yeah, there was something. Not nearly as strong. I had wondered if it was just my imagination working overtime. Because of what we'd sensed earlier." She shrugged. "I blew it off and went inside."

"Back to what I said earlier." Gabe faced her, settled his back against the truck door. "Whatever that is, it's emanating from that hillside, maybe centered there. And it only comes to awareness at night."

"Excuse me?" Rily twisted in her seat, faced him.

"Granted, we only have two nights to go by for that hypothesis. You're sure last night was the first time you sensed this thing?"

"What the hell are you thinking? Saying?"

His brows drawn together, Gabe raised his hands, palms upward. "Do you really think, believe, that what we felt was human?"

"It has to be human."

"Why?"

"Because what you're talking about, implying, can't exist."

"And what is it I'm implying?"

"Something straight out of science fiction. Horror. Some kind of intelligent being, an entity, a *critter* of some kind, stalking me. Stalking us." Geez. She shoved her hands through her hair, gripped two handfuls before letting go and scrubbing her hands down her face.

"Stalking you, yes."

"Dammit, Gabe. You can't really believe this pile of shit you're trying to feed me."

"Come on, Rily. Regardless of what Garrett says about you, you're not so naive to believe in only the things you can see or touch."

"Psychic ability is one thing. Hunches, gut instincts. You're talking about something completely unnatural. Something *other*."

"It's unnatural because whatever that is doesn't fit into your preconceived, ordered view of the universe?"

"Yes."

"Rily —"

"So what you're saying is this seems to be active at night and only at the station?" She pressed both hands to her face, moved her index fingers so she could watch him. "Such B.S."

"Do you have another theory? One that fits more comfortably into your world?"

Rily held his dark gaze for a long moment. Damn him, anyway.

She dropped her hands and shook her head before pushing open her truck door. "Come on."

"So I don't have to sleep in the truck tonight? Figured after this conversation, there was no way you'd let me in the front door."

"Ha. Ha." Jumping down, she turned and reached for her pack. "Letting you sleep outside isn't worth facing my mother. Indoors, she might never know. Outdoors, she'd have a detailed account of every move you made before ten in the morning. And that's with her being out of town."

"Small towns. Gotta love 'em."

"Right."

GABE SET HIS DUFFEL, with his gun tucked safely inside, on Rily's living room floor beside the dark brown leather couch. She'd left him here a few moments before, muttering something about letting the dog inside.

He took a slow turn, cataloging the room. Comfortable, subtly feminine without being frilly. The colors were muted, mostly browns and greens.

Earthy. Peaceful.

Not at all like the bundle of fire that emanated from Rily Carrigan. He'd half expected to see bold splashes of red, like her truck, not this enclave of comfort.

More of her framed photos lined the wall on either side of the stone fireplace. People. Friends and family. They were so much a part of her, where she came from.

He stomped down the envy tightening his chest.

A mother who didn't want him, a father who probably never knew of his existence. What did he know of family dynamics?

And the Garretts sure hadn't been a shining example, any way he looked at that. Talia. She hadn't been here, at Rily's. Not yet. And there had been no sign of her earlier, when he'd scanned the perimeter. Or now, from inside the house.

He shoved his hands in his pockets, as much to keep from rubbing the scar on the back of his neck as to keep from punching a wall.

Ben. Why hadn't he been in touch? Gabe had left several messages. He knew Rily had left at least two herself. Maybe more. She certainly didn't have his patience.

He smiled at that and glanced at the huge wall clock she had attached to the stone wall above her fireplace. Not that his notorious patience was much in evidence tonight.

Too late, or early, to try again. But he would phone Ben in a couple of hours. Wake him if that's what it took to catch the man.

Whatever lurked around the police station had bearing on what would ultimately take Rily's life.

Of that much he was certain.

He hunched his shoulders forward, paced a few steps across the polished wooden floor. Rily was right, being here in her home, this was stupid.

She should be safe, for rest of the night anyway. As long as she stayed inside. Here. If he was right, whatever was waking up underneath that hill didn't seem able to leave the hillside.

If he was wrong –

He didn't want to think about being wrong. Hell, he didn't want to think about being right.

Nails scratching hardwood flooring warned him an instant before a big, black lab bounded into the room. Gabe crouched down, offered his hand to the friendly fellow whose entire body wiggled with excitement. He sniffed Gabe's fingers, licked them twice and bounded out of the room through another door.

Priorities. Gabe guessed they both had their own.

He turned to face the side hallway, to watch Rily make her way back towards him. Awareness thrummed along his entire body, every nerve ending, every skin cell.

Shit. How could he be so conscious of another individual this quickly? Her presence, her moods, her thoughts.

God, she was gorgeous.

And the thoughts running in his head were asinine. Completely off the stupidity chart.

Rily stopped under the hallway arch, her arms wrapped around her middle, the edge of her bottom lip caught between her teeth.

The thought she was as unsure of him as he was of her brought him no comfort at all. She needed to blast him again, tell him to go sleep outside in the truck.

No matter how cold it was out there.

Why the hell had he insisted he stay here anyway?

Stupidity.

He cleared his throat. "Your couch looks long enough for me."

Her arms still around her middle, she leaned against the wall where she stood and nodded. "Both my brothers are tall. And since I'm the only one with a place actually in town, that couch gets used a lot."

She frowned, worried her bottom lip again. In his pockets, Gabe's fingers tightened into fists. God, he wanted to chew on those lips himself.

"Was used a lot before, anyway." Rily shoved both hands through her hair. "With Jake gone off with Hannah and Ben, and Craig ... gone, it's not used as much now."

From where he stood, he could see a light coat of moisture glistening in her eyes. Dammit. He couldn't touch her, didn't trust himself to do that right now. Because as much as he wanted her, if he touched her now he knew where it would lead. That wouldn't be right. Not now.

He stood, legs braced apart and his hands still curled into fists in his pockets, and watched her. With her fingers laced through her hair and her palms on the top of her head, she stared at him for several long moments.

"Ah, crap." Her eyes simmering, more gold than green, she let go of her hair. And advanced.

Chapter Ten

THE LIVING ROOM lights blazed. Gabe simply stood there, unable to pull his gaze from Rily's as she moved so purposefully forward.

This was stupidity at its finest.

He had to hold on, be the one to say no. Only, how the hell was he going to manage *that*?

His feet planted and refusing to backup, his gaze devoured her. Devoured the easy sway of her hips, the purposeful, lithe steps of her Tiger stalking its prey.

Prey. Mesmerized by her gaze. Unable to move.

Unable to just say no.

Hell.

She stopped a mere few inches from him, so close he could see the way the room's light reflected in the burnished gold burning through the green of her eyes, the ever so faint scattering of freckles over the bridge of her nose and across the top of her cheeks.

If he took her to the islands, would those freckles darken? Would her skin only burn? A bright pink she'd hate. Or would the sun kiss that skin until it gleamed a golden hue to match the flecks in her eyes?

Why couldn't they simply leave? Head to his islands. Jump on his boat. Sail away.

Away from here, away from murder, death.

Visions.

His jaw tight, he closed his eyes. Damn, this was difficult. "Ri –"

Light, almost non-existent, she trailed the tips of her fingers over his jaw. His eyes snapped open and locked with hers.

"Rily." Hoarse, his voice scraped his own ears. Over his cheek he laid his hand on hers. "We –"

"Are grown adults and can do whatever the hell we want."

He slid her hand to his mouth and pressed a kiss to her palm. Then he wrapped his fingers around hers and pulled her touch away from his face. God, how could a hand so strong have skin so damn soft? "This isn't a good idea. At all."

"I know."

"So why –"

"I'm tired of being good, Gabe." She tugged at their linked hands, pulled him slightly off balance and against her. With her head back, she pressed the length of her body against his. "Make love to me. Now."

"God, Rily. This is taxing my self-control about to the limit."

"So let it go, Gabe." Rising up on her bare toes – when had she kicked off her shoes? – she nuzzled his neck. Her tongue, warm and damp, sent alarms racing to every nerve ending he had.

Shit.

He wrapped both arms around her, crushed his mouth to hers. Explosions, loud in his head, bright behind his closed eyes, rocked him back a step. With his lips locked on Rily's and his arms tight around her, he pulled her with him, in a half circle.

Heat, from every point she pressed against him, pierced his skin underneath his clothes, spread like fire across the planes of his body.

God, he needed more.

Her arms snaked around his neck and the tip of her tongue stroked his. Like the nectar of honeysuckle, pure sweetness exploded in his mouth. He groaned.

Spicy hot and sugar in one seductive package.

He was a walking dead man.

Her greedy mouth devoured his. One of her legs slid up behind his, her ankle hooked behind his knee. With her mouth still locked on his lips, she arched her back, pushing her pelvis against him. And rocked.

His jeans, already tight against his erection, constricted even more.

She moaned.

"Where the hell is your bedroom?" His voice little more than a growl against her mouth, he cupped her rear and lifted her, wrapping both her legs around his middle. "God, woman. You're going to kill me."

"Not yet." She arched again, pressing her breasts against his chest then leaned closer to bite his earlobe. Her tongue traced the contour of his ear. "I haven't finished with you."

"Where's your damn bedroom?" He shoved her shirt up, her skin cool to the heat of his hands along her spine.

She tightened her legs around him and leaned back to pull the shirt over her head, tossing it somewhere behind her. Red, barely there lace cupped her breasts.

"Rily." His breathing harsh, as if he'd run a marathon, he glanced away from the red lace and up into eyes even more gold than green.

"Now, Gabe." She crushed her mouth against his. Sliding down his body, she slipped her hands between them and fumbled with the buttons of his jeans. Her fingers brushed over him and his breath stopped in his chest.

"Let me." Those were the only words he managed to choke out of his constricted throat. With one arm around her, he stilled her fingers, flicked open his pants and did the same for hers.

Lowering his head, he skimmed his mouth over the top bit of lace covering her left breast and slipped his hands under the waistband of her jeans. The calluses on his palms and the pads of his fingers seemed too rough to be touching something as silky soft as her skin.

But he did and wasn't going to quit. Unless she told him to stop.

And from the way she pressed herself against him, there didn't seem to be any danger of that happening.

Thank God.

Without letting go of his hold on her, he shoved her jeans down her legs and to the floor. Still within the circle of his arms, she stepped back and out of the jeans, kicked the pants aside, and moved back closer to him.

Skimpy red lace panties to match the barely-there bra. How the hell was he going to survive the night?

"You." Her mouth back on his, her fingers slid under his sweatshirt. She pushed at the cloth and he leaned back, yanking the damn thing over his head. The cold air brushing his skin barely registered as he reached for her again.

Skin against hot skin.

"Your bed."

"Back that way." One hand waved behind her, but then she had those fingers threaded through his hair. She nipped small bites along his jaw line, kissed his neck.

His stomach muscles clenched.

Rily. God.

He had to get them both horizontal while he could still stand. With a control tightly held on to, his hands all but shaking, he slid them over her almost bare curves, her silky soft skin. Lifting her, he cradled her in his arms, nuzzled her throat.

Her sigh deep, she arched her neck, giving him greater access.

Bedroom. Now.

With her tight in his arms, he headed down the side hallway. In what seemed an eternity, he had them in her darkened bedroom. She flipped the switch on the wall as they passed it and from the night stand a warm glow enveloped a king-sized bed covered in a comforter the color of a deep forest.

One knee on the mattress, he laid her down, pressing both hands on the bed on either side of her. She lay there with a purely feline look, gazing up at him, her eyes more golden in the warm light.

Her hands stoked down his bare chest, her touch light, but the sparks of electrical current racing through his system centered from the tip of each of her fingers.

He was weak and strong, both at the same time. Both for her ... this woman he needed so badly he hurt with the pain of wanting her.

"Rily." He closed his eyes, arched his neck. Her mouth closed over his left nipple. The sudden shock of the wet warmness of her mouth against him sent wild currents through his body. He stiffened then gathered her against him, twisted to land on the bed with her on top of his body.

He fastened his mouth to hers, ran his hands down the length of her spine, under the edge of lace barely covering her bottom. In one smooth and graceful move that left him groaning, she pulled her legs up his sides and straddled him.

Her arms braced on either side of his chest, she again smiled that purely feline smile.

"You're wearing too many clothes, Nicholetti."

"You're killing me, woman."

"Not yet." She wiggled down his legs, her fingers tracing the bulge in his pants.

A groan, from deep in his chest, escaped.

He reached for her, but she swatted at his hands.

"Stay where you are." Her gaze on him, she slipped her fingers under the waist band of his jeans, tracing it behind his back. He lifted his hips and she pulled the worn denim down his legs, trailing her hands over his skin along the way and leaving a trail of electric heat in her wake.

She knelt on the floor and pulled each boot off each of his feet.

Then she finished with his jeans, tossing them aside. Like the lithe cat she was, she stretched her body up and over his. At each point of skin contact those electric sparks arched between them.

Could she see the sudden flares of light, feel the heat of them?

He wrapped his arms around her, rolled her onto her back. She gazed at him, her smoldering eyes liquid gold, full of dark secrets. Secrets he had to have, needed to wrap around himself.

Rily.

Biting her bottom lip, she slid her palms down his chest, between their bodies, to his briefs. There she cupped his erection, stroked her fingertips over the ridge.

"God, woman." He reached for her hand.

She slid those hands behind his back, underneath the band of his briefs and pushed the material over his ass. Her fingers lingered over the sensitive skin of his butt cheeks, stroking ever so lightly.

Another groan escaped. With one hand, he shoved the briefs down and pressed against her as he kicked the underwear across the room.

He smiled at her sharp intake of breath then rocked hard against the lace of her panties. This time she held her breath, her eyes half closed, her mouth partially open.

He took advantage of that and crushed his lips to hers, his tongue invading her hot, moist mouth. She met his tongue thrust for thrust, her hips moving against him.

"Rily."

"Gabe. Please." Her breath whispered over his cheek, against his mouth. Under him, she arched her body and her back lifted from the bed.

He reached between them and shoved the lace of her panties down her legs, cupped her damp center. She gasped and pressed herself against his hand.

Only a few moments before, he'd thought her mouth was hot, but here, she scalded him.

He slipped a finger inside her. Moist heat incinerated what little control he had left.

Wet, ready. *Rily*. He couldn't wait any longer.

Her hands were on him, stroking him, covering him with a condom she'd somehow materialized from somewhere. *Thank God.* She pulled him towards the burning core of her.

His breathing heavy, harsh in the quietness of the room, he lifted his hips. Looked into the heavy gold fire of her eyes.

The tip of her tongue touched her bottom lip and she squeezed him. "Gabe."

His eyes fell closed, his chin fell to his chest and he thrust, sliding into that damp, wet heat. Her muscles contracted, holding him still for just that instant.

Then she relaxed, slid her legs up over his back and her hands up his chest. She angled him in deep, matching his thrust and rocking her hips back. Her breath came in short, raspy pants, faster the harder he pushed into her.

In, not quite out and then in deep again. A constant rhythm, his body tightening in response to hers.

The world only existed now, here on this bed, in this room with this woman.

Rily.

The precipice was there, just there, and she rocked with him, meeting him, joining him and falling over the edge.

With him.

SPARKLES GLITTERED ACROSS the early morning water. Cool water, sliding over Gabe, sluicing across his back, surrounding him. Thrilled at the touch, the feel of the water, he undulated his big body through the current, swimming in a race only in his mind.

In his dreams.

Part of him realized he dreamed, that this wasn't real. The Orca of his Totem, however, reveled in the pure, simple pleasure of being submerged in the water, of cutting through it and having it caress his body even as it whisked by him at enormous speeds.

He turned his mind's eye to the shore and there a Tiger, an orange and black stripped Bengal, raced with him.

If cats could grin, that one would have a huge one plastered across her face. She matched his speed, leaping over rocks and tree stumps littered along the shoreline, her head swiveling to see what was ahead and to keep an eye on his progress.

Rily. "Remember I Love You."

"What?" An impatient hand pushed at his heavy arm, shaking him to consciousness. "What the hell did you just say?"

The center of his palm tingling, he traced his fingers along her bare hip, opened one eye and got an amazing view of a red lace covered breast, the nipple barely held in place. With one finger, he traced the edge of lace, but then it was gone and Rily was gone, pacing beside the bed.

Damn shame.

Remember I Love You.

Knowledge, quiet in its intensity, slipped over him. "Your brothers, they named you. For that phrase. Your mother would put those initials, R.I.L.Y., in a note in their lunch boxes every day. When you were born, that's what they wanted you named. Rily."

She stopped moving, just stood there staring at him. In her red lace bra and no panties. No modesty whatsoever. But her face was pale, so white the hint of freckles across the bridge of her nose stood out in stark relief.

Damn. He was usually more circumspect with his inner *knowings*. Blurting them out like that was something he tried hard to keep in check.

"You need to leave, Gabe."

"Good morning to you, too, sweetheart."

"Nicholetti –"

"Was it that bad? That you're kicking me out of your bed so soon?" He turned on his side, propped his head on his hand and used the other to pat the bed beside him.

He shouldn't taunt her, but what the hell? The night had been spectacular. For her as well as him. No ego, just the truth. He wasn't going anywhere just yet. "Come here and let's try that again."

Rily shoved her hands through her hair. The lace of her bra barely contained her breasts, the one nipple he'd spied earlier had worked its way free. His groin twitched hard.

"You're not supposed to be here." She turned away, and then back again. "Go home. Back to your motel."

"Come with me."

"Dammit, Gabe. Go away. Go anywhere but here."

"Rily —" He sat up. A small surge of satisfaction welled inside him when her gaze caught and followed the sheet as it pooled in his lap. One side of his mouth lifted in what he knew was a dangerous smile.

He was feeling dangerous. Close to shoving all caution aside. That she brought this out in him, he wasn't going to examine.

"I don't do 'mornings after', Gabe. Never." Desperation lined her voice, clouded her eyes. "Go away."

His gaze narrowed. What the hell? Where had the feisty woman he'd held in his arms just hours ago gone? The one who knew exactly what she wanted and had made sure she got it? "You should have thought of that last night."

"Neither of us were thinking too clearly last night."

"What?" His voice deadly calm, he shoved the sheet aside and stood. This time, when her gaze swept downward a burning heat began to simmer in his belly.

She closed her eyes, wrapped her arms around her middle. When she opened them again, a film of something close to moisture coated them.

Shit.

"I don't do mornings after. I don't do relationships."

He fought past the tightness of his jaw. "Again, you should have thought of that last night."

She swallowed once, defiance mixed with panic and sparked from her eyes, making them huge in her face.

Dammit all.

"Go get your shower, Rily." He lowered his gaze, let it linger in all the right places. Damnation. "Unless you'd like company. I could scrub your back."

She moved back two feet, swung away from him and hit the bathroom and slammed the door.

The lock clicked as the deadbolt slid home.

IN THE SHOWER, Rily let hot water cascade down her back, let the heat work on her tense muscles. Her sweetly aching muscles.

How idiotic could she be?

Obviously pretty damn idiotic. Beyond idiocy.

For taking him to bed or for not keeping him there?

The best sex of her entire life and she'd kicked the man out. Almost literally.

With her head back, she let the spray pummel her shoulders, drench her hair. She had panicked. Because she didn't do mornings. Which she didn't. Or relationships. They were too damn messy.

But there was more, more she'd only admit here in the shower with no one else around. Him knowing what he had known, about her mother and brothers. About how she'd been named. As if he'd pulled it right out of the very air.

Maybe he had.

In less than forty-eight hours, the man had wedged himself into her world, into her psyche. And she didn't like that. Didn't know how to deal with that.

Damn woo-woo shit.

She panicked. Pure and simple.

Something she rarely ever did.

Crap and double crap.

She turned and lifted her face to the water, let the steam surround her deliciously aching body. Making him leave was for the best. She couldn't have any kind of future with this man. Any kind of relationship, which she didn't do anyway.

A man who was an agent for an institute that thrived on woo-woo. Like the two of them would get along anywhere outside of the bedroom.

Her gaze wandered to the door. But the sex, she could live on that for days.

She didn't want or need a man in her life. A man to complicate things, mess up her head. Her heart.

And Gabriel Nicholetti was complicated. Beyond complicated. And she wasn't going there. Not with him. They were going to solve Allison's murder. Then he was going back to Minnesota. Or those islands. Or wherever it was he'd come from.

End of story.

No more bed time.

The center of her palm tingled, she'd almost swear in protest.

What the hell?

Her eyes narrow, she pulled back from the spray of water and held up her hand, stared at her palm. Normal. Except for the invisible current seeming to pulse from the very center.

Her fingers closed into a fist.

Weird. She turned, leaned into the water, let it sluice over her head, down her back. Consciously willed her fingers to open, shoved her hand through her soaking wet hair.

She was going to ignore that tingling, it would stop and wouldn't amount to anything more than an overactive imagination. With more force than might have been necessary, she shut off the water, dried off, and scrubbed the towel over her hair. Blew out her breath.

Okay then. She'd made a big enough fool of herself. Time to get moving. Get to work. Focus. Face the music.

With her towel wrapped firmly around her, she sucked in a deep breath and unlocked the door. Utter silence met her. Then the clicking of Bogie's nails on the wood flooring as he careened into the empty room. His tail thumped against her bed – the made bed – and water dripped from his black face.

Rily sniffed the air. Bacon and coffee scented the house and her stomach rumbled.

But Gabe was gone. She didn't *feel* him in the house.

Shit, they had her doing *that* now.

Feel, her ass. That damn tingle started in the center of her palm again. She held it up. Warmth spread outward, but it looked normal. Just tingled.

Bogie woofed, wanting outside. Rily tucked her towel tighter and followed the aroma to the kitchen. Her coffee pot sat on its perch, down one cupful. An empty cup, except for the splash of milk in the bottom, sat on the counter next to the pot. Along with a note.

Rily,

Eat. Have your coffee. There's cream and sugar already in the mug.

I have phone calls to make and will meet you back at the station in an hour or so. I'll return the cup I took then.

G.N.

His handwriting firm and flowing, like the man himself, his words pricked moisture in her eyes. She curled her fingers over the pulse in her palm.

Damn him to hell anyway.

/

Chapter Eleven

ABE, WITH HIS CELL PHONE pressed to his ear, paced along the pier on the north side of his hotel. The stiff, cold morning wind lashed through his hair but did nothing to soothe the agitation prickling his skin.

If anything, the weather stirred his insides even more, added to his restlessness.

He'd showered, changed. Even shaved. Had two cups of coffee and managed to reach Ben. The bad connection had cut that conversation short. Something about a snow storm isolating the Institute. Now he couldn't even reach a busy signal.

Disconnecting, he shoved the phone in its clip at his waist and blew out a deep breath. He wasn't sure what Ben had managed to get from the aborted call. Wasn't sure when they'd be able to reconnect.

With both hands braced at his hips, Gabe stared out at the white capped river, let the wind blow his hair back, press his new sweatshirt against his body. Maybe he was getting acclimated to this damn area. The cold didn't seem as bad this morning. Even with the wind.

At least they didn't have snow to contend with here. Not today, at any rate.

And no visions to speak of since he'd arrived in Eagle Crest. Not that he was naive enough to believe the outcome had changed.

No matter how badly he wanted it to be different.

He leaned his head back, his face lifted to the wind.

Rily Carrigan.

A sigh, huge in proportion, stuck in his throat. How the hell was he going to save her? White knight to the rescue had never been part of his job description.

Save her.

God, he knew better than to let his thoughts head down that road. Knew better than to believe he could change the course of anyone's life. Anyone's destiny.

Sex with Rily *had* been a bad move. More than just a mistake. One he wanted to repeat over and over again.

As soon as possible.

Like a kid in high school with only one thing on his mind.

Gabe shook his head. *Focus on something else.*

Justin Doherty. How had the kid died? *Why* had the kid died?

How did that death connect to Allison Davis'? How did he circumvent that damn Grim Reaper and keep Rily alive?

The questions, round and round in his head, wouldn't stop. The major one, though, was *what the hell* was in that hillside?

He wiped his hand over his mouth, rubbed his fingers along his smooth jaw. The center of his palm tingled, pulsed. He fisted his hand before shaking it out.

Rily.

Linked whether either one of them wanted it or not.

WITH HER OFFICE door open, Rily heard the murmurs of greeting and Gabe's deep voice in reply. He stopped to talk with Kyle Samuels, and although she could hear the mumbles, she couldn't make out the actual words.

Maybe Kyle would keep him out there, going over the stuff he'd found on Irene Trent's imaged hard drive. Really nothing more than what the woman had already shown them, but they needed IDs on the people Allison had painted.

One more piece of a weird puzzle.

And that would keep Gabe out of her office for a few more precious moments. Not that she was avoiding him. With the investigation and the Chief reiterating the play nice comment, she didn't have that choice.

But she could gain a few more minutes to still the turmoil twisting her insides, eating at her gut. Making her feel like a fool.

And an ass.

Her shoulders tight, she forced herself to lean back in her chair. To stop herself from shoving her hands through her hair, she gripped her fingers together in her lap. That also stopped her from lifting her hand to examine her damn palm for the umpteenth time.

The weird pulling in the center had intensified the moment Gabe had entered the building. She hadn't had to hear his voice to know he was there.

Which was off the weirdness chart as far as she was concerned. She closed her eyes, trying to calm the staccato beat of her heart.

"Napping on the job, Detective?"

She snapped open her eyes, narrowed them. Straightened in her seat. "Go to – No, that's right. You already live there."

Gabe lifted one brow and she silently cursed herself. Foot in mouth seemed terminal when he was around. Why the hell was that?

With one shoulder propped against the door jamb, he stood with his legs crossed at the ankle, his arms loose and his thumbs tucked in his front jeans pockets. Sexy as hell.

Her stomach clenched and her breathing hitched. The pulse in her palm warmed, sending currents to other parts of her body she would just as soon not be aware of with this man.

That fast she wanted him again.

She lifted her chin and one corner of his mouth lifted in response.

Geez.

Did that simple movement of his lips have to be so lethal? Why was it enough to send her spiraling back down a path she'd sworn off of just minutes ago?

Why now, why him?

Her throat tight and chest constricted, she picked up her pen, leaned back in her chair. She pasted as bland an expression on her face as possible.

His almost smile widened for a bare fraction of a moment, then he lowered his chin and his eyes shuttered. "When are we planning to head out to see this doctor?"

Relief coursed through her system and the tension holding her shoulders tight lessened. Normal questions, normal work she could get behind. As normal as this case got, anyway.

She caught the slight quirk of his eyebrow, and regretted the way her body had responded to him getting down to police business rather than dwelling on funny business, physical or psychic.

He read her way too well.

"Now." She stood, started to stretch, caught his gaze on her chest and adjusted her weapon holster instead. He blinked a few times and that small, inner female voice laughed inside her head.

Snarky, yes, but that's how she felt at the moment. Along with being ticked with herself for the small pleasure at the realization she affected him as badly. That's what got her into this mess in the first place. She rubbed her palm over her pant leg. "Have you managed to reach Garrett?"

HE PULLED HIS gaze from her hand and rotated his head, lifted his mouth in a half smile. "Snowed in. Intermittent cell service."

"No help from that quarter then, for the time being." She rounded her desk and he pulled back into the hallway with a sweep of his arm.

Smart ass. Walking past him her palm warmed a fraction more and she curled her fingers over the sensation. How was she going to manage spending the rest of the day driving around Eagle Crest in the close confines of her truck? With him in such close proximity?

May as well get it over with.

"Let's go." Time to ruin the good doctor's first cup of organic brewed coffee, that part with pleasure.

HER STRIDE LONG and impatient, Rily led the way down the shopping district pier to The Coffee Hut, a small shop tucked into the corner where the wooden boardwalk jutted out over the river rocks. Small, intimate tables lined the railing area outside, semi-protected from the strong December winds kicking up white caps along the river.

Gabe followed a few steps behind. She wiped her palm over her hip. She was grateful he'd remained distant, seemingly as focused on the day's work as she was trying to stay. Even the ride over from the station had been quiet, no more than a few words between them.

She snugged her jacket tight and told herself she was grateful for that distance.

Exactly where she expected to find the man, Dr. James Sheldon sat alone, the only patron to brave the cool morning temperatures. Nice and private.

Last spring, Dr. Sheldon's daughter had been taken away, in a manner of speaking, for what had been done to Rily's now sister-in-law, Hannah. But Rily couldn't shake the deep belief Sheldon was actually behind everything that had happened to Hannah. The fact his daughter confessed and refused to implicate her father didn't sway Rily's strong certainty.

"Dr. Sheldon." Rily stopped in front of his tiny table. Nodded. Gabe flanked her left side, facing the water.

A slight tightening of the doctor's lips was the only sign of displeasure. When the man lifted his eyes, his gaze was benign. Pleasant even. "Detective."

He took several heartbeats to smooth his newspaper into a neat, three-fold rectangle and set it aside. He flicked a glance towards Gabe and the doctor's light blue eyes widened, his eyebrows rising sharply for a quick, unguarded moment.

What did the man see when he looked at Gabe?

"Allison Davis." Rily angled her body to box Sheldon in, to keep Gabe in her peripheral view.

The doctor blinked once, skimmed a hand over his steel grey hair. "I heard about her death. Tragic."

Rily lifted an eyebrow. "When was the last time you saw Allison?"

"Really, Miss Carrigan. I treated Allison's entire family back when they lived here."

"Detective Carrigan." No quarter given to this man, that had been her motto for months now. "When was the last time you saw Allison?"

His mouth set into a tight, thin line, the man lifted his chin.

"Did she or did she not come to you for treatment just before she died."

"I am no longer a practicing physician." His eyes like hard pieces of pale, flinty glass, he glared at her.

"Which doesn't change either of the questions I asked you."

"Allison came to see me. Yes. To visit me. Not to be treated."

"Really? You weren't aware she had P.L.S.?"

That minuscule twitch of the doctor's left cheek caught Rily's attention, but she kept her gaze focused on the man's entire face.

Yes, she wanted to scream. The man was giving himself away. Not with anything she could use in court, but enough for them to pursue him. She'd taken a shot and it had paid off.

The M.E. had said Allison was healthy. Irene Trent had told them otherwise. For now, Rily was pushing the P.L.S. scenario, one she was still finessing as she went.

"Detective Carrigan, just because someone dies an unexplained death doesn't make P.L.S. the cause." Sheldon touched his nose with his right index finger, rubbed the tip. "And if someone visits me, someone I have always held a great deal of affection for, that doesn't mean I am currently treating that person."

"Might be hard to currently treat her, considering the fact she's dead."

"Rily, really." Sheldon sighed, the sound long and suffering. "Don't you think you're taking this too far? Allison did not see me for treatment."

From her side vision, Rily saw Gabe frown, his gaze tight on the man's face. Yeah, she knew the doctor was lying. And not just because his lips were moving, although that played into it.

Her brow lowered.

So she was glad Gabe was here. *Sue me.* The idea he backed up her opinion of the lying doctor, giving credence to her contention she wasn't simply carrying her grudge against this man too far. Exactly as he, the doctor himself, was now suggesting.

She smiled, knowing it wouldn't reach her eyes. "Maybe she didn't come to you for treatment, maybe she came to you for advice. Either way, you're involved."

Sheldon's eyes sparked flint again.

"My earlier questions, Doctor. Are you going to answer them or should we take this to the station?"

His nostrils flared. He cast a quick glance at Gabe and then back to her. "I saw Allison early last week. She was in town, stopped in to see me."

"Asking you to treat her?"

"No."

Rily raised an eyebrow.

"Detective Carrigan, it was simply a personal visit."

"What day was that?"

"A day or so before they found her body. I'd have to look at my calendar to be sure."

"To see what day you'd scheduled her appointment?"

"No. Now that I'm *retired* –" The doctor aimed a glare at her. "All my days run together. Anyway, Allison only stayed a short amount of time. She actually spent most of what little time she was there talking with another visitor I had."

"And that visitor would be?"

His jaw tight and his eyes locked on hers, Sheldon huffed a breath out through his nose. "A young woman who showed up at my door a little bit before Allison. This woman said she was looking for my daughter, but anyone who actually knows

Althea also knows that Garrett character has her locked up somewhere. I told the woman to go away."

Gabe stiffened. Rily shot him a sideways look. How the hell had she *felt* that?

"Name?" She pulled her gaze back to the doctor.

This time Sheldon blew his breath out through his mouth.

"I don't have her last name, only her first. Talia."

Resignation, palpable in its intensity, centered in her palm, seeped over her hand. *What the hell?* Barely stopping herself from shaking out her hand, she speared Gabe with a sharp look.

With his dark gaze fastened on Sheldon and the line of his jaw stiff, Gabe lowered his chin. That expression on his face couldn't be good. At all. Rily's chest tightened and her breathing constricted.

How did Gabe know this Talia woman? What was her involvement in Allison's death? Rily resisted the urge to suck her bottom lip between her teeth.

Appearing weak or indecisive in front of Sheldon wasn't an option, not now. Not ever.

She braced her hands on her waist, just above her belt. Kept her focus on the doctor and ignored Gabe and whatever the hell was going on inside herself.

"So this Talia woman chatted up Allison there in your home?" Rily tapped two fingers against her belt. "What did these two – strangers – find to talk about?"

Sheldon lifted his fine china cup, stared into the creamy liquid before blowing gently across its already cooled surface. "I had gone out of the fore-room to answer my phone. When I returned they were talking about Allison's memories of times past here in Eagle Crest. When she was in high school, I believe."

Ah, crap. Back to that. Again. Only with a brand new player. Unable to stop herself, Rily's chin lifted a fraction and her left eye twitched.

"Weird conversation, Doctor, for two women who had never met one another."

"Perhaps. But Allison gave me a hug, said she was going to be back in town in a week or so and would stop back in. Then the two of them left."

"Together?" Gabe's voice held an intense, razor sharp edge.

She slanted a glance in his direction. His eyes, almost black in the shadows cast by the roof line, held a predatory gleam. Waiting for the perfect moment to strike. Under her jacket, shivers ran up and down her arms but she ignored those.

Sheldon glanced at Gabe, looked away and back. His throat worked, but then he nodded without saying anything.

"So, according to what you're telling us –" Rily lifted an eyebrow and squared her shoulders. "This Talia, No Last Name, could possibly have been the last person to see Allison alive?"

The doctor sniffed, stuck his chin out to look down his nose at her. Cool trick, considering he was seated and had to look up. "That's really not for me to say."

Oh, she wanted to nail him for this. In the worst way. But it had to be by the book, with everything done as perfect as she knew how. "Description of this mystery woman?"

"The first thing I noticed were her eyes. They almost seemed too big for her face. Dark, deep blue. She has short, pure white hair that curls around her neck. Maybe 5'3" or so. Tiny."

"Age?"

He shrugged. "Early thirties."

Rily pursed her lips. Sure as hell didn't sound like anyone from around Eagle Crest. She cast a side glance at Gabe. His body taunt and rigid, his entire focus was on the doctor.

Curious. Who was this mystery woman to him? She struggled against the urge to wipe her palm down her pant leg.

"Even though you were the person this Talia came to see –" Rily angled her head to glance out over the white caps on the river, then brought her gaze to Sheldon. "She makes conversation with Allison and leaves with her. Someone she supposedly never met before? And now Allison is dead. You didn't think this was important? Something we might be interested in?"

"I knew you wouldn't be able to resist seeing me, Detective Carrigan. So I waited." Sheldon touched the corners of his mouth with his paper napkin. "Are we done? Allison left with the woman. End of story. At least from this end. And rather than sit here sparring with you, I have other things to do with my time today."

"Such as?"

"Really, Rily. You act as if I killed that sweet child."

"Did you?"

Sheldon set his napkin on the table with precise, slow movements. Then he raised his sharp gaze and met hers. "No."

GABE FOLLOWED RILY'S determined pace away from the pier, away from the not so good doctor. The sway of her hips tantalized him, but the news Sheldon had dropped on them gnawed along the underside of every nerve he had.

He'd been afraid Talia was in the area. Had prayed he was wrong. Knew he couldn't be that lucky.

Once Rily reached the asphalt of the parking area, she stopped and spun to face Gabe. "Who the hell is this Talia woman? And don't give me that bullshit about not knowing what I'm talking about."

"Wouldn't dream of it, Detective." Gabe shoved his hands in his front pockets, rocked back on his heels. "Talia Garrett. Ben's daughter."

"What?" Rily's eyes widened then narrowed. "And?"

"My one time lover. One time fiancée."

Chapter Twelve

ABE ABSORBED THE SHOCK in Rily's eyes along with the way she immediately shut down inside. In the mostly empty parking lot she physically turned away from him, first her face and then her entire body. Her legs braced apart and hands on her hips, she stared across at the buildings lining the pier.

The center of his palm ached, the pain sharp and biting.

Shit. He stopped himself from reaching for her. Not because she'd snap his head off. That he could handle. He stopped himself because he understood the need for space. And he would give her that, what little they could spare.

Talia Garrett being here wasn't good. Talia involved in Allison's death was worse.

His chest constricted on itself, the tightness threatening to cut off his air supply. Whatever was out there stalking Rily certainly didn't need his ex's help. His real question now, though, was what in damnation did Talia want with whatever those kids had awakened all those years ago?

Coincidences didn't exist. At some level everything connected to everything else, even if that level wasn't completely obvious on the surface.

Something resided in that small mountain the locals called a hill. Had Allison's return reawakened it? Or had Talia, somehow, managed that on her own?

And what did the freaking entity want with Rily?

He'd wager it was nothing good.

He resisted the urge to rub the back of his neck. Space, his own, sounded like a good idea. Time alone to process this, to check the link connecting him to Talia. However, leaving Rily alone wasn't an option. Now or in the foreseeable future.

Which would only serve to further piss Rily off. Ticked off or not though, she now had a constant shadow. He might not be able to save her life, but he wasn't about to let Talia be the one to kill her.

"So your ex-lover may have been the last person to see Allison alive?" Rily's voice bit across the distance between them.

"Looks that way."

At least she was now talking to him.

"And you can be impartial – How?" She tossed her words over her shoulder.

"The same as you." He glanced towards the river, at a large, white bird of prey diving into the water for its morning meal. "Taking each moment as it's thrown at me."

She angled her head, spearing him with a sharp look, her eyes a chilly, flat green. She let several beats of silence pass before jerking her head towards her truck. "Let's go. Once we're done at the dump site, I have an appointment with the M.E."

Relief scoured through him. For now he wasn't going to have to fight her. The deep breath he sucked in burned all the way to the bottom of his lungs.

How the hell had she become so damn important to him in such a short amount of time?

RILY PULLED HER TRUCK into the same parking area as she had the morning Allison's body had been discovered. Today the place was vacant, no one around.

No fog.

A cold wind rattled the branches of the surrounding trees, bringing with it the fresh, clean scent of pine, belying the fact death had visited this field a measly two days before.

Bright, midmorning sunlight shone across the field behind the dumpster. Brown pine needles lay scattered across the dormant grass.

Her team had done a good job clearing out the area. She wasn't really sure what Gabe hoped to find, but she was willing to have another look with him. In spite of the day's emotional bombshells.

Shocks she was trying to ignore. For now.

Together they moved behind the dumpster and onto the field. "This is where she was found. Whoever left her here covered her body with pine needles."

"To conceal her or protect her from the elements?" Gabe turned in a full circle, his gaze moving along the perimeter of the field.

"Good question." Rily shoved strands of her windblown hair behind her ears and stuck her hands in her back pockets, as much to keep from rubbing her palm down her leg as to keep from touching Gabe. "My first impression was for protection. More of a caring gesture than for concealment."

He stood so close she could tell the earthy, woodsy scent came from his aftershave, different than the pine forest. Sexier.

Dammit to hell and back again.

"And your people are on that angle? Forensic wise?"

"Unfortunately, the weather that night played havoc with any evidence that might have been left behind." She needed to reel in those wandering thoughts. Get a handle on them. "Between Samuels and Malory, the M.E., they're doing what they can."

"Protection from the elements." Gabe looked down at her, his eyes hooded, although she could see the heat lurking in the shadows of his gaze. The wind pushed through his dark hair and her fingers itched to do the same.

SHE REALLY NEEDED to get a grip. Last night was supposed to have settled her, to have taken that physical edge off and leave her satiated.

At least that had been her rationale at the time.

Instead, every other one of her thoughts circled back to him, to the way his body moved, to the way her body reacted to his. In her back pocket her fingers curled over the pulse at the center of her palm.

"Which brings us back to the good doctor." Gabe scanned the area then brought his gaze back to her. Her skin tingled at the light touch from his eyes. "As far as we can tell, you and Sheldon are the only ones left who would care enough to protect her in that way."

"*Your* Talia wouldn't cover her?"

Crap. She hadn't meant to sound so bitchy. Standing this close, the heat of his body practically radiating through her, the twitch of muscle along his jaw was hard to miss. Neither was his raised eyebrow. Double crap.

"She hasn't been mine in a long time. I prefer it that way." He rubbed his hand over the back of his neck, grimaced. "And no, she wouldn't bother taking the time to protect Allison's body from the elements."

Rily's breath stuck in her throat. She pulled her hands from her pockets and brushed her windblown hair out of her face. With her gaze locked on Gabe's, she took a step back and rubbed her fingers over the sleeves of her sweater. "Do you have any pictures of your ex? I'm going to have my officers do a sweep through the local hotels, see if anyone recognizes her."

He shook his head, rubbed the back of his neck again. "I didn't keep anything like that."

"Okay then." Why the hell did that please her? "Samuels can go back over the photos he took of the surrounding area. Of the people that were hanging around. See if she showed up in any them."

Gabe nodded. "She's distinctive. Hard to miss."

"Well, then." How did she do this? How did she act normal? They'd had one night together and now his ex was at the top of her suspect list. Didn't that just figure? "Tell me about her. Do you think she killed Allison?"

He made a face, shrugged. "She may be more than capable of doing so. But to what purpose? With Talia, there's always a purpose. She never does anything without an aim towards her own selfish goals."

Bitterness laced his words. Rily frowned. So the bitch had hurt him on some level.

Geez, she hadn't even met the woman yet, hadn't interacted with her, hadn't gotten the feel of her and she was already thinking of her as a bitch.

"That's the question, isn't it?" She yanked her thoughts back to the case, back to business. "What is gained from Allison's death? Who benefits?"

"The doctor?"

"Straight out, I would love to pin this on him." She stared out into the line of trees. More business that smacked of the personal. "I don't know how much Ben actually told you. Althea, Sheldon's daughter, was doing research on P.L.S., that Psychic Leukemia Syndrome, and used my sister-in-law as an unknowing guinea pig. I haven't been able to prove it, but I suspect Sheldon is still using gullible people in the same fashion."

"The John Does? Are you thinking whoever killed them, killed Allison?"

This time she shrugged. "There are some similarities. And some differences. The first being the other victims were all male."

"But in perfect health, with no apparent cause of death."

"Which is why Malory Quinn, the State M.E., was out here in the first place, and the whole reason Ben sent you."

Gabe glanced away, towards the ring of trees surrounding them. "But you're not discounting any connection to the doctor?"

"I can't. Except for Sheldon and the P.L.S. angle, I've got next to nothing on any of those cases." Frustration simmered just below the surface, like bile coating her stomach. There had to be a connection. Why couldn't she see it? What was she missing? "And now Allison."

"With ties to your past and, through Talia, possibly mine." Gabe held Rily's gaze.

A cell phone rang, the sound shrill against the rustle of the wind through the pine branches. She snatched her cell from the holder at her waist.

"Ben Garrett. Finally." She held the phone to her ear and paced a foot away before facing Gabe "About time you called back."

Give him hell. Gabe moved a few more steps away. Close enough to hear her end of the conversation but with enough distance to scour the area psychically for any hint of Talia.

Ben could keep Rily busy for the small amount of time he needed.

"Talia Garrett." Speaking into the phone, Rily's voice took on a hard edge. "What the hell is your daughter doing in my town?"

One corner of Gabe's mouth lifted as he turned slightly away. *Lots of hell, sweetheart.* In spite of the thought, he hoped that with the bad connection earlier Ben had at least gotten the part about Talia being here and possibly involved.

Time to find out if the conniving bitch had been out here.

With his eyes partially closed, and using as much of a filter to hide his presence from Talia as possible, he stretched his senses outward. Several times he spanned the perimeter in his mind, tightening the circle with each pass.

Nothing.

After a side glance at Rily, standing a few feet away with the phone pressed to her ear and a scowl marking her face, he deepened the mental probe.

Still nothing.

He leaned his head back, stared at the tops of the pine trees. The wind, ripping through his hair and pressing his jacket against his body, seemed to mock him, to laugh at his inability to find any answers.

Either Talia had covered her tracks with more finesse than normal or she hadn't specifically been out to this location within the last few weeks. He wasn't sure which.

Was hoping for the latter.

Rily's feet apart and her eyes narrowed with simmering anger, she held out her phone. "He wants to talk with his *agent.*"

Gabe slanted a half hooded glance her way and took the proffered phone. Pissed off, burning ire brought out the gold fire in her eyes almost as effectively as flame hot passion.

His body reacted, tightening his gut and jeans in one quick moment. In spite of the chill in the air and the fact his boss waited on the other end of Rily's cell.

"Hello, Boss Man." Gabe kept his gaze on Rily, on the hard set of her lips. If he pulled her against him, pressed his mouth to hers, how long would it take for those lips to soften, to part and open for his tongue?

The tip of her own tongue touched her top lip, swept along the bottom one. She frowned at him.

"Am I interrupting something?" Ben's voice grated in his ear.

"Would it matter if you were?"

Rily turned her back to him, although he knew she listened as effectively as he had done earlier.

"No." A deep sigh echoed through the cell. "So Talia is out there?"

"She is." Gabe blinked once, shook his head twice. *Focus, man.* And not on Rily's sweet mouth. Or ass. "I haven't laid eyes on her myself, but with the description Sheldon gave, I'm positive it's her."

"Haven't laid eyes." Ben took a deep breath. "Okay. But you've sensed her?"

"Yes."

"Where?"

"Allison Davis' home."

Rily started, slanted a glance back at him. With a sharp movement, she turned to face him and folded her arms over her chest. Her lips compressed into an even thinner line.

"Great." Weariness coated Ben's voice. "Rily says you're at the dump scene. Any trace there?"

"None." Gabe aimed a non-humorous, half smile in her direction. Her eyes narrowed more. "No trace at the police station or at Rily's place. Nowhere in town, for that matter. At least no place I've been."

"All right. I'll see if I can track her movements for the last month or so. See where she's gone to ground."

"I'd appreciate that. The sooner, the better."

"Are you thinking she'll wind up having something to do with your vision?"

"Too coincidental, her showing up here."

"Neither of us believes in coincidences." From Ben's end papers rustled. "I'm going to email Rily a photo of Talia. Anything else I need to take care of?"

"Do some checking on the Davis' old property. From when Allison and Rily were in high school."

"Am I looking for anything specific?"

"Yeah. The hill between that property and the police station. Anything tying them together. And a Justin Doherty. He died around that same time. Rily's senior year."

Silence greeted him for a few moments. "Want to tell me why?"

"Not really. Not now. More a hunch than anything else."

"Fair enough. When would be a good time to reach you?"

"There isn't. Keep your phone nearby."

"Doesn't do much good during a snow storm." Ben disconnected and silence echoed in Gabe's ear. He held the phone out to Rily.

"Want to explain all of that to me?"

"No."

She snatched her phone from his hand. "Do it anyway."

The corner of his mouth lifted. "Such a bossy woman."

"You haven't seen bossy yet."

"Promise?"

With her head back, she let out an exasperated sigh. "Nicholetti –"

He lifted one brow.

Her head came forward, her chin resting on her chest and her eyes downcast. "It's more of that psychic mumbo-jumbo, isn't it?"

"Yes." He shoved his hands into his front pockets. "Why does that bother you so much? Justin, Allison and the Talking Board? It all seems to stem from that incident."

"I think Justin dying is more than a simple *incident*."

"Never said it was simple."

She closed her eyes, but not before he saw the moisture coating them. Hell, he didn't want to hurt her. He glanced away for a second, focused on easing the constriction tightening his own chest. Unaccustomed flutters he didn't like.

"I'm not sure about the Sheldon or Talia angle." He swallowed, trying to ease the pressure in his throat. Talking to Rily about Talia wasn't something he wanted to do. The fact he needed to, sooner or later, that stuck in his craw. "I am sure there is something stalking *you*, something tied to that hillside, maybe even the whole damn mountainside. Something possibly from your past, from the night Justin died."

"Stalking me?" She blinked several times, grimaced and shoved her hands through her hair. Then she turned in a complete circle, her gaze following the line of surrounding pine trees. After several silent seconds, she pinned him with a tack sharp stare. "That's quite a leap. Based on what? Really, Gabe. We need to deal with facts, not feelings or psychic impressions."

He held her gaze, refusing to look away.

She sighed, the sound long suffering and completely female. "You *felt* Talia Garrett at Allison's yesterday?"

He nodded, not sure he liked this new direction any more than the other one she had headed down. He sure didn't like the way she jumped to accurate conclusions based only on his side of a phone conversation.

"And you didn't bother sharing that *feeling* with either Ramon or me?"

"With this kind of reaction, can you blame me?"

With her palms open and fingers spread, Rily held her hands in front of her. "Facts, Nicholetti. Facts and real, solid evidence are what is going to solve this case. That is what is going to put Allison's killer behind bars and keep him – or her – there. Not unreliable feelings and impressions that don't mean a damn thing."

THE CLOSER RILY came to the morgue door, the slower she walked. Bumps raised along her arms, the way it always did whenever she found her way to this basement area.

Mustiness filled the still air, almost as if Death itself was telling them it waited on the other side of that door. Although she thought it might be her imagination, the chemical smell seemed to permeate the long hallway.

She hated being down here.

Behind her, Gabe was quiet. Did he feel the heaviness, too?

The fact he was with her, literally at her back, eased a tiny corner of her mind, a corner she roped off with crime scene tape and refused to look at right now.

With a deep breath, she pushed open the door.

Inside the room the odor was even stronger. Along with an even heavier sense of doom.

Malory Quinn glanced up from the gurney she stood next to, a perplexed look marking her heart shaped face. She frowned and pulled the sheet over the body.

Gabe's steps as quiet as Rily's, he followed her into the room. She made the introductions.

"Allison?" His hands in his front pockets, he motioned with his chin towards the gurney.

He didn't seem as taken by the M.E.'s striking looks as the male members of Rily's department. A small inside part of her did a silent happy dance. Not that she felt in competition with her friend, but Nicholetti meant more to her than those guys did.

And she hated that. Go figure.

Malory nodded at Gabe, eased the sheet back, exposing the body from the neck upwards. He studied the face. Rily watched him.

His expression tight, his dark eyes shuttered, the lines at the sides of his mouth seemed deeper, more pronounced. His nostrils flared a slight bit and a twitch pulsed along the line of his jaw.

The center of her palm throbbed in response and she lifted her hand, had it stretched part way to him before she realized and twisted both of her hands together in front of her. Against her own body.

What the hell had she been thinking?

The knot inside her stomach squeezed in on itself.

Sleeping with the man didn't make her responsible for soothing his demons. Or his twitchy jaw.

She needed to just ignore him. Ignore the feelings, ignore the way she wanted to curl up against his side. To inhale the pure male scent of him rather than the stale, chemical induced one down here in the basement. She puffed out a huff of breath.

"No sign of acute illness?" Rily turned away from Gabe, towards Malory. Unable to be still, she paced the small confines of the hospital morgue. "No long term illness? You're sure? Nothing?"

"I'm sure." Malory raised one eyebrow, shrugged and pulled the stark white sheet back over Allison's face. "Like I told you earlier, no illness, no trauma to the body, healthy organs. Not even a sign of recent sexual intercourse. Nothing. No reason for her to be dead. None.

Awareness of Gabe's move away from them, to the not so far side of the room – the way he leaned back, one muscular leg bent with his foot braced against the wall, his broad shoulders tense, belying his apparent ease – sent scurries of shivers along every inch of Rily's skin. Obviously ignoring him wasn't working so well for her.

Dammit.

From the not so subtle side glances Malory threw at both of them as she moved around the gurney, Rily also guessed her friend was picking up on her distraction. And the darkly handsome, silent reason behind that.

Great.

Malory tucked her chin against her chest, but the move didn't hide the small grin playing over her lips. Rily narrowed her eyes. Her friend blinked several times, but the innocent act didn't wash.

At all.

Dammit, Rily needed to focus on the case. On work. Not on her hormones or whatever the hell it was Gabriel Nicholetti affected.

Malory, the smile gone, waved Rily over to her corner desk. Piled half a foot high with several stacks of folders, the surface was barely visible.

"My project before Allison took precedence." Malory addressed Gabe, waved a hand over her desk then loosely crossed her arms at her middle and leaned her hip against the desk. "And I have to admit, I'm wondering if Allison fits in there somewhere."

"With the John Does?" Gabe frowned. "We were wondering the same thing."

Flutters, small and hardly noticeable, spiraled in a tight circle in the middle of Rily's chest. What the hell was that? Gabe threw her a startled sideways look.

Malory nodded. "Maybe it means nothing. Maybe it's only coincidence."

"If you trace coincidence back far enough, there's a link. Somewhere." Gabe shot another shuttered look at Rily. "At that point it ceases to be coincidence."

"Exactly." Rily matched Gabe's look, held that dark gaze of his for a long moment. What the hell was going on with the flutters in her chest? She was not a flutters kind of girl, dammit.

Malory shrugged. "Well, I've found questionable circumstances surrounding cause of death in five other cases spanning the last ten years."

What? Rily focused on the M.E.'s words.

"Eight deaths total?" Rily set her hands on her hips and stared at the ceiling for a moment – anywhere except at Gabe. "In ten years?"

"And if Sheldon is doing this –" Malory waved her hand over her desk. "He's getting better at it."

Chapter Thirteen

"WHAT, EXACTLY, IS SHELDON DOING?" Gabe swung his gaze between Rily and Malory. He pushed away from the morgue wall to stand a short distance from them.

The two women exchanged a glance.

"If I knew that, I think we'd have all the answers." Malory shrugged, tossed another veiled look at Rily before picking up the top file from one of the stacks.

Easy to see these two were friends. The M.E. was a beautiful woman, a Sea Otter with the deepest, darkest brown eyes he had ever seen. Eyes that saw more than she let on, eyes with dark secrets of her own. Ones that had nothing to do with Rily or this case.

But as beautiful as the M.E. was, Rily had a fire inside her, one that sparked something primal in him. With his hands shoved into his pockets, he curled his fingers over the burning prickles lacing his palm.

That damn connection. To Rily.

Her gaze on her friend, she wiped her own palm over her hip, stretched out her fingers. He hadn't expected that, not this physical manifestation. Wasn't at all sure what to do about it, either.

He glanced at Malory. A sea creature would be a better match for him. Much more suitable than a land animal. Especially Tigers. He knew that one from experience.

If he was actually looking for a match.

Damn good thing he wasn't.

Regardless of any damn connection.

"This file is the last John Doe before Allison." Malory, a smug glint in her eyes, held the file out to Gabe. "Rily knows this case backwards and forwards."

He flicked a glance at a pacing Rily, her long legs eating up the short distance between the morgue door and Malory's desk, before taking the manila folder.

"That was one of my brother, Jake's, cases." Rily stopped for a brief moment beside him, tapped the folder he held before she paced off again. "I was his sounding board. Then after we found Hannah, I revisited this one along with a couple of others."

Gabe opened the folder. Attached to the inside cover was a photograph of the dead man from the shoulders upward. Dark hair, thin face. Nothing remarkable. He flipped through the meager details in the file.

Perfect health, no discernable cause of death. No needle marks, no sign of any kind of drug in his system.

Dr. Sheldon's signature, a thick and bold script, scrawled across the bottom of the last page.

With a frown, Gabe glanced at Rily. "If the doctor's responsible and attempting to hide that fact, why didn't he fabricate a cause of death?"

"My personal belief is that Jake was so rabid about this case he scared the good doctor." Rily paused in her pacing to shrug once. "This case and the other John Doe were both ones Jake obsessed over."

"The other possibly connected cases I've found weren't John Does." Malory's humor filled gaze followed Rily's progress around the room. "In those instances, their identities were established, as was their cause of death so they didn't get any attention. If it wasn't considered foul play, the death wouldn't be flagged. Nothing to investigate."

"Partially because the two John Does couldn't be identified, as a detective, my brother was on those cases quick as lightening. Sheldon didn't have time to cover his tracks on the medical angle."

"Or he really couldn't find a cause." Gabe drummed his fingers on the folder, met each of their skeptical gazes. "Devil's advocate here. Maybe it was his daughter all along, as they both contend. And the two John Does were her first victims."

"That's always been a possibility." Rily tilted her head to the side, made a face. "Just doesn't feel right."

"Going with the gut, Detective?" Why the hell was he pushing her, now of all times? "Psychic intuition?"

The look she shot him would have scalded a lesser man. One who hadn't been inside her, hadn't held her when she came hard – her legs wrapped tight around him. Who hadn't spent the entire night in her bed.

Her eyes narrowed and chin lifted, Rily wet her lips before she turned to Malory. "The other cases you found?"

"That's where it gets interesting." Malory, a slight tilt to her mouth, glanced between them before moving to the side of her desk. Her palm flat, she rested her hand on a smaller pile of folders. "On a well thought out hunch, I pulled all the cases where Sheldon was the deceased primary physician."

"Because Sheldon had been my sister-in-law's doctor?"

Malory nodded. "Wasn't she supposed to have had leukemia? Acute, without any previous warning?"

"Yes." Rily stopped a few feet from Malory, her body suddenly still. "The deaths you're questioning?"

"These five died from leukemia." The M.E. lifted the folders and handed them to Rily.

Leukemia. Normal or psychically induced? Gabe met Rily's quizzical, still temper-filled gaze.

If he got to her the way she got to him, at least he wasn't alone in this craziness.

Pulling his hands from his pockets, he moved to stand next to her, to look at the files over her shoulder. The musky scent of her perfume distracted him, swirled inside and settled somewhere near the vicinity of his heart. He inhaled, softly, and shut his eyes for a brief, quick moment.

When he reopened his eyes, Malory met and held his gaze before lifting one brow and then refocused on her friend.

Well shit. Rily wasn't going to be happy about the interrogation that look promised. *Might be fun to watch from a distance.* His lips quirked. A safe distance, like from across town.

"I remember this guy." Rily opened the top file, fingered the picture attached to the folder. "He was sick, but then seemed to get better. We were all surprised when he died. What, five years ago?"

"Yes." Malory rested her rear-end against her desk, braced her hands on either side of her body. "He lived in town. As did one of the other cases. Another one lived about an hour south of here and two were Portland residents."

"Portland?" Rily, her voice coated with a thin edge of excitement, closed the top file and shuffled through the other folders. "Yet Sheldon was their primary doctor?"

"Were they originally from here, like Allison?" Gabe resisted the urge to rest his hand on Rily's waist. Barely.

God, he wanted to touch her. Pull her against him, tuck her under his arm. Protect her. Keep her from dying.

"No." Malory, her deep brown eyes glistening with something akin to dark laughter as she looked between them, shrugged one shoulder. "Not that I can discern anyway. You two will have to figure that out."

Still flipping through folders, Rily shook her head. "How many other leukemia deaths in that time frame? Where Sheldon wasn't the doctor? Is this a lot to have died under the care of one man?"

"When he's a primary care physician and not a specialist? Yes. I'm still sorting through the other county deaths. So far I've only found one other leukemia related death here in this county where Sheldon wasn't the doctor."

"Irene Trent said something about an underground doctor —"

"For leukemia patients? Why?" Malory tilted her head back, starred at the ceiling for a moment before spearing them each with a disgruntled look. "From what I've been able to dig up about these people, not one of them was destitute. Each of them should have had the means to afford decent treatment from any number of places specializing in this disease. Whether through insurance or on their own."

"You said Sheldon was getting better. At hiding what we suspect him of doing." Rily still stood next to Gabe, her body coiled tight, ready to move. To pounce.

The depth of her energy echoed through him, vibrating to the soles of his feet.

"Yes." Malory nodded, looked between them. "The earlier cases seem more … sloppy, less data to substantiate the leukemia death."

"How long was Sheldon the County Coroner?" Gabe glanced at Malory, but concentrated on keeping his breathing even. Rily's building tension spiraled into a tight knot in his stomach. He wanted to push off, pace the room, like a tiger stalking its prey.

Like Rily, pacing to loosen the nerves bundled into one solid tangle inside. To throw off her nervous energy so she could think, could put the pieces together.

"Thirteen or fourteen years." Malory glanced between them.

"You went back through the files ten years?"

"Started with five." Malory's gaze narrowed in on her friend. "Then went to ten."

"Need to go back fifteen." Rily, balanced on the balls of her feet, bounced once. "To the year before he became coroner."

Her lips pursed, Malory's gaze lingered on the stacked desk then she looked back. Rily arched a brow and Malory lowered hers into a frown.

"Oh, all right. Okay." Malory sucked in a breath. "Fine. I'll go back the fifteen years."

Rily's cell phone buzzed once.

"Email." She met and held Gabe's eyes.

He drew in his own deep breath and energy swelled at the center of his palm. Power, an almost tangible current, flowed between them.

Rily blinked several times. Frowned. She wiped her hand down her jeans, curled her fingers over her palm.

With a shake of her head, she plucked her cell from her side and broke the lock she had on his gaze. She swiped at the screen on her phone. "From Garrett. With that photo of Talia."

OUTSIDE THE PIER HOTEL, Rily's head back against the head rest of the driver's seat of her truck, she drummed her fingers over the steering wheel. Waiting on Gabe to finish up whatever the hell it was he was doing, she pulled up a mental image of the picture Ben had emailed her.

Talia Garrett. A beautiful woman. Big, blue eyes – Garrett eyes – holding all manner of secrets. Sexy secrets any man would want to decipher.

So what had gone wrong with Gabe and this woman?

He actually seemed to hate her.

And hate was so very close to love.

Wasn't it?

She'd heard that somewhere.

Her fingers tightened on the steering wheel.

Crap and double crap.

She was jealous. And it ate at her insides, the pure acid of it, leaving her a little queasy. Disgust, with herself, oozed over her skin, coated her insides.

Geez.

Maybe she needed to eat. Breakfast had been hours ago.

Breakfast.

Food Gabe had cooked and set out for her.

Crap again. Why was everything circling back to that damn man?

She wiped her hand over her face then let it rest on her chest. Maybe she just needed more sleep.

Right. Food and sleep. What she needed was for Gabriel Nicholetti to leave town and never – ever – come back.

Movement from the side entrance to the hotel caught her attention and there he was, striding towards the truck, his long muscular legs eating up the distance between them.

Think of the damn Devil.

He yanked open the passenger door, slid into the truck. "Lunch?"

So he was a friggin' mind reader now? "Drive through on our way out to the old Davis place."

Where she didn't want to go. Not now, not ever again.

He made a face, his nose scrunched and mouth turned down.

She stamped down the instant desire to trace her fingers over the line of his lips. Crap, crap and more crap.

"Drive though?" He sighed, the sound deep and vibrating all through her insides. "If we must."

Oh yeah. They must.

GABE STOOD AT the center of the narrow field, his legs braced apart, hands loose on his hips. The breeze, chilly in the mid afternoon sun, raked bony fingers through his hair and brought the almost acrid scent of death.

Real or imagined?

Shivers chased themselves down his spine. He wasn't sure if that was from the cold or from the place itself. Or maybe from his thoughts. He hunched his shoulders forward.

The wind earlier, by the water, hadn't felt nearly as cold.

Rily, her body tense and her head down, paced several feet away, near the forest line. Thick coverage there, the few pines green against the overwhelming barrenness of the deciduous trees.

Too similar to the trees in his visions for his peace of mind.

But right now, Rily paced, very much alive.

Lunch, such as it was, hadn't helped her disposition. Not one bit.

He'd hoped, but knew better.

They rubbed each other wrong, yet right at the same time.

Her spasmodic thoughts echoed in his head like images just out of reach, not coherent or with any substance, just there. Like a transparent layer.

And her pent-up feelings, those reverberated through his heart, cutting right to his center. He'd never been so attuned to someone else. Not even Talia. Not like this.

After Ben had sent the email with his daughter's picture, Rily had pulled herself in, closed herself mostly off from Gabe. If this could be called mostly closed off.

But in comparison to earlier, she had definitely pulled back. And he wasn't happy about that.

Although he should be thrilled.

His fingers curled over his palm. The connection was still there, wasn't going to go away until –

He hit the brakes on the course of those thoughts. Going there, not smart. Not safe. Not at this point.

Grounding was what he needed.

Before he lost focus and crushed her body against his. Before he hauled her through the forest to the spot they'd left her truck, shoved her into the passenger side and drove them both straight to the nearest airport.

Preventing her fate or just delaying it?

It is what it is.

Fate wouldn't be denied.

How many times did he have to learn that lesson?

He turned away from Rily, took several deep breaths.

After a moment, he stretched his mind, touched the earth with his thoughts. Although a stickiness surrounded the area, coated the very air along with the ground's surface, deep down the earth itself remained pure.

He stood with his legs shoulder width apart and with a quiet, soft inhale of air, he pulled the anchoring energy up through his feet. Letting the power pulse and swirl upwards throughout his body, the strain tightening his muscles eased. Relaxed. On a deep and silent out breath, he let go of his hold on the earth energy, let it slide down through his body and puddle at his feet before the earth absorbed it back into the ground.

Stickiness still reamed the air, Rily still paced and his body still buzzed with want, need, for her. Only now that desire slid to the back of his mind, leaving him more in control. His focus sharpened on the small details of their surroundings along with the large.

Talia *hadn't* been out here. Not yet.

At least not to this exact spot.

He turned in a slow circle. Daylight spun wavering shadows through the trees to the west yet shone bright on the ones to the east, marking a dense line along the base of those trees.

Tall, dried grasses, burnished gold in the light, waved in the strong breeze, filling the entire field and marching up the slope of the hillside to lie flattened against the ground. Although trees grew near the top of the hill and bordering the field, this expanse seemed stunted, not lifeless but sucked dry.

Struggling without hope of ever succeeding.

Like him with his visions. Seeing dead people alive and walking, no hope of preventing what he first saw in his sleep. What he *saw* becoming sharp and in focus, with increasing clarity as the days moved on.

Death.

Gabe's lip curled, he shoved the ugliness to the back of his mind. He took another deep breath and continued to turn, scanning the surrounding area.

To the southeast, through a narrow break in the healthier, denser forest, a rutted road wound away from the field towards a house hardly visible through the bare, deciduous branches.

Large rounded boulders, possibly granite, sat scattered around the field's edges, almost as if some giant had dropped them and forgotten to pick them up. The entity's marbles?

Gabe's lips twitched.

Rily stopped moving, stood near the rutted road, and faced him. The wind whipped the fine strands of her hair around her face. "Well?"

Not seeing any reason to make this easy on her, he arched a brow. She seethed. He saw it, *felt* it echoing though his own body.

Not a damn thing he could do about it.

Her brows drawn down, she tore her gaze away from him, stared at the top of the hillside for a brief moment before swinging her hot gaze back to his. "Any *impressions* Mr. Psychic-man? Any ideas?"

Plenty, none he was sharing with her at the moment. His left eyebrow arched, he cocked his head to one side.

Her mouth tight, she spun in a half circle, tilted her face to the sunshine. The line of her neck taut, her chest rose and fell in an erratic tempo. Gabe shoved his hands into his pockets.

After several deep breaths she twisted around to face him. "Why the hell are we out here?"

"Connections. From the past. To the present." He moved the few feet to stand next to her. Not close enough to invade her personal space, but closer. "Where did Justin die?"

She cringed. And he flinched with her.

Justin's sprawled image, legs twisted at an unnatural angle, blew through his head. There, then gone.

Rily jerked her chin towards the largest of the rounded boulders, set off by itself and near where the hillside began its upward slope in earnest. She wrapped both arms around her middle. "Over there."

GABE NODDED, set off towards the rock. After several heartbeats, she fell in behind him.

Tendrils of unnatural, unseen, slime suddenly pressed against him. The intelligence from the night before, at the station, wasn't present. Only the stickiness of defiled, tainted air so thick the breeze couldn't dispel it, couldn't budge it from where it centered on the stone at the foot of the hillside.

What had those kids connected with that night?

Without a doubt, something evil.

Did this hillside contain it? Hold it prisoner?

Or did it roam freely?

Gabe shook his head. If it roamed freely it would have followed Rily home, wouldn't be contained within.

If I'm right. God knows, I could be completely wrong.

But, whatever the hell they were dealing with, what did it want with Rily? And what did Talia want with it?

Gabe stood next to the rock, scanned the skyline along with the area immediately around them. Rily stopped just to the side of him. He turned towards her. "Why here?"

Her face a mask of misery, her arms still wrapped around her waist, she hunched her shoulders forward. "Allison was in the lead and this is where she headed. I bought up the rear."

With a nod, he squatted next to the rock, balanced on his heels. He stretched his hand out, not quite touching the surface of the rock.

The wind stopped completely. The air itself seemed to hold its breath.

A small, choked sound came from Rily. He paused, but only for a short moment.

She was going to have to maintain for a while longer.

His palm down and fingers spread wide, he closed his eyes and concentrated on the energy emanating from the stone. Mixed alongside the natural earth energy springing up to greet him, a thread of residual memory twisted itself around his hand. Stinging prickles of sensation centered at his palm, bit into his skin.

Rily's neck arched, her head back. Her arms, no longer wrapped around her waist, stiffened at her side. The green of her eyes darkened, as deep as the shadows marking the tree line. Without light, blind to what was around her.

What the hell was happening?

Gabe curled his fingers over his palm. His gaze locked on her, he eased himself into a standing position.

Fine tremors shook her, echoing down through his own body. He held out a tentative hand, touched the back of her hand. Her eyes widened, focused on something he couldn't see, then her eyelids fluttered and closed.

Shit. Gabe moved, one arm around her waist, the other at her shoulders, crushing her against him. Her body limp in his arms, he stumbled several steps back from the stone.

Images, sharp and in crisp detail, sprang full blown before him. Gone was the sharp light of a cold and crisp December afternoon. Night now enveloped them, a full moon illuminated the field. Grass, tall and the deep green of midsummer, waved in a non-existent breeze.

A much younger Rily, terror staining her face, crouched on the ground with one hand outstretched. Blood oozed from a wound to her temple. Her eyes wide and dark, unblinking, she stared at the teenage boy hovering over her.

Justin Doherty.

Gabe recognized the boy from his photo. With one arm tight around the real Rily's back, Gabe tucked her head under his chin and held her there. Her breath, warm against his skin, came in shallow, short puffs.

What Gabe saw, Justin and the young Rily, couldn't be Rily's memory. At least not from this angle. Otherwise, he'd see this from her eyes, from her level, there where the young Rily crouched on the ground.

This vision from the past, this memory, seemed to belong more to this place rather than to Rily.

A residual memory? A haunting?

Did that make it more accurate? Less?

Or was something messing with them?

The image wavered, solidified again. Justin lunged forward, grabbed the young Rily's wrist. She cried out, her mouth forming the scream, but no sound accompanied the sight. Justin yanked her up, pressing her against his body.

Much the same as Gabe held the real Rily.

Except the young Rily struggled, her fists beating at Justin's chest. The boy smacked her across her cheek. Her head snapped to the side but her eyes shone with sudden deep gold sparks.

Asshole.

No sound, but Gabe saw her mouth form the word as clearly as if he'd heard it. Young Rily lifted her knee, jamming it home between Justin's legs. Hard.

The boy barely budged.

In one move he twisted her arm behind her back, trapping her other one between their bodies. With his free arm he pressed her against him, holding her tight and unable to move.

Eerie, soundless laugher shook the boy's body. Fury lined young Rily's face.

Justin leaned forward, bending her backwards. He rocked his pelvis hard against hers and again soundless laughter shook his shoulders. Young Rily struggled, turning her head to each side, but the boy found her mouth with his, trapped hers.

In Gabe's arms Rily's moans were more like whimpers.

Although her eyes were closed, he'd bet she was seeing exactly what he saw played out in front of him.

If that boy hadn't already died, his life would be in serious jeopardy right now. Gabe fought with himself to stand still, to hold Rily in his arms and *not* leap forward to smash the bastard's face in.

As if he could.

"Shush, sweetheart. It's just a memory. This can't hurt you." God, he'd better be right. He splayed his hand at the base of Rily's head, his fingers threaded through her hair.

From his peripheral vision another young girl tore onto the scene. Her long, blonde hair streaming behind her, the girl leapt on Justin's back, her fists pummeling his shoulders.

Justin howled, that eerie soundless noise locked in whatever realm these three inhabited. Young Rily's struggle intensified. The other girl – Allison – gripped her legs around Justin's middle and held to his back with her arms around his neck.

The boy twisted his body back and forth, trying to knock Allison aside. His grip on young Rily loosened and she shoved at his chest. His face contorted, his mouth open and screaming silent curses, he staggered to the side with Allison clawing at his back.

Now free, the young Rily stumbled backwards. Justin lunged to grab her and she scrambled a few steps back, slipping on the grass. Justin backhanded her across her face and she went down.

Unconscious.

In Gabe's arms, Rily gasped. He pressed his lips against her forehead. "It's okay, sweetheart."

But was it? What would regaining these memories cost her?

How the hell did he stop this from playing out?

Helluva time to ask that.

In front of them, Justin reached behind and shoved his hands through Allison's hair. He gripped her head. In one smooth motion, he swung her off his back and tossed her onto the ground.

Allison lay there, stunned, her chest heaving and her eyes locked with Justin's. He kicked her side, and when she doubled up he aimed his foot at her head. She rolled away, lay curled in on herself.

Soundless laughter again shook Justin's body. He pressed his foot against Allison's back, but the girl only curled into a tighter ball. His mouth lifted into a spiteful mimicry of a smile, he kicked her again.

Allison didn't move.

For a long moment, Justin stood looking down at the girl. Then he turned his head. Met Gabe's gaze.

Smiled.

What the hell?

Gabe stumbled back, Rily tight in his arms.

A jolt of pure malignant energy shot through Gabe's aura, coated his skin. His fingers splayed at Rily's back, he set an instant sphere of protection around them. That nasty, electric energy from outside dissipated in an instant.

How the hell could a memory attack them?

None of the figures had a totem. No animals. How was this more than a memory being played out? And how was Gabe going to stop it with a semi-conscious Rily in his arms?

Justin leaned his head back, his suddenly too real laughter boomed across the field and shook his entire body.

Shit. Gabe retreated two more steps.

As quick as the laughter started, it ended.

Justin, with his chin lowered, stared at Gabe. Eerie green light glistened around the edges of Justin's hazel eyes. His mouth twisted, widened. "She's mine."

Chapter Fourteen

"**L**IKE HELL SHE'S YOURS." Gabe, his arms tight around Rily's limp body, glared at the teenaged boy who stood a short distance away. A boy who shouldn't be there, in this field, who couldn't be there. Who'd died long ago. Gabe flung extra energy into his protective sphere. In his arms Rily shuddered. "You can't have her."

The edge of Justin's lip curled. His eyes, locked on Gabe and full of that unnatural green light, glowed brighter than the moon above them.

In one move, Justin bent and scooped the young Rily into his arms. He threw Gabe a malicious glance before laying her on the large stone. His fingers rough, he shoved his hand under the collar of her T-shirt. Ripped the shirt at her shoulder.

Smiled.

Ran his hand over her left breast. Ripped the shirt from her other shoulder, snapped the bra straps.

He looked back at Gabe, began unsnapping his jeans.

Oh no, the hell you don't. Gabe's grip on Rily tightened. This didn't happen. Rily's father had taken her to the hospital. That had been specific. No rape.

How was he going to prevent that from happening this time?

Now?

This being the past didn't seem to make any damn difference. Rily pressed her face to his neck. Her warm tears scorched his skin.

Shit.

Young Rily opened glazed eyes, blinked several times. Those same eyes widened when Justin leaned over her, shoved her bra down her abdomen. He shoved his fingers into the waistband of her pants, fumbled with the buttons.

Her face in full panic, she gripped his hands but he batted hers aside. His own pants gaping at the front and slipping down his hips, her struggles only seemed to excite the bastard.

"No. No. No." Rily whimpered against Gabe.

He heard his Rily's words, saw the young Rily silently scream the same ones. Her neck arched and her chin up, the young Rily twisted her body to the side. She reared her legs back and planted her feet on Justin's chest.

Allison sprang in from somewhere to their side, a game board gripped in both hands. With her own soundless scream, she swung the board towards Justin's head as the young Rily shoved him backwards with her feet.

Light, brighter than the full moon, exploded and an eerie screech pierced the air. Darkness descended again, the moon dimmer than before.

Gabe and the Rily he held tight in his arms were the only two in the field.

He blinked, shook his head. With one hand on the small of Rily's back, he cradled her against him and turned them both in a full circle.

Late afternoon sunlight, filtering through the far tree line, brightened and sparkled along the granite of the stones scattered in the field. They were back in the present.

Alone.

How much time had passed?

At least half an hour. Maybe more, judging by the angle of the sun. Yet the events had seemed to happen so quickly.

Rily trembled in his arms, her shivers racing through his skin and across every nerve ending in his body. His own body shaking in reaction, he pressed his mouth against her forehead.

With his index finger, he tilted her chin to look at her face. Her eyes seemed too big for her face, as dark a green as the far tree line. Smudges of exhaustion lined the area under her eyes. Her freckles stood out against the paleness of her skin.

He gave in to the temptation to crush her against him, leaned his forehead on hers and wrapped her tight in his embrace. She wound her arms around his neck, pulled his head down and found his mouth with her own.

The taste of her filled him. Her lips parted and he shoved his tongue deep into her mouth. She sucked and his groin tightened. Rock hard.

Right here. Right now.

She rubbed her chest against him. Pressed her mouth to the side of his neck.

"God, Rily."

Take her. Now.

The words, full of malice, echoed in the air around them.

What the hell? Gabe seized Rily's upper arms. Held her away from him. She frowned, blinked. Reached for him.

"Rily." He pulled in a deep, scalding breath. "Not here."

"Why not –" Her eyes widened. She took a fast look around. Her chest expanded, heaved several times. "Oh, God."

"We need to get out of here." He pulled her back to him, tucked her under his arm. "Now."

SO COLD.

Rily spared a glance out the passenger window of her truck. Scenery passed by in a rush. Sunlight sparkled off the river far below the road.

Can't get warm.

The heater on full blast, the spare blanket she kept in the back seat tucked around her and still she was freezing. Would she ever be warm again?

She cast a sideways look at Gabe. The hard set of his mouth didn't invite conversation. Neither did the grip he had on the steering wheel or the twitch along his jaw line.

That was okay, though. She didn't feel like talking either.

With her shoulders hunched under the blanket, she rubbed her hands up and down the sleeves of her soft sweater. And watched the swells of the river as the truck ate up the road back into town.

Memories she didn't want welled up, along with whatever that crap was they'd had for lunch. She was so *not* going to be sick in front of Nicholetti. Swallowing hard on the bile, she lowered her chin to her chest and closed her eyes.

"So Justin *did* have a seizure after attacking me and Allison." Rily opened her eyes and blew out the breath she hadn't realized she'd held. Dammit. So much for not talking.

"Why do you say that?" His tone clipped, Gabe swung the truck around one of the many hair-pen curves along River Road.

He didn't know. Rily sat straighter, gripped the edges of her blanket tight. After the intensity of the returning memories and the way he'd hustled her out of the field, she'd just assumed he saw what she did.

How stupid was that? Showed how over reactive she was. Crap. Now she was going to have to talk about it after all.

She should have just sewn her lips shut.

"Rily —"

"I remembered, okay? You're experiment was a success."

"My experiment?"

"Wasn't that what this was all about?" Could she get any cattier? "Back to the scene of the crime, so to speak?"

"This was your first time back there? In all the years since that boy died?"

Rily's chin jutted up, she couldn't help herself. "Yes."

"And now you think you remember what happened?"

"Yes." The word dragged itself out of her. What did he think she was talking about?

Gabe swung her truck into a wide spot along the road, slammed the gear shifter into park. He turned to her, his eyes darker than she had ever seen them. "You can't trust what you saw out there."

"What do you mean? You were the one who insisted on going there." She gripped the blanket at her neck. "I remembered. That's what you wanted. Justin attacked me, had a seizure. End of story."

"No." Gabe stared at the roof of the truck, wet his lips with his tongue. The muscles of his neck taut, he took a deep breath before looking at her. "Tell me what you saw."

"*Saw?*"

"Your memories." Exasperation lined his words. "Tell me what happened."

Underneath her blanket she shuddered and looked away from the intensity in his dark eyes. Outside her window pine trees lined the cliff where they had stopped, not quite blocking her view of the river. The limbs of the trees swayed in a light breeze.

How precarious was the cliff's edge? How far down to the river, to the water? How did she delve deep enough into those memories to satisfy Gabe? Without falling over that edge? Without drowning?

"Rily?" His voice, soft and husky, slid over her skin.

Moisture coated her eyes. She could have gone all day without him being this nice to her.

After blinking a couple times, she turned her head back towards him. He sat, one arm draped over her steering wheel, his big body tense and facing her.

Such concern mixed with the darkness in his eyes. She pulled in a deep breath, looked down at the truck's dash. Wet her dry lips. "Justin hit me. Several times. Knocked me out. When I came to he had my clothes ripped and was taking his pants off."

She had been *so sure* Justin would never hurt her. How could she have been *so wrong*?

"I kicked him in the chest at the same time Allison hit him in the back of his head with the Talking Board. He must have had the seizure then. I blacked out after that."

"Rily, what happened in the field today –" Gabe wet his lips again. "I *saw* what happened. At the same time you relived it."

Her gaze on him, she leaned back in her seat. Shivers chased themselves down her spine. That was what she had assumed earlier. Had told herself she was being silly. "How?"

He shrugged.

"So why did you make me tell you what I remembered?"

"I needed to know I was seeing the same thing as you."

"And?"

His eyes on hers and his movement slow, he nodded. "I don't think that was a memory."

Her eyes narrowed, she puffed out a breath. "Gabe –"

"I never promised any of this would make sense." A slight smile lifted one side of his mouth.

She glanced at the roof of the truck. "Why don't you try and make it make sense."

His chuckle, warm and sexy, followed the chills and slid over her skin. "Bossy woman."

"I do my best."

Heat from his gaze scalded her and she let her tight grip on the blanket ease. The small confines of her truck didn't seem quite as chilly as before.

Gabe looked down, ran a hand over his mouth. "We talked about something stalking you."

She frowned. Back to that?

"What you saw out here, what *we both* saw, was what it wanted you to see." He glanced out the windshield before swinging his gaze back to hers. "Wanted *us* to see."

"Why?"

"I –" His throat muscles worked and he swallowed once. "What we saw is what it wants to have happened. What it plans for your future."

"Excuse me?" She shook her head, sure she wasn't hearing this right. The flutter tightening her chest she ignored.

"What part of stalking you don't you get? What the hell do you think it wants with you?"

"I don't even think *It* exists, so how would I know what it wants with me?"

"What does any stalker want?"

Her heart thumped hard against the inside of her chest. All of a sudden her skin didn't fit her body, it was too tight. Constricting. "What does that have to do with the way Justin died? Or with Allison's death?"

"We're going to find out."

"Dammit, Gabe."

"No coincidences, Rily. None."

She held his gaze, her own jaw tight. This was beyond ridiculous. Why the hell was she even listening to him? Why was it so hard to catch her breath? "You *really* think Allison's death is related to Justin's?"

His expression leery, Gabe nodded.

"And this *thing* is responsible and now wants me?"

Gabe glanced away from her, his tongue working around his mouth. What was he thinking? What didn't he want to say?

"I think you've been the target ever since you got away."

"Got away?" Damn, sounding like a parrot again.

"High school. The first time. What we saw in that field."

"That you said wasn't real. And now you're saying it's been *stalking* me ever since?"

"At some point you need to get past that stubborn streak and actually *look* at what's going on around you. Get past that fear of everything different."

"I'm not –" She shoved the blanket down, the cab warmer than it should be. Her too tight skin burning through to her muscles. "The things you say make no sense."

"And things that make no sense are going to get you killed."

Her stomach contracted as if he'd just slammed a fist into her gut.

His eyes dark and unreadable, he stared at her.

The buzz of a text message coming across her phone broke the taunt line holding her gaze to his. She fumbled at her waist, pulled the phone out. Read the message.

"Well." Her chin jutted upwards, she glared at Gabe. "Looks like your ex has surfaced."

RILY STRODE THROUGH the local market's parking area a good two feet ahead of Gabe. Nervous energy riddled her spine, making her steps fast and long.

The ride into town had been quiet. And short. Not nearly enough time to absorb the events of the day or the fact she was about to come face to face with Garrett's daughter.

Gabe's ex.

She rotated her shoulders, scanned the area one more time. There would be time later to dwell on things she couldn't change. Right now she had to focus on this coming *encounter*.

In plain clothes, Officer Kyle Samuels stood near the market's front door with a newspaper tucked under one arm. He nodded at Rily, indicating the market itself.

She stopped and turned to Gabe. "You're here, but wouldn't you rather wait in the truck?"

"Really, Detective." Dark sunglasses hid his eyes, but that damnable brow lifted and his lips quirked. Just once. "Why would I want to miss all the fun?"

"Suit yourself." She pursed her lips for a moment. "Right now we're only going to question her. Here, over a cup of coffee if she cooperates. The station if she doesn't."

He inclined his head. "After you, Detective."

She spun away, hoping she wasn't making a mistake in having Gabe there for this interview. Sure as hell, she didn't want him around. Didn't want him in the same zip-code.

How pathetic. She didn't even believe the lies she told herself.

With a deep breath, she approached Kyle and stopped just to the right of the market doors.

"She's inside, at the back in the café." Kyle gave Gabe a nod before continuing. "Early dinner or late lunch. She's having a sandwich. No one has approached her."

"Good." Time to get this over with. Time to move on. "With any luck she'll give us something."

Warm air, filled with the nauseating, yeasty tang of just baked bread, hit Rily the moment she entered the building. She ignored her still tender stomach, ignored the way it churned.

Her stride long, she shed her jacket on her way to the back of the store. Checked her gun. Not that she expected that kind of trouble from the woman, but a little intimidation never hurt.

Gabe followed right behind her.

"Talia Garrett?" Her jaw loose from the way she'd worked it on her way to the back of the market, she gave the woman sitting alone at one of the small tables an easy smile.

Fake, but easy. Warm even.

"Yes?" The woman looked up from the hardbound book she had open next to her plate. Annoyance, along with something harder to read, flashed across the porcelain features of her delicate face. She took her time examining Rily before she glanced to the man standing behind Rily.

Those Garrett blue eyes widened. Her lips parted and her expression softened.

"Gabriel." The word came out in a hushed wash of sound.

Damn, the woman was good.

Her bottom lip trembling, Talia blinked several times. She pressed one hand to her mouth. The other hand she threaded through her short, pure white hair and tucked the strands behind her ear.

Gabe twitched and the feel of it settled over Rily's skin. She resisted the urge to glance back at him. This hyper awareness was getting on her nerves.

In more ways than one.

She aimed another insincere smile at Ben's daughter. Flashed her badge. "Detective Carrigan. Obviously you already know Gabe. Mind if we join you?"

Talia looked from the badge to Gabe, twisted her hands together before indicating the two empty seats at her table. "Please."

Rily took the seat across the table, adjusted her gun. She laid her jacket across her lap and pulled her pen and a small notebook from the pocket.

That left Gabe the seat between the two of them. She ignored the twinge in her palm, resisted wiping it down her pant leg. He pulled his chair out and angled it more to her side. Slouching in the flimsy chair, he stretched his legs out and crossed them at the ankle.

Those damn sunglasses still covered his eyes.

Since they stepped inside the market, he had yet to utter a word. She'd wanted cooperation from him, but this silence might be going too far.

"Ms. Garrett." Might as well jump right into it. Rily uncapped her pen. "We have reason to believe you were one of the last people to see Allison Davis alive."

Sudden sparks of pure heat wound into a spiral at the center of her hand. In his lap, Gabe's fingers curled in on his own palm. One eyebrow arched above his sunglasses, but he kept his face angled toward the other woman. Much as Rily didn't want to, they were going to have to talk about this weird crap later.

When she didn't have a bitch to interrogate.

Talia sat forward in her chair, her gaze moving from Gabe to Rily. "Me? You're kidding?"

What the hell? The woman sat across from Rily yet it felt as if she'd just had her personal space invaded.

"Not at all." Rily leaned forward herself, mentally adjusted her space back to a comfortable level while she tapped her notebook with her pen. "So what I want to know is why you followed Allison to Eagle Crest and what you have to do with her death?"

Talia, her brow drawn deep in a frown and her mouth open, sat back in her chair. Her gaze darted between Rily and Gabe then back again.

Rily rested her elbows on the table and rolled her pen between her palms. "No answers?"

"Detective Carrigan, I didn't know Allison before a few days ago." Talia pulled her gaze from Gabe. With her hands clasped in her lap, she shook her head. "I met her here in town."

Right. "Where?"

"At Dr. Sheldon's."

"Why were you at Sheldon's place?"

Talia lowered her chin. "That's personal."

"Murder trumps personal." Rily gave her another fake smile. She laid her pen on the notebook, linked her fingers and stared at the other woman over her hands. "Want to try again."

Talia turned her gaze to Gabe. He sat slouched and un-moving with one elbow on the chair's arm, his chin cupped in his hand. He could be asleep for all the surface interaction he offered to the conversation.

"You won't get any help from that quarter, Talia." She sure as hell better not. Rily angled her head, narrowed her eyes.

"Why the hostility, Detective?" Talia, her Garrett blue eyes sharp and intense, met her gaze while she picked up her cup of steaming hot chocolate, cradled it above her lap. "I didn't know Allison well enough to want her dead. Much less kill her."

Rily sat back, not bothering to resist a small, satisfied smile.

The bitch had no idea who she was toying with, something Rily intended to remedy.

Chapter Fifteen

"IF YOU BARELY knew Allison, what were you doing in Portland?" Rily pressed the thumbs of her linked hands to her pursed mouth. Watched Talia Garrett across the table in the café at the back of the local market. "In her home. *After* she was killed."

Gabe sat between them. Quiet and unmoving with his sunglasses covering his eyes. Rily didn't bother glancing at him.

Talia frowned, but didn't look at Gabe either. Her chin lifted a small fraction. "What makes you think I was?"

"Evidence linking you there."

"I don't think so, Detective."

"What were you looking for, Talia? In Allison's home?"

"I wasn't there." Talia lifted her cup of hot chocolate to her mouth. Sipped. "I've been here, in this area, for over a week."

"Really?"

"Staying where?" Gabe's voice, quiet yet demanding at the same time, pulled both their gazes towards him.

So the sleeping giant awakens. Although he hadn't moved. He still sat with his elbow on the chair's arm and his hand cupping his chin. Rily looked back at Talia.

"Are you going to stop in and see me?" A slight smile lifted the other woman's lips.

"Answer the question, Talia." Gabe pulled off his sunglasses.

Her gaze held by his, Talia's chin lifted. Her nostrils flared.

What the hell had just passed between them? Rily picked up her pen, tapped her notebook. "Well?"

Lowering her chin, Talia slid her a narrowed look and rattled off the name of a pricey hotel on the coast, maybe fifteen miles southwest of Eagle Crest.

Rily jotted down the information. "Back to Dr. Sheldon. Are you ill? Is that why you wanted to see him?"

"Hardly." Talia glanced at Gabe from under her lashes before lifting her chin. She met Rily's gaze. "It's business."

"You just said it was personal."

"I take my business personally."

"Ms. Garrett —" *Bitch*. Rily moved her lips into what might resemble a smile. "You can cooperate with us — here — and answer our questions. Or I can haul your ass down to the station and keep you there for a minimum of twenty four hours."

"Are you threatening me, Detective?"

"Stating facts."

Talia looked down her nose. Impressive, considering how much shorter the woman was than Rily.

Gabe drummed his fingers on his cheek. "Maybe we *should* take this down to the station."

"Gabriel." Talia sat forward, set her cup on the table. "You would let this woman put me in jail?"

He shrugged, gave her a cold smile. "Isn't that where you belong? In a cage?"

Talia's mouth tight, she stared at him. The tiny muscle under her left eye twitched.

Rily looked between the two of them. Dammit. What had she stepped into here? "I'm asking for the last time, why did you visit Dr. Sheldon?"

With a frown, Talia gave Rily a quick glance before again staring at Gabe. A light sheen coated the woman's big eyes, but Rily doubted they were tears of anguish.

Pissed off tears, maybe. They glistened in the café light.

Definitely ticked off.

Rily pushed against the table, moved to stand.

"My employer wants to hire Sheldon." Talia lowered her head, picked up her cup and sat back in her chair. Her jaw still taunt, she lifted her chin again. Looked at Rily over the rim. "He sent me to make the offer."

"Asking about his daughter was part of that offer?" Rily settled back in her chair.

"His daughter was what brought the doctor to my employer's attention."

"Why?"

"I'm not privy to all the inner workings, but I would guess my employer is interested in the research Dr. Sheldon's daughter was doing."

On my sister-in-law. "And you know about this, how?"

"Rumors." Talia blinked, shrugged one shoulder. "None of that is my area of expertise."

"Your area is in convincing old men to come work for the company."

"Ouch. So catty, Detective." Talia aimed a smile at Gabe without letting her teeth show. She batted her lashes at him. "Are you going to be able to declaw this one?"

Gabe raised one eyebrow. "Why is that any of your business?"

"Now, Gabe." Talia's gaze razor sharp, she glanced between them then ran the tip of her tongue along the edge of her top lip. "Since when did that ever stop me?"

"That's why you left with Allison?" *Were they getting to the root of something?* Rily leaned forward. "Nosiness? The doctor wouldn't cooperate so you latched on to her as a possible means to an end?"

"The doctor did turn me down." Talia blew across the top of her hot chocolate, looked up and shrugged. "Allison offered to show me around town."

"That simple?"

"Sometimes it is, Detective."

"And sometimes it's not."

"True."

"So why are you still in town?"

"I haven't got what I came for."

"The doctor."

Talia smiled, her blue eyes cold.

"Who do you work for?"

"Milford Enterprises."

Rily *felt* Gabe stiffen. So he hadn't known that little fact. She sent him a look from under her lashes. His narrowed gaze stayed locked on Talia.

Okay then. Rily jotted down the information in her notebook. "Where are they located? Contact numbers?"

The corners of Talia's mouth turned down but she rattled off the information. Rily added that to her notes.

"Anything else?" Rily addressed Gabe.

"Not right now." He straightened in his chair, stood.

"I have a question of my own." Talia took a tentative sip of her hot chocolate, looked at Gabe. "How is my father doing?"

"Why don't you call and ask him yourself?" His eyes dark and shuttered, he stared down at her.

She frowned then pursed her lips. Shrugged one shoulder. "Doesn't matter that much."

Rily stood herself, glanced between the two before spearing Talia with a direct look. "You need to stay in the area."

"No problem, Detective. Like I said, I haven't gotten what I came for." Talia's face smoothed, her eyes glittered. She cast a short glance at Gabe and her lips lifted in a semblance of a smile. "Besides, now I have even more reason to hang around."

GABE'S SUNGLASSES BACK IN PLACE, he trailed Rily towards the front of the market. The chill of the late afternoon, swooshing inside each time the automatic doors opened, was just beginning to give way to evening.

He rotated his neck, the scar there throbbed to the point of pain. His palm pulsed, the erratic tempo adding its own brand of hurt to the mix.

But he refused to touch his neck. Not here. Not now. He wasn't going to give Talia that satisfaction.

Small victories, like his success at blocking her knowledge of his presence in the area, were few and far between. He intended to savor this one.

Ahead of him, Rily was one mass of seething wrath.

He let his sun shaded, shielded gaze linger on her ass, on the way her muscles tightened as her stride ate up the distance to the front of the market. Along with the small victories, he was going to take the small pleasures where he could.

Before the explosion that was sure to come.

And that should be spectacular.

His past had just collided with his present and he wasn't sure of the fallout. For now, though, he'd walked away from it. In a manner of speaking.

He had no illusions about his future.

Talia's presence in town had upped the stakes considerably. She wasn't just nosing around, being curious.

Everything with a reason, nothing without a specific purpose. One benefitting Talia Garrett.

Milford Enterprises.

That changed the dynamics.

But his shields had worked.

At least they had when she hadn't been aware of his presence. He was going to have to work on beefing them up now that she knew he was here.

He also needed to figure out how to protect Rily from the insidious invasion of her mind. This talent of Talia's, such as it was, could prove a real threat.

After the text alerting them to Talia's presence, he'd gone over a dozen different scenarios and still didn't have a solid game plan on that front.

Shit.

With the way Rily had gone for the throat in there, he was running out of time. She'd challenged Talia, something the other woman didn't take lightly. He had to come up with something. And convince Rily to work with him on her own protection. Soon.

She had abilities. The way she'd pushed back at Talia's initial probe had completely startled the other woman. And Gabe. He'd *felt* the subtle invasion, *felt* Rily's resistance. But that natural, protective instinct of hers wouldn't be enough if Talia decided to get serious.

When. There would be no *if* with Talia.

Outside, Rily paused to scan the area. She nodded at Samuels. "Keep a tail on her for the time being."

"Will do." The officer nodded.

"Wait a minute, Kyle." Rily frowned. "Why are you the one out here? Shouldn't you be working on Allison's computer?"

"Needed some fresh air." Samuels grinned. "Besides, I was finished with everything I could personally do. I have some scans running, but I don't need to be there for that."

"And?"

The officer's grin widened. Gabe rocked back on his heels, liking the guy just for the way he baited her.

"Kyle —" Rily's eyes narrowed and her chin came up. "I am so not in the mood."

Samuels shrugged, his grin slipping a little. He patted the pocket of his heavy jacket and pulled out a white plastic sleeve holding several CDs. "As far as programming goes, Davis really didn't have much on her computer. Here are copies of the folders she did have, the data."

Rily took the discs. "What am I going to find on these?"

"Lots of artwork, which is quite good. In addition to the Celtic flavor of what you found at her place, it appears she was also working on a Tarot deck with a definite American Indian influence. Actually, local Indian influence."

"Local?" Gabe frowned.

Samuels nodded. "She had several files on local Indian myths. Along with word processing files detailing her own interpretation of the stories." He focused on Rily. "There was one in particular she seemed stuck on. Maybe she was going to write a book or something."

"Yeah. Or something." Rily sent Gabe a dark look from under her lashes before she tucked the discs into her jacket pocket. She nodded at Samuels. "Keep me posted."

The officer nodded in return and Rily turned on her heel, heading across the lot. Gabe hung back until they reached her truck. She dug into her pockets, swung around to face him with her hand out.

"Looking for these?" Knowing he shouldn't bait her either, he held up her keys – the ones he hadn't given back when he'd parked her truck.

Her eyes lit with gold, she snatched her keys and jabbed the open button. The truck beeped.

"Did you think it went that badly with Talia?" His neck throbbing, Gabe gave Rily a bland smile. She'd never know what this calmness cost him.

"No. It didn't go bad at all." She turned on him. "Get in the damn truck."

"Bossy, bossy woman." He wiggled his eyebrows.

Her jaw clenched, she yanked open her door. "Your ass in the truck or it stays here."

"Can't have that." He rounded the hood, climbed into the passenger side. Looked like Rily was back in control. As in control as the day she'd had would let her be, anyway. "Dinner?"

She shoved the key into the ignition. "Is that all you ever think about? Food?"

One side of his mouth lifted. "A certain bossy woman is right up there in my thoughts."

Rily's mouth opened. Closed. "I could toss you in the river. It's really cold this time of year."

"Join me?"

She scrubbed both hands over her face, threaded her fingers through her hair. Shaking her head she started the truck. "I need to write up my notes. File a report."

Gabe glanced to his right, at the lowering sun. Another thirty minutes and it would be full dark. December in the

Pacific Northwest. "That can't wait until the morning? You've already had a long day."

"Life of a cop."

"Let's go, then."

"I'll drop you by your hotel first."

"No."

"Gabe –"

"I'm not leaving you alone, Rily." Even though he'd have to watch her die, he wasn't leaving her side. "Not happening."

"I'm a cop, dammit. I don't need a freaking body guard."

"It'll be dark soon."

"For Pete's sake –"

He shrugged, hooked his seat belt before settling in his seat. "What Talia has to do with all of this, I'm not sure. Her presence doesn't negate what happened this afternoon. Doesn't change the fact something has you on its radar."

Or that it just might be getting stronger.

Her mouth tight, Rily slipped the gear shifter into reverse and backed out of their spot. With the truck in drive and her foot on the brake she slid him a sideways look. "What about Talia's radar?"

"Oh, we're both on there now. No doubt about that."

Rily nodded, pulled out of the lot and concentrated on her driving for several streets. "How did you know she'd been at Allison's?"

He'd been half waiting for that question, wondering when she'd work it all around in her head to the point she had to ask. "So you believe me, then? That wasn't just a shock tactic to see her reaction?"

"I believe you. Not sure why though." She flipped her blinker on for a left turn, eased to a stop and waited on an oncoming car. "There's absolutely nothing to back that up. No evidence. But, yes. I do believe you."

And? Gabe waited.

She swung the truck into the station lot, parked in a space much closer to the building than she had before and let the truck idle for a few moments before she turned off the vehicle. With her keys in one hand, she stared at the palm of the other one. "How did you know?"

He tilted his head to each side, worked the kinks in his neck. *How did he start this? How did he explain?* "There's a connection of sorts between us –"

"Like this one?" She held her hand out between them, palm upwards.

Gabe laid his own palm less than inch over hers. "Similar."

Energy hummed in the confines of the cab, stretching and rebounding between the surfaces of their palms.

Rily fisted hers, clasped both her hands together, one over the other, in her lap. She wet her lips and glanced at him from under her lashes.

Her glance no longer dark or accusing, it seemed more muddled. Confused. Weird shit she didn't appreciate, but she'd have to suck it up. They needed this out in the open.

Question was, how the hell did he explain without her running for cover?

"So you connect like that to every woman you have sex with?"

Okay, so that was putting the subject right out there. *Should've given her more credit.*

"Could have warned me." Rily stared out the windshield. "That seems like it should be right up there along with any diseases you might have."

But then again, this was Rily. He let his chin drop to his chest. "No. I don't *connect* with every woman I have sex with."

"How many so far?" She angled her head, looked at him from the side. "How many have you connected with?"

"Two."

"Me and the psycho bitch?"

"The cop and the psycho. Story of my life."

"Why us?"

Oh boy. That wasn't necessarily where he wanted this *conversation* to head. "Hell if I know."

Her dry chuckle filled the truck's cab, eased a small portion of the vise constricting his chest. "Not good enough, Nicholetti."

"If I tell you I really don't know?"

"I won't buy it. Did you love her?"

"Once. I thought I did, anyway."

"So…." The hesitation in her voice was palpable.

"That connection wasn't because of any affection I had for Talia."

"The psycho bitch."

"Yeah." If she only knew. Gabe glanced at the side mirror, at the colors spilling across the dusky sky. "You need to get your paperwork handled and we need to get the hell out of here before it gets completely dark."

Rily scanned her mirrors along with the area outside the windshield. "Because of whatever is out there?"

"Stalking you."

Rily cleared her throat. "Right. Let's finish this discussion first."

"Rily –"

"I'll log into my computer from home. File my report that way."

"So why are we still sitting here?"

She rubbed her fingers across the top of the steering wheel. Shrugged. He understood her unwillingness to let this go, didn't blamed her. Not really. He'd be the same.

"My connection to Talia didn't happen with sex."

Rily glanced down, masking the spark in her eyes. "Okay. But it did happen."

"Yeah." He angled his head to look directly at Rily. "When she tried to kill me."

"What?" Rily's gaze snapped to his.

He made a face. Not the most pleasant of memories. His mouth lifted in a non-smile. "Remind me later to show you the scar on the back of my neck."

"How —"

Now wasn't the time. He jerked his chin to the windshield. "Let's get out of here."

She glanced around, looked back at him. "I don't *feel* anything."

"And I'd rather be away from here and still *not* feel anything."

"Leaving here isn't going to get you out of this conversation."

"Oh, believe me, I realize that. But let's continue over dinner."

She narrowed her eyes.

He gave her a real smile. "Steaks?"

RILY LEANED BACK, away from her home desktop computer, and stretched. Night had fallen but the heavy drapes lining her living room windows kept it at bay. The room glowed with warm light from all the lamps she'd switched on.

Silly, maybe. She didn't care.

Between the disturbing memories from the afternoon, the interview with Talia Garrett and what she'd found in the files

Kyle had given her, Rily was in dire need of warmth. Of normalcy.

And she hadn't even finished reading the files. She'd skimmed a few, printed others to read later.

They were a bit disturbing. A bit out there, even for Allison.

"I never would have guessed you had a computer tucked away in that cabinet." Gabe leaned against the entryway into the kitchen, two wine glasses held between the fingers of one hand and an opened bottle of wine in the other. "I may have to incorporate something like that on my boat."

The aroma of fresh cooking, not steaks but something chicken with lots of Italian herbs, wafted into the room. Her treacherous stomach growled. "Do you cook like that on your boat?"

"All the time." Laughter lit his dark eyes. "Come away with me?"

God, the thought tempted her. Get away from here and all the weirdness. Just her, Gabe, his boat and all that lovely, warm water. Still, she shook her head.

He pushed away from the wall, set the glasses on a book case near her and poured the Chardonnay into them. Swirling the gold liquid around the bowl of the glass, he handed it to her then held his up in a toast. "The offer stands, Rily. Anytime you say the word, we're out of here."

"So serious."

He sipped his wine, watching her over the rim. Her gaze locked on his, she watched him back. What was it about a sexy man who could cook?

One with eyes so dark she could get lost in them?

She slammed the brakes on that train. *Not going there.* With a sip of her wine, she turned away from the intensity of his gaze.

You don't do relationships. Remember, dip-shit?

So why did running away with him sound like such an exhilarating idea?

Bad boys. Oh yeah, she did like those.

Ones with no thought of commitment. No desire to settle down. Who were thrilled she didn't do mornings. Those kind of men she could deal with.

Gabe might look like a bad boy, but he wasn't.

Bogie padded into the room, turned in a circle in front of Gabe and sat down with his tongue lolling out of his mouth and an expectant look on his canine face.

"You've been giving him scraps?"

"What makes you say that?" Gabe frowned and he made a face at the dog. "Rat fink."

Bogie barked once and his entire body wiggled.

"You keep spoiling him like that, what am I going to do with him when you leave?"

"Bring him and come with me." He took another sip of wine. "Leave this town, leave the damn cold. Sail with me from island to island. Work on your tan."

She met and held his gaze. Live with him. In Paradise.

On a boat.

Her stomach gave a little flip, quivered. Was he serious or just flirting? The thought he might be serious scared her shitless.

"I don't tan. I burn."

"All the more reason to rub you all over with sun screen. Often."

Tingles chased themselves over her body, following the trail of his hands in her imagination. *Get a grip.* And not on him. She gave him a rueful smile. "We have a murder to solve before I can think about anything remotely like running away."

A shadow darkened his already dark eyes. There and then gone. He nodded and moved the few feet to stand next to her. "What was in Allison's files?"

Glad to have anything else to talk about, she set her wine glass down and picked up the pages she'd printed out earlier. "Kyle wasn't kidding when he said Allison had an interest in the old myths. She was obsessed with the legends. Especially this one."

Gabe took the stack she handed him, scanned the first page. He frowned. She watched him read it again, slower this time.

"According to this –" He looked at her with his brows furrowed. "There's an ancient Shaman trapped in the hill between the station and the Davis place? A shaman who wants the Chief's daughter."

"An old legend –"

"Being played out again. Now."

Chapter Sixteen

"ARE YOU OR are you not the Chief's daughter?" Like puzzle pieces snapping into place, the details in the pages Gabe read made sudden sense. His chest tight, he set his wine glass next to Rily's, flipped to the second page.

From her chair in front of her home computer, Rily shook her head. "My dad is retired. And as far as I know, we don't have any Indian blood."

"Doesn't matter. When Justin died your father was the Chief of Police. It's the Chief part that's important."

The image of a young Rily lying on that damn stone, the wound at her temple oozing blood onto the surface of the rock flared in his mind. Shit. If that part was accurate, and right now he was assuming it was, that meant the thing had tasted her blood. If any of this had any basis in truth, they were in a world of hurt.

"This is simply a legend. A myth Allison dug up. We're taking this off her notes, who knows if this is even a real story and not something she put together based on her own conjecture." Rily leaned back in her chair, threaded her fingers through her hair. "Or maybe she made the damn thing up."

"A good many myths are based on some type of fact."

"Irene Trent didn't mention any of this. And I didn't see any of this Indian artwork at her place. She must have done all of this as part of whatever assignment she had. Drawing on the local color for her work. Maybe Kyle is right and she was working on a book."

"Show me the artwork files."

Rily let go of her hair and pulled her keyboard to her. Gabe gave in to his urge and smoothed the wild strands sticking out from her head. She closed her eyes for a moment, leaning into his touch, before snapping them open and hitting a few keys.

"Have you read all of this?"

"Only the first paragraph. I did read those notes Allison made on the story though. The ones you just read."

"We can read it together then." As Allison's images floated across the flat monitor, Gabe shuffled the pages until he found the actual story.

"Two Winds wanted the Chief's daughter as his own. But the girl was promised to another Chief in a village farther down the coast. A powerful shaman, Two Winds sent disease to the other Chief, causing him to die within two days." Gabe glanced at the screen and then down at Rily. "Pretty handy trick."

Her gaze on the screen and the artwork depicting the story, she nodded.

"Two Winds demanded the daughter. But because the dead Chief's family believed Two Winds worked for this Chief, they declared war between the two villages. The Chief lost both of his sons in the battle. Afterwards he refused to let Two Winds take his daughter. So Two Winds stole her."

"Bastard."

"They rescued her, killing Two Winds. But the shaman wouldn't stay dead and the next month he stole the daughter again."

"Tenacious bastard."

"Her family saved her once more, but at the cost of two of the Chief's nephews. Again they killed Two Winds. Again he returned to life. As luck would have it —"

"Always."

"A traveling shaman from another village came through. He had heard of the trouble with Two Winds and told the Chief he knew how to imprison the shaman. But the cost would be the Chief's daughter."

"She must have been something. All those men wanting her."

"No kidding." Gabe glanced at the monitor. Allison's haunting imagery infused her artwork. The Chief's daughter was indeed beautiful and bore a striking resemblance to Rily.

With dark hair and no freckles.

"The Chief agreed. They sent a messenger to Two Winds, telling him they had enough of the fighting. That they would meet him at the base of the little mountain."

Rily, her gaze on the images, picked up her wine glass and sipped.

"Once they were all gathered there, the traveling shaman sent the daughter across the field to join the other shaman. Two Winds gathered her in his arms, laughed to the sky. He picked her up in his arms and sat her on top of the largest boulder, all the while laughing. He ripped her dress from her."

Rily shivered and chills chased themselves over Gabe's skin.

"The traveling shaman lifted his bow and shot an arrow straight through the daughter's back and into her heart."

Rily gasped.

"Her blood spilled over Two Winds, across the stone. The traveling shaman chanted and waved his arms. Two Winds screamed but the winds of his name swirled around him and pushed him into the ground.

"The Chief cried out for his dead daughter, demanding an answer to why she'd been killed. The traveling shaman answered that he had told the Chief the cost was his daughter."

On screen the bloodied image of the daughter wrapped in her father's arms seemed too real. Rily sat her glass next to the keyboard.

"But do not be saddened, the traveling shaman told the Chief. Together they had vanquished the evil soul of Two Winds, trapping it inside the hill where it would spend eternity. He also told the Chief his own Guardian Spirit would accompany the daughter's soul on her journey."

RILY PULLED IN an audible breath and clicked the slide show to off. She sat back in her chair. "Wow."

"Yeah."

"This had to have been for a book."

"Maybe."

"What else would she have done this for?"

"As a warning for you?"

"You don't seriously think there's a shaman's soul trapped in that hillside?"

"I've seen weirder things, Rily."

She held up her hand. "Please, don't even go there."

"Even if it will save your life?" Who the hell was he kidding? She had a death warrant tattooed to her skull. *When* was just a matter of days.

If that long.

The question was whether it would be Talia or Two Winds. And if it was Two Winds, what the hell would be the fallout?

How did he make a freaking shaman's soul pay?

Rily exploded from her chair. "You're taking this paranoia too far."

"Am I?"

"You stand there so calm, but you're the one who's nuts."

"I'm the one making dinner." He knew when to back down. For the moment at least. There was going to come a time, sooner than later, when he wouldn't have the luxury of backing down. "And it should be just about ready. Bring your wine and let's eat."

RILY PACED BACK and forth in her kitchen. Dinner had been excellent and the conversation light and easy. Neither of them had broken the unspoken dinner truce. In addition, the wine had mellowed them both.

But now dinner was finished and she'd made short work of the dishes while Gabe had called Ben. The deep timbre of Gabe's voice carried from the living room.

She'd thought about listening in, but she knew what they were discussing. Allison's story. That damn Two Winds.

What was it about that tale that made her nerve endings raw?

Gabe had said those weren't her memories out there in that field this afternoon. That she – they – were being toyed with.

By Two Winds?

And how did that play into Allison's death?

That was the most important item on the agenda. Who killed Allison and how did they find that person?

Because a living, breathing *person* was responsible, not some mythical ghost stuck in a hillside.

She still wanted Sheldon for it. Or maybe Talia Garrett. She glanced at the kitchen archway, let Gabe's voice drift over her.

The other woman was a class-A bitch. Yet, once upon a time, Gabe had fallen for her. Men. They could be so oblivious.

But Talia was beautiful. Exotic, with that tilt to the corner of those big blue eyes, that pure white hair and the delicate features. Fragile, even. But she'd bet Talia could take care of herself better than most men.

The other woman's name came through from the living room, the sound harsh. Angry. Rily stopped pacing and made her way into the living room.

This she wanted to hear.

Gabe, standing by her bookcase, studied the spines of her books while he listened to whatever Ben was telling him on his cell. The pages she'd printed earlier sat on the top of the case. Spread and gone through. Ben must be as up to date as they were.

"No." Gabe spoke into the phone, shook his head and rubbed the fingers of his other hand over his forehead. "I don't see how that's a good idea."

Rily settled in the corner of her couch, her legs drawn up under her. She pulled the beige afghan from the back of the couch and tucked it around her thighs. Gabe tracked her movements, a banked fire in his eyes.

"I realize she's your daughter." He turned away from the bookcase and openly watched Rily. "And you should realize your presence is only going to muddy the situation."

Gabe's sharp bark of laughter startled her.

"Yeah, about like that. Two cats with their claws out." He listened for a moment. "I think I can handle it. If not, you can pick up all the pieces. You're good at that."

One more laugh, this one more natural, and he shut off his phone. He stood still, his phone in one hand and the other fisted on his hip. His gaze locked on hers.

Predator. And she was his prey.

Why the hell did that thrill her?

"So Ben wants to come out here?" Unable to look away from his eyes, she plucked at the yarn of the throw.

Gabe nodded.

"You don't want him here?"

He shook his head.

"Cat got your tongue?"

"Here, kitty-kitty."

"Meow."

In two strides he was there, looming over her. He leaned forward, braced his hands on the back of the couch on either side of her head. "Don't tease me, Rily."

"I'm not teasing." She pushed herself up and wrapped her arms around his neck, pressed her mouth to his.

She didn't give a damn if this was a good idea or not.

Not tonight.

Motionless, not even his mouth moved, for one short moment and then he crushed her to him. He twisted his body to land on the couch, her on top of him and the afghan tangled between them.

Mouth on hers, he shoved her shirt up her back and ran his palms over her bare skin. She eased up, away from his greedy mouth and straddled him with her legs on either side of his hips. Then she pulled her shirt over her head, tossing it aside.

She stared down at him, his heat filled gaze scalding her exposed skin. With one finger, he trailed the tip from her chin, down her neck and chest. There he traced the edge of the black lace cupping her breasts.

What clothes she still wore seemed too tight, too warm.

Too constricting.

His gaze locked on hers, he slipped two fingers underneath the lace, rubbed the top of her breast. Then he eased the lace aside. Still watching her, he slipped his other hand behind her, pressed her closer.

Closing his eyes, he lifted his head and licked her exposed nipple. Shock waves of pure electric heat coursed through her, gathered between her legs. Her knees gripped his waist and he pulled her tightened nipple into his mouth.

"Gabe –" Her hands kneaded his chest and a rumble from his body echoed through to hers. "Let me take off your sweatshirt."

"Please." The word breathed over her skin. His mouth closed back over her sensitized nipple, the bite no more than a scrape of teeth before he let go and leaned back.

She sucked in her own breath and slid her hands under his sweatshirt, inched it up his stomach. For a moment she got lost in the way his muscles contracted at her touch.

"Rily." His breathing harsh, he arched his neck.

She couldn't stop the smile sliding over her mouth. With both hands under his shirt, she splayed her fingers over his chest. Rubbed his nipples with her thumbs.

His stomach contracted again.

In one sudden movement, he grabbed the hem of his shirt and had it over his head and across the room.

"Well." She held fast to the side of his chest.

"You're taking too long, woman."

"And if I told you that you had to lay there and let me take as long as I want?"

His head back and his eyes closed, he groaned. "I'd stay here and take the torture."

"Torture?"

"I want inside you. Right now." His eyes open mere slits, he leveled his head and held her gaze. "So bad I can't think straight."

"I want that too."

"So why are you torturing us?"

She let her gaze glide over his naked chest before she scooted backwards, taking the bunched afghan with her. Trapping his legs between hers, she ran the palm of her hand over the bulge in his jeans.

His head went back and he groaned.

Unable to keep her hands from shaking, she worked the button loose and eased his zipper down. His hands warm, he cupped hers and pushed his jeans and underwear down his legs to bunch against the afghan.

Rily pulled one of her hands from his, wrapped it around the hard, hot length of him. Stroked once.

"God, woman." He sucked in a raspy breath, wrapped his hand around hers. With his eye half closed, he rocked his hips.

She eased forward and with the tip of her tongue she licked the top of him. His body jerked.

In a smooth, single move he sat up and pulled her forward to straddle his hips. The hard, long length of him prodded her belly. He kicked the afghan onto the floor, followed by his jeans and underwear.

"Your turn." His words, thick and husky, scraped in her ears and down along her spine. He reached between their bodies and with one hand undid her jeans and had them down over her bottom.

She lifted her own hips and wiggled out of the confining pants. She pulled the condom from the packet she'd stashed in her pocket earlier, when she'd wondered if she'd be able to resist her burning desire to have him again.

Gabe shoved her clothes away and ran his hands down her back. Cupping her rear end, he scooted her back up his body.

Taking both her hands in his, he guided her fingers as she eased the condom over him. Then, his eyes daring her to look away, he cupped one of her hands around his shaft. Held her there.

He kissed the palm of her other hand, then covered hers with his and slid their joined hands down her stomach and between their bodies.

With his hands locked on hers, he dipped their fingers into the wet, hotness of her core. She couldn't stop the sudden gasp or the way her hips rocked all on their own.

He lifted his shoulders, found her mouth with his and rocked his own hips, tightening his grip on her hand holding him. Squeezing. At the same time he pushed their fingers inside her with the same slow rhythm.

She was going to die.

Right here. Right now.

"Gabe –" She nipped at his lips.

"See what happens when you torture me?" He slid his tongue between her lips, increased the tempo of their hands.

With their bodies rocking against each other, his hands working hers between them, her breath came fast and erratic. Everything hot whorled into a tight hole inside her. "I'm about to lose it here."

"Not without me." Gabe pulled her down to his chest and pushed himself into her, in one hard and fast stroke.

She'd only thought she'd died before. Now that edge rose up, grabbed her and sent her spiraling over the side.

She had died and didn't give a damn.

THE LIGHTS IN Rily's living room still burned bright and warm, but everything seemed softer somehow. Nothing was urgent, nothing needed to be taken care of, not right then.

Right now, the most important thing was the bare chest under her hands, Gabe's naked body pressed tight between hers and the back of the couch.

"You know, I still don't do –"

"Hush."

"Gabe…."

"Sweetheart, whatever tomorrow brings it brings. Right now, let's just enjoy this for what it is."

That was the biggest part of her problem. She didn't know *what* this was and it scared the crap out of her. But maybe he was right. Maybe she should just let it go. For the moment.

Gabe stretched, pulled her closer and plucked the afghan from the floor and tucked it around them. "Sleep, Rily. Tomorrow will take of itself soon enough."

With her head resting on his arm and the warmth of him at her back, she fell asleep.

GABE'S BACK AGAINST Rily's couch, he cradled his head against one hand and traced the side of her face, slipping a wayward strand of her hair behind her ear. Light from all the damn lights she had on made it easy to watch her sleep.

Dawn peeked through the slit in the drapes, the only reminder of the outside world. Here, cocooned away from reality, they were all that existed.

If he could only extend that, make each minute – each second – last.

Even with all the disturbances in his sleep patterns these last few days, he was still on Island time. Four hours later than here.

Only here looked more appealing with each hour that ticked by. He brushed her hair back from her neck and she turned her face into his palm.

A lot more appealing.

Why the hell did she matter so damn much? His hard edged, soft hearted Rily. His doomed Rily.

He held her close while Allison's story played out in his head. Two Winds. An ancient, trapped shaman.

That made as much sense as anything else these days.

That line of trees along the edge of the field was where he'd seen Rily dead in his visions. Of that he was positive.

What had woken the shaman, this time?

He brushed his lips over Rily's forehead. She snuggled closer and sighed. Really, he should take his own advice and get some rest.

Hard to do, though, when time mocked him and slipped through his fingers so damn fast.

WATER SLUICED DOWN Gabe's back as he braced his arms on either side of the shower. Lowering his head, he captured Rily's mouth with his, swallowing her laughter.

With both of them in there, the shower stall was tight, although not as confined as the one on his boat. He could get used to this communal showering. If only they had that opportunity.

Rily wound her arms around his neck, pressed her slick and soapy body against his and fed off his mouth. He wrapped both arms around her waist, lifted her so that her legs encircled him. *Damn, I could get used to this.*

Her hands threaded through his soaking hair, massaged his scalp.

"God, Rily." He pressed her back against the corner of the stall. Entered her in one smooth stroke.

She gasped, her breath warm against his face. Although not nearly as hot as the core of her surrounding him, squeezing him as they moved together.

Yeah, he really could get used to this.

THE OVERSIZED DARK GREEN ROBE Rily had wrapped around her body intensified the depth of her eyes. Sleepy eyes that stared at Gabe from where she sat at her kitchen table, sleepy eyes sated with a look of utter satisfaction.

A look he'd put on her face.

Her hair, nearly dry, fluffed around her face in a way that made her look almost angelic. Especially with the sun filtering through the window, adding a halo of gold sparks around her head whenever she moved. He knew better. Had the nipped bite on his bottom lip as evidence.

Somehow he didn't mind.

Her own lips were swollen. She had the aura of being thoroughly loved. Something he knew to be true.

He set a plate of scrambled eggs and bacon in front of her and she pulled her leg up to rest her heel on the top rung of her chair. Taking a piece of bacon, she munched on it and watched him settle in his own chair.

"We are going to have to head into the station soon." She picked up her fork, frowned at it.

"Duty calls."

"Yeah. It does." She took a bite of the fluffy eggs.

"What's bothering you, sweetheart?"

One corner of her mouth lifted, although her eyes stayed pensive. "I'm not sure anyone except my dad has ever called me sweetheart."

He gave her a wolfish half smile. "I ain't your dad."

"Thank goodness." She grinned, but the shadow remained. "Everything. The case. Allison. All the weird stuff."

He waited.

She set her fork back down, lowered her foot to the floor. Squirmed in her chair. "You told me, yesterday, to ask about the scar on the back of your neck."

Shit.

He had, indeed, done that. With his fork he shoveled a bite of eggs into his mouth. Chewed and rummaged in his mind for a simple way to explain the damn scar.

Without getting in too deep.

As if you aren't already. He shoved that aside.

"Why did Talia Garrett try to kill you?" She snapped a piece of bacon in half.

He took another bite of eggs.

Great breakfast conversation.

The problem was where did he start? At the beginning? Or at the stage where everything had finally seemed to come together for him, where it looked like he and Talia had a future together?

Or what about at the point where the bitch had stuck a knife in his neck and left him for dead?

Gabe shoveled another fork full of eggs into his mouth.

The scar on the back of his neck throbbed, mocking him.

Again.

Chapter Seventeen

RILY STUDIED GABE from across her kitchen table. He swallowed the bite of eggs, took another one. Morning light sparkled across the table, belying the heaviness of the morning.

"Talia may end up being important to this case." She resisted the urge to squirm even more in her seat. With the ball volleyed into his court, she needed to wait. See what he did with it.

"I know, Rily. Eat your breakfast and I'll tell you the tale."

She nodded and picked up her fork, took a bite of her eggs. Gave him a somewhat worried smile. She'd asked the question, only now she wasn't sure she wanted the answer.

Not really. How was that for wishy-washy?

Even though she knew, as a cop, she needed the infor-mation. Some instinct, deep in her gut, whispered this was going to change things.

More than they'd already been changed.

Status-quo was looking better every second.

"From the time I was five or six or so – I really don't remember how old I was – I'd lived at the Institute." He set his fork down, braced his elbows on the table and linked his fingers. Studied her over his hands. "Ben was, in a very concrete way, my surrogate father."

"Where were your real parents?"

He shrugged. "I don't have any memories of my father. I have his last name and know he was from Italy. But that's all I know. My mother – she couldn't cope and left me at the Institute with a note pleading for them to take me in."

"Why?" She pushed the image of him as a small boy aside. Right now she needed to focus and not let empathy sidetrack her.

His chin on his linked hands, he covered his mouth with both index fingers. Tapped his lips.

"What couldn't she cope with?"

"Me." The glimmer of past memories deepened his already dark chocolate eyes. "My gifts. Which even then were over the top. She died later. I really don't know how much later. At the time, as a kid, it seemed that forever later kind of time. As an adult –" He shrugged again, rubbed the edge of his nose with the knuckles of his linked hands. "Maybe a few months later. A hit and run driver."

His mouth tight, he looked down at his plate. Away from her. What was he seeing, in his mind's eye? What didn't he want to share with her?

She fought to keep her face neutral, to keep a semblance of distance. Because of her job, she'd heard all manner of horrific stories. She knew what people could and did do to each other. To the people they were supposed to love.

But this was Gabe, a small inner voice whispered. *Go away*. She didn't want to hear that. So she'd welcomed the fact he spent the night this time, she'd showered with him, that didn't mean he *meant* anything to her. Anything more than an annoyance and a means to solving this case.

And glorious sex. So what? Sex to the point she wasn't going to be able to walk straight for a very long time.

And he'd fed her again.

What did it matter if she sat here, her heart breaking for a small child, different and abandoned by the people who were supposed to love and protect him?

None of that mattered. Unless she let it. And she wasn't going to let it matter.

"Your mother left you at the Institute because …?"

"The weird shit you mentioned, that's what they do there. Even back then. I was the only child in residence for quite a number of years."

"You said Ben took you in?"

A dry chuckle escaped Gabe's throat. "Yeah. He didn't feel he had much choice. My mother had been explicit about what I was able to do. How my manifested *gifts* scared her." His lips lifted in a rueful half smile and he met her gaze. "Somehow she had found Ben's name in connection with the Institute. Named him my guardian. It must have been easier back then. No one else claimed me. No one questioned the legality."

"What about schooling?"

"I lived in a research facility with teachers everywhere I turned. I do believe they all took it as their duty to make sure my education didn't suffer. I'm probably overeducated."

"So you were everyone's pet?"

"Until I hit my teens."

"Rebellious?"

"Understatement." His shoulders tensed and he glanced away. He lifted his chin, stretched his neck before looking back at her. "When my *talents* began to manifest beyond what they could control, I scared the shit out of each and every one of them. Except Ben."

"So Ben understood you?" Rily frowned, let that roll around her head and ate the last bit of egg on her plate.

"In a manner of speaking." Gabe snapped a piece of bacon in half. The rest of his food had to be getting cold. "Mostly he just wasn't going to take anything off me. Period."

"Now that sounds like the Ben we all know."

"If he hadn't been there, who knows if I would've made it into adulthood?" Gabe shoved a large bite of eggs into his mouth. Chewed. He gave no sign if the food had any taste at all, cold or otherwise.

"Life was that bad?"

"Ben and I –" He laid his fork across his plate. "Our relationship was – still is – complicated."

"Does Ben have a non-complicated relationship with anyone?"

The edges of Gabe's mouth lifted a little and a light sparkled in his eyes for a second.

"Wait a minute." Rily frowned, pushed her empty plate away. "If you were the only kid there, where was Talia? She is definitely Ben's daughter. She has his eyes."

"That she does."

"And she's not that much younger than you."

"A couple of years. Closer to your age."

"So where was she?"

"Eastern Europe, with her mother."

Rily raised an eyebrow, tilted her head. Man, this just kept getting more and more interesting.

"Okay." He braced his elbows on the table again, blew out a huge breath. "I never knew Ben's wife. She left before I came to the Institute. She also never told him she was pregnant."

"Oh." More fascinating by the moment. She braced her own elbows on the table and rested her chin on the heel of her hand.

"That's not what Ben said when a teenaged Talia showed up at the Institute's door."

"I bet."

"Talia had somehow found him. Had run away from her mother straight to Ben."

"From Europe? That's quite a trek for a teenage girl."

"TALIA WAS – still is – quite resourceful." Gabe reached up, touched the side of his neck and paused. He frowned before pulling on his ear.

Resourceful my ass. When they'd showered, she'd had a cursory look at that scar on the back of his neck. He was damn lucky to still be alive.

"From what I've pieced together after the fact –" Gabe placed both hands on the table in front of him, palms down and his thumbs hooked on the edge. He met her gaze. "Ben's insistence about operating on the side of right when it came to the use of talents, gifts – curses – was in direct conflict with Talia's mother."

"Who wanted what?"

"To be able to use her talent in any way she saw fit. Damn the consequences. Especially when someone else usually paid for those consequences anyway."

"So Ben's the standup guy in all of this?" *Right.* Where was a bridge to sell when you needed one?

Gabe smiled, that half smile that made her heart flip in her chest. "He's fairly rigid on that point."

"Like he doesn't bend the rules or the law when it suits him."

"Of course he does. Whether you like it or not, his agency – and his agents, of which I am one –" Gabe rolled his eyes. "I can't believe I'm defending him."

Rily grinned, she couldn't help herself.

"As a whole, the agency works for our government and that occasionally entails some rule bending."

"You just said –"

"I was talking about the use of psychic ability. Ben's strong on not using that to harm another."

"So he and Irene Trent would get along great."

"Probably. At the core, with Ben, is taking responsibility for your actions. Especially along the psychic angle."

"Hmmm." She could see that, just didn't want to give in too soon. "So wifey-poo got her tail twisted in a knot, took off and neglected to let Ben know he was a soon-to-be daddy."

"Yes."

"Fast forward to Talia showing up to surprise Daddy Dearest. How did Ben take it?"

"As well as could be expected. A few harsh words in private, but on the surface, not much fazes the man." He pressed his lips tight.

"Until she decided you were the next best thing to hard candy?"

With humor lurking in his eyes, he shook his head. "That's one way of putting it."

"Did all of Ben's protective fatherly instincts come to the fore at that point?"

"During those first few years I managed to resist Talia. That was easier with Talia going back and forth between Minnesota and Europe. Something Ben insisted on. And then I left for college, determined to never go back to Minnesota."

"But you did?"

"Talia's mother died, some kind of freakish accident, and when Talia came back – I did, too."

"For her?"

Gabe shrugged. "Ben offered me a job."

"As an agent?"

He nodded.

"Talia was just a nice addition?"

"That's what I told myself."

"And Ben?"

"Hated it."

"Was that a nice perk, that it got to Ben?"

Another flash of humor lit his eyes. "You could say that."

"And?"

"We became a couple, more or less. Dating in between my job assignments and her school. She went to a local college, only because Ben insisted she continue her education."

"Did Ben send you away a lot? Keep you apart as much as possible?"

"At first, yes. But then he just seemed to accept that we were together."

"Did Talia work for the agency after college?"

"For a while, but not originally as an agent."

"Why not?"

"I asked myself that many times. She seemed a natural. At the time I wondered if Ben was simply being over protective of his daughter."

"What was the real reason?"

"Looking back, I believe Ben never fully trusted her."

"Because of her mother?"

Gabe made a face. "Possibly part of it. Ben is an excellent judge of character. As much as he loves his daughter, he sees right through to her core."

"And it's not a pretty core?"

"Not even a little pretty."

"But you didn't see that then?"

"Hell no. She was beautiful, exotic and completely focused on me. I saw what she wanted me to see. I heard what she wanted me to hear."

"Did she love you? Back then?"

"In her own way, maybe. Who knows?" Gabe leaned his head back, hating this discussion. Maybe he owed it to Rily. Maybe he didn't. But he was willing as long as it made her understand what they were dealing with when it came to Talia. "I'm not even sure what my feelings were for her then."

"And now?"

He leveled his gaze at her from across the table. "Hatred. Contempt."

"But you're still connected to her?" Her gaze locked on his, Rily bit her bottom lip.

He nodded. One of them would have to die for the connection to be broken. That was something, although he'd touched on it earlier, he really didn't want to share with Rily.

Looking away from him, Rily turned her hand over and rubbed her palm with the fingers of her other hand. Gabe lifted his own palm towards her. Her gaze drifted to his hand and she made a fist, one hand wrapped over the other one.

Pretty definitive, that.

No, he couldn't tell her death was the only way to sever their connection. Not when he was going to lose the connection to Rily all too soon.

What would happen to him once that was severed? The blowback, would it kill him also?

He fisted his own hand and lifted his chin, watching her.

"How did you get the scar?"

"Talia got tired of working in the office, she wanted to get out in the field." Gabe glanced up at the ceiling, gathered his thoughts back to the subject of Ben and his daughter. "Utilize her talents."

"So she's a psychic also?"

"A powerful one."

"Ben knew this?"

"Suspected. It turns out Talia's mother did a good job training her daughter in the skill of flying under the radar."

"Talia fooled him?"

"To a degree. Like I said, I believe there was a reason Ben tried to keep her from the field. That he let us both believe he was being overprotective."

"He was waiting for her true colors to show?"

"That's what I suspect."

"HOW LONG DID all this last?"

"Several years." Gabe shook his head at the level of patience Talia had shown. She'd fooled him completely.

"But she eventually made it into field work?" Rily traced a whorl pattern on the wooden table with the tip of her index finger.

He nodded and watched the way her hand moved. "Small cases, where Talia couldn't do a lot of damage. She knew Ben was testing her and she shone like a bright star. Made all the right moves. He moved her up to bigger cases, keeping a close eye on her all the while."

"The two of you worked together?"

"Not much when she first came out in the field, more later, after she became more seasoned. She worked hard, closed a lot of cases. At the time, I thought she was trying to please her father, to show him she was capable. I was her biggest defender."

"That changed?"

"Yes, Detective, that changed."

She shrugged without any evident apology. Straight forward, that was Rily. Bands tightened, constricted his chest.

They should be on a plane half way to the islands. Not going over all of this.

"My relationship with Ben became more strained." He rolled his head, side to side on his neck. Damn it all. "Hell, it's still strained."

"Ben is Ben."

"Yeah. Well, my talents lie in finding killers. So in my own way I was an invaluable asset to the agency. He kept me around, kept a close eye on me, too."

"Finding killers with an investigative talent or a psychic one?"

"Both."

She frowned at him. "Where do Talia's talents lie?"

"All over the damn place."

"Bitter."

"With reason." He shoved both hands through his hair. Shit, how the hell did he explain any of this? How did he make Rily understand this wasn't something to ignore? "Talia's like a receptor, transmitter and amplifier all wrapped up in one tiny little package."

Rily cocked an eyebrow, tilted her head.

"Receptors pick things up, seemingly out of thin air. Thoughts, data. There were times I would have the radio on and she would know – actually able to hear – what I was listening to, from all the way in Europe."

"That can't be real."

"Oh it is."

"And you let me walk in that market yesterday without warning me." She frowned and braced her elbows on the table, her chin resting on her palm.

"Would you have believed me?"

"I'm not sure I do now."

"My point exactly. You have a natural protective shield in place. Plus I was running interference. And she didn't touch you."

"Touching is bad?"

"With Talia it is."

"Okay, so no touching the bitch. What about transmitting?"

"That may be the strongest of her talents. Although I didn't realize that until much later. In reality, most of us are transmitters to some degree or another. Transmitting constantly."

"Most? As in psychics?"

"Most as in all of us. People in general. Thoughts are energy. And as such are out there, in the ozone, to be picked up by anyone with the right type of mental receiver. Talia is better able to direct her transmissions than most people. Or to block them."

Rily's frown deepened. "I'm not sure I even want to know what an amplifier does."

"Just what it implies."

"Amplifies the thoughts, the energies you're talking about?"

He nodded. "With the added caveat of increasing whatever has been left at a scene, of making it easier to get a read. Most murders are, by their nature, violent."

"No argument there."

"And that residual energy is left behind. To be read by anyone who knows where and how to look."

"Read? Like a book?" She frowned.

"In a matter of speaking. Although different for each person, for most it's not a visual process. It's more of a feeling, a knowing type of sensation."

"And having an amplifier there?"

"Makes the residual energy easier to read."

"How does that work? I mean, is she re-transmitting this energy? Wouldn't that taint it? When it's read?"

"Always the cop." He let himself smile, just for a moment. "No. Her energy doesn't mix with it, merely enhances what is there. Like turning up the volume on a radio so you can hear it."

"Does she have to do anything specific?"

"Specific as in what?"

"If I knew what I meant, I wouldn't be asking."

He lifted his eyebrow. "So testy."

"Is it just her presence that does this amplifying? Or does she have to willfully, on purpose, amplify whatever the hell it is that she's amplifying?"

"I think there's a degree of it that goes on just with her being in the vicinity."

"And?"

"There's probably a certain degree that's she's able to manipulate on purpose."

"Okay." Rily's eyes widened and then narrowed. "She's able to deliberately transmit what is there to someone else?"

"Bingo."

"That could be … handy." Rily's eyes still narrowed, she drummed her fingers on the table.

"What the hell do you mean by that?" Gabe narrowed his own eyes, watched as she fixed an innocent look on her face. "Not only no, but hell no."

"Gabe –"

"Stupid idea. First of all, Talia won't help you. Second, you can't trust anything about her. Anything she says."

His throat tight, he held Rily's gaze for a long moment. Surely she wasn't that stupid.

Mule-headed, yes. But not stupid.

"Don't bait me, Rily."

"Why not, when you're so easy?" She batted her lashes. Smiled.

He ran a hand over his face. Yeah, why not?

"You still haven't told me how you got that scar on your neck."

He waited a few moments, held her gaze with his own. "A few years ago I caught her transmitting to someone I considered an enemy."

"What?" Rily sat straighter.

"The primary suspect in a murder case. The man I was about to nail." Gabe let his lip curl on one side. "I had him, dead to rights, and had just found the missing piece of evidence.

"Not wanting to believe what I suspected, I headed over to confront the bastard. He'd left town. Bailed. And the evidence trail I'd so painstakingly followed dried up completely. Gone as if it never existed."

"What did you do?"

"Confronted Talia."

"She denied?"

"Hell no. She laughed in my face. Went so far as to invite me to join her. When that didn't go over the way she wanted, when I went to walk away from her, she pulled a knife and jumped on my back. Still not sure why I'm not dead."

"She tried to kill you to keep you from ratting her out?"

"No." He laughed, the sound unpleasant even to his own ears. "To stop me from walking away from her."

Chapter Eighteen

RILY, SITTING AT HER kitchen table, sat back and stared at Gabe. She tilted her head to one side and rubbed at the area behind her left ear. "I couldn't have heard that right."

Slouched across from her, Gabe, his gaze shuttered and face devoid of expression, linked his fingers and rested his hands on the table in front of him.

Morning sunlight dappled across his skin, across the empty breakfast plates.

"Talia stuck a knife in your neck, with the explicit purpose of killing you, yet she is *still* walking around." Rily pushed away from the table, paced to the kitchen sink and back all the while tightening the belt on her robe. "Why isn't her ass in prison?"

"That is where she belongs. In a cage."

"So? Why isn't she in one?" Her legs shoulder width apart, Rily set her hands on her hips. "You said she didn't want you walking away from her. What's to stop her from doing something like that again? Since *obviously* you're not with her now. And since it is *extremely* obvious she still wants you."

"So many questions."

"Dammit, Gabe. The woman tried to kill you –"

"And I'm still here, aren't I?"

"Yeah. That's what I'm asking. How did you manage that one?"

"She left me there, on the floor to bleed out. Then called Ben, telling him we'd been ambushed. That I was dead and she was chasing the bastard that had stabbed me."

Whoa – ballsy. "And?"

"She hadn't counted on Ben being close by."

"Trailing you guys?"

"I never did get the answer to that. But he saved my sorry ass, got me to the hospital. If the knife had been slightly to one side or the other, I would've been dead before Ben could get there. In the meantime, Talia killed the bastard we were investigating."

"The one she'd been transmitting to?"

He nodded. "She used my gun on him, supposedly in self-defense."

"No one to rat her out."

"My word against hers."

"Surely Ben believed you."

"Surely he did. By the time I was coherent enough to tell my side of the story, Talia had left for Europe. She said she couldn't stay, knowing I was gone. That if she'd been quicker she might have been able to save my life. To have stopped the man from killing me."

"Excuse me?"

Gabe's mouth lifted in a humorless smile. "Ben kept the fact I was still alive quiet."

"Sneaky."

"Talia wasn't as convincing as she'd thought and Ben has always been the suspicious sort."

"So why wasn't there a warrant for her arrest after you were able to tell your side of what she'd done?"

Gabe closed his eyes, tapped his thumbs together.

This was difficult for him. She got that.

Tough shit.

They needed this out in the open. Period.

For the case she was working and for their *non*-relationship.

"Well?" She sat, braced her elbows on the table and hooked her foot around the front leg of her chair. And waited.

After a drawn out moment he sighed and looked across at her. "It's complicated, Rily."

"Life is, in general."

"My word against hers."

"I'd say yours carries more weight."

"Yeah, well her actions after she stabbed me – with a knife known to belong to the perp – opens up reasonable doubt."

"So she's a conniving bitch. That isn't an answer."

"We're going to nail her another way. Another time."

Rily pursed her lips, not believing she was hearing this. "You and Ben are letting her walk around. Free. And neither of you are doing a damn thing about what she did."

"I didn't say nothing was being done. Just that it was complicated." He scrubbed a hand over his face. "The scar on my neck, where she stabbed me, is a two way street."

Oh. Rily sat back, rubbed her palm along the soft material of her robe. *That connection between them.* "Her obsession with you forged that?"

Gabe nodded.

"When you rub your neck, it's because of her?"

He nodded again.

"She's thinking about you?"

Another nod.

"Come on, Gabe. Help me out here. Your neck hurts and that tells you she's in the area?"

"Sometimes. She's good at blocking. Other times, she could be anywhere and is thinking about me. Hard to tell just from the scar alone. There are too many variables involved."

"So this goes along with that transmitting you were talking about?"

"In a way."

"How does this forged connection manifest for her?"

"Manifest." Gabe smiled, although it didn't quite make it to his eyes. "Fancy word for someone who doesn't really believe any of this."

"Deflection is another fancy word and it's not going to work." She showed her teeth in a parody of a smile.

He rolled his eyes. "No idea how it manifests for her. Maybe I can ask the next time I see her."

"As long as you're not alone with her when you do that. She still wants you dead."

"I know."

They stared at each other across the table.

"I'm serious Gabe. She belongs in prison."

"I agree. It's just not always that simple."

"What is?" Rily leaned her head back, glanced at the ceiling than back at him. "So her ... passion at that point in time, when she knifed you, is what cemented this connection you talk about?"

He stared at her.

"Just being specific here. Covering my bases. Making sure I understand."

"Defensive, too."

"Hmmm. Beats being evasive."

"Yes, Rily. I believe that's what happened. Why that happened."

"So she knew you weren't dead fairly quickly?"

"I think that's why she ran to Europe. Despite the reasons she gave."

"Makes more sense." Rily made a face at him. "Okay, I'll quit harping on the fact she should be locked up. For now."

"Appreciate that."

"Bet you do. I need to get dressed and head into the station."

"Rily —"

"You need to quit harping, too."

"We don't have any idea if yesterday's events strengthened Two Winds."

"Two Winds." She sucked in a deep breath. "Right."

"He is as good an answer to what's out there, to what happened to Justin, as anything else."

"So is the seizure theory."

"You felt that presence at the station."

"I felt something … at night time."

"That was before yesterday."

She frowned at him. Hard. "You're thinking he can pull this crap during the day now?"

"He? As in Two Winds."

Her gaze narrowed, she glared at him.

"Daytime is a distinct possibility now."

"Why now? I've been in and out of that station for as long as I can remember. First as my dad's daughter then as a cop myself. Not until —"

"Allison came back did you feel anything. You said yourself this was her first time back. Maybe she did something out there before she came into town. Maybe her mere presence is all that was needed. You'd said the Talking Board had been her idea."

"Maybe it was the right alignment of planets and the moon. And the stars."

"Maybe."

"An awful lot of damn maybes."

"In my line of work, that's a normal day."

RILY WATCHED GABE pace the hallway outside her office. Back and forth. Sometimes he had his phone to his ear, other times he just meandered across, deep in thought.

He was driving her nuts.

And they'd been here less than hour.

She pushed her keyboard back, laid her pen across her notebook and stood to move towards her door. This was enough.

"Gabe." She gestured him into her office and shut the door behind him. So her gaze lingered on his back when he passed her. On his ass.

Sue me.

That was a major part of her distraction.

The desire to run her hands down that back. To grab that ass. To take him right back to bed. Or to the couch. Possibly back into the shower.

Any of those places.

She smoothed her achy palm across her hip.

He turned to her, that same fire banked in the depths of his dark eyes. Her stomach muscles clenched and she lifted her chin.

How was she supposed to focus when he looked at her like that?

"You need to stop with the pacing." She took the few steps to the safety of her desk, the width between them.

"Oh? You have the corner market on that?" That damn brow of his arched.

"In my office, yes."

"Technically, I wasn't pacing in your office."

"Gabe –" She shook her head. With her hands braced on her desk, she leaned forward. "What did Ben say about Allison's myth?"

"He's found the kernel of the legend." Gabe rotated his shoulders, stretched his neck. "No specifics on exact location. But the story is real."

"What does *real* mean?"

"The story is part of the local lore. Local being relative. Back in the late 1800s and early 1900s, there was a man who translated quite a few of the legends for the tribes up and down the North Pacific Coast. Ben found the story in those translations."

"Oh."

"Yeah."

"That doesn't mean –"

"Give it a break, Rily."

"Earlier, when we got here, you agreed there wasn't anything out there. Not today."

"What's your point?"

"I don't know if I have a point." She straightened and ran her fingers through her hair, rested her hand on top of her head. "All this psychic stuff is making my head hurt. Besides, you're going to wear a hole in the floor out there."

"Been thinking."

"Come up with anything useful?"

"Not a damn thing. However, if you will stay here – inside – until I get back, I'd like to run back out to the old Davis' place. Unless you have something else for me?"

"No. Go." *Please go.*

"You'll stay here?"

"I'm not promising anything."

"Then I'll keep pacing."

She fished her truck keys from her pocket, tossed them across the room. He caught them mid-air.

"Go."

"You'll stay?"

"Unless something comes up."

"God, you're difficult."

"I do my best."

He stared at her for several seconds. "I'll be back before you need to go anywhere."

After he left, pulling her office door closed behind him, Rily sat. With her elbows on the desk's surface, she rubbed her face, threaded her fingers in her hair.

Difficult.

What a colossal understatement.

Leaning back, she picked up her pen and tapped it against the edge of her desk. Not any closer to finding Allison's killer than she'd been two days before, she had nothing. Zilch.

Not a damn thing, as Gabe had said.

Sheldon and Talia Garrett.

What, besides Allison, linked the two of them? There had to be something.

She pulled her notebook to her, flipped through a few pages. Money? Talia was supposedly in town to entice Sheldon to work for her boss.

Had Allison gotten in the way of that? How? Why hadn't Sheldon and Talia simply talked another time?

Milford Enterprises ... who were they and what the hell did they want with a local doctor? Rily sat straight, pulled her keyboard closer. There had to be something.

She'd just see what she could find on that business. See what kind of possible links they might have to one Doctor Sheldon and/or his daughter.

Gabe could go chase illusionary shamans all day long if he wanted. A soul trapped in a hillside hadn't left Allison's body out at that rest stop.

And that soul hadn't covered her with pine needles.

Someone very human had done that and Rily intended to find *the who* and *the why*.

She'd have her answers and have justice for Allison.

If it was the last thing she did.

"WHAT ARE YOU doing here, Talia?" Gabe, glad his sunglasses were in place, didn't glance at the woman stepping out from between the trees. Didn't acknowledge her beyond his words.

He didn't turn his back on her, either. Once had been enough of a lesson.

"Here? As in right now, with you?" She stopped a few feet away. Close enough for their energies to interact, not close enough for him to grab her. "Or here, as in this town?"

"Take your pick." His hands, shoved in his pockets, fisted. The scar on his neck throbbed, had been doing that almost since he'd left the station.

Maybe he was being reckless. Maybe he wasn't. But once he'd realized she was behind him, trailing him, it had become a risk he'd decided he needed to take.

Had she shaken her own tail? Was he on his own out here with the bitch? Or was the Calvary, even now, being amassed?

"Yesterday I told your detective why I'm in the area." Her own sunglasses as dark as his, she lifted her delicately boned face to the sun shining across the area. Almost as if she didn't have a care, as if they were just two people having an innocent conversation.

Like there had ever been anything innocent about her. Or delicate. Looks and actions could be so deceiving. That was a lesson he'd also learned well.

"Milford and Sheldon." He scanned the area around them, visually and psychically. Nothing. They were alone. Nothing preternatural or human.

Where was the officer who had been following her? Even she wouldn't take the risk of hurting the man. Not yet.

"Yes." Her expression unreadable behind her sunglasses, she angled her head towards him. "I told the two of you about the job offer as well."

"I'm sure you left a few pertinent details out."

"Now, Gabe, I'm crushed you would think that."

"Right. What's in this alliance for you?"

Talia, a slight smile lifting the corners of her mouth, mirrored his stance with her hands in her jeans pockets. She shrugged.

"You're not sick. You don't have P.L.S. Why the interest in Sheldon and his daughter?"

She laughed, the melodic sound washed over his skin. There had been a time that was all it had taken to give him a hard-on for her.

Now, her pleasure left him as cold as the breeze that had picked up and stirred the tall, dried grasses and limbs of the nearby pines.

"Money." Glad, considering the chilled air, he'd worn the heaviest of his new sweatshirts, he rolled his shoulders. "Power."

"You really do know me so well."

The center of his palm burned. His hands still in his pockets, he flexed his fingers a slight bit. How much of this was Rily picking up?

Any? All? Or none?

Given time, Rily and he would make a hell of an investigative team. He glanced at the edge of the field.

Time. Something Rily didn't have much of, the one thing he couldn't give her.

And thinking about time, he didn't have any to stand here and play Talia's games either. But he didn't see an alternative. Not if he was going to get to the bottom of any of this.

Talia sighed, the sound as soft as the sweep of air through the field. "But if Sheldon doesn't want to play –"

Gabe frowned at the deliberate *play* on his thoughts. He was going to have to do better at shielding, sharpen his focus. "I can't say that I blame him, considering *who* Milford sent to recruit him."

Just above her sunglasses, Talia's brows drew down in a frown. "And here I thought you loved me."

Gabe angled his head, studied her. "Not anymore."

Her mouth widened in a secretive smile and she lowered her chin. "No, Gabe. That's where you're wrong."

"How so?"

Maybe Rily was right and they were all crazy.

"You're mine. Always have been. Always will be."

"That ended with that knife you put in my neck."

"No. That solidified it. Consecrated it."

"What?"

"You know I'm better than that. If I'd intended you to die, you would be dead."

"What kind of fantasy world are you living in, Talia?"

She stepped closer to him. Tilted her head to look at his face from behind her dark glasses. "Don't you think it's rather interesting we have both ended up here?"

"Interesting is one word. Not the one I'd choose." He held his ground, eased his hands to the edge of his pockets.

"No, really Gabe. We belong to each other and the knife sealed it. Sealed our fate, one to the other."

"Mental illness isn't a defense. Not one you can use."

Her smile, full of secrets, widened. She tilted her head to the side, listened. "Are you sure?"

Okay. This was a good act. The question was why. What was she up to? He waited.

"I rather think it might work."

"You belong in a cage, Talia. One of these days you will be."

She shrugged. "So says you."

"And your father."

Her chin lifted, she turned her face away from Gabe. "My father doesn't have a say in any of this."

"You tried to kill me. You were one of his agents. It's just a matter of time before he catches you. Before he puts you in that cage himself."

"You're so sure of that, aren't you?" She pulled her hands from her pockets, turned to look towards the line of trees. "I told you. If I'd tried to kill you, you would be dead. Why do you think I called Benjamin? I knew he was close by – I could always tell – knew he wouldn't let you die."

"Lovely story you're spinning there."

"It is, isn't it?" She shrugged again, laced her fingers together and pressed the back of her thumbs against her mouth. "And it's all true."

"If you're lucky, maybe Ben will put you in cell near Sheldon's daughter. You might even be able to ferret out her secrets that way."

"I'd get quite a bonus for that one." She laughed again, soft as the breeze lifting her hair back from her upturned face. "But I don't intend for Daddy Dearest to have that opportunity. I'm going to have to find another route to my bonus."

"RILY?" The male voice accompanied a knock on her partially opened door.

She glanced up from her notebook and gave Kyle Samuels an absentminded smile. Milford Enterprises was proving to be quite interesting. Not for what she was finding, but for what wasn't out there. She rubbed her aching palm over her thigh. "Yes?"

"Thought you'd want to know. The officer I had tailing Talia Garrett called in."

Rily straightened in her seat. Trepidation eked into her gut. Slow and deliberate, she sat her pen on the pad. "And?"

"Seems your buddy, Nicholetti, picked himself up a tail of his own. They've all ended up out at the old Davis place. My officer is hanging back, but the Garrett woman went after Nicholetti on foot."

.

Chapter Nineteen

CRAP AND TRIPLE CRAP.

"Gabe has my truck. You're driving." Rily didn't wait for Kyle's agreement. She pushed away from her office desk, checked her gun and grabbed her jacket from the back of her seat. "Let's go."

She strode through the station with him behind her. Outside, unsure where he'd parked – if he even had a patrol unit today – she paused.

"My truck is over there." Kyle waved towards the edge of the lot and passed her, leading the way.

Sharp arrows of awareness darted across her shoulders, tightening the area between her shoulder blades. *Like someone watched her too closely.* A shudder, one she couldn't stop, trembled through her body.

Great. Talia was following Gabe with who knew what on her mind, and now Two Winds decides to spend the afternoon, *in daylight dammit*, tweaking her. Just what she needed to round things off.

Perfect.

After a quick, cursory glance around, she caught up with Kyle and climbed into the passenger side of his old truck. Once in, she slammed the door – the only way to make sure it stayed shut – and settled in.

The freaking awareness dissipated the further Kyle got from the station. Two Winds could stay right where he was, she didn't need any more shit from him today.

She rubbed a hand over her face, glad Kyle was quiet and concentrating on getting out to the Davis place as quick as he could. The town flew past and after only a few minutes they were on one of the dirt access roads that crisscrossed over the hills in the area.

Grateful for the fact Kyle took his beat up truck over these roads on a regular basis, Rily stared out her window at the passing trees.

Talia following Gabe wasn't good. Not any way Rily looked at it. What the hell did the woman think she was doing? She had to know she had a tail. From everything Gabe had said, her awareness on that level was intense.

So maybe all Talia wanted to do was talk to him. She also had to know if anything happened to Gabe, Rily would be parked right at Talia's doorstep. Wherever that happened to be. Didn't matter where. And she'd see to it the woman stayed in the cage where she belonged.

If Talia didn't realize that, she was more stupid than they'd given her credit for. Rily bit the inside corner of her lip.

Gabe had to be okay.

The heat in her palm intensified, heat she'd been trying to ignore since Gabe had left her office.

You're not giving him enough credit. Yeah, well the bitch had managed to stab him in the back of the neck once.

Her shoulders tight again, Rily leaned her head back and rotated her shoulders to work the kinks out. That damn prickliness radiated down her back and up to the back of her skull.

She blinked twice, slow.

Crap.

She sat straight, glanced around and paid closer attention to their surroundings.

They were traversing Two Winds' hill.

Perfect.

GABE STOOD, his fingers curled over the warmth radiating from the center of his palm and his fists on his hips. With his legs braced shoulder length apart, he stood in the center of the field and watched Talia from behind his sunglasses.

She had moved away from him, had scanned the area. With more than just her vision. What else had she picked up?

Could she sense the ancient shaman?

He had no illusions about why she was out here.

Power.

The doctor wasn't cooperating with her, but she sensed another less tangible source of power. And if she could screw Gabe over in the meantime, he had no doubts about her willingness to do just that.

He just had to make sure she didn't get the opportunity.

An energy signature, one Gabe didn't recognize, hovered just at the edge of the Davis property. Near the road leading to the farmhouse. Strong, the signature moved in a twisted circle, in and out of his range.

The officer who had tailed Talia out here?

Or someone else?

"I didn't hurt him." Indignation lined Talia's voice.

"Didn't say you had."

"But you wondered." She shrugged one shoulder. "Injuring that policeman would have not gained me anything."

This time. Gabe heard the unspoken words.

She stopped near the large boulder where Jason had laid a young, unconscious Rily the afternoon before. A frown lined Talia's forehead and she held her hand out over the stone.

Gabe waited. For a brief moment he wondered if he let his guard down would he be able to zone in on her purpose. Would their connection flare up, would he be consumed or would he be able to control it and figure out what was going on inside of her? In her head?

He already knew what was in her heart. And that, he reminded himself, was why he sent extra energy into his shields. Not less.

"What happened out here?" Talia turned in a slow circle, scanning the area.

"You don't already know?"

She pulled off her sunglasses, slipped them into the vee at the neck of her black, fitted sweater. She glanced at him through half closed eyes before scanning the area again. Her gaze on the top of the hill, she shook her head. "This must be what Allison was talking about, though."

"What would that be?"

Another half-smile softened the edges of her mouth. "I have the distinct impression you know more about that than I do."

"Why don't you share, anyway?"

"What fun is there in that?" She cast him a sideways look. "Unless you want to go first."

"Hardly."

The heat at the center of Gabe's palm ratcheted a notch. He flexed the fingers and slid his gaze around the perimeter of the field. Again he opened his senses to what was out there while staying shielded against Talia.

Someone else was in the woods. He'd bet that someone was Rily. Another someone was making their way through those same woods towards the officer at the edge of the road. Samuels?

The Calvary had arrived after all. Not that it looked like they were needed. So far, talking was all Talia seemed to want. But then, appearances could be deceiving. Especially with Ben Garrett's daughter.

"Ahh." Talia tilted her head to the side and her lips curved. Deep blue Garrett eyes, awash in dark humor, gazed at him. "Your pretty detective has decided to join us. I was wondering how long she was going to take to get here."

"What are you up to, Talia?" Gabe shoved his hands back into his pockets. "Why do you want Rily here?"

She shrugged and settled onto the stone, pulling her knees up and wrapping her arms around her legs. "So suspicious."

"With reason." He angled his body in order to keep her in his line of vision and to also be able to watch the trajectory of the approaching person.

Rily slipped from between the trees. A frown marred her forehead. Pain or aggravation?

She is mine.

Rily's eyes widened and her gaze flew to Gabe's.

Shit. Two Winds was awake. And he knew Rily was here.

Talia sat on the boulder and seemed oblivious. Thank God for small favors.

Rily followed his glance at Talia and then met his gaze. She stopped a few feet away and with both hands on her hips, glowered at them both.

"What's the matter, Detective?" Talia rubbed her chin on one of her knees. "Upset we didn't invite you to the party?"

"Wondering why there was a party to begin with." Rily tilted her head to one side, spared a glance for Gabe before focusing on the other woman.

Good. Don't underestimate her. God, he wanted to shout that at Rily. Instead he could only hope she got the message anyway.

Between Talia and Two Winds, he wasn't sure of today's outcome. He glanced at the tree line, the image of Rily laying there – not moving, not breathing – with the yellowed grasses surrounding her, superimposed itself in his vision.

Mine.

This was the place. Would Two Winds win? Would he possess Rily's soul? Was Talia here to help the shaman?

Did the bitch even know what that hillside held, locked inside?

Or was it so much simpler than that? Would Talia kill Rily outright?

The heaviness that had steadily been settling in his chest all morning thickened. Time was drawing closer and he didn't have a way to prevent the inevitable.

He pulled his thoughts back, ignored his shifted vision and the sights taunting him. Mocking him with what he couldn't change. He focused on the two women in the field with him.

Both very much alive at the moment, claws out and each figuratively circling the other. If he was lucky, he wouldn't end up with any swipe marks.

Luck hadn't been good to him lately.

"What are you doing out here, Talia?" Rily squared her shoulders.

"I hadn't seen Gabe in such a long time." She swung her gaze between the two of them, a quizzical frown in place. "When he drove past me, I took that as a sign we should talk."

"Really?" Derision coated the word and Rily arched a brow.

"I'll bet not much gets past you." Talia shrugged, the frown gone and a sly smile hovered on her lips. "Gabe and I *really* do have a lot to catch up on, don't we *darling*?"

"No." Gabe shook his head, rotated his shoulders. "Can't say that we do."

With Gabe in her peripheral vision, Rily watched Talia's smile fade into a pout. Games. That's all this was. Manipulations for what purpose?

That was one thing Rily had taken from what Gabe had said about the other woman. Nothing without direct personal motivation.

Personal gain.

Maybe Talia did just want to see Gabe. Talk with him. Feel him out. Rily frowned. Looked between the two of them. As long as there wasn't any actual touching going on.

Geez. She sounded jealous, even to herself.

Mine.

Two Winds voice echoed in her head. As it had from the moment she'd moved out from the line of trees surrounding this field.

At least she hoped that voice was an echo. The hike down from where they'd left Kyle's truck had ratcheted her nerves to the point she thought they might implode. That awareness, the overwhelming sense of being stalked had settled over her shoulders with each step she'd taken, the weight hard to shift around.

Two Winds, or whatever that damnable sense pressing against her was, needed to just back off. Leave her the hell alone.

"What has Gabriel told you about me?" Talia laid her cheek on her knees, her narrowed gaze sharp on Rily.

"Besides the fact you're a bitch with a knife fetish?"

Talia blinked once then her laughter rimmed the field. "Oh, I like that."

Gabe tensed and Rily frowned. How did she know that his muscles had tensed? She wasn't even looking at him from her peripheral vision. And she wasn't going to, not yet. The way Two Winds pushed against her mind was enough of a distraction without adding a hyper-awareness of Gabe into the mix.

Talia's smile once again sly, she pressed her chin into the narrow gap between her knees. "What I really want to know is if Gabriel told you that I'm there, with him, when the two of you have sex. Has he told you about that? About how he feels *me* in his head?"

What the – Rily heard Gabe's words echo through her head, but refused to react to him. She clamped down on her own visible reactions, steeled her body.

The bitch was baiting them. Pure and simple.

Gabe's jaw, tight with a pulse ticking along the edge, locked. Rily *felt* that, too.

"He did mention something about the delusional world you live in."

Talia's smile widened. She glanced at Gabe, then back to Rily. "Oh, that's a plus. That you amuse me. Screwing you while he's thrusting inside you just got that much more pleasurable."

"Talia." Gabe's harsh voice cut across Rily's mind. He pulled his sunglasses off, his dark brown eyes sparked with deep emotion.

Hatred?

With his lip curled, he shoved the ear piece of his glasses into the collar of his sweatshirt.

The other woman lifted her head, arched her neck and caressed her throat with the tips of her fingers. Her low, throaty chuckle prickled along Rily's spine.

"What do you like best?" Her head still back, Talia watched Rily from half closed eyes. "Running your hands over his hard, tense body? His hands on you? Or that moment just before –"

"Too bad you threw all that away, Talia." Rily forced herself to smile, well aware it didn't reach her eyes.

All mine. Two Winds' words reverberated through Rily.

"Mmmm. But I didn't." Talia ran the tip of her tongue over her bottom lip. "I especially like the way he lays between your legs and sucks on your breasts, while you're still wearing your lacy bra."

Rily kept her chin level, her brow arched. She couldn't stop the twitch at the corner of her mouth or the way her stomach recoiled as if she'd been sucker punched.

Gabe had some explaining to do.

"That's enough." His hands fisted, he rolled onto the balls of his feet.

Talia looked over at him. Smiled. "But I love how it feels when you're moving deep inside her. Screwing her. Feeling *me.*"

"Bullshit." Rily lifted her chin, watched Gabe from her side vision. He took several steps forward, his fisted hands raised in front of him.

Laughing, Talia scrambled from the stone, put the boulder between them. Rily surged forward, grabbed his arm at the elbow. She wanted to plow her fist into the bitch's face, but she couldn't let Gabe. He stopped, his chest heaving, his mouth in a snarl and his gaze locked on Talia.

"Oh, Gabriel. You've been so naughty." Talia skipped back a step. "Don't you think she deserves to know what she's getting into with you? With us?"

"There isn't an *us.*"

"Of course there is. Only now there's a three of us. For the time being anyway."

"You really are delusional." And dangerous. Rily let her hand fall away from Gabe's arm.

"And Gabriel really should have let you in on the fact that sex with him will never be *just* with him." Talia ran her gaze down Rily's body. "I'll always be there. *Always.*"

Always mine.

Rily ignored Two Winds and cocked her head to one side. Did the bitch wear lacy bras, too? She was going to burn hers. Tonight. "So you say."

"I *do* say." Talia twirled in a small circle, glancing back over her shoulder at Gabe. "Just as you're always there for me. Tell me, did you enjoy my last lover? He was quite – inventive."

Rily spared a sideways glance at Gabe. Devoid of expression, his gaze shuttered, he stared at Talia.

Acid in Rily's stomach churned in on itself. The things Talia was saying couldn't possibly be true. They couldn't.

Why wasn't Gabe denying what the bitch said?

"Although, unlike the good Detective here, Byron didn't know you existed, Gabe. He never knew you were there. Watching. Feeling every thrust." Talia's head fell back and she sighed. "He could move that body of his, but was a bit lacking in the brains department. Too bad about him."

Too bad, my ass. Rily forced her hands to stay lax, to not curl into fists. Gabe simply stood there, staring at Talia. No expression. Nothing.

They were going to have quite a talk once they got back to her house.

And then he would be gone. Outta there. No more sex. No more working together. He was so gone. Right now she didn't give a damn what the Chief or Ben had to say about it.

Having sex with this bitch, her ass.

"How does it feel, Talia –" Rily studied her nails, pinched a piece of nonexistent cuticle from her thumbnail. Her insides roiled, acid dissolving the bile. But she managed to rub her fingers together, to act like none of this mattered. She aimed her stony gaze at the woman. "To know you'll never have Gabe again? That he will never – *ever* – be inside *you* again?"

"*Bitch.*" Talia spat the word, her face contorted and the blue of her eyes darkened to the point of near blackness against the natural paleness of her face.

"No." Rily drug the word out. "That would be *you.*"

Her gaze locked on Rily's, Talia licked her top lip. Then her bottom one. Rily refused to look away.

Her mouth tight, Talia swallowed once before looking away, upwards. A half smile parted her lips and she blinked a couple of times before glancing back at Rily and then settling her gaze on Gabe.

"It's her, isn't it?" Talia shook her head and the light streaming across the field glistened through her white, spiky hair. "I should have seen it before now. There is no connection to Allison. Not for you."

"What are you babbling about now?" Rily set her fists on her hips.

Ignoring her, Talia paced forward. Keeping the boulder between them, she spread her hands in front of Gabe. "It's her. Your pretty detective. Your other *Tiger.*"

Gabe's jaw jerked, the pulse throbbing in time to the way Rily's own heart pounded. His eyes narrowed and his nostrils flared. The bile in Rily's stomach doubled.

"You're the one." With malice glinting in the depths of her eyes, Talia turned to Rily. "Oh, this is too precious. Too, too precious."

"Talia." The one word, clipped and caustic, echoed between them. "Don't."

"Oh, but I must. I really, really must." Talia clapped her hands together. "Seeing as she won't be here long, I won't hold your feelings against you, darling." She turned back to Rily, delight replacing the malice in her eyes. "Consider that a farewell gift."

"What kind of crap are you trying to feed us now?" Rily widened her stance.

"I will explain later." Gabe jerked his head towards the dirt road. "We should leave."

"Hah." Talia shook her head. "That's Gabe-ese for you don't need to know. He has no intentions of enlightening you. And maybe that's a more gentle, kinder way of letting you muddle through these last remaining days."

"Gabe?" Rily kept her gaze on the nut-job that was Garrett's daughter. "What is she talking about?"

"Oh, let me tell you." Talia glanced up at the sky, then back at Rily. "You really do deserve to know."

What the hell else was this day going to bring?

"That's not your decision, Talia." Gabe wrapped his hand around Rily's arm. His thumb rubbed circles over the material of her jacket, but the heat spiraled through her just the same. "I left your truck at the farmhouse. I'm sure Kyle and your officer are wondering where we are."

Talia's expression suddenly closed and with her mouth tight, she glanced between them before she took a step back from the stone. "So I am right. It is *her*. Not Allison."

"We're leaving." Gabe sent a dark glare at Talia, one Rily could only describe as a warning. An involuntary shiver chased itself over her body.

What else could there be, that Gabe didn't want her hearing? Standing here, with the two of them, the air had continued to take on an oppressive, thick feel. Now it even hurt to breathe at all. Still, she filled her lungs and turned to Gabe.

"No." She touched his hand, turned her gaze to Talia. "What does any of this crap you're spewing have to do with Allison?"

Talia dropped her gaze, scuffed her shoe in the dirt before looking up at Rily. "Do you know Gabe's nickname? What the other agents call him?"

A low growl, from Gabe's chest, punctured the air.

Talia gave her a tight smile, her eyes glinting in the sunshine. "The Harbinger of Death."

The shivers coursing through Rily doubled. What had Ramon told her? Something about Death being Gabe's companion and stalking those close to him. Her shivers tripled.

"That's one of Gabe's gifts, you see."

"No. Actually I don't."

"Yes, well … he actually calls it a curse. He sees Death. In visions. Usually in his sleep. Which is why his sleep is always so disturbed."

"What?" Unbidden, in her mind's eye, she saw the lack of sleep etched on Gabe's handsome face when they'd first met. Remembered the thoughts about time change and travel doing him in. She threw Gabe a swift glance. "He looks rested to me."

"Yes, he does. But then he's here. Where his visions insisted he come. You know he's a psychic?"

"What does that have to do with Allison? Are you saying he saw her death in a vision? That's why he's here?" Rily slid another glance at the man standing next to her. Had that been why Ben had been so insistent about Gabe working with her?

Made as much sense as anything else.

Right. Listen to her. A not-her-lover-any-longer self-proclaimed psychic, a first class crazy bitch and the soul of a trapped shaman trying to get her attention.

Could the day get any weirder?

Talia's mouth compressed into a tight oh before she shook her head and gazed at Gabe from under her lashes. "I had thought, when the two of you walked into the market yesterday, that it was Allison's death you had seen, Gabriel. I couldn't quite figure out the connection you had with her, so I followed you out here."

Gabe closed his eyes, when he opened them he glanced upwards before his gaze fell on Talia. What the hell had just passed between him and the woman?

Rily shoved the zipper tab of her jacket higher. The air had become distinctly colder in the last few minutes.

You're mine. Two Winds' call echoed with the breeze. Was she the only one hearing it?

"It's *you* Gabriel is here for. You he wants to save. Even when he knows he can't." Talia visibly pulled her gaze from Gabe's and focused on Rily. "But what is the connection? How did he –"

Talia's eyes narrowed. She pulled her lips in, making them a thin line as she looked between the two of them.

"Oh my. It's Daddy Dearest, isn't it? He's the link between the two of you. He's why you had the visions of Rily's death. How priceless. I love it." Talia clapped her hands again. "So tell me, Rily. Were you my father's young lover? Did he discard you the way he did my mother? Does he know about Gabriel?"

Rily choked on her response. *Her* death? Never-never land was looking pretty damn decent right now. Where was Peter Pan when she needed him? Or Tinker Bell? Hopefully not locked up with Two Winds.

"How will *Daddy* take the news?" Talia batted her lashes at Gabe, spun in a tight circle.

He smiled, the light in the deep darkness of his eyes treacherous. "Your daddy's going to miss you."

Talia stopped, faced him. "Don't be ridiculous. My father doesn't –" She splayed both hands on her hips. "Good try. But you wouldn't be here to find *my* killer. Except to thank him."

"Really?" Gabe watched her. "My loyalties are to Ben. Not you. Then, of course, there's always the reward."

"What reward?"

Gabe smiled again, took Rily's arm. "I think we're done here. I know it's early, but I'm starving. How about that steak dinner I promised you."

"Beats fast food." Rily, not sure she wasn't shell shocked at this point, slipped her arm through the crook of his. Heat settled in the pit of her belly, warming her from the inside.

She walked away with Gabe, conscious of the woman at their backs.

"Are you sure this is a good idea?" Rily hissed the words at him. "She's not entirely stable."

"That's what she wants you to believe." Gabe's voice, low, held a trace of fatalistic humor.

He thought this was funny? "She did a damn good job of convincing me."

Silent, he nodded.

They hit the dirt road, rounded a curve where neither Talia nor the house or her officers were in sight. She yanked her arm free, spun around to face him.

"What the hell was all that about?"

"Rily –"

"Don't you 'Rily' me."

"This isn't the place. She's not far behind us."

Rily turned to peer up the dirt road. She swung her gaze back to Gabe. "Fine. But this isn't done."

"Didn't think it was." Gabe shoved his sunglasses over his eyes and took her arm. She resisted, but he simply tucked her arm against his side and held on with a vise grip.

Bastard.

She let it stand, nodding at her officers as they rounded the last narrow curve along the dirt road. Kyle, leaning against the other officer's truck, scanned the area behind them.

"Didn't hear any shots, so I figured things hadn't gone to hell yet." Kyle pushed himself away from the vehicle.

"Not yet." Rily jerked her chin towards the small, blue rental car sitting a few yards from the truck. "I assume that's hers."

The other officer nodded. Rily arched a brow and Kyle shook his head0.

"Nothing."

Not surprised Kyle hadn't found anything worth finding in Talia's vehicle, Rily shrugged. "Worth a shot."

Gabe rolled his shoulders, his grip on her arm still tight, and smiled. "Something else for us to talk about later."

"Fat chance."

Both officers straightened, their gazes locked on something behind Rily and Gabe. Or someone.

"Are you ready to go?" Talia, her sunglasses firmly in place, tossed the words at the other officer as she waltzed past them.

The officer, flustered, sent Kyle a desperate look. Rily shook her head once and Kyle did the same to the other man.

"Suit yourself." Talia pulled the key from her jeans and headed for her car.

"Don't leave the area." Rily kept her voice level. Pleasant even.

"Whatever." Talia climbed in her vehicle, inserted the key and threw Kyle a dark look. Once started, she swung out around the two trucks and hit the gas, leaving them choking on her dust.

"Juvenile." Rily pulled away from Gabe, with success this time, and wiped at her face.

"Temper. You got to her. Not many do."

"Points for me." She held out her hand. "My keys."

The corner of Gabe's mouth lifted. "Of course, Detective."

"If you don't mind, Rily, I'll hitch a ride back to my truck with dufus here." Kyle pointed his thumb at the other officer. "Did you want someone else to pick up her tail once she gets back to town?"

"I don't think that's going to be necessary. We'll just keep loose tabs on her."

Kyle nodded and Rily climbed into her truck.

"Where are we headed?" Gabe settled into the passenger side.

"Home. To burn a certain bra."

Chapter Twenty

WHAT HAD BEEN a light breeze out in the field near the old Davis farm was now a cold, buffeting wind along the river's shoreline. Gabe hunched his shoulders forward and stood his ground on the decrepit pier.

The wind matched the chill radiating from Rily.

How the hell had he gotten into this predicament? Why did she mean so much? Why her?

She hadn't said one word after they left the Davis place. She also hadn't gone to her house and she hadn't burned that bra. Not yet. That still might be coming.

Even though none of what Talia had baited her with was true. Not the sex part, anyway. He had no idea how to make Rily believe him.

Now, her pacing done for the moment, she stood at the edge of the pier. The burned out hulk of a warehouse behind them left Gabe worried the entire pier was going to fall apart. With them on top. As it was, near the edge where Rily stood, several bare pylons jutted up from the river bed, rotting in the water that beat against them.

He scrubbed one hand over his face before shoving both hands back in his pockets. Now what? He wanted to respect her privacy, her time alone with her thoughts. But this was killing him.

She hated him right now, and he didn't blame her at all.

He hated himself just as much.

"Rily."

Her shoulders tensed and her head came up, but she continued to face the river. Continued to ignore him.

He kicked a lone rock into the water, the splash swallowed by the wind driven waves pounding against the wood. Shit. He lifted his face to the wind, let it push at his hair, sting his cheeks.

At least out here Two Winds couldn't taunt them. A good thing considering he was beating himself up enough without that bastard shaman spouting off.

"How much of it is true?" Rily's voice, barely audible under the onslaught of the wind, touched his nerve endings. Sang along his spine.

He lowered his head. Rily stood facing him, her back to the river, still at the edge of the pier. She caught and held his gaze with her own.

"Which part?"

"Any of it. All of it."

With a deep swallow, he moved a few steps closer to her. She tensed again but held her ground. He didn't want her falling into the river, but suspected she came out here a lot. His worry was probably misplaced. He didn't care, he still worried.

If she drowned, then the vision won't happen. Gabe's lip twitched. She'd be just as dead. The vise in his chest twisted another notch, tightening and constricting his breathing.

"The bra thing –" He leaned his head back for a moment and then met her gaze again.

"Yeah. Top of my list in the questions department."

"That one's not true. Talia can't *feel* us. She can't see us. Has no bearing on us."

Her eyes narrow and her mouth compressed, Rily studied him. "She sounded awfully convincing."

"Yes, she did."

"But she's lying?"

"Yes."

"And I should believe you?" Rily held up her hand, palm facing forward. "Why?"

"Rily –"

"No. If she wasn't there, with us in your head, then how did she know any of the details?"

"She guessed. Took a lucky shot. She's *good* at that. I told you, she's a receptor. Picks things up out of the ether."

Rily scrubbed her palm across her hip and shook her head. "She was too specific. Unless all your women wear lacy bras. Unless that's a requirement for you to have sex with them."

"God, Rily." He pulled his hands from his pockets, fisted them in front of him. "This is exactly what she is trying to do. Drive a wedge between us, just like this."

"There is no us."

Gabe wet his bottom lip, stared at her. "So, she wins."

Rily's chin came up, fire sparked gold in the green depths of her eyes. "That's low."

"It's the truth."

She dropped her gaze, turned her head to stare out at the water. Her bottom lip between her teeth, she blinked several times.

Was that more than mere moisture, were those real tears? In his strong Rily's eyes?

He swallowed around the sudden lump in his throat, shoved both hands through his hair. How the hell did he make this right?

"What about the rest of it?" She kept her gaze fixed on some distant point, didn't look at him. "If that part was a lie, what about the rest of what she said?"

Crux of the whole thing. What did he say now?

Damn Talia and her black heart.

But that didn't help, didn't solve the issue of what to say to Rily. Here. Now.

"This is where Craig was ambushed." Rily turned her head, her luminous green eyes stabbed at his heart.

"Your oldest brother?" No wonder he had the impression she came out here often.

"Yes."

Gabe waited.

"Ramon was in the hospital and Craig set up the guys that put him there. It went bad. They burned the place down, but that's not what killed him. He bled out from a gunshot wound. Jake, my other brother, tried …." Those tears welled in her eyes, slipped over her lashes. With the edge of her hand she swiped one cheek and then the other. "And then Hannah died. Or we thought she did."

Gabe took a step forward. With short, little shakes, Rily shook her head. He stopped.

God. He wanted to pull her to him, wrap his arms around her. He wouldn't even mind the tears. She could ball all over his sweatshirt, soak him to the skin. If she'd only let him hold her.

"I don't want to die, Gabe."

In two strides he was there, wrapping her in his arms, pulling her away from the edge of the damn pier. Her fingers clutched his sweatshirt and sobs racked her body.

With his chin resting on her head, he rocked her back and forth.

WITH THE SHARP EDGE of her knife, Rily sliced off a piece of steak. She sat there, in the town's finest restaurant, with the knife in one hand, fork in the other, and stared at the meat on her plate.

I'm going to be sick.

Good and sick.

Clutching the toilet all night sick.

This had to all be a bad dream. Some kind of flu induced nightmare. Allison was still alive in Portland. She, herself, was snuggled under the covers in her warm bed. Waiting out the flu bug that had to be ravaging her system. The fever giving her nightmares.

And she'd never met Gabriel Nicholetti.

She set her utensils down on the plate and looked at Gabe from under her lashes. He sat across from her, no more of his steak eaten than hers. His wine glass in his hand, he twirled the deep red liquid and watched her across the rim.

The sigh burgeoning in her throat threatened to choke her. There was no waking up from this. Just as there hadn't been after Craig had died.

So she might as well quit moping. Moping hadn't changed anything with her brother. She didn't see how it would change things now.

Besides, why should she go down without a fight?

Where was the honor in that?

With one fingertip, she traced the stem of her wine glass. "Two Winds is active again."

Gabe closed his eyes for a moment. When he opened them a cautionary light glinted in their dark depths. He nodded.

"Tell me about the field. About what you sensed out there before I came on the scene."

"Nothing."

Rily tilted her head.

"There was nothing there. No power source, no weird energy vibrations. Just a normal, empty field on a cold, December afternoon."

"Was that what you expected?"

"Pretty much."

"And after Talia arrived?"

He raised an eyebrow.

She allowed herself a small smile. "You said she was an amplifier. Did she amplify anything?"

"Not while we were alone." Gabe sat his wine glass down and braced his elbows on the table. "Although she did look rather funny when she held her hand over that boulder."

"The same one she was perched on when I got there?"

"The same. She asked what had happened there, but then got off subject with your arrival."

"And once I was there? What did you feel?"

"I could hear Two Winds. Muttering, trying to get our attention. Your attention."

"Yeah." Wasn't that the shits? "When I left the station that started."

"Him talking to you?"

"More of a pressure. We took Kyle's truck over Two Winds' hill and it intensified. Then, once I was on foot heading towards you, even worse."

"Just pressure?"

"A heavy sense of being watched."

"Once out at the field?"

"That's when the muttering started. When I heard actual words." She took a sip of her wine. "With Talia being what you called an amplifier, is that why we could hear his words?"

"Maybe. Could very well be why." He sat back. "But Talia didn't hear anything. Not once."

"Is she usually aware of what she's amplifying?"

"In the past, yes."

"So what's different now?"

Gabe stared at her, unblinking, for several moments. "Me."

"You?" Understanding she focused on this to keep from dwelling on the things Talia had said, Rily picked up her wine glass and settled back in her seat. "How so?"

"At one time, I was quite tuned into Talia."

"Now you're not?" Rily leaned her head back, ran her tongue over her teeth. "Excuse me, but doesn't that scar on the back of your neck negate that?"

The smile he gave her a little sad, he shook his head. "No. Before the knife attack, I was a willing participant. Afterwards, I've done everything I can to minimize the two way street."

Rily lowered her head, looked at him again from under her lashes. She wanted to believe him. But didn't.

The things the other woman had said had been too … personal. Too on target. And if the bra thing was from personal experience on the bitch's part – as in things they'd done to each other in real time – she didn't want to know that. Either way she was done with Mr. Nicholetti.

But life is so short, especially for you. She shoved aside the thought. That was nothing but lies, too.

He didn't deny that one, though. She hadn't given him the chance. Ugh. She needed to stop torturing herself.

Their waiter approached, worry lining his aged face. "The steaks are not to your liking, Detective? Sir?"

Rily gave him a gentle smile. "Not feeling well. We'll take them to go, though."

He nodded and took their plates with a soft muttering about boxing them up special. Rily's gaze followed him. When she turned her head her glance collided with Gabe's.

"Rily. She lied."

"Okay."

"Just okay?"

She shrugged. "What do you want me to say? It's not my head she's in."

"She's not in my head. She *can't* see or feel what I see and feel." Gabe set his wine glass down again. He leaned forward, crossing his arms on the table. A frown drew his brows down and anger sparked in the dark depths of his eyes.

Her own wine glass cradled in her hands, Rily leaned forward herself. "You told me about the connection between the two of you."

"Yes I did, dammit. It's an awareness, Rily. Like Two Winds, only amped up."

"Like Two Winds?" She leaned back again, chewed on the inside corner of her mouth.

"Yes."

"What about the lace bra? And all that goes with that?"

Gabe rubbed a hand over his face. "You're a beautiful woman, Rily. She took a shot you would wear lace."

His gaze shifted down to her chest, just for a quick moment. But her nipples tightened and wet heat pooled between her legs.

Damn him.

She wasn't doing this. *They* weren't doing this. "Okay."

"Is it really okay this time?"

She nodded. "But you're sleeping in your hotel room. Alone."

IN RILY'S LIVING ROOM, Gabe paced back and forth. From the hallway Bogie's nails heralded the dog and Rily's arrival from the back of the house. Gabe turned and faced her.

"This is stupid, Rily."

"Really?" She gave him a false smile and set a pillow on the arm of her couch. "You could always go back to your hotel."

"We've been over that."

"True." She unfolded a blanket then spread it over the cushions of the couch. "And I even agreed with you."

"You said you were okay about the bra thing." And it hadn't hit the fireplace yet. Would be a total shame if she did that.

"I am."

"Then what is wrong?" He touched her arm and she spun away from him.

"Do you always have sex with the women you see dead? In your visions?"

Gabe sucked in a deep breath. He should have expected this. Should have seen it. But he hadn't.

"And I thought I was the one who didn't do relationships. Talk about a way to avoid commitment." She pressed a hand to her head, pushed her hair back from her face. "I sound like a damn shrew. Go to sleep."

Gabe watched her weary steps across the living room, Bogie at her side. She didn't turn back, didn't even pause as she headed down the hallway. The soft click of her bedroom door galvanized Gabe.

He took the pillow and slammed it on the couch.

Damn it all to hell.

Several hours later Gabe lay on the couch, his hands behind his head, staring at the ceiling. This was total bullshit.

The blanket was snug, the room toasty enough. But Rily slept down the hall away from him and he couldn't sleep. At all.

The idea of slinging her over his shoulder and heading to the nearest airport still held great appeal. No Two Winds. No Talia. Just Rily, her dog and him.

Sounded like paradise.

Too bad that didn't really exist.

PRESSURE BUILT ON Rily's chest. She tried to suck in a deeper breath, but her lungs wouldn't expand any more. Shallow puffs of breath left her gasping for more air.

Laughter rang through the room. Eerie, evil laughter right there, beside her bed. Inside her head.

Mine. Always mine.

She twisted to the side, but the laughing continued. Louder.

"No." The moan tore through her body.

She pushed at the pressure, pushed at the sheet and blanket tangled around her legs. Her bare feet touched the wood floor. The December night chilled her entire body.

She tried to move but unseen arms wrapped around her, held her still. Spread warmth through her trembling limbs.

"Hush." A big hand brushed back her hair, slid down her back. Cradled her closer. "It's only a dream."

Mine. The ugliness faded to a grim whisper.

She burrowed into the warmth, pressed one ear against a solid chest and covered her other with her hand. The sounds vanished. The pressure disappeared.

Her shaking subsided. Cautious, she pressed both palms against the hard chest and looked up. Gabe stared down at her.

"Are you all right?"

Her throat dry, she swallowed once and nodded.

Gabe brushed a strand of hair away from her face. His dark eyes held her captive. Time stopped. He blinked and the corner of his mouth lifted before he kissed her forehead. He wrapped his arms tighter around her and she closed her eyes.

She wanted to stay right here. Nowhere else. Here where the voice couldn't touch her. Here where warmth and security surrounded her.

Even if Gabe wasn't supposed to be in her bed. Wasn't supposed to be holding her.

If that made her a wuss, right now she didn't care.

"Just a bad dream." His breath, soft and warm, traced over her temple.

"I think so." Even to her ears, her voice sounded hoarse. Raspy. As if she'd stood screaming at the top of her lungs. "I hope it was only a dream."

She eased a little away from him. His arms tensed, but then he relaxed and loosened his hold. The luminous glow of her alarm clock mixed with the nightlight making the soft light in the room almost eerie.

She hadn't noticed that before.

Her sheet and blanket lay in a tangled pile in the center of her bed. Bogie pressed against her and his wet tongue swept across her bare foot.

"Oh geez." She twisted and Gabe held her firm, stopping her from falling. "I hate when he does that."

Gabe held her tight again, for a long moment, kissed the top of her head and eased away. "Come on. Let me fix you some hot chocolate and you can tell me about your dream."

Hot chocolate. That sounded … wonderful.

And so normal.

"I THINK IT was just a dream, Rily." Gabe set the wooden spoon on the small plate she had set out as spoon rest. Chocolate scented the kitchen, making it seem homey. Quaint even.

Rily nodded. She sat at her table, slippers on her feet and the heavy green robe wrapped tight around her. Pity, that. He rather liked the thin pajamas she wore. Long sleeved and long pants, but they hugged her in all the right places.

Bogie was outside doing his business and investigating the three in the morning yard. A dog's life.

Gabe turned the stove off, poured the hot chocolate into the mugs he had set out. Rolling his shoulders, he set a mug in front of Rily. He turned his chair at an angle and settled across from her with his legs stretched out. He set his mug on the table.

"You didn't hear him, then?" Rily leaned forward, both hands wrapped loose around her cup. Steam wafted up from the hot chocolate, the wispy tendrils caressing her face.

"Two Winds?"

She nodded.

"No. I didn't hear anyone." He ran his thumb along the rim of his mug. "And Bogie didn't react until you cried out."

"That's what brought you in there?"

He nodded. The fact his heart had stopped with her scream, and then went into overdrive … he was going to keep that to himself. He'd also have to fix her bedroom door lock. Maybe. And maybe he'd leave it broke. "You stood in the middle of the floor, your eyes wide. Unfocused. Bogie yapping."

"I never heard him."

"I could tell." He took a tentative sip of the hot liquid. "Tell me about the dream."

She pulled in a deep breath. Swallowed once. "I don't remember that much. It was more like impressions than anything else."

"Give me your impressions."

She inhaled the steam from her mug, nodded. "Pressure all around me. That awful voice whispering *mine. Always mine.* I fought to get away and then you were there, holding me."

"A dream, Rily. Nothing more." That's what it had to be. "The last few days have been stressful. Especially today."

She nodded again.

"It's no wonder you had a nightmare."

"I don't want to die, Gabe."

"Rily —"

"You didn't deny that part of what Talia said."

"No, I didn't."

"What you saw in your vision, that's why you asked me to run away with you. To your islands. Your boat."

Gabe rotated his neck, worked the muscles. Then nodded.

He could damn Talia all he wanted, but he still had to deal with this. With Rily.

"Has it ever worked before?"

"Has what worked?"

"Running away like that. To your islands."

"You're the only one I've ever asked."

"Oh." She lowered her head, took another small sip of her hot chocolate. Looked up at him through her lashes. "Have you ever saved anyone before? Anyone that you saw die?"

"I don't see their actual death." That would be too simple, would give him a starting point to work with. To maybe actually saving some of them. "I only see them … dead."

"Oh." She set her mug back on the table. "Where do you see me … dead?"

He closed his eyes. "Rily —"

"You never said if you've managed to save anyone yet."

He wet his lips. Opened his eyes to stare at the ceiling.

"I'll take that as a no."

He tilted his head to look at her. "There's always a first time."

"But you don't really believe that."

"I want to believe it." He worked his tight jaw, ran his tongue along his teeth. "I have to believe it."

"How long?"

He glanced away and then back at her.

She sat there, so damn serene, asking him questions about her own death. He pushed his cup away, stood and ran his fingers through his mussed hair.

"Rily –"

"How long?"

"I have no idea." He paced to the stove, turned and leaned against the counter.

"Will it be Talia?"

He shrugged one shoulder. "Possibly. Maybe Two Winds."

Maybe both working together.

She pushed her own mug away, looked at him. Her eyes, so big and so green, shimmered in the harsh light of the kitchen. "I don't want to die."

Gabe sucked in a sharp, raspy breath. "I'm going to do everything I can to prevent that from happening."

"But your vision –"

"Screw that." He shoved away from the counter, took the strides to her side and pulled her from her chair. With his arms wrapped around her he pressed his forehead to hers. "You can't give up. We have to try. Maybe together –"

"We'll kick both their asses." Rily leaned back, her eyes glistening with unshed tears. "Then you can show me that boat I keep hearing about."

Chapter Twenty-One

TWO MUGS, a small pot and a single wooden spoon took no time to clean. Still, Rily stood with her hands covered in sudsy dishwater and let the heat seep into her skin.

Dawn wasn't even a glimmer on the horizon, but sleep held no appeal. None. From the way Gabe leaned with his back against the counter, his ankles crossed, he was content where he stood.

Patient.

Silence stretched between them, marked only by the swish of the second hand on the wall clock.

She'd meant what she'd said, she didn't want to die. Not today. Not tomorrow.

She wanted to see Gabe's islands. Make love to him with the lapping of the ocean against the hull of his boat.

The sudden peal of the front door chime startled them both. Their gazes met. She grabbed a dish towel at the same moment he pushed away from the counter. On tip toe, she retrieved the loaded gun she had stashed at the top of the cabinet next to the back door.

He raised one eyebrow, jerked his chin towards the other room. She nodded, led the way.

The doorbell pealed again.

In the living room, Gabe snatched up his own weapon and moved to stand on the right side of the door. She spared a quick glance through the peep-hole.

Ramon Ortega. His dark hair mussed in the night time wind and his dark eyes unreadable, he stood with his hand poised over the doorbell and stared hard at the door.

Her shoulders slumped. Gratitude welled with the swell of moisture blurring her vision. She pursed her lips to keep them from trembling.

Gabe's eyes narrowed. He didn't lower his weapon.

She opened the door and Ramon moved across the threshold. He wrapped her in a full body hug, his arms pressed tight against the thick robe enveloping her. He leaned his forehead on hers.

"*Mi Corazon.* You are all right."

She kissed his cheek, stepped back but not out of his embrace. "I told you I was."

"For the moment. I heard the unspoken words."

"I didn't mean to worry you. Or have you drive all the way out here."

"What are you doing here?" Gabe stood, legs braced apart and arms crossed, his gun still in his hand.

Ramon looked at him, an eyebrow raised and disdain marking his face. Testosterone. Too freaking early in the morning for this. Rily straightened the thick collar of her robe.

"I called him." She hugged Ramon then stepped back to meet Gabe's gaze. "I couldn't reach Jake, or he'd probably be on his way here, too."

"Rally the troops?" Gabe raised his own eyebrow before he tucked his gun in the waistband at his back.

"Circle the wagons." She lifted her chin. Let him make what he wanted of her.

The side of Gabe's mouth lifted. "Then you won't get upset when I tell you Ben should be here in a few hours."

More pleased than she should be, she blinked back sudden, stupid tears.

The noise from Ramon's throat might have been a snarl.

Happy for the distraction, she turned to Ramon. "What do you have against Ben?"

"He is like a *dog*, sniffing around *Mi Abulita.*"

Gabe smiled, the look still not friendly. "The big mean kitty doesn't like his grandmother playing with alpha wolves?"

"Alpha my ass." Ramon, his dark eyes almost black, cocked his head to the side. "Your wolf needs to go play with his own kind."

"How do you know your grandmother isn't his kind?"

Ramon's top lip curled.

Rily slipped her arm through Ramon's, patted Gabe's shoulder. "Leave the big, mean kitty alone. Let's scramble some eggs and heat up those steaks we didn't eat."

"MI CORAZON." Ortega pushed his empty plate forward, leaned back in his chair.

Gabe resisted the urge to slam his own seat back, to smash his fist in the guy's face. From the slight deepening of the lines bracketing his mouth, Ortega knew he pushed buttons. All the more reason to resist.

"Tell me now, what this is about." Ortega touched the back of Rily's hand.

"Maybe we should wait for Ben." Rily spared a glance for Gabe.

He shrugged. Rily was stalling.

Ortega met his gaze. "Or maybe Nicholetti can simply catch *el lobo* up on the ground we've covered once he arrives."

Why not, seeing as Ben already knew most of what they knew? Gabe inclined his head. Ortega had many undercurrents, more talent than the man himself realized. Or utilized. Push to shove, he'd rather have Ortega as an ally than an enemy.

He'd also rather him miles away from Rily.

Not that he was jealous.

Much.

Since Ortega away from her wasn't looking feasible – not at this moment – he'd sit back, see how the man reacted to what Rily had to tell him.

Should be interesting.

Rily speared Gabe with an unreadable look. He answered with a genial smile and his hands spread. *Go for it, Sweetheart – you called him, I didn't.*

Her eyes narrowed to thin slits, her Tiger peered at him through the green. They weren't telepathic, but damned if he didn't get exactly what she was telling him.

His smile widened to an actual grin.

With one last swish of a tail only he could see, she focused on the other man. "What do you know of the local Indian legends?"

Ortega looked between the two of them, frowned. The lines at the side of his mouth deepened. "Not much more than the stories Craig used to tell. Late nights on stakeout."

Rily told him the tale of Two Winds.

Ortega listened, pressed the tips of his fingers together over his mouth. "Allison Davis had several Indian illustrations on her computer? Ones that she did?"

"Yes."

"She was killed over an old Indian story?" Ortega frowned. "A myth?"

"We don't know for sure."

"And what does this have to do with the threat against you?"

Gabe lifted his coffee cup to his lips. Rily sent him a dark look. She wasn't comfortable, admitting she was buying into any of this, but she'd called Ortega. As far as Gabe was concerned, this was her show.

"Two Winds is still stuck in that damn hillside. He wants out, thinks I'm his ticket."

Blunt. To the point. Impressive.

Silence reigned until Gabe sat his cup on the table. He watched Ortega stare at Rily.

After another drawn out moment the man picked up his own coffee cup. "So how do we stop him?"

Rily closed her eyes, let out an audible breath. "Thank you."

"Don't thank me yet." Ortega lowered his chin to his chest, glanced between the two of them. "I've never fought a mythical shaman trapped in a hill before."

"I was afraid you would tell us we were nuts."

"I still might." He shrugged one shoulder. "You forget who raised me. *Mi Abulita* is a self-proclaimed *bruja*. A witch."

"Craig said you pretty much shook your head over that."

"Let's just say I'm a bit more open minded than before I spent so much time in the hospital."

Gabe cocked his head to the side. He hadn't met the grandmother, the High Priestess in Allison Davis' deck, but Ortega himself had several layers of untapped abilities. What happened in the hospital – or before – that changed the man's outlook?

The closed expression on Ortega's face stopped him, for the moment, from asking.

"Also, I was there when you found the paintings and tarot cards." Ortega grimaced. "Since my face showed up more than once on those cards, I would say I have an interest in figuring out what is going on here."

Rily pushed away from the table, paced to the archway leading to the other room. She turned to face the table. "I wish I could get any kind of grasp on any of this. None of it makes sense. Not this bullshit, not Allison's death. Not Talia."

"Back up." The frown back, Ortega glanced at Gabe then back to Rily. "Who is Talia?"

"His ex-girlfriend." She waved a hand at Gabe. "Ben's daughter."

Ortega's eyebrows shot up a fraction, the side of his mouth twitched. "Interesting."

"Okay. Let me think." Rily shoved her hands through her hair, scrunched it between her fingers on top of her head. "I'm too scattered, jumping from point to point. Not making any kind of sense."

She lifted her chin, stared at the ceiling. Gabe stared at the elegant line of her exposed neck. The pulse throbbing there at the base. He couldn't ease the agitation, hell he was at least half the reason for it.

She snatched a yellow legal pad of paper and a pen from one of the drawers near the sink. With a huff of breath, she settled back in her seat. Gabe exchanged a look with Ortega.

"Allison's death." Rily started to write.

Gabe touched her arm. "Justin's death."

She paused, tapped the pen on the page.

"At the beginning."

"Wouldn't that be with your mythical shaman?"

Gabe and Rily looked at each other.

She wet her bottom lip with the tip of her tongue.

"Yeah." His stomach muscles tightened. He had to stop fixating on her mouth. "That's one place we could start."

With effort, Rily pulled her gaze away from Gabe. She swore she could *feel* what he was thinking. All that hot, sexual content. Nice distraction from what she *didn't* want to feel. Didn't want to think about.

Maybe later she would take him up on that heat. Maybe. Once she laid the rawness over Talia to rest. She wasn't quite *there* yet.

Thank God Ramon had shown up.

His presence should keep her from throwing herself at Gabe. She hoped.

Distraction or not, she had to deal with all this crap.

How the hell did they figure out what was real? If she couldn't touch it, feel it, how was she supposed to know?

Even with her brother, Jake, Rily had to *see* Hannah's apparition standing over her own body before Rily truly believed him. She was hoping like hell she wasn't going to actually *see* Two Winds, in the flesh.

She had to get a handle on this now, before that became a possibility.

Then there was Justin. What really happened with him?

"Rily?" Gabe touched the back of her hand. Sparks of pure warmth spread across her skin.

She wanted to turn her hand over, lace her fingers with his. Instead, she shook herself, wiped her hand down her leg and got up again, went to the other room and came back with the pages they'd printed from Allison's computer. She handed them to Ortega to read. Once she settled back at the table, she wrote Two Winds at the top of her paper.

Then she wrote Justin's name underneath.

She bit her lip and met Gabe's frank gaze. His directness steadied her. She could do this.

"Tell me about this person." Ramon tapped her pad of paper, looked between them before he laid the printed pages on the table. "How did Justin die?"

Rily swallowed. Gabe reached over to squeeze her hand and the lump in her throat loosened. He let go, sat back in his chair. With a breath, she sighed and told Ramon about Justin, Allison and the Talking Board incident.

He listened without interrupting. She laid out the facts as she knew them. Nothing extra, nothing expanded. She gripped her fingers in her lap, as much for comfort as to keep them from trembling.

"So somehow, back when you were teenagers, the three of you awoke this shaman?"

"It seems as if that may be the case." With two fingers, she rubbed the spot between her eyebrows. Talking this out, putting it on paper – she'd hoped those activities would ground her, make it all more real. More solid. Make it something she could fight against.

She pressed her fingers to her lips. So far that wasn't working too well.

"And you haven't felt anything from this shaman in all these years?" Ramon glanced at Gabe then swung his gaze back to Rily. "Until Allison came back?"

"Nothing. I shoved that whole incident to the back of my mind –"

"Suppressed it." The muscle at Gabe's jaw twitched.

Rily pulled her gaze away from the thin line of his mouth. Her chest tight, she took a couple shallow breaths to even out her breathing. They didn't help. "The authorities at the time, my dad and the coroner, believed Justin had a seizure. That he attacked us and –"

Gabe and Ramon both sat, quiet, in their seats. With both her hands flat on her kitchen table, she closed her eyes, pressed her lips together.

Okay, she could do this. She took three deeper breaths through her nose. All she had to do was concentrate.

But the panic lay just below the surface.

Dammit. She'd relived it, accessed those memories – hadn't she? Why were they still so hard to talk about?

Focus. All she had to do was focus.

Again a hand covered hers, warm fingers wrapped around her own.

Gabe.

She squeezed his fingers, opened her eyes. With his dark, concerned gaze locked on hers, she nodded. He lifted her hand, brushed his lips over her knuckles, and settled her hand under his on the table. Then he turned his gaze to Ramon.

She did the same, gave her friend a smile that only trembled a little. Ramon, his near black eyes full of concern, inclined his head.

She swallowed once. "I had suppressed those memories. Selective amnesia, the doctor called it."

Gabe rubbed his thumb over the back of her hand.

"Yesterday –" God, it seemed like years ago. "Was the first time I'd actually been out there."

"In all this time?"

"I was good at the suppression thing." She gave him a half smile, made a face.

"And you remembered?"

"Gabe isn't sure what I saw out there yesterday was real."

"Saw?"

"In full color. I had my eyes closed, but watched the whole scene unfold. Justin attacked me. Allison and I fought him. I kicked him in the chest. Allison hit him over the head with the board. He had a seizure."

"And?"

"I heard Two Winds in my head." She closed her eyes for a moment. "If what I saw wasn't real and if I don't ever remember, we won't know what happened to Justin."

The two men were quiet.

"For whatever reason, Allison's death has reawakened all of this." She held up a hand. "Not just the Two Winds crap. Justin's death. The question of why he died."

"Have you figured out what Nicholetti here has to do with any of this?" Ramon glanced between them. "Because there's a reason he's here. Now. Isn't there?"

One side of Gabe's mouth lifted in what wasn't quite a smile, an eyebrow lifted then he lowered his chin.

"There is a reason. I think. Maybe." Rily shrugged. "That's part of why I called you. Something you'd said the other day."

Now it seemed so ... girlish and silly. Over reactive. But she couldn't bring herself to be sorry she'd called.

Ramon sat straight in his chair, his brows drawn down in a frown. "Who else is going to die, Rily?"

"Me."

GABE PACED THE length of Rily's fenced back yard. The sun had risen, the early morning cool through his sweatshirt.

How the hell had he gotten used to the chill?

He *hated* the cold.

Ben would be here in within the hour. Ortega was snoozing on the couch. Rily was in the shower. And he was out here with Bogie wondering why her seeming acceptance of her own death was pissing him off.

He stopped at the back edge of the fence, wrapped his hands over the metal railing, let the freezing cold bite into his bare skin. Puddles of water sat in the ruts of the dirt back alley separating her and her neighbors from the back of the houses on the next street.

She needed a wooden fence, not this chain link crap. A tall one that matched her home, gave her a semblance of privacy.

He did a mental calculation of the cost and time.

Shit, what the hell was he doing?

Building a picket fence in his head? For Rily.

His fingers tightened on the metal.

God. She mattered so damn much.

He turned, braced his back against the back gate. Bogie came running, scudded to a stop next to him and sniffed at his feet before tearing off across the yard.

Love.

Wasn't that a bitch?

RILY PACED THE length of her living room, stopped to scowl at the three men. What right did they have to order her around?

And using the safety card.

What a crock. Did it really matter if they were right? She was going to protest, no matter what. She knew it, they knew it.

Man, she hated this.

All of it.

"Rily —" Gabe stood behind the couch with both hands shoved into his pockets.

"What?" She rounded on him, past caring how unreasonable her behavior looked.

Ramon's lips curved in what could only be a smirk. She swung her narrowed gaze to him. He leaned back on the couch and covered his mouth with the tips of his fingers, but the light sparkling in his nearly black eyes gave him away. Her own lips tightened.

They could all go to hell.

That blasted shaman could meet these three there.

Ben Garrett shrugged on his jacket, met Gabe's gaze and nodded. In the center of the room, she planted both feet with her fists on her hips.

"So now I can't even be alone? By myself?" Her chin jutted upward, she met Gabe's impassive look. Her insides roiled, vibrated. God, she wanted to stomp her foot. Hard. "Now I need a freaking babysitter?"

"Yes." Gabe's lips lifted in a small smile. A mean smile.

Damn him all over again.

"I will guard your body with my very own." Ramon laid a hand over the center of his chest. Grinned.

"Just make sure you don't *touch* her body with yours while you're guarding it." Gabe's brows drawn down in a deep frown and his jaw tight, the words seemed to ground out of his mouth.

One of Ramon's eyebrows lifted. Ben coughed into his fist, but his blue eyes glistened with laughter.

Shit. Gabe actually sounded jealous. Yesterday that might have thrilled her. Today it pissed her off.

She combed both hands through her hair, gripped it in her fists at the back of her neck. "I have work to do. A murder to solve. I can't sit here on my ass all day while you two run around trying to commune with an ancient shaman."

"Testy today." Ben opened the front door.

Gabe, still standing next to the door, turned and speared her with his shuttered, dark gaze. "So, go investigate. Stay away from Two Winds. And Talia."

Ben flinched. The movement quick and barely discernable.

Rily pressed her lips together, bit back the smart remark on her tongue. For a short moment there, she'd forgotten Talia was his daughter.

That he was here, because Gabe called him, said a lot. She just wasn't sure what that lot meant. In the long run.

"Then we'll be at the station." She lifted her chin, challenging him to try and tell her what she couldn't do.

Gabe's eyes narrowed. "Inside."

She held his gaze but then shrugged. Stubborn might be a huge part of her reputation, but right now she didn't want *stupid* added to it.

"When the two of you return, Garrett can give me the Two Winds Tour." Ramon leaned forward. Something dark and not altogether pleasant passed between him and Ben.

Rily frowned.

Ben nodded once before Ramon inclined his head.

Great.

A male understanding. Bonding.

Screw them all.

The shaman included.

Chapter Twenty-Two

A T THE FIELD, a few feet behind the big boulder, Gabe stood with both hands fisted at his waist. Frozen drops of rain, left from an early morning thunderstorm, sparkled across the field like cold diamonds scattered throughout the flattened and yellowed grass.

Bright sunlight, sharp in its mid-morning intensity, cut at his eyes, almost blinding him. He slipped on his sunglasses.

Garrett stood next to him with narrowed eyes. The man waited a few heartbeats before he wiped a hand over his face and then shoved his own sunglasses over his eyes.

This was hard on Ben. Gabe got that. He just wasn't sure he gave a damn. Not right now. Not here.

Not with Rily's life at stake.

How the hell were they going to protect her? How did you save someone when you didn't believe you could?

"This is where it all happened?" Ben turned his head, appeared to be taking in the entire field. In more than a visual way. "Where Justin Doherty died?"

Gabe's jaw tightened, but he nodded.

"This is where Rily is slated to die?"

No. Gabe's nostrils flared, but again he nodded.

"Any ideas how to stop that from happening?"

A single bark of bitter laughter, welling from deep inside his own chest, caught Gabe off guard. He wiped a hand over his mouth. "I was hoping you'd come up with something on your flight over here."

One corner of Ben's mouth lifted. He leaned his head back, took a deep breath of air. "My daughter was out here. Yesterday, you said?"

"Yes." Gabe shoved his hands in his pockets, rocked back on his heels.

"How did she seem?"

"Pleased with herself. At first anyway."

His shoulders tense, Ben nodded. "She would be."

Gabe waited.

Ben wet his lips, shook his head. "Recriminations aren't going to help Rily."

"No, they're not." And he didn't have the time or energy. Not today.

"Beyond what you told me happened out here, what does your gut say?" Ben angled his head towards Gabe. "What does my daughter want? This time?"

"That's a damn good question."

Behind his sunglasses Ben's eyebrows drew together.

"I don't know if she knows what she wants. This feels –" Gabe leaned his head back, stared at the clear sky before lowering his gaze back to the man standing next to him. "Opportunistic."

"Sounds like her."

"Yes. She claims to be here to entice Sheldon to work for Milford, but I believe meeting Allison changed Talia's priorities somewhat. Especially since she hasn't been back to see Sheldon."

"Do you think she killed Allison?"

Gabe stared at the trees ringing the field. God, he wanted to say yes. Wanted to pin that poor girl's murder on Talia. "No."

Ben's shoulders sagged a small amount.

"Not that she isn't capable of it."

"I know very well what my daughter is capable of." Ben squared his jaw. "We both know."

Change the subject, before they went further down that ugly road of no return. Gabe angled his head to study the far tree line. "What about Allison and Irene Trent? Any surprises we weren't expecting?"

"Not really." Ben's energy leveled out. "Allison was doing well in her illustration business, kept her nose out of anything that didn't have bearing on that and appears to have considered Irene part mentor, part surrogate mother."

Gabe nodded, brought his gaze back to Ben.

"Once this is over, before I head back to Minnesota, I'd like to meet Irene Trent."

I bet you would. Question was what would the domesticated Himalayan kitty think of the wild wolf? That might be worth watching. "What are you picking up out here?"

One corner of Ben's mouth lifted. "Not a lot. On the surface the place seems almost tranquil."

Gabe snorted.

"I said seems." Ben paced a few feet away, turned to face Gabe. "There's something underneath. Something not quite right, but I'm having a hard time pinpointing what that is."

"Two Winds."

"Without a doubt. But what, *exactly*, is Two Winds?"

"Beyond a vindictive son of a bitch?"

That one side of Garrett's mouth lifted again. "Yes."

Hands balled in fists in his pockets, Gabe rocked backed on his heels. "You don't feel him? Specifically?"

"I don't know what he *should* feel like, so I'm not sure. But there's nothing malevolent out here. Again, not on the surface." Ben took the few steps to stand in front of the stone. He bent forward and, with his fingers spread, held a hand over the top of the boulder. "Whatever Two Winds is, he doesn't register with his own personal signature."

"Because he doesn't truly exist or because he's not anything we've come across before?"

"That's another good question." Ben straightened, took another scan around the perimeter of the field. "When those images played out of what happened here, when Rily was struggling with Justin, did he have a totem?"

"No. He didn't have one when he turned and looked straight at me, either. But none of them did."

Ben, his gaze on the tree line, nodded. "So whatever Two Winds is, he might not be alive."

"Doesn't make him any less dangerous."

"I'd say it just might make him more of a danger."

Right.

Gabe stared out across the field that sparkled in the cold light. At the forest's edge, the place where the woman he loved would die if he didn't figure out something.

Soon.

RILY SLAMMED THE passenger door of Ramon's low slung BMW coupe. She liked the sleek lines of the convertible, the barely restrained power. The fact that when the weather was nice, he could drive around with the top down. What she didn't like was *having* to be driven around when she had a perfectly fine *truck* sitting in her driveway.

Dammit all.

As if she'd run off and leave Ramon's ass here at the station.

Well.

Still. She didn't like it. At all. "Come on."

"Temper, temper." Laughter threaded Ramon's voice.

Rily resisted opening the car door so she could slam it again.

How was she supposed to do her job with so many damn restraints?

They're trying to keep you alive. Yeah, well, she'd like that to be the outcome, too. But she also had a murder to solve. Clipping her wings wasn't making that any easier.

Mine. Always. Two Winds' voice, sinuous and loaded with conviction, echoed through her mind.

Oh, shit.

Her head lifted, she scanned the hill behind the station. Ramon, his eyes narrowed, did the same.

"Did you hear him?"

"Two Winds? No, Rily, I didn't."

"But you believe I did?"

He nodded. "Let's get inside the building to discuss this."

She let a smirk cross her mouth. Relief welled when Ramon gave her answering one. Still, getting inside seemed like a fine idea. She led the way to the building and through the sliding doors.

An hour later she wondered if she'd have to strangle Ramon.

She tapped the tip of her pen against the pad of paper she'd pulled from her desk drawer and scribbled Allison Davis across the top. The rest of the page was still blank.

Ramon had taken one of the chairs from in front of her desk and angled it against the wall so he could see both her and her closed office door. Right now, he slouched in that chair with his legs stretched out in front, crossed at the ankles, and his hands folded together in his lap.

"So." Rily tapped the page again.

He canted his head a slight bit towards her, his nearly black eyes unfocused, before he turned that gaze back to whatever the hell he'd been staring at before she'd spoken.

Whatever he was looking at wasn't anything here or even now, that was for damn sure.

Damn freaking inside time. Hell, she was fine with that. Used it herself, once in a while. But going on an hour?

What happened to discussing Two Winds and what she'd heard outside just after they'd arrived?

Pissy, that was her mood this morning. Although it was now nearing noon. How long did Gabe intend to take out there with Ben? Show him around, do the woo-woo shit, allow Ben to get a *feel* of the place. Get their asses back here.

How long could that possibly take?

She tapped the tip of her pen harder against the pad of paper. The nearly empty page mocked her.

With a silent growl, she wrote Sheldon on one side and Talia Garrett on the other then stabbed a line underneath both names. Her pen tore through the top sheet of paper.

"So." Ramon's voice startled her.

"What?" The snarl lifted her top lip.

His mouth curved in a smile and those dark eyes focused completely on her. Well, hell. Maybe it was better when he was off in la-la land.

"Two Winds."

"What about the bastard?" She set her pen on top of the pad and shoved it away from her.

"According to the reading material at your house, he was trapped inside that hill by another shaman. One who used the Chief's daughter as a sacrifice to, in essence, seal the deal." Ramon's face impassive, those dark eyes held hers. "Did you and your friends, back in high school, wake Two Winds or has he always been awake, in limbo, waiting for you to return?"

"What do you mean, waiting for me?"

"Is it *you*, specifically, Two Winds has been waiting for?"

"You mean, like am I the *reincarnated* soul of the original Chief's daughter?"

Ramon nodded.

"How am I supposed to know?" Frustrated, she stared at the ceiling for a moment before again holding Ramon's gaze. "Before Justin died, Allison and I were over that hillside almost every single day. After school we'd stop at the station and Dad would take us over the hill to Allison's."

"Your dad was the Police Chief then?"

"Yes."

"Nothing weird on that hillside?"

"Nothing until that day."

"With the homemade Talking Board."

She nodded.

"How did Two Winds know your dad was the Chief?"

"Unless Two Winds was actually *listening* to our conversations, and if he was, he'd have known a lot sooner, the only thing I can think of is that day, when Allison set the board up, she made this whole big production about who each of us was, like she was already talking to whatever it was she was trying to contact through the board and introduced each of us."

"And she called you the Chief's daughter?"

"Yeah."

"So, that is probably the point Two Winds decided he had to have you."

"Okay. That makes as much sense as anything else."

"If that is the case, and you aren't the reincarnation of the original Chief's daughter, and your father isn't the original Chief, then any daughter of any Chief will do for the sacrifice."

"Excuse me?"

"For all intents and purposes, Benjamin Garrett is also a Chief."

Rily, still holding his gaze, narrowed her eyes. "So."

"His daughter happens to be in town." Ramon smiled, the effect chilly in the warm room. "And that daughter has a completely unhealthy fascination with Two Winds."

"You think Talia is reincarnated –"

"No, Rily. I think Two Winds wants what he believes he was promised long ago and will stop at nothing to get what he wants. Regardless of *who* that daughter is."

"What are you saying?"

"That although Two Winds is focused on *you* right now, there are other alternatives."

"I don't care for Talia Garrett, but I'm not going to sacrifice her to save my own life."

His eyes darkened. "No one is asking you to, *Mi Corazon*."

"Ramon."

"The first choice is always that everyone comes out alive."

"No bait and switch."

"Of course not."

"Ramon."

"Muddying the waters, however, that is something I think we need to examine."

"Talia isn't going to help save my life and I don't see Ben agreeing to endanger his daughter."

"Asking Talia wasn't on my agenda." Ramon stretched then stood. "Don't underestimate Benjamin, he is capable of many surprises."

Rily's skin prickled at Ramon's words, at all the implications of what he'd said, something she didn't want to examine right then, so she ignored them. "Where are you going?"

"Out to examine the hill from this side." He frowned. "I'd rather do that alone. You will wait for me here? Stay in your office?"

"Why not?" *Men.* "Without you in here doing your commune with whatever the hell you were communing with, I might actually make some progress."

The barest of smiles lit Ramon's eyes. "I won't be long."

The door clicked closed behind him. *Focus.* Right. Rily picked up her pen and the pad of paper then leaned back in her chair.

Dr. Sheldon.

Talia Garrett.

Rily didn't believe Talia had killed Allison. If, indeed, Allison had been killed.

Although they *knew* some kind of foul play was involved, had Allison actually been murdered? The M.E. was asking that same question.

How did Rily prove the not-so-good doctor was behind this? That he was still experimenting on patients and discarding his mistakes?

Behind a dumpster, covered in a pine needle blanket.

Talia Garrett knew more about that than she was admitting.

Rily's pen tapped out an erratic tempo. That missing link, tying all this together. What the hell was it?

Fifteen minutes later a soft knock on her office door distracted Rily.

"Come in." She scribbled the last of her note before glancing up as the door opened.

Talia Garrett slipped inside then closed the door to lean against it. In skin tight jeans and a dark blue turtle neck sweater, she crossed her legs at her ankles and wrapped one arm around her waist while she toyed with the long, light blue beaded necklace she wore. The artful mess of her spiky, short white hair made it seem she'd only been awake a short time, but the sharpness in those deep blue eyes belied that.

"What are you doing here?"

"You aren't happy to see me?"

"I had enough of you yesterday." *Always the games.* "What do you want?"

"Such manners."

"I'm working, Talia." And wanted answers. "Since you're here, do you have anything constructive to add to my investigation into Allison's death?"

"I'd rather not talk about Allison."

"I bet." Rily rolled her pen between her fingers and settled back in her seat.

"At least not her death."

"That's pretty much all I'm interested in right now. When you were at Allison's house –"

"I never said I was there."

"We both know you were, so quit the lies."

"*That* wasn't a lie, Rily. I just said I'd never admitted to being there. Not the same thing at all."

"You like word games."

"Games can be fun." She let go of her necklace and pushed away from the door. Seemingly restless, she prowled around the room, touching books in the short lawyer's book case along one wall, skimming her finger along the edge of Rily's desk.

Rily waited.

"I saw one of the paintings Allison did of you."

"Really? I thought you *said* you hadn't been to Allison's home." Rily frowned at the sudden sense of her personal space being invaded, so similar to the first time she'd met this woman. As she'd done that time, Rily shoved the sensation back.

Talia's fingers gripped the edge of Rily's desk then she let go and continued wandering around the office. "Allison had several images on her phone. You make an excellent Fool. Of course, at the time she showed me those images, I had no idea who you were beyond the fact you were the reason she decided to do her own deck."

"Do you know where Allison's phone is now?"

Talia pressed her lips together and shook her head.

"What other images were on there?"

"I really wish she'd had the entire deck, but there were only three cards. The Fool, The Magician and The Chariot. Can you imagine my surprise in seeing Gabriel's face staring up at me from a *painting* on Allison's phone screen?"

Rily ignored the heat radiating outward from the center of her palm. She couldn't be distracted by Gabe, not now. She had to focus.

What other images were on Allison's phone? The ones of Two Winds, the ones they'd found in her computer?

Rily bet Talia had that phone stashed somewhere. It sure as hell hadn't been out behind the dumpster or in Allison's motel room.

"She swore she didn't know him, or most of the people she painted for that deck." Talia shook her head back and sighed. "But there he was, tall and so manly in that transparent scrap of white linen, standing in his chariot while he struggled to control the two tigers whose reins he held. Is it any wonder I thought Allison was the reason he was here? Of course, now I realize you are the other tiger and are as tied to him as I am."

Rily curled her fingers over the warmth spiraling in her palm and leveled a dismissive stare at the other woman.

Talia grinned and spun away to stop in front of the black and white photos on the wall. "Great shot of my father."

Rily nodded once. That was the same photo Gabe had commented on not so many days ago.

"So, if you weren't my father's young lover, does he think of you as what? A *surrogate* daughter?"

"Hardly."

"He cares about you." Talia slid a sideways glance her way. "Otherwise Gabe wouldn't have been able to pick up on your death."

"We went over this ground yesterday."

A sly smile twisted Talia's lips. "And since then I've done more research on you, Rily Carrigan. The Fool. The start of Allison's tarot journey. You're the key, you always have been. Allison more or less alluded to that, but she was gone before I could get all the answers I needed. Before I understood the scope."

"You killed her?"

"Goodness, no. That's also ground we've already covered. Why would I kill her? I needed her alive. She still had so much to tell me. Like why *you*, in particular, are the key. For Gabe and for the shaman she called Two Winds."

"What do you mean by key?"

"To awakening Two Winds, of course."

"Why would anyone want to do that?"

That sly smile in place, Talia turned away from the photos. "To harness all that lovely power."

"You're a sick bitch."

Talia's eyes lit with laughter. "Maybe. Didn't you hear Gabe yesterday? He knows me so well."

"Yes, he does."

"That didn't sound particularly nice."

"Wasn't meant to."

That sly smile slid back over Talia's mouth. "Power is everything, Rily. I will have Gabe on his knees. He will beg *me* for his life. Shame you won't be around to see that happen."

Rily lifted her chin. "It's against the law to threaten the life of a law enforcement officer."

"Gabriel isn't the law." Talia shrugged. "And I didn't threaten you, Rily. Just stated a fact. You're a dead woman walking. Otherwise, Gabe wouldn't be here."

The office door opened.

"Rily." Ramon stood there, hands on his black jean clad hips. One dark eyebrow quirked upwards. "I can't leave you for even a few minutes, can I?"

Talia turned slightly towards the door. "Oh my. Our Magician. Where has Rily been hiding *you?*" With her bottom lip between her teeth, she tilted her head and her gaze took in all of Ramon.

Rily rolled her eyes.

"Enough of that." Ramon held up a hand, palm forward, fingers spread. "I'm surprised Garrett didn't teach his daughter better than to probe someone without their permission."

"What fun is that?" Talia brushed a lock of hair back from her face. "I'm at a disadvantage considering you know who I am but I have no idea who you are."

One side of Ramon's mouth lifted. Rily settled deeper into her chair. She'd have to ask about that probe shit later, but right now she was going to enjoy the show.

"Back off." His voice low and dangerous, he curled his fingers over his palm then flicked them open. Static electricity tainted the air.

Talia's eyes widened in shock then narrowed in pleasure. Her gazed locked on Ramon, she slowly ran her tongue over her lips. "Yum. He tastes completely sinful, Rily. Rich and full of unleashed power. I wonder, have you had a bite of him, yet? Does Gabe know about this one? You know, Gabriel really doesn't like to share."

"Funny, that's not what you said yesterday."

Talia slanted a quick glance at Rily before her gaze went straight back to Ramon. "Hmm. Seems I asked if he'd told you I was there, I don't remember saying he liked it."

"Implications."

"I'd say Garrett's daughter is full of those." Ramon, his hand still open in front of him, came further into the room.

"Talia. My name is Talia."

"I'm well aware of your name."

"Use it."

"Why?" Ramon shrugged his left shoulder. "When it bothers you so much that I don't?"

The air between them tense, the two held each other's gaze for several drawn out moments.

"Who is he, Rily?"

Ramon's mouth curved into that non-smile that didn't quite reach his eyes.

"Allison's Magician." Rily smiled.

Talia flashed a quick, calculating glance at her before dropping her shoulders a small fraction. "There's that. Another player in our little drama."

Rily leaned forward to set her pen on her desk. Time to get this back on track. "Talia, where's Allison's phone? In addition, when you were at Allison's the other day, did you take any of her artwork?"

Talia's gaze slid between her and Ramon.

"No lies, Talia. No half-truths."

"Allison was extremely talented. She's also extremely dead." Talia took several steps towards the office door. "What good do her paintings do her now?"

With a look from under her lashes at Ramon, Talia waved a hand towards him as she passed on her way out the door. "Bye for now."

Ramon flinched then moved to shut the door behind the bitch's exit.

"Did that hurt?" *I can't believe I asked that.* "Whatever it was she just did."

Ramon shook his head, settled into the chair he'd occupied earlier. "An annoyance. Like a bug bite."

"Hopefully not like a spider bite where the venom lasts a long time."

Chapter Twenty-Three

A T THE SHARP, single tap on the office door, Rily glanced up from the sheets of paper she had spread across her desk. Before she could answer, the door swung open.

"Talia has been here." Gabe threw the words at Ben as they crossed the office threshold. His dark eyes scanned the room.

With more than his vision? *Just listen to me. Neverland, here I come.*

"Tell me how you know that." Rily spared a glance at Ramon, barely resisted sticking her tongue out at him. She shoved her hands through her hair.

"What did Talia want?" Gabe stood in the center of the room, his hands fisted on his hips.

"Answer my question first. What is it she left behind? That you sense? That tells you she was here. This essence or whatever the hell it is. What does it feel like?"

Gabe exchanged a quick glance with Ramon.

"No. He's been closemouthed ever since that bitch left. *Talk to me.*"

Gabe lifted his hands, palms forward, and nodded. Ben, his expression closed, shut the door then took the other remaining chair. He set it against the lawyer bookcase and sat to face Ramon.

"There's a curious sense of dissatisfaction that is feminine, but doesn't belong to you. That just *feels* like Talia." Gabe lowered his hands as he flicked a glance towards Ben then brought his gaze back to Rily. "And if I had to guess, I'd say you tweaked her tail. Again."

"Damn right, I did."

Gabe's smirk aimed straight for her heart. She nodded back at him.

"What did she want?"

"To rattle me, I think. Again."

"Did she succeed?"

"What do you think?"

"I think she's pissed you off more than rattled you."

Rily pressed both hands against her desk, pushed herself backwards before leaning back in her chair. "She has the paintings Allison did of the Two Winds legend."

"She admitted that?" Gabe moved around the desk, sat on the corner.

"It's the fact she didn't deny it that tells us she has them."

His expression guarded, he took her hands in his, rubbed at her palm with his fingers.

Heat swirled at the center of her hand, seeped into her skin. She tried to pull away as she glanced at the other two men in the room. "What?"

Gabe pulled her up and ran his hands over her arms. "She didn't touch you."

Like she'd let the bitch close enough. She shrugged off his hands, sent another swift glance towards the others then her gaze rested on Gabe. She frowned. "You told me before that touching her was bad. But why would it matter if she did?"

"I don't want her tagging you."

That didn't sound good. "Like when we put surveillance on somebody? That kind of tag?"

"Very similar." Ben crossed one leg over the other knee and let his hands hang loose over his leg.

"Why would she do that?" Rily shook her head. "No. Wait. *How* would she do that?"

"Obviously by touching you." A thin thread of laughter laced Ramon's voice.

Too much amusement at her expense. She aimed a disgusted look his way.

Gabe frowned then again ran his hands down her arms.

"She didn't touch me, okay?" She again brushed his hands away. Even without him touching her palm, heat swirled there. "She just seemed to want to stir the shit, to be a pain in my ass."

"Definitely your daughter, Garrett." Humor still lurked in Ramon's voice.

"And she was all bent out of shape because she couldn't figure out who Ramon was and he wouldn't tell her. Even tried some kind of mental probe thing. Which reminds me, what the hell is that about?"

Ben's chin came up and his eyes narrowed.

Cool. Focus their attention elsewhere. Rily rotated her shoulders, let a smirk buffer her uneasiness. "Ramon told her he thought you would have taught her better than to do whatever the hell she did totally uninvited."

"Some people believe they are a law unto themselves. Regardless of the consequences." Ben sucked in a deep breath, exchanged another of those unreadable glances with Gabe. "Did she try this probe with you, Rily?"

"I'm not sure. That's why I'm trying to get to the bottom of what all this feels like." She brushed by Gabe. Too much sitting, too much thinking. She needed to move. "The first time I met Talia, at the market café, there was a moment when it felt as if someone had stepped into my personal space. No one was close enough to have done that."

Right now, she could *feel* Gabe's gaze following her as she paced. *Add too much* awareness *to the 'too much of' stuff.*

"At this café, where was Talia?" Ben's voice held a trace of self-recriminating resignation.

Because his daughter had previously tried to kill Gabe? Or because she might succeed in killing Rily?

Crap, crap, crap.

Lord, there were too many damn people in her suddenly too small office. She barely managed to keep from shoving her hands through her hair.

"Talia sat across the table from me." She threw the words over her shoulder.

"And Gabe, where were you?"

"Between them."

"Was it Talia?"

Rily reached her office door and swung around to face the room.

Gabe nodded, his gaze locked on her. "And Rily pushed her back."

"It's that don't mess with me attitude." One side of Ramon's mouth lifted. "In addition to the sarcastic tongue."

Rily scowled at him.

Ramon shrugged. "Shielding is a first line of defense against psychic attack."

"And Rily's defenses aren't completely negligible." Ben drummed his fingers on his leg.

"That's all there is to that, then? Pushing back mentally?" She paced forward two steps.

"It's a start." Gabe shoved his hands into his pockets. "You need to learn to control your shielding. Make it work for you instead of it being reactionary."

"Will that stop Talia from tagging me if she happens to get the chance to touch me?"

Ben shook his head.

"Then what good is learning to control it? Why go through whatever that entails when I recognized, on some level, what she was doing. And stopped it."

"Cockiness can get you killed, Rily." Ben's narrowed gaze focused on her.

She was going to die away.

Damn.

When had she become so fatalistic about all of this? She wasn't a quitter, wasn't going to just roll over and let it happen.

"It's not cockiness. Now that I know what it is, what it feels like –" Sudden pain prickled along her nerve endings with electric heat scalding across her skin.

Oh, crap. What the hell was that?

Her breath lodged in her throat. As fast as it came on the pain eased then dissipated, leaving her weak and her knees trembling.

"What the hell, Ben?" Gabe shoved away from her desk and in three strides had her in his arms.

Rily, her hands gripping Gabe's arms, stared at Ben.

"She needed to know it's not always so simple."

"You could have given her a definition, a description. Not a damn demonstration."

"Rily is from the school of hard knocks. A definition is something she would completely ignore."

Rily shook herself, but didn't step away from Gabe's embrace. "That was you, Ben?"

He nodded.

"That was … weird. It hurt."

"And your shields are better than any of us thought they were, Rily." Ben wiped a hand over his mouth before he leaned back in his chair. "I got in, but you kicked me out and slammed the door in my face."

"Really?" She lifted an eyebrow.

"Again with the cockiness. You might have just got lucky."

"Dammit, Ben." Gabe pulled her even closer. "She isn't one of your students."

"I'm also not some kind of fragile flower that needs to be coddled." She pushed at Gabe's arms and turned to face him. "What I felt from Talia wasn't that intrusive. She could do that to me?"

"If she chose to do so, yes."

"Was that what she did to you, Ramon?" Rily angled towards him.

He shook his head. "Although the mechanism is probably the same, what she did to me was less of an attack and more of an actual probe. She wanted to know what I was, what my defenses were like. My shield alerted me as soon as she made contact."

"It seemed to me that whatever she was doing she did it almost automatically. Without thinking."

"As effortlessly as breathing." Gabe touched Rily's shoulder. "At least with men."

"I believe she discounts you, Rily." Ramon shrugged. "Stupid on her part."

"Unfortunately, in that regard, she's like her mother." Ben sent Gabe a quick glance, one full of dark remorse.

So many damn undercurrents. Rily squared her shoulders before she looked up at Gabe. "Can you teach me to protect myself from that sort of invasion?"

"Yes." Resignation lined his face. Resignation with an underlying hint of determination.

He *wanted* her to kick some Talia butt.

She was going to do her damnedest.

Ramon stood, faced Ben. "While school's in session, why don't you show me around Two Winds domain?"

THREE HOURS LATER, sitting in Rily's kitchen, Gabe wiped his brow with the back of his hand and threw an underhanded mental probe at Rily's defenses. She deflected it as easily as if it didn't exist.

The student caught on fast.

She could be dangerous if he ever got her to really believe in this stuff. Got her to really hone what turned out to be natural abilities.

If I can keep her alive long enough to believe.

Her grin pierced his heart. She was too much *alive* to die so young.

His feelings for her aside.

Rily.

Remember I Love You.

He'd found her and would lose her all in the course of a few days.

Fatalistic.

He'd never saved anyone before.

He'd never had the same level of motivation before.

Rily *had* to be different.

His reasons why didn't matter. Not if they could save her life.

But, dammit, how?

Rily perched on the stool next to him. "How do I make sure these shields are up and running so I'm not blindsided?"

Right to the chase, that was his Rily.

"Intent."

"Okay, what does that mean?"

"You know how you can wake up before the alarm clock ever goes off?"

She frowned but nodded.

"Intent. You intend to be up at a certain time and your internal clock makes sure you're awake before the alarm can wake you. Same sort of thing." He touched her hand, laced his fingers with hers. That connection between their palms flared. "At first, like now, you need to consciously decide that your shields are up and running. That they will remain up and running. You need to reach out, every so often, and take mental stock. Are they as strong as you want them to be? Have they been breached when you weren't paying enough attention?"

"How do I know that?"

"You will."

Her gaze dubious, she nodded. "So I do all that, then what?"

"Then they become second nature."

"Like what happened with Ramon, today?"

"Yes."

She pulled her hand from his, rubbed at her palm then folded hers in her lap before she met his gaze again. "But I don't have time for it to become second nature, Gabe."

"Rily —"

"Tell me what's going to happen."

"I don't know. I'm not able to see that part."

"Then tell me what you do see."

God, this was hard. He blinked at his suddenly blurry sight. "When I was on my boat, for several days in a row, every time I closed my eyes to sleep, I would see you lying in a forest."

"The tree line along the field out by Allison's?"

"I believe so."

"And?"

"You're stretched out, lying on your back, staring at me. But —" He ran a hand over his face, through his hair. "Your eyes are lifeless."

She pressed her lips together.

"There's no soul left there, Rily."

"You didn't even know me, then. How could you have seen that?"

"I know Ben and in spite of his prickly exterior, he cares for you."

"And you see the death of those connected to the ones *you* care about." She touched his hand. "How often does this happen to you?"

He frowned. "Often enough."

"How hard for you."

"Rily, don't go all sympathetic on me."

Her turn to frown. "Who says I am?"

"I do."

"Eat shit, Nicholetti."

"Right." He turned his palm over. She slipped her hand in his.

"Just saying that has to be hard, is all."

No way to deny that one.

"So, until you dragged me out there, I hadn't been to that field or that part of the forest since I was in high school. Why can't I continue that and avoid this whole lifeless in the forest stuff?"

"If it worked that way, we'd be having a beer on my boat right now. And you'd be in a bikini." He wiggled his eyebrows.

"Lech."

"Yep." He squeezed her fingers. "Once Ben's back, he'll be testing your shields. Keep them up. Keep them strong."

She nodded. "Then we get down to the nitty-gritty of what to do about Two Winds and Talia Garrett."

"Rily –" He tugged on her hand, tugged her off her stool to stand between his legs and into his embrace. She pressed both palms to his chest. Her troubled gaze held his. He pulled her closer, laid a gentle kiss on her lips. "You're going to live, Rily."

How the hell was he going to keep that promise?

ALTHOUGH THE HOUR wasn't late, darkness had already fallen. Another early December evening in the Pacific Northwest.

Rily rubbed at the soft sleeves of her green sweater and stood staring out the square pane of glass in her kitchen's back door at the dark landscape beyond the feeble circle of light illuminating her porch. Behind her, Gabe, Ramon and Ben sat in three of the four stools around the island in the center of her kitchen.

She half blocked their words, half listened to the psychic jargon. None of it, as far as she could tell, was going to keep her alive.

Almost Christmas. And she was supposed to die.

Helluva Christmas present for her parents.

Regardless of the almost promise Gabe had made, he was here to find her killer. Not to keep her from being killed.

Because he didn't really believe he'd be able to save her.

She got that. Didn't make her any less mad at him or at the situation, though.

Also didn't mean she was going down without a damn fight.

She wasn't one of those people who accepted *fate* as a reason to quit trying.

Fate could kiss her ass.

"Sex magic." Tension lined Ben's voice.

What? Rily spun to face the men behind her.

"That's what Two Winds is using to try and break free of his prison." Ben met her gaze.

"How did you three jump to *that* conclusion?" Rily wrapped her arms around her middle. She refused to ask what sex magic was, she just wasn't going to do it.

Ramon and Ben exchanged glances.

Gabe's gaze held hers. "She doesn't remember what happened after Two Winds enacted his little show for us."

"What are you talking about?"

Gabe laid out the details.

"I came on to you afterwards?" She shook her head. "And he was in your mind? Trying to control you? Why the hell didn't you tell me that part before now?

"Didn't think you were up to all those details."

"Anything else you're keeping from me?"

Gabe's dark eyes held hers.

"Dammit." She spun away. *Sex magic.* Crap. She faced the men again. "So how do we fight this?"

Gabe's dark smile matched the intensity radiating from his eyes.

"I'd suggest carefully." Ramon, with his elbows on the island, leaned forward. "Considering the shaman is using your feelings against you."

"Because I cared about Justin back then?"

"And Gabe now."

Her chin lifted.

"No sense denying it, *Mi Corazon*. It's completely obvi-ous." Ramon shrugged his left shoulder. "And the shaman will, as he's already shown, attempt to use that to his advantage."

"By inhabiting Gabe's body?"

"As he did Justin's in the past."

"So Justin didn't really attack me? It was Two Winds all along?"

Ben ran a hand over his face. "We believe Two Winds used Justin's body as a *host*. What we're not sure about is what would have happened if he'd been able to rape you."

She flinched.

"That was his intent, Rily." Ben's voice was low, his blue gaze locked on hers.

"I realize that. But Gabe is stronger than Justin, and he knows what Two Winds is trying to do so he can stop him, right? Like he did earlier."

Okay, so I've officially slipped over the edge here.

"It's not that simple." Ben exchanged a shuttered glance with the other two men.

"Why not?" *Made sense to her.* At least as much as any of this made any kind of sense. For the moment, anyway.

"Two Winds is looking to escape his prison. According to the story Allison left behind, the traveling shaman used the Chief's daughter's blood to bind him in that hillside."

"A myth. A legend." Rily shoved both hands through her hair.

Why the hell was she buying into all of this? Where was her common sense? Where was *all* their common sense?

Hiding in that hillside with Two Winds?

"We're basing a lot on something that may or may not be accurate." She spun towards the back door, paced the few feet then spun back to face the island and the three men who stared at her. "A story that might be nothing more than a *story* Allison was writing. That might be pure fiction."

"You forget that story of hers is based on an actual legend transcribed over a hundred years ago." Ben's voice held sharp traces of exasperation.

Tough. She set her hands on her hips. "And forgotten until Allison dug it up."

"Until you, Justin and Allison brought him back with a Talking Board." Ramon's smile was grim and didn't reach his dark eyes.

"You know, it's hard to be the voice of reason when there are three of you buying into all this woo-woo crap."

"Rily." Gabe pushed his stool back and stood. "These protests of yours could be what will get you killed. This belief that none of what we say is real."

She stared at him, her brows low and tight, as he came around the island and advanced on her.

"That tomorrow, out there in that field, when I yank you against me and start to rip off your clothes, you believe it's me doing that and that when we have sex out there, there won't be any consequences. That's what you believe?"

"We're not going to have sex out there. Not going to happen."

"How will you stop me? Especially when my entire focus will be on having you."

"I'll make sure there's a damn board game handy to beat you over the back with."

"You wouldn't do that to me." He stopped his advance less than two feet from her.

"If you have a crazy shaman stuck inside you, I will."

"See?" He reached out and ran his hand down her arm. "You do believe in spite of your protests."

"That was dirty pool."

"Maybe." He pulled her forward then in front of him to face the other two. "But we need to formulate a plan. The four of us need to be on the same page with that plan."

She took one reluctant step towards the island.

Gabe leaned forward, his breath warm on her neck. "And you *will not* beat me over the back with a damn board."

Chapter Twenty-Four

GABE, FROM HIS POSITION on the polished, wooden floor with his back against the wall of Rily's living room, glanced at the ornate wall clock. Nearing midnight and although the four of them had, many times, been over the details they knew, they weren't any closer to figuring out what to do once they lured Two Winds out to play.

No real plan, good or otherwise, to keep Rily alive.

Her dog, Bogie, lay beside Gabe with his eyes closed and his big body warm against his leg. Calm and comforting. Ben sat in the only recliner, less than a foot from Gabe, and every once in a while he'd reach down and scratch behind Bogie's ears.

"So the players, as I see it, are me, Gabe and Two Winds." Rily, her pacing done for the time being, leaned against the archway.

Down that hallway was her bedroom.

That's where they should be, in her bed, lost in each other. If the world hadn't gone completely insane.

If that hadn't happened, though, would he have ever met her? Held her in his arms? Made love to her?

"Don't forget the Chief and traveling shaman." Ramon, who'd been fairly quiet for most of the night, now sat on the couch with his legs stretched out and crossed at the ankles. He linked his hands over his stomach.

"Just where do you intend to find a traveling shaman? Besides, my dad, the Chief, is not in town and not involved in any of this. Since they don't plan to be back until after New Year's, I'd rather keep it that way."

The smile Ramon aimed at her was lethal.

"No." Rily pushed away from the wall. "I told you, Ramon, I might not like her, but we're not *sacrificing* Talia to save me. Shove her ass in jail, maybe, but that's the extent."

Talia. An integral part of the puzzle, one Gabe had hoped to leave out of the equation. He tilted his head to the side to look at Ben.

"Technically I am a Chief." Ben, his hands linked, steepled his index fingers. "And, technically, Talia is therefore a Chief's daughter."

Gabe kept his mouth shut.

If it'd keep Rily alive, he'd willingly sacrifice Talia any damn day of the week. But he wasn't the Chief. And in the past, in the myth, the Chief had willingly given his daughter in trade for trapping Two Winds.

That the Chief hadn't realized his daughter had to die was neither here nor there.

If they had to use Talia to save Rily, so be it. If Talia caused Rily's death, she'd pay with her own life.

"No." The set of Rily's mouth firm, she stood with her legs braced and her hands on her hips. She met each of the men's gazes. "We're not trading one life for another."

"I have no intention of trading my daughter's life for yours, Rily." Ben's eyes narrowed as he tapped his mouth with his index fingers. "However, Ortega may be on to something."

"No, he's not." Rily glanced between Ben and Ramon. "According to the *legend*, the spilt blood of the daughter set this up and her death entrapped him. If we're going with that scenario, how does *another* daughter enter into this?"

"We make *you* unavailable."

"How do you intend to do that?" Rily stared at the ceiling for a moment before she brought her gaze back to Ramon. Derision practically dripped from her voice. "When, according to you three, I have to be there to lure Two Winds out in the first place? Because without me, no one even hears or senses him. Are you going to put me in a psychic cage where he can't touch me? Toss Talia's blood on that stone to throw his scent off and go from there?"

Ben, one eyebrow raised, threw a sideways look at Gabe.

Good luck with that one, Garret. Gabe let one corner of his mouth raise in a semi-smile. Personally, though, the idea had merit.

"What the hell?" Rily's gaze swung from Ben to Gabe then back again. "You mean a cage like that actually exists?"

Ben's own smile turned secretive.

Rily frowned. "Unless you guys are successful, I'd be stuck there, wouldn't I? In that psychic cage thing."

"You'd be alive." Ben held her gaze.

"Trapped as effectively as Two Winds."

"Only until we figured out what to do with him. How to keep you safe."

"But, if I have this right, he's not alive any longer. And you guys don't know what he is. Makes it a little hard to figure out what to do with him."

"We need another trap for him." Ortega glanced at Gabe. "One we can control."

"You mean, take him *out* of the hillside and stick him in one of those cages Ben seems to like so much?" Rily shook her head. "Again, how?"

"If we had all the pieces, it'd be easy." Ben continued to tap his mouth with his index fingers. "Gabe kept his head when Two Winds tried to take over his body."

"Because he's more psychically savvy than Justin ever was." Rily wiped a hand over her eyes. "And he has those shields that still didn't completely stop this from happening."

"But Gabe was *aware* of what was happening."

"I don't remember. Not with Gabe. But that's what Two Winds tried on me with Justin?"

"You were young, then, Rily. Out there in that field with your friends for some fun. I doubt that, with Allison and her board game, sex was on your mind." Ben shook his head. "From what you've said, I think Two Winds believed all he had to do was control Justin and you would be his. Finally."

"Does that mean Two Winds has learned that since force didn't work last time, coercion might?"

"I think he's adapting."

"I'm sure he is. But there is one thing we need to keep in mind." One at a time, Ramon met all of their gazes. "The shaman's violence with Justin may have been necessary. Rily's blood *had* to spill on that stone as part of whatever reversal the shaman had in mind. He's had a very long time to think about this."

"And since that blood has already been spilt, we have to assume the first part of his plan is in place. Gabe kept his head before, but Two Winds has been getting stronger."

"Which is why we can't attack him at night, when we know he's strongest."

"Daytime. Check. Not that much of an advantage." Rily sat on the edge of the couch, a few feet from Ramon. "How do we give ourselves more of one?"

"My daughter and her gifts may very well be a part of the answer."

A chill seeped through the warmth of Gabe's sweatshirt, raising bumps along his skin.

Rily's eyes narrowed and her gaze speared Gabe right through to the center of his chest. "Amplification."

Damn. She was too quick a study. He nodded. The question, the one icing his veins, was whose abilities would Talia amplify?

Theirs or Two Winds?

RILY SHUT HER front door behind Ben and Ramon. After one in the morning and the two men were heading to the hotel. Ben had his own room and, since Gabe wouldn't be using his, he'd given his key to Ramon.

Rily hadn't argued.

She wanted Gabe here tonight. In her bed, in her arms.

For the rest of this night, the rest of the world didn't matter.

Talia Garrett could rot for all she cared. Rily had never considered herself the vindictive type, but if any of the poison the other woman spewed was accurate, Rily hoped like hell she *felt* her intentions tonight.

She was going to rock Gabriel Nicholetti's world. Was going to be one woman he would never, ever, forget.

And she only had a few hours left to do that.

Ben and Ramon would be back here by eight, to collect them and head out to the field. To force the issue before they were the ones forced.

Not much of plan. Especially considering she still had no idea how they were going to accomplish any of that.

"So." Rily led the way back into the kitchen where she let Bogie out into the back yard for his last run of the night. While she waited for the dog, she shut off the coffee pot, dumped what was left of the liquid into the sink and made a face at the burnt coffee smell before she turned to face Gabe. Suddenly chilled, she ran her hands over the sleeves of her sweater.

His expression shuttered, he stood a few feet away with his guarded gaze locked on her. That was fine. She had a few things to get out of the way first, no matter how uncomfortable they made either of them.

"This whole mess seems pretty hopeless."

Silent, he continued to watch her.

"Talk to me, Gabe. Tell me why this next time out in that field will be any different from the other times we've been out there. How are we going to be the ones in control? This time?"

For a long moment she didn't think he was going to give her an answer. Then he lifted his gaze to the ceiling before he dropped it back to capture hers.

"We know more than we did before. We're better prepared."

"Are we? Or are we fooling ourselves?"

"What choice do we have?"

She shook her head. "I want to go back to not believing any of this."

"You can't."

"So this non-plan of ours involves me invoking Two Winds then denying him just to piss him off." Edgy, unable to stay still, she paced the length of the table. Opened the back door for Bogie, resisted slamming it shut after the dog bounded inside. Instead, with her hands at her hips, she twisted to face Gabe. "How do you know Talia will be there?"

"She won't be able to help herself."

"Really? Her self-control is that lax?"

"When it comes to power. She believes Two Winds' is there for the taking. Her taking."

"We will not sacrifice her for me."

"Whatever happens won't be because we sacrificed her."

"But you're not going to take responsibility if she gets in the way?"

"I won't be responsible. She's a grown woman. Makes her own choices."

"But you're counting on those choices, aren't you, Gabe? Counting on her not being able to resist all that lovely power."

"I'm not her keeper."

"So her shortcomings are what will, ultimately keep me from dying? Feels to me like I, at least, will be responsible. Like I'll owe her for my life."

Wasn't that just a wonderful kettle of smelly fish?

Gabe's shuttered gaze held hers.

He doesn't believe. Rily swallowed hard. She knew that, but here it was in her face. "You don't think I'll make it."

"I didn't say that."

"You don't have to. It's there in your eyes." Her hands fisted. "Dammit, Gabe. Don't do this to me. If you don't believe, how the hell am I supposed to?"

"Rily –"

"No." She swiped at her cheeks with the back of both hands. She would not cry. She would not die tomorrow. Fate was damn well going to have to wait. "Tell me how it's even possible Talia could steal Two Winds power from him."

Gabe's dark gaze continued to hold hers. "She called you the key."

Rily shrugged one shoulder. "So?"

"If you're the key and you head out there, she won't be able to stop herself from heading out there, also."

"How will she know?"

He didn't look away, didn't even seem to flinch, that she could tell anyway.

"Right. The scar." Wasn't that the shits? "Does she know you're here? In my house. Now?"

"Probably."

"And?"

"And nothing. That's all she knows. I could probably block that knowledge from her, but why? In light of everything we discussed, we want her to know I'm here. We want her to know you're important to me. We want her to follow us out there tomorrow."

"And tonight? When we make love, will you block that from her?"

"When we make love, Rily –" He closed the distance between them, stood staring down at her. "That has always and will always be between us and us alone."

With her gaze on his, he cupped her face between his hands and ran a thumb over her lips. She curled her fingers over the tingling in her palm, an electric current pulsing in time with each stroke of his thumb.

Her lips parted and he slipped his thumb between her teeth. She bit lightly into the padded area. One side of his mouth lifted. Her stomach tightened at the dark light shining in his eyes.

Tonight he was hers. Only hers.

"Rily." Her name no more than a hoarse whisper, he brushed his lips over her forehead before he threaded both hands through her hair. He claimed her lips in a soft, almost feather light kiss.

This was what she wanted. Right now, tomorrow didn't matter. Only Gabe mattered. Only this moment mattered.

She slid her palms over his chest, over the soft material of his sweatshirt and leaned into him, parting her lips and deepening the kiss.

His mouth locked on hers, he gathered her into his arms.

Closer. Lord, she needed to be closer to him.

Skin on skin.

No barriers.

"Wait." His voice low and rough, he pulled a few inches back from her but kept her against him.

"No." She pressed her face to his chest, inhaled the dark, woodsy scent of him. "No more waiting."

On an oath he lifted her and she wrapped her legs around his waist. With his hands cupping her butt, he nuzzled her neck. "Bed."

"Now."

He took two steps forward, stumbled then cursed.

"Don't trip over Bogie."

"Too late. Damn dog needs to come with a warning label."

A giggle tickled her throat and she nipped Gabe's ear then rubbed her cheek over his hair.

"Are you laughing at me, woman?" He squeezed her butt, stepped over the dog and headed down the hallway.

"Yeah, I am." She kicked her shoes off and tightened her legs around his waist.

Inside her bedroom, with her still wrapped around him, he kneed the door shut and used an elbow to click on the wall switch for the lamp on her bedside table. Then he kicked off his own shoes. "Bogie's going to have to sleep in the living room tonight. I'm not sharing you, not even with him."

"Poor Bogie." She slipped her fingers through Gabe's hair then flicked her tongue over the top of his ear. At his shudder a surge of pure feminine power swelled through her.

They'd take care of life and death later. Right now, this man wanted her as badly as she wanted him.

With her legs still around his waist, he sat on her bed and ran his hands up her back to tangle his fingers in her hair. She met his mouth with her own.

So much heat, the fire inside her hot and scorching. She was going to incinerate right there in his arms.

"Gabe?" Too far gone to care about the pleading in her voice, she pulled away from his mouth to brush her lips over his jaw. "Help me. I'm burning up inside."

His low groan vibrated through her, his hands found the hem of her sweater, his fingers swept up over her back as he lifted the sweater over her head and the coolness of the air hit her overheated skin.

She shivered. Then, with her eyes half closed and her neck arched, she ran her fingers down her throat.

Yes.

His dark gaze followed the path of her fingertips to the swell of skin over the top of her black lace bra. Her nipples, both already taunt, tightened more when he cupped her breasts. His fingers massaged the bare skin above the lace.

Heat swirled low in her belly. Ached. She pressed the top of her legs together, swayed forward. "Gabe –"

"Yes?" His gaze flicked to hers then, with his hands slipping to rest at her bare waist, he leaned away, leaned back to rest on her bed with her straddling his midsection and the bulge underneath his jeans. He rocked against her. "Tell me what you want, Rily."

"You have to ask?"

"Tell me."

"You. Me. Naked. Nothing between us."

Those dark eyes, nearly black now, held hers while he inched the hem of his sweatshirt up his flat stomach then over his wide chest and then finally, finally, over his head.

Lord, he was killing her. She leaned forward, braced herself with one palm on the bed. With her other hand, she trailed the tips of her fingers down his chest, over his warm skin, down his stomach to circle his navel. "What do *you* want?"

His arms came around her then she was on her back with him above her, resting on his elbow and one hand hovering over the top button of her slacks. "This is a good place to start."

Her smile slow, she tucked her fingers in his waistband. In seconds she had his jeans unsnapped and unzipped and her hand inside his underwear, her fingers wrapped around him. "Now?"

With his eyes closed to mere slats, he rocked forward twice. She squeezed. A groan shuddered through him.

"I'll take that as a yes." She let go of him, pushed him flat on his back before she slid the straps of her bra off her shoulders and undid the latch at her back.

He lay there, his dark, hooded gaze never leaving her face. She stood, undid her slacks and let them pool around her feet. Then she slid her panties down her legs and stepped out of the puddle of clothes, holding his gaze the entire time.

Standing there, naked, in front of him, her skin burning from the heat of his gaze, she paused to let the sensation fill her, empower her. Tonight, she was all woman.

And she knew exactly what she wanted.

Her touch light, she leaned forward to trail her fingertips over the material of his underwear. She licked the tip of her finger, ran that tip up the length of him. Watched his eyes go even darker.

Still he lay there, his muscles tense and his gaze locked on hers.

Emboldened, she slipped her hands inside his pants, cupped his buttocks then shoved at the material of his underwear and jeans. He lifted his hips, allowing her to ease those clothes away and then down his legs.

His breathing heavy, almost labored, he remained quiet.

Waiting.

This night, he was hers.

She again ran her fingers down her arched throat before stretching out, like a cat, next to him, on her side, so that her body pressed against his. Her touch barely there, she lay her pulsing palm on his hip. Stroked up his stomach to his chest then down to his groin.

Lashes fluttered over those dark eyes and he moaned.

Her hand around his shaft, she squeezed and leaned forward to press her mouth to his ear. "Tell me, Gabe. What do you want?"

COLD MORNING AIR stung Rily's cheeks as she stood watching Bogie take his sweet time sniffing around the perimeter of the back yard.

Almost as if he'd never been there before.

In a way, she envied that innocence. Every day being new, new scents, new adventures. Being alive with possibilities.

Especially when this day might be the last of possibilities for her.

She huddled in the warmth of her jacket, her shoulders hunched forward and her hands curled into the fake fur lined pockets.

A damp, cold morning. No wind, but chilly just the same.

In more ways than one.

"Hey." Ben's deep voice settled over her when he stepped out of the house. He pulled the door closed behind him.

She met his deep blue gaze for a second then swung hers back to her dog. "Do we know where Talia is this morning?"

"Yes."

"Through Gabe?"

"No." Ben stopped next to her, slid his hands into his pockets. "After we left last night, Ortega and I took the liberty of stopping by her hotel to slip a tracker on her vehicle."

Technology over woo-woo? "Cool. You carry stuff like that around with you all the time?"

He shrugged. "Ortega is extremely resourceful."

Ramon would be.

"And she doesn't know you were there?" She shook her head. "Never mind. It's you. Of course she doesn't know. So, is she active yet this morning?"

A small smile lifted the corners of Ben's mouth. "Looks like she's having breakfast on Main Street."

"Less than a mile from here."

"Close enough to move when we move."

Rily locked her gaze on her dog, pulled her hands from her jacket pockets and flexed her fingers before balling them into fists. "Do you really believe we'll succeed out there today?"

"Depends on your definition of success."

She closed her eyes for a moment then wiped the back of her hand over her mouth. "Cut the double speak, Garrett."

"You will be alive when this day is over."

"Even though Gabe has seen me dead in his visions?"

"Fate isn't absolute."

"Gabe doesn't believe that."

"Up until now, he's had no reason to believe. Prove him wrong."

"And your daughter?" She cut him a sideways glance.

His blue eyes dark, he stared across the yard but didn't really seem to be watching the dog. "I'm not blind to who she is, what she is or her potential to become a true monster. We have to keep her from finding and tapping into that power supply she's so desperate to plug in to."

"So we sacrifice her to stop her from something she may or may not try to do." Rily pressed her lips together. God, she had so much to say. So much she couldn't quite wrap her mind around it all or how to say it all.

"Why are you sure a sacrifice is necessary? That it's you or her?"

"Aren't you?" She shoved her hands through her hair. "Bottom line, someone died to trap Two Winds in that hillside. If you look at this in a linearly fashion, someone has to die in order to release him or the original sacrifice has no real meaning. And if he's the big ugly we think he is, that isn't acceptable."

Ben remained quiet, continued to watch as Bogie sniffed around the far perimeter of the yard.

"That sacrifice, all that time ago, has to have meaning, because it's kept him trapped all these years. Arrow through the heart. Pretty damn straight forward. If it's not me, then it's Talia. Chief's daughter. And I can't see her willingly stepping in to take the arrow."

"No. Talia has no interest in self-sacrifice."

"Ramon means what he says, Ben. If it comes down to me or Talia, she's toast." Rily faced the older man. "Gabe, too. Even knowing I can't be saved, he's going to try."

"That's who he is, Rily."

And that, more than anything, was breaking her heart. "Are you going to be okay with that, Ben? Push to shove, she's your daughter."

"Are you asking who I'd save? Who I'd sacrifice for the other?"

She shook her head. "I'd understand, Ben. That's all I'm saying."

Chapter Twenty-Five

GABE STOOD IN the center of the empty field, a few feet from the boulder. His arms at his sides and his hands loose, he kept his gaze moving and searching the perimeter.

Not much after nine in the morning and the members of their makeshift team were in place, each on edge. Each having no idea what they would face.

A few feeble rays of light tried to poke through the heavy clouds, but the morning stayed damp and dark. Although his sweatshirt was no match for the cold breeze going right through him, he'd left his jacket in Rily's truck.

Freedom of movement.

Nothing to slow him down.

From what, he wasn't certain, but he'd face whatever he had to face.

For Rily.

To keep her alive.

Or die trying.

Destiny and visions be damned.

She was out there, nearby, in what she'd referred to as Ben's woo-woo cage. Protected for now. At least as well as they could.

No guarantees.

So far, Two Winds didn't seem to realize Rily was here. The field was quiet. Rain from the night scented the air, leaving it fresh and damp.

Serene. Except for the damn breeze.

Gabe twisted his neck side to side. Worked on the kinks.

Game time.

He let his guard down in increments. All at once went completely against what was left of his comfort zone. So little by little he deliberately lowered the outside layer until all he held in place was the barest of shields.

On an intake of breath, he mentally touched the scar on his neck. The lightest of strokes. An answering flare swelled over his skin.

His hands fisted.

Damn.

Talia was close, closer than he'd thought. She'd be here soon.

Less than ten minutes passed before he heard the approach of her car. With a last rotate of his shoulders, he faced the direction of her pull, of where he could *feel* her making her way from the area they'd parked Rily's truck.

No jacket for Talia either. The oversized dark pink sweater she wore hit just below her ass, the arms cuffed at the wrist. Slim black jeans, tucked into a pair of black hiking boots, covered her shapely legs. Her short, white hair, tousled by the wind, fluffed around her face to make her look more pixie than evil sorceress.

But he knew the deviousness of her heart and how deceptive her appearance.

His shields slammed back into place.

Shit. Reflex actions.

On an inhale, he released a small fraction of his hold, just enough to let her think she was in. Just enough to, hopefully, entice Two Winds once all the players were in place.

Talia paused at the tree line, a frown marking her brow, before she moved forward. Her deep blue gaze swept over him, over the field, then back to him. The scar on his neck twinged as she again stopped. They stood staring at each other across several feet of sloped ground.

"I'd hoped you would come to your senses, Talia, and stay away from here."

"What's the fun in that?" She gave him an insincere smile, one that didn't touch the cold depths of her vibrant blue eyes. "Where's your new girlfriend."

"Safe."

"How boring." She stepped closer, lifted her head to stare out at the tree line. She ran the tip of an index finger over her lips. "You know who's not boring? That delicious hunk of a man in Rily's office yesterday. I'd love a taste of him."

"Is there a point to this?"

"You never were any good at small talk." Her fingers curled at the base of her throat. "Where's my father? I can't imagine him missing out on all the fun."

"Really, Talia."

Temper tightened her features, flared hot against a momentary glimmer of doubt in her cold eyes. "I haven't done a damn thing wrong."

"So speaks a guilty conscious."

"Here. In Oregon." She flicked him a sideways glance as she ran a hand down and over that ass of hers. "I've done nothing illegal. Nothing against any kind of law here in Oregon."

"Yet." Gabe rocked back on his heels. "What do you have in your back pocket?"

She tossed her head, shaking her cap of pure white hair back from her face. "Nothing."

But her hand stayed at her back.

In seconds Gabe cleared the remaining few feet separating them, pressed one hand at her shoulder to turn her so her back was open to him. He wrapped his fingers around the hand over her ass, twisted her wrist and shoved her arm up and tight against her back between her shoulder blades.

Trapped before she could blink twice, she hissed then cursed.

"Such language."

"Really, darling." She tossed him a dirty look over her shoulder. "Rough is fine. All you had to do was ask."

"Asking is overrated." With his free hand, he shoved the hem of her sweater up to run his palm over both back pockets.

A switchblade knife.

Some things didn't change.

He yanked the knife out then tucked it into his own pocket before he finished patting her down. Then he shoved her away from him.

"While that was fun –" Her blue eyes sparking with icy heat, she rubbed her wrist. "I wasn't planning to use that knife on *you.*"

The scar on his neck pulsed. "Like I trust you near me with anything sharp."

"Trust is something else that's overrated." She shrugged.

"Did Allison trust you?"

"I told you before, I didn't kill her." Her lips pursed, Talia cradled her arm against her stomach. "In spite of what you think, I don't go around killing people willy-nilly, just for the sheer joy of it."

Right. But you're quite capable of that if it gets you want you want. "Then why is she dead?"

She shrugged again. "Allison had P.L.S. That's why she was at Sheldon's the same day of my visit. Thanks to my father and your new girlfriend's brother, the doctor doesn't have all his daughter's notes. He tried to help Allison, but he really doesn't have the cure."

"You're saying Dr. Sheldon killed Allison?"

"I think he was trying to make her better, but as they say, sometimes the cure is worse than the disease. I suspect he left her body out there at that rest stop. His daughter used to take care of all of that for him. Now, he's left to fend for himself."

The bodies. The ones he couldn't cure. The ones who had no one to miss them, no one to realize they were gone.

Nothing more than what they already supposed.

No proof, though. Of anything.

"Sad that Allison died, but meeting her that day was so fortuitous." Talia's eyes sparkled and a sly smile slid over her mouth. "For me."

She spun in a small circle then looked skyward.

Checking the perimeter. Making sure Gabe was alone.

He flexed his hands. Ben and Ortega had better be on their game. The slightest kink in their shields, in Rily's woo-woo cage, and Talia would be all over them.

And it wasn't time yet.

Talia's smile widened. "I'm going to contact him."

"The shaman."

"Yes." Her laughter, as light as the fairy she resembled, scraped at his nerves. She bounced on the balls of her feet. "He's *real*, Gabe."

No shit. "How are you planning to get his attention?"

"A ritual. So, it would be nice to have my knife back."

"Cold day in hell."

She laughed again as she skipped her way to the boulder. His steps reluctant, he trailed her but stayed several feet away.

"Join me."

"Why would I do that?"

"Two Winds is going to need a body. A host."

"You think I'm going to offer mine?"

"You're strong enough to resist him. Strong enough to keep him from taking over completely."

"You think I'm going to offer up my body so you can have his power? Why the hell would I do that?"

"Because you're a moral person. Because you won't be able to stand watching anyone else have sex with Rily Carrigan. Because if you don't, I will make you watch."

Bitch.

"I can see I'm right about your feelings for her, Gabe." Talia's eyes narrowed and she lifted her chin. "I'd say I'm sorry she has to die, but that would be a lie."

The nerve along his jaw throbbed.

She shrugged one shoulder. "Not that I'm going to be the one to kill her. Nothing illegal, remember. However, I am sure Two Winds will do the honors. He wants her soul, after all. So after the sex, Rily dies and we trap him."

"There is no we."

"Really, Gabe, we both want the same thing. Essentially. You're here because you want justice for her death. I want the one responsible in a cage. *My* cage, one that I control. You help me, I help you."

Mine.

The word whispered on the breeze. Whispered and surrounded them.

Two Winds.

Gabe scanned the perimeter of the field. Rily must be out of *her* cage. No time left.

Mine.

Talia frowned and also scanned the area. "Did you hear that?"

"Yes."

"Two Winds." Excitement bubbled in her voice. She crouched down next to the stone, felt along the edge where it sat and pulled a dagger, its blade long and curved, from underneath.

Gabe's stomach knotted.

Shit didn't cover that.

He eased back.

"You wouldn't give me the other one back, so I'm improvising."

Right. Improvising his ass.

Her smile wicked, she climbed on top of the boulder. "Stay back, Gabe. I really don't want to hurt you again."

"What are you planning with that knife?"

"I'm not going to hurt anyone with it. I'm going to use it like an anthame. To aid in my summoning."

"Since he's already here, what good is that going to do you?"

"Really, Gabe. He may be here, but he's not under my command. Not yet. Stay back." Facing him, she held her arms out to her side, shoulder height with the quasi sword extended. "We need to welcome Two Winds."

"Seems presumptuous of you, considering this is his home." Gabe waved a hand towards the hillside behind them. "You're not a witch, Talia. Do you have any clue what you're doing?"

"Semantics." She spared him a glance. "And I did a lot of reading."

"Not the same thing. You're messing with things you have no idea how to control. Summons, cages, Two Winds."

"You sound like my father." A shadow darkened her eyes as she shook her hair back from her face. "Where is he, by the way?"

"Here." Ben stood a few feet from the tree line, his hands braced on his hips.

"Hello, Father." Talia's chin lifted and defiance replaced the shadows clouding her eyes. "Happy you could join us. Where's the lady of the hour?"

Mine.

"Here." Rily, her head high and her shoulders back, stepped out from the line of trees to stand beside Ben. Fear tinged her gaze, but defiance, more than anything, shone in her eyes.

My lady. My love.

Pressure squeezed, bands wrapping tight in Gabe's chest. Invisible fingers pressed at his throat.

Always mine.

No. Rily was Gabe's. Not the shaman's. Not anyone else's.

Gabe, his gaze locked on hers, twisted his head to the side. He would not fail. His fingers curled into fists. Not this time.

Take her. Now.

"No." The word squeezed through Gabe's clenched teeth.

"Yes." From on top of the boulder Talia grasped the hilt of her blade with both hands and began to trace an unseen circle around herself. Power radiated, pulsing there in the air around her perch.

Her words nothing more than chanted whispers, Gabe barely glanced at her.

He couldn't. Too big a risk.

One slip, one small loss of focus, and Two Winds would have an opening into his mind. Gabe *couldn't* allow that to happen.

That pressure built inside his head, blurring the edge of his sight, pulsating a low, erratic beat in his ears.

In painful increments, he lowered his chin to his chest but forced his gaze to continue scanning around him.

He *had* to stay aware.

"Talia, what the hell are you doing?" Ben took several long strides forward.

"No, Ben." Each movement a small torture, Gabe held up a hand. "Don't come any closer."

"Listen to him, Father." Talia's giggle rippled across the air. "Soon his mind won't be completely his own."

"Talia —" Rily eased forward to stand next to Ben. "This is too dangerous. For you as well as me."

"The danger isn't important. Not if the end result matters." Talia lifted the blade over her head. "I, Talia Garrett, summon the powerful shaman, Two Winds, to stand in my circle. In my presence. To be *mine* to command."

Wind, stronger than the earlier breeze, rushed down the hillside, swirled in a rising spiral around the boulder. Talia's laughter skittered across the field, along Gabe's skin and mixed with the dirt and grass that bombarded him.

Focus, Nicholetti. Hold on.

The pressure in his head backed off a fraction. He blinked once.

Abruptly, as sharp as Talia's knife, a pop vibrated between his ears, rocked him where he stood. Breath filled his lungs, burned there.

Wind continued to whip around him and light blasted the area. No longer in agony, he lifted his hand to shield his squinted eyes.

Through the haze, a few feet north of the boulder, stood a man.

The wind stopped as sudden as it had started.

Gabe's chin came up, his hands fisted in front of him as his gaze locked on the stranger.

Shorter than average, but muscular with thick shoulders, the nearly naked man wore a short swath of dark leather around his waist. On his head sat a feathered headdress, the plumage the deep browns and lighter tans of a hawk or a golden eagle. His hair, as black as his eyes, hung down his back in a twisted braid of sorts.

Two Winds.

As alive as the totem animal hovering around him, over him and above him.

Bear.

A snarling, nasty bear.

Grizzly, but bigger.

A lot bigger.

Meaner.

Kodiak.

Shit didn't begin to cover this.

Gabe's fists tightened.

They hadn't counted on a blood and bone shaman. *But in the flesh, the shaman could be killed, like any other man. Couldn't he?*

Two Winds leaned his head back, closed his eyes. Round and broad, his tanned face relaxed. He breathed in deeply through his wide, flat nose. He lifted his arms, palms turned upward, out to his side. "I am."

"Yes, you are." Talia's voice cut across the field.

Dread and tension swamped the void left inside Gabe by Two Winds' withdrawal from his mind.

Talia had no clue what she was dealing with.

None of them did. The man had manifested himself, something that shouldn't have been possible. Because of Talia's uncontrolled amplification?

Two Winds frowned, the heaviness of his dark brows slashed across his forehead. He opened those small, beady eyes and turned his gaze on her. "Who are you?"

"The one who summoned you."

"Only a Chief's daughter can summon me." Two Winds turned his head to spear Rily with his gaze.

Gabe took one involuntary step forward. The shaman's gaze flicked to him then returned to Rily.

Her face pale, she lifted her chin and held the shaman's gaze as Ortega shoved through the bramble at the tree line and moved to stand beside Rily, opposite Ben.

They were all in place. Gabe's insides clamped down on themselves. Game time.

The look in Two Winds' eyes lethal, he smiled at Rily. Then he shifted his gaze back to Talia. Pulsing energy, nearly visible, followed his eye movements. "You are also a Chief's daughter. Who of these men do you call Chief?"

"You don't question me, Two Winds." Talia, with her anthame clasped in both hands in front of her, shook her hair back. "I summoned you. Therefore I control you."

The man's dark laughter skated across the field. "No woman controls Two Winds."

"I do."

Two Winds shook his head once before he lifted his hand and flung open his fingers. A sudden gust of wind knocked Talia off the boulder and onto her ass.

Sprawled on the ground, the anthame beside her, she glared at him. "You can't do that."

"Looks like he just did." Gabe loosened his shoulders, twisted his head from side to side with his gaze on the shaman all the while. "Why don't we talk this out, Two Winds? Find some kind of compromise."

Unseen weight settled on Gabe's shoulders as the shaman shifted his gaze to him.

"No." Two Winds frowned. "I have come for the one called Rily Carrigan and this time I will not be denied. She is mine."

"Going to have to disappoint you on that score." Gabe lowered his chin to his chest, charging the few feet toward the shaman. The impact sent electrical shockwaves through his body. Two Winds' roar echoed along his nerve endings as wind again rushed around them.

Gabe twisted aside then back to wrap an arm around the shaman's throat. He wrapped the fingers of his other hand around his own wrist and wedged the crook of his arm under the man's chin.

The damn shaman wasn't getting away.

Two Winds struggled for several moments before he stilled.

They stood that way for several heartbeats. Two Winds took several deep breaths, breaths that vibrated through Gabe's body.

Shit.

The shaman was centering himself.

That couldn't happen.

Gabe squeezed his arm muscles, cutting off the man's oxygen.

On a choked, shallow out breath, Two Winds reached up behind and grasped Gabe's right shoulder. Fire, instant and painful, seared through Gabe's sweatshirt to torch his skin. Flames licked his ear.

Shit. His shirt was burning.

Drop and roll.

The shaman was going with him, dammit. He'd snap the man's neck before he let go.

Gabe dropped, rolled to the right and the fingers Two Winds dug into his shoulder loosened as the man struggled to break Gabe's hold on his throat.

A loud pop, near Gabe's right ear, sent sharp, shearing electrical pulses along his shoulder to split at his neck and travel up across his jaw line and down his chest.

The flames disappeared in an acrid puff of dark smoke but paralyzing pain followed the electric trail across his skin. Two Winds gripped Gabe's arm and shoved him aside with ease and a dark laugh.

"She is mine." The shaman stood.

Dammit. Gabe couldn't move.

And his shirt was smoldering. Acrid smoke filled his nose.

"Two Winds." Talia stood on top of the boulder again. She held that damn curved knife above her head. "I brought you here. Obey me or I'll send you back."

The shaman's gaze locked on Gabe, he lifted fisted hands before turning his head to stare at Talia. "You overstep, woman."

Air rushed back into Gabe's lungs. His tensed muscles eased and he eased onto his back.

He could move again.

"You're an arrogant son of a bitch." Talia's voice held a slight hint of desperation.

That wasn't good.

But she was keeping the bastard occupied.

Gabe spared one glance toward where Rily stood between Ben and Ortega. Their shields had better hold.

Rily was the reason they were doing this.

On an inward count of three, Gabe pushed himself into a semi squatting position, the tips of his fingers on the ground and his gaze on the shaman.

"That may well be, little cat." Two Winds bark of laughter mixed with a sudden, single gust of wind. "I shall enjoy declawing you."

The shaman turned again towards Rily and her two protectors.

Gabe's muscles tightened.

Two Winds cocked his head to the side, studied the trio.

The air stilled and completely died.

"Come to me, Rily Carrigan." Palm upward, Two Winds held out a hand.

"Like hell."

"Your guards are no match for me." He beckoned at her with his fingers. "Come now and I won't have to hurt them."

"Go to hell." Ortega's calm voice carried across the field.

"Where do you think I've been?" Two Winds smiled before moving forward while holding both hands out. "Come, Rily Carrigan."

"Noooo." Her eyes wide and full of fear, she shook her head and took several steps back.

Ben and Ortega exchanged a glance as they moved in front of her.

At the center of Gabe's palm, where he connected with her, pain swirled.

What the hell was happening to her?

From where he crouched on the ground, he pushed up and launched himself at Two Winds.

On impact the shaman stumbled. His mouth in a snarl, he fisted a hand and swung at Gabe. "You will not stop me."

"Yes I will." Gabe sidestepped the swipe, countered with his own punch and connected with Two Winds' jaw.

Pain laced Gabe's right shoulder, pounding along the edges of the burn. But that didn't matter. He swung his left fist and hit the shaman in the stomach on the right side.

Two Winds' bent forward, the snarl still covering his face. With the fingers of both hands spread, the man shoved a ferocious wind forward, blasting Gabe backwards several feet.

Dammit, he was sending that asshole back to hell.

Alone.

Chapter Twenty-Six

SUDDENLY ABLE TO breathe again, Rily bent forward at the waist and sucked air deep into her lungs. That bastard, Two Winds, had tried to invade her mind. She didn't know how else to describe it, wasn't sure he hadn't at least partially succeeded.

But he wasn't there now.

Because Gabe had, somehow, stopped him?

Ramon and Ben stood in front of her, partially blocking her view of what was happening across the field.

Looking like a damn pink pixie, Talia stood on top of the boulder, with that damn curved knife clutched in both her hands and brandished in front of her body.

Rily, with her elbow, touched the gun she had tucked into her waistband under her loose jacket. That bitch was a problem.

Talia, her gaze, hot and intent and just this side of crazy, followed the skirmish paying out a few feet from her.

Gabe was fighting Two Winds. Physically throwing himself at the shaman. Getting punches in and then knocked back on his ass.

He shoved himself up from the ground, pushed a hand through his hair then round-housed a kick to the shaman's side. Two Winds backhanded him across the shoulder, hitting the seared edges of his sweatshirt and the exposed, burnt skin underneath.

Pain grimaced across Gabe's face.

He was doing this for her. To save her life.

Gabe.

She straightened, threw energy into her shields as Gabe had taught her to do. Then she mentally pushed outward, felt Ramon and Ben's invisible touch just there on the periphery of her invisible shields. Their layers of protection.

Oh, God. Listen to her.

She choked on the derision.

No time for that. No time for self-doubt.

No time for disbelief.

Ramon and Ben weren't helping Gabe fight the shaman because their job was to protect her. Time for her to help herself, dammit. Gabe needed *all* their help.

No matter what she'd promised.

A shudder quaked through her body. She couldn't let Two Winds hurt him.

"Hold tight, *Mi Corazon.*"

"But —"

"No buts, Rily." Ben's voice, low and firm, scraped over her nerves. "Gabe can handle himself."

"If you just shoot the bastard Gabe wouldn't *have* to handle this himself." She hated the tremor in her voice. The weakness that said she was scared shitless.

For Gabe.

"Rily."

Right. Unknown consequences. They were *all* in over their heads. How the hell did you beat a supernatural, whatever the hell Two Winds was, and come out on top?

"We can't just stand here —" Dammit. "Put me back in that damn cage, then. Go help him."

"We may have to." Ben's shoulders stiffened and he rotated his head. "With the shaman corporeal instead of trapped in that hillside …."

They had no idea what would happen if she disappeared from Two Winds' radar. And whatever he was couldn't be allowed to roam free.

To threaten the general populace.

Looking to steal a Chief's daughter.

Shit. Shit. Shit.

"Fine." Her fingers clenched over the painful heat swirling in the center of her palm.

Gabe slammed his fist into the shaman's face again. Two Winds' snarl rent the air. Rily's fists tightened in front of her.

Being helpless sucked.

Two Winds angled his head and, from the center of the field, made direct eye contact with her. His dark eyes glittered in the gloomy light.

Mine.

Always.

"In hell, you bastard."

Two Winds dark laugh skittered along her skin. He swung his arm out to the side, towards Gabe, opened his clenched fist and flung his hands open.

Something, energy maybe, nearly translucent, shimmered briefly in the air then appeared to gather itself before hurling in a tight ball at Gabe's injured shoulder.

The impact spun Gabe in a complete circle. His eyes rolled back before he dropped to the ground, unconscious.

"No." Rily, her fingers gripped on the butt of her gun, shoved forward.

Ramon wrapped an arm around her, locking her in place against his side.

"No, Ramon. I have to –"

Tentacles of pressure pressed inside her head.

"Ramon. Ben. We have to –"

"Rily?" Ben's voice, laced with concern, flitted over her.

Invisible fingers shoved inside her skull. Dug sharp nails into her head. Red, nearly black, exploded across her vision. Heat seared down through her chest, inflamed her lungs.

What the hell?

"Shit, Ben …."

DISORIENTED, Gabe forced his eyes open. He lay on his back. Heavy clouds pressed down. Muffled noise pulsed in his ears. Wind scratched over his skin, abrading the raw edges of the wound lancing his shoulder and stinging the abrasions along his jaw.

He'd been fighting the shaman.

Rily.

Every muscle aching, Gabe forced himself up on his elbows then into a sitting position. He shook his head to try and bring sound back. The near silence was deafening.

In front of him, Talia stood at a ninety degree angle, on top that boulder. She had her feet braced apart and that damn knife gripped tight in her hands. Her attention focused in front of her, she seemed oblivious to him.

Between Talia and the tree line, Two Winds stood with his back to her, one hand open to the clouds and the other holding a carved wooden staff aloft. Dark feathers twisted in the heavy breeze.

Where the hell had that come from?

The shaman's posture stiff, his body completely still, he had his head back and his chin lifted.

Gabe followed the direction of the man's gaze.

Across the field Ortega held a limp Rily against his body while Ben stood in front of them, his arms open wide and a scowl on his face.

Everything inside Gabe tightened then went still.

Several feet above them, on a level he knew only he could see, Two Winds' growling Kodiak bear stood on two legs facing Rily's crouched and snarling Bengal tiger.

Gabe lurched to his feet as the tiger's muscles bunched and she sprung forward to slash at the side of the bear's face. The Kodiak's head snapped back.

Long, jagged claw marks swelled with blood along the bear's right jaw.

Two Winds' bear screamed, the piercing sound reverberating across the field. He launched himself at the Bengal, wrapped both forelegs around her torso.

Teeth displayed, they snapped at each other as they rolled across an invisible ground.

Dammit. Gabe had to do something, had to stop the Kodiak.

Stop Two Winds.

Gabe ignored the pain in his shoulder and hunched forward. Like a football player, he charged with his head down and barreled into the shaman.

Two Winds' grunt rented the air.

Gabe's fist connected with the man's right jaw. Blood welled in the gashes suddenly visible along Two Winds' cheek.

From Rily's tiger?

Manifesting on the physical level?

Focus, Nicholetti. Focus.

He shook his head once, steadied himself.

No time for questions.

"You can't have her." Gabe's left fist plowed into the shaman's gut. Then his right.

Two Winds' curled forward, but his gaze remained upward and his arms out to the side.

Gabe spared a quick glance over his shoulder. The tiger lay on her side, her green eyes dim and unfocused. The air around her shimmered.

No, Rily. Sweetheart, keep fighting.

He shoved his right fist back into Two Winds' stomach. "Asshole."

The shaman bent over, his gaze locked on Gabe. "She is mine."

"No." Gabe clocked the man's jaw with his left fist.

Two Winds' head snapped to the side. Blood from the claw marks dripped down his cheek. A sly glint shone in his eyes. "Yes."

Rage boiled inside Gabe. Bubbled to the surface and erupted.

His fists tight and his elbows close to his side, he slammed the shaman's chin then his gut.

Right fist. Left. Right.

Two Winds' body twisted with each punch. Gabe advanced until he had the man against the boulder.

"Gabe!"

Talia. Gabe registered the voice. Ignored it. His right fist buried itself in the shaman's stomach, his left again connected with the man's chin.

"Gabriel." Ben this time. "Stop."

Not until he's dead.

Right fist again.

The copper tinge of spilt blood scented the air.

The shaman's or his own?

What did it matter?

Left fist into the kidney.

Shit.

He shook his head.

In front of him, Two Winds bent over, his staff held in both hands across his body. Not fighting back.

The man's bear totem loomed over them, its beady eyes watching.

Had it given up fighting Rily? Or was she already gone?

Gabe spared one quick glance over his shoulder.

The tiger still lay on her side, her eyes open but no one there.

Her essence gone with only the shell remaining.

Just the way he'd seen Rily in his vision.

Grief welled in his gut.

He swung his gaze back to the bear.

But if Rily was dead, why was her totem still visible?

What had Two Winds done with Rily's essence?

Gabe leaned forward, wrapped his hands around the man's neck, and forced him to look up.

He squeezed. "Let her go."

Even if it meant she died. That was better than her soul trapped in whatever cage the shaman had created.

A snarl curled Two Winds' lips. "Mine."

Gabe squeezed tighter.

"Gabriel." Ben's hand cupped his uninjured shoulder. "He doesn't do us any good dead."

"So?" *Without Rily, what difference did it make?*

Ben's fingers dug into his skin.

Shit.

He loosened his grip.

Two Winds' dark eyes shifted between him and Ben.

"Where is she?" Gabe snarled the words.

"Where you cannot reach her."

"Then I'll kill you."

"And she'll be trapped for eternity."

"Bastard." Gabe tightened his fingers again.

Wait. Trapped? Shit.

He cast a quick, wary glance to where the tiger still lay, hovering just above Rily's prone body. The tiger's green eyes remained dull, unfocused. Lifeless.

Ramon had lowered Rily's body to the ground and even now pressed his hands to her forehead.

Gabe's throat tightened.

Had they already lost her?

Was all of this for nothing?

Dammit it all to hell.

They couldn't lose her. Not like this.

Not now. Not to Two Winds.

Vision be damned.

Between Gabe's hands Two Winds' body drooped as the man's tension began to seep away. The shaman's eyes practically glowed.

Oh, hell no.

"What did you do to her?" Gabe pulled one hand back then slammed his fist into the man's jaw. Anger boiled in the black cauldron of Two Winds' gaze. Again Gabe punched his face. "Just what the hell are you?"

He shoved Two Winds to the ground. With his hands balled into fists, he towered over the shaman. Then he planted his heel on the man's chest. "A soul stealer? That's what you've become?"

Ben stopped beside him but Gabe ignored his startled glance.

"You can't have her, bastard." Gabe's harsh breath burned his throat.

"She is already mine." Two Winds lay prone on the ground, not even trying to move his body. His gaze though, that he shifted towards Ben. "You are Chief."

Ben, his eyes narrowed, focused on the shaman. "Why does that matter?"

That slyness coated Two Winds gaze. He glanced at Gabe with a questioning look.

Gabe ground his heel harder into the man's chest.

"Now what?" Talia, from her perch on the boulder a few feet away, shifted her stance. With her hands still gripped around the hilt of her curved knife and her Garrett eyes a hardened blue, she resembled a merciless sprite. All bent on revenge.

No mercy.

Sounded like a plan.

But how to execute it without trapping Rily's soul?

"Now –" Two Winds opened his hand, palm upward, and the staff that lay a few feet away flew into his grip.

Shit.

Gabe dropped, one knee on the man's chest with the other on the ground, and gripped both of Two Winds' wrists in his hands.

"To extract my vengeance on the Chief." Two Winds closed his eyes. On an out breath he sunk into himself.

"Like hell." Whatever the bastard was trying, Gabe had to stop him.

Two Winds opened his eyes. An eerie, silver glow circled the dark irises. Cold, electric pain, biting sharp, hit Gabe's nerve-endings. All of them. All at once.

"Bullshit." Gabe dug his fingers into the shaman's wrists.

The silver in Two Winds' eyes widened, darkening to pewter. Gabe's muscles stiffened, screaming in agony. But he held on to the bastard.

Two Winds, his gaze locked on Gabe's, arched his neck. Veins bulged as his back lifted from the ground. Silver electric currents danced over the arms of Gabe's sweatshirt, sizzling in the abrupt stillness of the air.

Suddenly, Ben hit him, full body, and thrust him aside.

Gabe landed on his stomach, on the ground, a few feet from Two Winds.

"You're on fire. Roll." Ben's urgent command, against his ear, pierced Gabe's stunned mind and he rolled onto his back. Ben pushed him onto his stomach.

"What the hell?" Gabe shook his head once then shoved himself to his feet. Pain pulsed through his body.

"Take it off." Ben yanked at the hem of Gabe's sweatshirt. "You're still smoldering."

Shit.

Grabbing the hem, Gabe wrenched the shirt over his head, threw the shirt on the ground and stomped on the thick material.

Two Winds' deep laughter coated the air. The sudden, slimy breeze skidded over Gabe's bare arms and pierced the thin material of the black, A-Frame T-shirt he'd worn under his sweatshirt.

The burn on his shoulder, the one Two Winds had inflicted earlier, throbbed.

With a glance at where Rily's tiger still lay several feet above her body, Gabe slowly turned around.

Two Winds now stood, a few feet in front of Talia. He held his staff with the end planted on the ground next to him, and shook his head back. "I have waited too long for this. You cannot stop me."

His movements fluid and quick, Two Winds braced his legs apart and swung his staff in a graceful arc. Then, with both hands gripping the wood, he slammed the bottom portion into Ben's midsection.

Pain lanced Ben's face as he doubled over.

"I will kill you, Chief." Two Winds straightened, his staff held horizontal, in one hand, in front of him. "Here. Now."

The shaman flung open the fingers of his free hand. A sudden, powerful wind thrust at Ben, its invisible fingers gripped his throat and lifted him off the ground.

"No!" Talia's cry echoed around the field. She jumped on the shaman's back and wrapped her legs around his waist. With one arm wrapped around his shoulders and her knife at his throat, she hissed in his ear. "Let him go."

Gabe rushed forward and grabbed Ben just as whatever had held him suspended in the air let go. For a brief moment Ben collapsed against Gabe's body.

"Go ahead and slice me, Chief's daughter." Two Winds lifted his chin. "Slice me and seal your fate."

"Talia, wait." Ben, his hand at his neck, shoved against Gabe and stood on his own.

"Why should I?" Talia ran the sharp edge of her knife along Two Winds' throat, not quite cutting, but threatening.

Gabe shook his head once.

Killing Two Winds might mean the end for Rily. Or the beginnings of hell for her. Not that Talia would care one way or the other about that. Talia only cared about herself.

But she risked herself to help Ben. To save her father.

Gabe refused to think about that.

She was still at risk. Was still a risk.

"I brought him here, in this form." Talia tightened her legs around the shaman's middle. "Why shouldn't I take him out?"

"You may have aided in bringing me here, Chief's Daughter, but I am the one with power." Two Winds' face a mask of calm, an eerie half smile lifted the corners of his mouth. He dropped his staff. The wood made a soft echo in the sudden stillness.

"Really, shaman? Looks like I'm the one holding the knife."

"Talia." Shit. Gabe held both hands up in front of him, palms forward. This didn't *feel* right. *Felt* more wrong than simply being completely out of control. "Don't. He wants you to cut him. Why?"

There wasn't any kind of good reason Gabe could figure out.

Two Winds, his gaze locked on Ben, lifted his own hands in a parody of Gabe's. A split second and the shaman covered Talia's hands with his own. Then, his movements quick and as sharp as the curved blade, he ran the edge of the knife over his own throat.

Crimson blood oozed along a thin, angry red line.

The cut wasn't deep, just enough to seep.

Talia tried to pull her hands away, but Two Winds jerked her around his body. He held her like a rag doll and twisted their hands until the knife's thin blade, bright with Two Winds' blood, lay against Talia's throat.

"You are now my bride, Chief's Daughter."

"Rot in hell." She spit in his face.

A sudden gust of wind, harsh and cold, swept down the hillside to merge with the shaman's laughter.

"Possibly. But you will be with me, at my side." With the tip of the knife, Two Winds pricked her neck then ran the flat of the blade over her throat, mixing their blood. "Forever."

Gabe rushed forward to slide across the dirt. He scooped up the shaman's staff before twisting to face the man.

Two Winds dropped Talia then spun and kicked her out of his way. In a fighting ready stance, he faced Gabe with both hands on the hilt of the curved knife.

Talia rolled onto her side then curled into a tight ball.

"What did you do to her?" Ben stood a few feet from Gabe, fists tight in front of him, between the shaman and his daughter.

"I took what was promised."

"No one here ever promised you anything."

That corner of Two Winds' mouth lifted in a damn half smirk. "Who promised isn't important."

"Like hell."

Two Winds ran the tip of his index finger over the blade then smeared the blood from the knife over his own neck.

Gabe's eyes narrowed. "He's mixing Talia's blood with his own."

"Why?"

Talia moaned.

"You can save her, Chief." Two Winds again ran the tip of his finger over the blade. "Take your protection from the one called Rily and I will release this one from my binding."

The knot clenching Gabe's chest tightened like a vise forced that last few centimeters. He shot Ben a hard look.

If the shaman was concerned about the shields around Rily, then he didn't have her.

Not completely. Not yet.

There still had to be a chance.

To save her. Save her soul.

"Cold day in hell." Ben rolled up on to the balls of his feet.

"Hell is colder than you realize, Chief." Two Winds' chin lifted. His eyes closed for the briefest of moments before they sprung open, that silver again circling the irises. He lifted the knife and twisted toward Talia.

"No." Gabe hefted the staff in one hand, the weight balanced and near perfect. On an outward breath, he swung the wooden rod at Two Winds' side just as Ben tackled the man at his knees.

The three of them hit the ground a foot from where Talia lay, prone and unmoving. Rising, Gabe smashed one end of the staff against Two Winds' head.

After a moment of struggle, Gabe had both of the shaman's arms behind his back with his wrist bent and locked in his grip. Ben shoved himself into a standing position then kicked the staff out of the way before he dusted off his jeans.

"Get that damn cage ready, Garrett." Gabe, pressed on Two Winds' wrist, increasing the pain.

The shaman growled, low in his chest.

Two Winds stilled, his struggles stopped. "I will not be put into a cage of your making."

"Tough shit."

Wind again swirled around them, stronger than before. Invisible, icy fingers scrapped over Gabe's skin.

"Doesn't matter what you conjure up, asshole. I'm not letting you go."

That wind shifted, lifted the staff from where it had lain on the ground.

Gabe blinked once, tightened his fingers around the man's wrist.

What the hell was the bastard up to?

The staff thrust forward, impaling Two Winds in the chest.

"Yes." The shaman's whispered word echoed in the now still air as he slumped forward. Gabe scrambled to hold on to the limp body but that body began to dissolve into black smoke. Slow at first then rapidly. In seconds there was nothing for Gabe to hold on to and his hands were empty.

An acrid scent filled the air. Coated his lungs.

Burned.

What the hell?

On the ground, Talia's back arched and her eyes opened wide.

"Shit." Ben lowered his hands from the makeshift psychic cage he'd been constructing and rushed to his daughter.

"Daddy?" Talia's voice, low and full of fear, ended on a soft sob.

Ben knelt beside her, gathered her into his arms.

Gabe spared a quick glance around the field then towards Ramon. Rily still lay as still as ever and her tiger still lay prone above her.

Where the hell was Two Winds?

Wiping his hands down his thighs, Gabe knelt next to Talia, across from Ben.

"Talia?" Ben pushed her hair back from her forehead. "Come on, baby, talk to me."

She arched her back again, those Garrett blue eyes widened and something black and sinister coated her eyes. There then gone.

Bile rose in Gabe's throat.

They'd found Two Winds.

Locked inside Talia's mind.

Chapter Twenty-Seven

RILY FLOATED, her eyes closed, unable to do more than that. Pain seared every inch of her body if she tried to even lift her eyelids, much less a finger or her hand. Or an arm.

And she'd tried.

Was this death?

Purgatory?

How her sister-in-law had felt all those months ago when Dr. Sheldon's daughter had held her hostage?

Rily gave herself a mental shake.

Hannah was fine. Was with Rily's brother, Jake. Both working for Ben.

But wasn't that the shits?

She'd never be able to nail Sheldon, that bastard.

Being dead kind of trumped that scenario.

Damn.

Ben would make the doctor pay, but she wanted to be there to see the bastard taken down.

Was this the regrets part?

Gabe.

A different kind of pain, mixed with sorrow, swelled to fill her body and matched the hot liquid suddenly filling her eyes.

Dammit. She didn't cry.

Ever.

Heat from the tears tracked down the side of her face and pooled near her ears.

So, she was flat on her back.

Wherever the hell this place is, wherever I'm going to be spending eternity.

Without Gabe.

Fingers, their touch as light as air, swept over her face and threaded through her hair. A palm, warm against her chilled skin, settled against her forehead.

"Dammit, Rily." A deep voice – Gabe's? – "Fight."

Really? How the hell did he expect her to do that? When she couldn't even move a damn finger to flip him off?

And what the hell was she supposed to fight *against*?

Bastard.

That palm against her forehead, not Gabe's, pressed harder. Those fingers tangled in her hair dug into her scalp. Pain, laced with a heat hotter than she'd ever felt and completely different from what held her paralyzed, spiraled from those fingertips, twisted down into the center of her head.

What the hell?

"Shi –" The word burned low in her throat, caught on thick, stagnant bile. She couldn't swallow.

"You've got her, Ortega. Hold on. Don't let her go." Hands gripped her upper arms. Gabe's hands. "Come back to me, Rily. Please."

Gabe.

"I –" A spasm shuddered through her chest. Electricity dipped in hot coals rippled from the center of her head, down her spine to run along her nerve endings. Searing pain scorched her skin.

"Rily." Gabe's voice, lined in desperation, echoed against her ears. "Open your eyes."

Her eyelids flickered, the lashes beating against the tender skin beneath.

"Come on, Rily." His hands cupped her shoulders. "Quit being such a pansy and open your damn eyes."

"Basta —" Her throat seized. But her eyelids flickered again. This time they opened, the small sliver of light too bright to see anything except white.

"Rily." This time, his lips pressed against her ear, Gabe breathed her name.

"Not a —" She sucked a small amount of air around the solid lump of bile. "Pansy."

THIS WAS HEAVEN.

Rily gazed at the dark, star strewn sky above her, the only real light coming from the top of the mast of Gabe's sailboat. A sigh locked deep in her chest held, paused at the simplicity of the balmy, brine-filled air whispering across her skin. Warm, Caribbean water lapped against the side of the boat while Gabe lay stretched, bare-chested, beside her on the bow, his fingers laced with hers.

New Year's Day night.

And maybe not the heaven she'd been terrified had rejected her those few days before Christmas, back in Oregon.

That sigh held tight in her chest released itself on a soft outbreath of air.

But heaven none the less.

Bogie was with her parents, traveling in an RV with Sadie, Jake's dog. And she was here, moored in a hidden cove along the shore of a private island in the British Virgin Isles. Wearing nothing but a bikini and a barely there smile.

Still alive.

She'd survived.

And Gabe was still with her. By her side.

A sudden pinpoint of light flashed across the dark sky, its graceful arc ending at the horizon.

"Did you make a wish?" Gabe rubbed his thumb against hers.

"Isn't that tempting fate? When I have everything I want right here?"

Water slapped against the side of the boat, loud in the lingering silence.

He squeezed her hand. Finally. "We nearly lost you."

Damn.

Of course he wanted to talk about that now.

They'd been here several days already and she'd neatly avoided *that* subject completely.

He'd been giving her time to heal. To come to terms inside her own head. She got that.

Just wasn't sure she was ready to talk about it.

Not yet.

"I'm alive." She pulled her fingers from his and turned on her side to brace her elbow so she could rest her head on her hand and trace the line of his jaw with the fingers of her other hand, to barely touch the edge of the burn on his shoulder. A burn that was nearly healed. "Let me show you how alive I am."

He captured her fingers with his. "Rily."

"Gabe." She leaned forward and brushed her lips over his forehead. "Let me show you."

"I almost lost you."

Panic clawed at her throat. "But you didn't. I'm still here."

The darkness of his eyes seemed to deepen, to call to her. To pull at her.

Dammit.

She wasn't ready for wherever it was he was headed.

With the tip of her tongue she wet her lips and pulled back. Put a little distance between them.

The better to watch those eyes of his.

"What about Talia?" Another area she wanted to avoid, but the lesser of the two evils.

She hoped.

His gaze flicked away from her, for less than a second.

Great. That didn't bode well.

She pushed herself up to sit cross-legged beside him. "Talia's going to be okay, right?"

"Why do you care?" His gaze caught hers as he linked his fingers behind his head. "She planned to sacrifice you to gain control over Two Winds."

"Didn't work out so well for her, did it?" Rily shrugged one shoulder. "But she ended up sacrificing herself for Ben. That counts for something."

"Does it now?" Doubt coated his words.

"Where is she? Now?"

"Ben has her some place safe."

"Safe for her? Or safe for us?"

"Safe for all concerned."

"Oh." Rily glanced around the boat then back at Gabe. "So she's going to be okay?"

"I didn't say that."

"No, you didn't."

Gabe's gaze flicked to the dark sky and then back to her. "Ben will figure it out. Might take some time, but he will figure it out."

"And he'll get Two Winds out of Talia's head?"

"Didn't say that, either."

Damn.

"It is what it is."

"Glad you didn't have that attitude about me, Gabe." She leaned forward just a slight bit, close enough to trace a fingertip along his bare arm.

Damn this need to touch him.

To reach out. To connect.

His head tilted back then he braced himself up on his elbows. That dark gaze of his caught hers. Pain lurked in the depths of his eyes.

She sucked in a breath. "Gabe."

"I did have that attitude. At first. Rily –"

"It's okay."

"Now."

"Isn't that all that matters?" She leaned in closer and traced two fingers over his mouth. "Stop beating yourself up. Let me show you how alive I am. Now."

His lips parted and she slipped one finger inside his mouth. He bit down, light, on the tip.

Heat spiraled from between her legs to swirl through her belly and opened her entire body. Her entire being.

Lord but what his touch did to her.

No wonder she was addicted.

"Gabe."

He covered her hand with his, pressed his lips to her palm in a soft kiss. Then he sat up, mirroring her position with his legs crossed and his knees inches from hers. "I nearly lost you."

Panic welled, replacing all that delicious heat with frozen icicles of dread.

Why was he doing this?

Why couldn't he simply live in the moment? Why bring up the past?

But the past wasn't what she was afraid of, not any more.

The future loomed overhead, as wide as that dark, starry night sky.

And that scared the crap out of her.

All of it. All of the implications, the possibilities.

Her need of him. His touch.

"Rily." He leaned forward, took both her hands in his. "Your hands are like ice."

Duh.

Somehow, she didn't think her old friend, sarcasm, was going to save the day. Not today. Not with this.

Dammit.

"You haven't even asked *why* you're not dead."

And I wasn't going to ask.

He squeezed her fingers again.

"So, I'm not dead. You were wrong." She tugged her hand, but he held on so she quit. A girl had to choose her fights. This wasn't one, at least not yet. "Hope that doesn't stick in your craw. Being wrong. Considering."

A wry smile tilted the edge of his mouth. "I wasn't wrong."

"Really? Pretty arrogant, don't you think?"

"No." Light glinted in his eyes as he lifted his head to stare past her, towards the shore. "I didn't save you, Rily. You were gone."

"Then why am I alive now?" She frowned. "You're not suggesting I'm some kind of – what? Vampire? Daylight and I do just fine together, thank you very much."

His eyes crinkled and his lips lifted. "Thank God."

Dammit. Okay, so he wanted to hash this all out. "If you didn't save me, then why am I alive now? How did I survive dying out there in that field?"

Unless …?

"I thought it was all over." She jerked her hands back from his, rubbed her palms down her bare arms. "That we've moved past whatever it was you saw out there in that field."

"It is over. And you were dead. I saw you dead." He braced his hands on her knees. "Ortega brought you back."

"Ramon?" She frowned again. "But –"

"Ben says he's a healer of some sort. A powerful one."

"Oh, wow." She'd seen some of that with her brother and his bride. "I died and *Ramon* brought me back?"

Gabe held her gaze.

"Bet that just makes them both happier than shit." A giggle lodged itself in her throat. "Ramon doesn't want anything to do with Ben's woo-woo crap."

"Ortega healing you made me happy, sweetheart." Gabe's thumbs drew circles at the edge of her knees.

"Even if Ramon is the one who saved me." She wiggled her eyebrows. A laugh escaped when Gabe growled low in his throat. "So it does stick in your craw. Going to have to remember that."

"I'll give you something to remember." He leaned forward until his forehead was barely an inch from hers. "My endgame, Rily, is marriage."

She sucked in a startled breath.

"I –" *What?* Words disserted her. Completely.

"Don't do marriage?" Gabe's gaze bore into hers while his fingers rubbed circles on her knees. "I get that."

She shook her head. "I don't think you do."

"I do, actually." His eyes crinkled again. "Just don't give a damn."

"Gabe –" She sucked in a needed gasp of air. Hyperventilating was next.

"We can take it slow. Get you used to the idea."

"Mighty big of you."

"Actually, it is." He squeezed her knees. "My instinct is to haul your ass to the nearest magistrate here in the islands. Make this legal and binding."

"I –" She shut her mouth and glared at him.

"You died back there, Rily." He held up his hand, palm towards her. "I *can't* lose you again."

Why the hell didn't he play fair?

Reluctant but unable and unwillingly to resist, she lifted her hand until her palm was a few inches from his. Heat swirled in the center, vibrating between the centers of both their palms.

"I can wait, Rily. Wait for you to get comfortable with the idea of marriage. As long as you understand that this connection that pulses between us is real." He held her gaze. "It might have been forged in danger, but it's bound by love."

"Love?"

"Rily. Remember I Love You. Always."

"Gabe –"

"Commit to me, Rily." He cupped his hands over her cheeks, one palm warmer than the other, and gazed into her eyes. "Commit to waking up with me. Not just the mornings on this boat, but every morning. For a lifetime."

Oh God. She closed her eyes. Closed him out.

Could she do that? Make that commitment?

The last few days had been *heaven*. Going to sleep each night in his arms. Waking up, curled against him with his arms around her waist and his face buried in her neck, his breath warm on her skin.

Could she really give that up? For what? Her pride? Her fear?

Could she really be that stubborn? That much of a coward?

"A lifetime?" Was that her voice, trembling like some school girl's afraid of the answer? She opened her eyes.

He nodded once.

"I don't know about the whole marriage thing, Gabe. A ring, a wedding. I just don't –" She wet her lips. Swallowed over the lump stuck in her throat. "I do love you."

"I know you do." That almost smile crinkled his eyes. "A day at a time, Rily. As long as I know you're mine, I will wait. Commit to me, Rily Carrigan, as I commit to you."

"I can do that." She let go of the breath she'd held. "For a lifetime of waking up with you, a day at a time –" Leaning forward, she pressed against his mouth. "I can do that, Gabe."

If you enjoyed BLIND SIGHT and would like to see more stories in the PSI Sentinel series, please consider leaving a review for this book with your favorite ebook seller.

Every review is appreciated.

To stay up to date with Pamela and to learn more about her upcoming releases, sign up for her newsletter:
http://eepurl.com/bbOUjv

You can also visit her at the following places on the web:

www.PamelaMoran.com
www.facebook.com/pamelamoranauthor
www.goodreads.com/PamelaMoran
www.pinterest.com/pamelamoran/
Twitter: Pam_Moran

Available now:

STOLEN SPIRIT
(PSI Sentinels, Book One)

Hearing his dead ex-girlfriend's voice in an empty room is enough to make a man question his sanity. Worse is when that ex insists she shouldn't have died. Broken cop Jake Carrigan has no interest in delving into a past full of heartache and regrets. But he can't deny she still matters, even if she's simply a voice in his head.

Hannah Dixon is having a hard time believing she's dead. How can she be when she feels so much inside? She can see Jake, can talk to him, but she can't touch him. And right now, touching Jake is all she wants.

Jake's probe into Hannah's death stirs up a sinister psychic link, something dark that will stop at nothing to keep its secrets. To protect her own heart, Hannah left Jake once. Can she leave him again to protect his life?

GAVIN'S WOMAN
(A PSI Sentinel, Darkwater Guardians Novella)

Gavin Dunbar, liaison between the PSI and the government, is a low-level psychic himself. A man of the present who believes the future is too nebulous, too fluid – that it can't be trusted. His reasons are mired deep in a past he has no desire to examine. After all, in his world, having a soul-mate doesn't equate to happily-ever-after.

Tragedy has brought Calea Fontaine to a crossroads and has her reassessing her future without the man she loves. A seer from a long line of seers, Calea knows, firsthand, that while Fate might try to guide a person along a path, Free Will has a way of trumping Destiny.

Or does it?

Along the storm ravaged Oregon coast, a predator stalks Calea with an obsession born of a dark ache, an overwhelming need to control and possess at any cost. The only obstacle standing in his way is Gavin Dunbar's own obsession.

ELSIE'S SECRET
(A PSI Sentinel Novella)

A PSI agent, Sebastian Alexander has secrets that once came between him and the woman he still loves. Finding her prowling around where she doesn't belong turns his simple reconnaissance into a rescue mission threatening to blow everything apart. Is he willing to risk his secrets to save her life?

Elsie Quartermaine has one goal. Save her nephew from a sadistic kidnapper. Sebastian is the one man who can help her. But divulging her secret puts more than her life in jeopardy. Can she trust Sebastian with her nephew's life? Her own? What about her heart?

As dawn creeps over the horizon, can they find enough trust in each other to stay alive?

Coming Early Summer 2015

Darkwater Echoes

PSI Sentinels: Darkwater Guardians, Book One

By Pamela Moran

Footsteps pounded across the deck above. Trent Sawyer, awake at the first thud, rolled from his berth and snatched his gun from under his pillow.

Barefoot and wearing only a black pair of shorts, he moved silently across the dark cabin to the door. He waited several heartbeats before letting the motion of a small wave hitting the side of the sailboat cover the sound of him opening the door a small fraction.

Light from the upper galley spilled through the crack and into his room.

Voices carried down to him, voices that shouldn't have been there – much less arguing over who was going to start the freaking boat's engines.

His boss' boat. Neither of those rough voices belonged to the man.

Trent wasn't letting whoever was up on deck steal *this* boat. Not on his first night. He hadn't even been on the boat – or in Key Largo – for more than a couple hours.

Not going to happen.

With his gun leading and his body crouched low, Trent slipped into the narrow hallway. He slid one bare foot onto the bottom stair, cringed at the soft groan of weathered wood then shifted his weight to ease his other foot up another step.

On a deep exhale of breath, he lifted his head above the solid railing. Two men, one a blonde giant and the other a squat redhead, both burly and wide through the shoulders, stood across the galley with their backs to him. Their voices lower than earlier, they seemed to be arguing over a sheaf of papers they had spread over the Captain's table.

Now was as good a time as any.

Trent straightened. He aimed his gun at Blondie's head. "What the hell are you doing on my damn boat?"

Both men whipped around, their faces slack with shock.

A small amount of satisfaction welled in Trent's gut.

Mongrels, both of them.

Their eyes brightened and their mouths widened into comical grins. They started forward.

"What the –?" Pain, sharp and sudden, splintered Trent's thoughts.

His world went black.

✧ ✧ ✧

Join Pam's newsletter to stay up to date on PSI Sentinel releases!

http://eepurl.com/bbOUjv

www.ingramcontent.com/pod-product-compliance
Lightning Source LLC
Chambersburg PA
CBHW072111250626
47159CB00007B/2395